THE
TUSCAN
CHILD

Center Point
Large Print

Also by Rhys Bowen and available from Center Point Large Print:

In Farleigh Field

This Large Print Book carries the Seal of Approval of N.A.V.H.

THE
TUSCAN
CHILD

WITHDRAWN

RHYS BOWEN

CENTER POINT LARGE PRINT
THORNDIKE, MAINE

The text of this Large Print edition is unabridged.
In other aspects, this book may vary
from the original edition.
Printed in the United States of America
on permanent paper.
Set in 16-point Times New Roman type.

ISBN: 978-1-68324-871-2

Library of Congress Cataloging-in-Publication Data

Names: Bowen, Rhys, author.
Title: The Tuscan child / Rhys Bowen.
Description: Center Point Large Print edition. | Thorndike, Maine :
   Center Point Large Print, 2018.
Identifiers: LCCN 2018017799 | ISBN 9781683248712
   (hardcover : alk. paper)
Subjects: LCSH: Large type books. | GSAFD: Mystery fiction. |
   Suspense fiction.
Classification: LCC PR6052.O848 T87 2018 | DDC 823/.914—dc23
LC record available at https://lccn.loc.gov/2018017799

This book is dedicated to Piero and Cajsa Baldini, who made my recent Tuscan experience so wonderful and provided insights for this book that only natives of the area could give me. My thanks as always to my brilliant agents, Meg Ruley and Christina Hogrebe; the whole team at Jane Rotrosen; and most especially to Danielle and the whole team at Lake Union, who gave me the chance to write the book I had always dreamed of writing! And finally, as always, to John for his love and support.

THE
TUSCAN
CHILD

CHAPTER ONE

HUGO

December 1944

He was going to die, that was quite obvious. Hugo Langley tried to examine this fact dispassionately. The left wing of the Blenheim bomber was on fire and flames licked at the cabin. Behind him, his navigator, Flight Lieutenant Phipps, lay slumped forward over his instruments. A trickle of blood ran down one side of his face, seeping from under his flight helmet. And Gunner Blackburn was already dead, shot in the rear gun bay by the first wave of Messerschmitts. Hugo wasn't sure whether he himself had been hit. Adrenaline was still pumping so violently through his system that it was hard to tell. He stared down at his blood-spattered trousers, wondering if the blood was his own or came from Phipps.

"Bugger," he muttered. He hadn't wanted it to end this way, this soon. He had looked forward to inheriting Langley Hall and the title someday, enjoying the status in the neighbourhood as the squire, Sir Hugo Langley. He thought briefly of his wife and son and found that their images stirred little emotion. She'd be all right without him. She could go on living at the Hall with the old man until she found someone else, which undoubtedly she would do. His son, that strange, quiet little boy, would be too young to remember him. They'd talk of him as a hero when in reality he was a bloody fool, a sitting duck. This was a bombing mission that should never have been flown. Everyone knew the Blenheims were out-dated, slower than the enemy planes. And in flying north from his base near Rome to reach his targets at the rail yards in Milan, he would have to fly over a hundred miles of German-occupied territory.

He tried to assess the situation rationally. The Blenheim couldn't make it back to base even if he could get the old crate to turn around, which wasn't likely with one engine on fire, one wing now useless. But he certainly wasn't going to sit there and go down in flames like a cooked chicken. He glanced out of the windscreen and tried to assess the terrain below but could see nothing. The night was as black as pitch. Cloud cover above. No moon. No stars. No lights down below. But there was also no sign of enemy planes, unless they were still tailing him. He suspected they had decided he was finished and was no longer worth bothering with. From their last reported position, he guessed he must be well over Tuscany by now. Maybe even north of Pisa and into territory still controlled by Germans.

Hilly, wild country. There was a chance he could hide out and make it safely to the coast if he could somehow parachute out without the chute going up in flames. It was a chance worth taking, anyway. He fumbled to release the glass hood of the cockpit. The latch came free, but the hood wouldn't budge. For a moment, he felt pure terror—that he'd be trapped in here to be slowly roasted or plummet to earth in a ball of fire, whichever came first. He pushed with all his strength and felt the glass hood finally yield and slide backward. Instantly, the flames licked at him.

"Go on, do it," he urged himself. He glanced back at Phipps. "Sorry, old chap," he said, "but I can't take you with me." His fingers, encased in their thick leather gloves, refused to obey him as he took off his flight helmet with the oxygen supply attached. Immediately, breathing seemed to be hard, but he was not flying that high, and it could have been just panic. He reached for his parachute and attempted to strap it on. It felt as if he was frozen in time, as if life had been reduced to slow motion. Eventually, he felt the harness snap shut. Trying not to rush, he attempted to stand, feeling pain shoot through his left leg. Damn. So he had been shot. Not much chance of running and hiding, then. Still better than being burned alive or crashing with the plane. With any luck he would land in territory no longer controlled by Germans. They had been driven back to what they called the Gothic Line, running across the peninsula just north of Pisa, and the Italians were no longer their allies. Having lived in Italy once, Hugo doubted the ordinary people ever had been incredibly pro-German or pro-war.

He hauled himself up and out until he was crouching on the good wing, out of reach of the flames, holding on for dear life as the wind buffeted him. Still he hesitated, picturing one of those Messerschmitts lurking to pick him off if he parachuted down. He listened but couldn't pick up the telltale rumble of an enemy fighter, only the deep growl of his own right engine—the left having died. He tried to remember that distant and brief session of parachute training—how to launch himself and how many seconds to count before pulling the cord so that the chute didn't tangle with the plane. His mind was a hopeless jumble of confusion.

He took a deep breath, then threw himself from the plane. For a few seconds, he felt himself plunging to earth. Then he tugged on the cord and was jerked upright as the parachute opened. The descent seemed to last forever. Somewhere above him, he heard the deep thump of an explosion as the fuel tank on his plane blew up. He watched the Blenheim spiral down past him. He didn't actually see the moment when it crashed to earth, but he heard the impact. Then he was aware of the dark shapes of hills around him—the ground rushing up to meet him. Again, he tried to recall his brief moments of parachute training. Brace? Roll? He seemed to be coming in awfully fast. Maybe the parachute had not opened fully. Maybe it had been damaged in the fire. He glanced up and could see the faint, whitish circle hovering over him. It seemed to be intact. Then he looked down, trying to make out what the ground looked like below him. He could just about see the shape of the land, the outlines of hills, some of them now level with him. And trees. Lots of trees.

There was the faintest hint of dawn in the eastern sky, silhouetting the dark outlines of the hills. No sign of rooftops or a town. At least that was good news. He wasn't likely to be observed or instantly captured. But he was also quite likely to find himself caught in the branches of a tree, hanging helplessly until he was found. He could actually hear his heart pounding in his chest. The night was so still that he almost believed the sound would carry for miles, alerting anybody who was up this early.

Then, as he came lower, he heard sounds: the rustle of wind through dead leaves, the creak of a branch, and the barking of a distant dog. So there were people nearby. And if they were peasants, they'd be rising with the dawn. The last seconds of the descent seemed an eternity. He felt helpless and horribly exposed, imagining German soldiers on the ground, standing by their vehicles, their rifles trained on him, waiting for him to come into range.

He could make out shapes now: to his left, a rocky crag of some sort, rearing above the gentler landscape. And trees—bare trees covering the hilltops and, below, more trees, in regular, orderly rows. But no empty fields. Nowhere guaranteeing a gentle landing. *It doesn't matter that much,* he thought grimly. He didn't have the skill to make the parachute go where he wanted it to.

The ground was coming up fast now. He could make out the rows of trees stretching up a hillside ahead of him. They were small, neat trees, still bearing their leaves and clearly cultivated. An orchard of some kind, with space between the rows to land if he could line himself up properly. He gulped in a big breath of frigid air. Branches snatched at him, knocking him off course. His feet made contact with the ground. His legs buckled under him, and he was half flung, half dragged forward.

"Release the chute, you idiot!" he yelled at himself. He tried to fumble with the harness release as his face bounced against frozen earth, then the parachute must have snagged on something. He lay still, smelling the loamy soil

14

against his cheek. He tried to get up and move, but a searing pain from his leg shot through him. The last thing he heard before he blacked out was the song of a bird, greeting the dawn.

CHAPTER TWO

JOANNA

Surrey, England, April 1973

I had never thought of my father as anything but old—old and bitter, remote and resigned, one who had long ago given up on the world. In my memory, his hair had always been grey. His face was deeply etched with lines that gave him a perpetual scowl, even when he was thinking happy thoughts, which certainly wasn't often, and he walked with a bit of a limp. So it was not a complete shock to me when I received the telegram notifying me of his death. What did shock me was to learn that he was only sixty-four.

I fought with conflicting emotions as I walked along the lane leading to Langley Hall. The countryside was bursting with spring glory. The banks were dotted with primroses. The first bluebells were appearing in the woodland beyond. The horse chestnuts that bordered the lane were sprouting their first bright green leaves. I found myself glancing up instinctively and thinking about conkers—the shiny brown horse chestnut seeds that would come later in the year. When I was a young child, the village boys would come out here with sticks to knock down the biggest and best conkers in their prickly green cases and then would thread a string through them and harden them for endless fights. I helped them in retrieving the conkers but was not allowed to join in the fights. Father did not approve of my mixing with the village children, even though our lifestyle was certainly no grander than theirs.

Overhead, a blackbird was singing, and in the distance I thought I could hear a cuckoo. I remembered how we had always listened for the first cuckoo of the year. Didn't the song go, "In April, I open my bill"?

Other than the birdsong, the world lay in almost complete stillness. I was conscious of the sound of my footsteps echoing back from the high hedgerows that bordered the lane. After the constant noise and bustle of London, it was a shock to the system to feel that I was the only person in this universe. I suddenly realised how long it had been since I had come home. Was it over a year? Not even for Christmas, because Father didn't approve of Adrian and had made it quite clear that he wasn't welcome, and I was too stubborn to visit without him. Actually, he didn't disapprove of Adrian per se. Who could find fault with a top graduate from University College London's law school who had been accepted as a pupil in one of the most distinguished

17

chambers at Temple Bar and was well on his way to becoming a successful barrister? It was only my living with Adrian that Father frowned upon. Father was of the old school, raised to do the right thing at all times. One did not live with a person of the opposite sex. Marriage was expected as soon as possible, and sex was something one anticipated on the wedding night. That was how the son of the squire at Langley Hall behaved, setting an example of morality and clean living to the peasants around him. Horribly quaint and anachronistic in a time when the rest of the world was enjoying a perpetual orgy of free speech, freedom of dress, and free love.

"Stupid," I muttered out loud and wasn't sure if I was referring to myself or to Father. I'd certainly been stupid enough, too, and if I'd only listened to Father's admonitions, I would not be in the position I was now. It was too bad he had died before he'd had a chance to say, "I told you so." He would have enjoyed that.

A pair of pigeons fluttered up from the grass in front of me, their wings making a sound like laundry flapping on a line, startling me out of my thoughts. I could detect other sounds now: a tractor working in a distant field, the hum of bees in the apple blossoms on the other side of the lane, and the rhythmic clickety-clack of a lawn mower. These were the sounds of my childhood: safe and reassuring. How long ago that seemed.

It was unusually warm and sunny for April, and I regretted wearing my one good winter coat. It was the only black garment I possessed, and I thought it was only fitting that I appeared at my birthplace dressed in mourning. I brushed a bead of sweat from my forehead. I should have sprung for a taxi from the station. In the old days, the two miles never seemed that far to walk. I had walked home from the village school until I was eleven, and that was a good mile away. I remembered coming home for holidays from university and managing the distance carrying my heavy suitcase. I realised I must still be quite frail. Understandable, really, since it wasn't too long that I had been out of hospital. They had told me my broken ribs would take time to heal. How long my heart would take they didn't say.

The tall brick wall surrounding the Langley estate replaced the copse of trees, and involuntarily I picked up my pace, driven by memories of coming home. I'd always broken into a run for the last yards when I was coming home from the village school. I'd burst into the kitchen, and my mother would look up from the stove, where she was always preparing some sort of food. The warm smell of baking would envelop me. She'd be wearing a big white apron, her face would be red, and she'd be liberally sprinkled with flour. She'd open her arms and wrap me in a big hug.

"How was school?" she'd asked. "Were you a good girl and did what your teacher told you?"

"I'm always a good girl. And I always do what I'm told," I'd replied, and added some minor triumph. "And guess what? I was the only one who could do the long division problem in sums today."

"Well done." She'd kissed the top of my head, then we'd looked up when my father came in.

"She was the only one who could finish the arithmetic problem in school today," my mother had said proudly.

"Well, naturally," he'd replied. "They are village children." And he'd gone through to the living room, settling himself with the newspaper. Mum had looked at me, and we'd exchanged a grin of understanding.

The memory of my mother brought sudden tears to my eyes. All these years gone and I still missed her. If only she'd still been alive, things would have been so different. She'd have known what to do and say. She would have been my refuge. Hastily, I brushed the tears away. I was not going to let anybody see me cry.

As this memory played itself out in my head, the wall came to an abrupt end, and I found myself standing outside the massive wrought-iron gates that led to Langley Hall. On the other side of the gates the raked driveway ran between manicured flower beds to the house.

The red brick of the Tudor façade glowed in the afternoon sunshine. The sun winked back from leaded paned windows. The front part of the house was pure Tudor, the property given to Sir Edward Langley by King Henry VIII for helping him to dismantle and plunder the monasteries. In fact, this very property used to be home to a monastery until my ancestor destroyed it, drove out the monks, and built himself a fine new house in its place. I suppose I should have guessed from this that a curse would eventually catch up with us.

The house was bigger than it seemed from the front. Subsequent Langleys had added on two fine Georgian wings and a touch of Victorian monstrosity in a corner tower and large conservatory at the rear. I stood still, gawking like a tourist, my hands wrapped around the bars of the gate, as if seeing it for the first time and admiring its beauty. My ancestral home. Home of the Langleys for four hundred years. And I was not unaware of the irony that I had never personally lived in the house—only in the small, dark, and poky gatekeeper's lodge.

The sign on the wall beside the gate proclaimed it to be "Langley Hall School for Girls." Instead of attempting to open one of the gates, I went past to a small door in the wall and let myself in the way I had always done. I turned off up the narrow path to the lodge and tried the front door. It was locked. I don't know who I'd been expecting to find there. My father had lived alone after I had gone to university. We had lived together there, just the two of us, after my mother died when I was eleven.

I stood outside the front door and noticed the peeling paint, the dirty windows, the tiny square of lawn that badly needed mowing, the neglected flower beds, with just a few brave daffodils showing through. A shiver of regret shot through me. I should have swallowed my stupid pride and come to visit. Instead, I had let him die all alone.

I hesitated, unsure what to do next. Langley Hall School was closed for the Easter holidays, but there should still have been someone in residence since the telegram had been sent from that address, indicating that Father had been found on school grounds. I presumed it had been sent by the headmistress, Miss Honeywell. She had a suite of rooms in the hall—what had been, according to my father, the best bedroom in the old days. I turned away from the lodge and willed myself to walk up the drive and confront my former nemesis from when I had spent seven miserable years at that school. After my father had been forced to sell Langley Hall and it had been turned into a girl's boarding school, he had been allowed to stay on as art master and to have the use of the gatekeeper's lodge. And when my mother had died, I was offered a scholarship to attend the school as a day girl. I suppose it was meant well—a kindly gesture. My father was delighted that I'd finally be mixing with the right sort of girls and would get the right sort of education. I would rather have gone to the local grammar school with the brightest of my classmates from the village, but one did not argue with my father when he had made up his mind.

And so I acquired a green and white uniform, with a striped tie, a panama hat for summer and a wide-brimmed velour one for winter, and a blazer with the school crest on it—which was our old family crest, acquired with the building. I entered what was for me a life of misery. Langley Hall could not be called an academic institution. Instead, it attracted the daughters of the upper class and of those who could pay to be considered upper class, and it readied these girls for good marriages. Of course, this was the nineteen sixties, and one did not actually broadcast this quaint notion. Girls were expected to learn useful skills to help them work in suitable jobs—PR, publishing, the BBC, maybe running art galleries or designing clothes—until they met the right sort of husband with the correct amount of money.

So from the very beginning I was an anomaly: I might have had a father with a title, but he was the art master at the school. I lived in the lodge and I was attending the school on a scholarship. And, worst of all, I was bright and driven. I asked questions of the teachers and longed for harder problems in maths classes. Some of the teachers loved me and encouraged my lively mind. The lazier and less qualified ones found me a nuisance and disruptive. They would send me to the headmistress and put me into detention, where I had to write out, one hundred times, "I must not interrupt my teachers," or, "I must not question my teachers."

Miss Honeywell's skull-like face with its high cheekbones and withering sneer came back clearly into my consciousness. "So you think that you know better than Miss Snode, do you, Joanna?" or, "May I remind you that you are only here as a gesture of my goodwill because your father is no longer able to look after you properly?"

The latter was undoubtedly true. My father had never cooked a meal or ironed a shirt in his life. My mother had taken perfect care of us both. And so my becoming a pupil at Langley Hall also included taking my evening meal with the girls and doing my prep with them in the study hall, going home only to sleep. I was glad of at least that small mercy. Sharing a dorm with my enemies would have been the last straw.

Not that all the girls were against me. I did make friends: quiet, studious girls like myself. We read and exchanged books and discussed them as we walked the grounds. But it was that core group of popular girls who moved in a pack, like wolves, and loved to pick on anyone weaker than them who made it quite clear that I did not belong.

"Sorry, there's no room at this table," they would say when I needed a place to sit with my lunch tray.

My gym shoes would mysteriously disappear. The wolf pack smirked as I got into trouble for losing my equipment. Unlike them, I'd had no private tennis lessons, and they mocked my feeble attempts to hit the ball. They talked loudly about where they would be going skiing or if they were off to a villa in France. As we got older, these pranks eventually stopped, partly because I never let the girls see that they were getting to me, but also because boys and parties became more important. Then they would talk loudly about which dances they would attend and which boys were being given fabulous cars for their eighteenth birthdays and might drive down to visit, giving the girls an incentive to sneak out at midnight. The trouble was that they were all part of the same social set—all interconnected in a giant web by family or business. I was one of the few outsiders.

And so I had endured until I reached the sixth form. I was driven by a burning desire and a plan for life. I was going to go to university, become a lawyer, be brilliantly successful, make a lot of money, and buy back Langley Hall. I pictured myself taking my father by the arm and leading him up the drive. "This is now ours again," I would say. "You are back where you belong— lord of the manor."

And to Miss Honeywell I'd say, "I'm so sorry, but I need you to be out of here at the end of this term." And I'd smile.

I had to smile now at my naïve optimism. Now my father was dead. I was the last of the line. The title would die out and there would be no point in restoring Langley Hall to its former glory. I took a deep breath as I went up the broad steps to the front door and pressed on the bell.

CHAPTER THREE

JOANNA

April 1973

I heard the bell echoing through the foyer, and then, after a long interval, the door opened, revealing Miss Honeywell herself. I had been expecting a porter or a maid and took an involuntary step backward when I saw that face. As always, her face was a perfect mask of makeup, her eyebrows plucked and drawn in as thin brown lines, and her hair, now greyer than I remembered, had been permed into perfect layers. What I had not been expecting was for her to be wearing slacks and an open-necked shirt. During the school year, I remembered her as wearing a tailored suit in winter with a gold pin on her lapel, and in summer a crisp linen dress and pearls.

She, too, looked startled for a second, then her face broke into a smile. "Joanna, my dear. I hadn't expected you so soon."

"I came as soon as I received the telegram."

"I wasn't sure we were sending it to the right place. Your father had several addresses for you, but we thought the firm of solicitors would find you."

"Thank you. Yes, they called me when the telegram arrived."

"Well, that's a relief. I am so sorry to be the bearer of such sad news. Do come in." She stepped back to allow me to enter the black and white marble-tiled entrance hall. Inside felt delightfully cool. Miss Honeywell shut the front door behind her.

"I was supposed to be in Italy right now, but I had some important meetings with the board of trustees and so I am stuck here," she said as she went ahead of me, her high heels tapping on the marble floor. "But it could have been worse. We are certainly experiencing some lovely spring weather, are we not?"

She was doing what the English did. When anything embarrassing or emotional threatened to come up, one discussed the weather. Always a safe topic.

"Are you planning to go away at all this year?" she asked.

"No plans as yet," I replied, certainly not about to admit to my current impecunious state.

We had reached the door of her study. I remembered it well, staring at that brass plate on her door—"Miss Honeywell, Headmistress"—and trying to breathe before I knocked and went in to face my doom. Now she opened the door and smiled at me again. "Do come in," she said. "Take a seat. I'll see if Alice is around to bring

28

us tea. As you can see, the place is pretty much deserted. Only a skeleton staff. Everyone else is gone for the Easter holidays. In fact, it was lucky that I always take a morning walk myself or your father might not have been found for days."

She picked up the phone on her desk and dialled. I watched her drum long red fingernails impatiently before she spoke: "Ah, Alice. Good. You're still here. I've Miss Langley here and we'd like some tea. Yes, in my office. Splendid." She put the receiver down and looked up at me with a smile as if she had done something rather clever.

"Where were we?"

"My father," I said. "You said you found him lying in the grounds?"

"I did. Quite a shock, I must admit. I was out with Bertie, my cocker spaniel, and he ran ahead and started barking. Well, he has a knack for finding disgusting things like dead birds so I shouted at him to leave it, and when I got there I saw it was a man lying face down in the grass. I turned him over tentatively and it was your father. Quite dead. Cold and stiff. So I ran back to the house and dialled 999. They've taken him off to the morgue and I expect they'll conduct an autopsy."

"So you don't know what he died of?" I asked tentatively. "He wasn't . . . I mean . . ." I couldn't say the word "murdered."

29

She looked horrified. "Oh no. Nothing like that, I'm sure. There wasn't a mark on him. Natural causes, I'm sure. In fact, if he hadn't been so cold and white, you'd have thought he was sleeping. Heart, it must have been. Did he have a weak heart, do you know?"

"I've no idea," I said. "You must yourself know that my father was a very private person. He never discussed anything that might be in the least personal. And I have to confess that I haven't spoken to him for some time. If he had been in poor health, he would never have told anybody."

"I had noticed he was rather more remote than usual recently," Miss Honeywell said. "Depressed, maybe." She paused. "I always thought of him as an unhappy man. He never quite got over the loss of his status and property, did he?"

"Would you?" I asked, my hackles rising on his behalf. "How would you feel if you had to live in the lodge of your former home and watch schoolgirls trooping through the rooms where you had grown up?"

"He need not have stayed," she said. "There were plenty of things he could have done. I gather he was a talented artist before the war. Up and coming."

"My father? An up-and-coming artist?"

"Oh yes." She nodded. "One gathers he

exhibited at the Royal Academy. But I've never actually seen one of his paintings, other than posters he did for school events and scenery for our plays. Competent, clearly a trained artist, but certainly not unusual."

"I had no idea that he ever painted," I said. "I knew he had studied art, but I never realised he had been a real artist. I wonder why . . ." I was going to add that I wondered why he stopped, but I answered my own question before I said the words—because his world had come crashing down around him.

"They say artists are temperamental, don't they?" Miss Honeywell said. "Highly strung. And of course he was from a high-born family, too. Inbreeding among the aristocracy does make for instability."

"You don't think he took his own life?" I asked sharply, the anger that she was suggesting my father had been somehow mentally unstable fighting with my own feelings of guilt that were threatening to engulf me.

She gave me a sad little smile. "If he had wanted to end his life, he would have had no reason to walk into the middle of the woods to do it. He could just as well have finished it at home. No one would have been there to stop him. Besides, as I mentioned, there was no sign of distress about him. Nothing like poison or a gunshot wound." She paused, looking out of

31

the window to where a starling had landed on a rose bush. "Of course, I rather suspect he had been drinking more heavily lately." She turned her attention back to me. "Oh, I'm not implying that he was drunk on the job or anything, but the groundskeeper did report that empty bottles went out with the rubbish, and Miss Pritchard, the history mistress, did bump into him in the off-licence buying Scotch."

I was tempted to ask what Miss Pritchard had been doing in the off-licence, but wisely stayed silent. "I expect we'll find out the cause from the doctor who conducts the autopsy," I said. "Not that it matters, does it? He's dead. Nothing can bring him back."

"I'm so sorry, my dear," she said, sounding almost human. "It must have been a great shock to you. He wasn't old."

"Sixty-four," I said mechanically. "Not old at all."

"He was very proud of you, you know."

I reacted to this with surprise. "Proud of me?"

"Oh yes. He talked about you often. How well you had done at university and how you were soon to be called to the bar."

This was completely unexpected. My father had resisted my desire to go to university. His attitude toward women belonged to the prewar era, to a time when he was the son of Sir Toby Langley of Langley Hall and life consisted of house parties and dances and fox hunts. A good match was made for girls, and they became mistresses of their own fine country houses. He refused to see that in the post-war era, girls like me had to make their own way in the world and could expect no help from their families. A good career was essential. And so quite without his help I had sat the entrance exams to Oxford and Cambridge and, as a backup, to University College London. I had been shattered with disappointment when I hadn't secured a place at either Oxford or Cambridge, but I had got into UCL. A good second best, I suppose. It had never occurred to me at the time that a headmistress's recommendation would have helped get me into an Oxbridge college, and I'm sure Miss Honeywell hadn't been flattering in her letter about me, if she even wrote one at all.

A government scholarship paid for my tuition, and I worked all summer at a seaside hotel as a chambermaid to pay for my room and board. While others of my generation had held protest marches, love-ins, and sit-ins, and chanted, "Make peace, not war," I had worked diligently. And so I had graduated with an upper second degree—not the first I wanted, but still pretty good. I then hoped to become a barrister.

Miss Honeywell must have been reading my thoughts.

"You are presumably working for the firm of solicitors to which I sent the telegram?"

"That's right." I saw no reason to tell her that I wasn't working there at the moment, nor the reason for my leave of absence. "I have been articled there and hoped to take the bar exam this summer, but it will now have to be in the winter. They haven't said whether they'd like me to stay on once I'm fully qualified."

"An interesting practice?"

"Not particularly. A lot of conveyancing and wills and the sort of routine stuff one gives to juniors."

"I should have thought a barrister was more your style," she said, staring at me keenly with those little bird-like black eyes of hers. "You always did like to plead your case, and you could be quite persuasive."

She broke off as an elderly maid came in with a tea tray. It was properly laid with a flowered bone china teapot, a matching milk jug and sugar basin, two cups, two saucers, and a plate of biscuits.

"Should I pour, Miss Honeywell?" the maid asked, but I noticed she was looking at me. When my gaze met hers she blushed and looked away.

"No, thank you, Alice. I'm sure we can manage," Miss Honeywell said, dismissing her with a vague wave. She picked up the silver strainer and placed it over a cup as she poured. "Ah, lapsang

34

souchong," she said. "She knows my preference. Do you take it with lemon or milk?"

I didn't happen to like China tea either way, but said, "Lemon, please," because I thought this was the right answer. I had become adept at sensing what people wanted to hear. I watched her pour the amber liquid into fragile china cups. How civilised this all was. A life so different from mine with rides on packed Tube trains and dinner from the Indian takeaway when I could afford it. And all the while my father was lying dead on a slab in the morgue. I decided I had endured polite conversation long enough. I dropped a slice of lemon into my tea and took a sip. It was too hot to drink, so I put it down.

"With regard to my father, I'm not sure what happens next," I said. "Should I arrange with the vicar for a funeral?"

"You should presumably visit the morgue first," she said. "They won't release the body for burial until they have signed the death certificate, and if there is an autopsy or there are any kinds of questions, then that could take several days."

She offered me the plate of biscuits. I rejected the chocolate digestive, not wanting to end up with it melting on my fingers, and instead opted for a custard cream. I nibbled delicately while I tried to put my thoughts in order. I hadn't considered being here for several days. I really hadn't thought things through at all, rushing out to take the next train from Waterloo, just knowing that I needed to be at my father's side—even though he was beyond help.

"Might I have the key to the lodge?" I said. "It seems a little far to keep going up and down to London."

"Of course," she said. "You'll want to go through your father's things anyway, and you could get a good start." She opened a drawer and took out a big, old-fashioned key, handing it to me with solemnity, as if she was presenting someone with the keys to the city. "Oh, and Joanna," she added, "I don't mean to rush you, and I want you to take all the time you need, but I should point out that your father was allowed the use of the lodge only as long as he was employed by the school. I have a new physical education teacher and tennis coach coming this term. He's also a man, and I would like to house him suitably far away from the girls. One can't put temptation in their way, and he is quite good-looking." She met my gaze and smiled. "You know what it's like with a flock of girls and an attractive young man."

I couldn't find anything to say or return her smile. All I wanted to do was escape from that perfect little room, from her self-satisfied smile.

"Do you have prospects in that direction?" she asked. "Any wedding bells on the horizon?" I saw her glance at my left hand.

"No," I replied. "No wedding bells."

"Still the ambitious career woman, I see." She smiled at me again. "So if you could have your father's belongings moved from the lodge before the start of the summer term, I'd much appreciate it."

CHAPTER FOUR

HUGO

December 1944

He came to with a start as something tickled his cheek. He brushed at it in alarm and saw it was only a stalk of grass bent over by the wind. He propped himself up, taking in the cold, damp soil around him, the rows of neat olive trees stretching up the hillside. It was still not quite light, but from what he could make out, the sky above him was leaden grey, heavy with the promise of rain. There was already a fine, misty drizzle coating him with a layer of moisture. He felt a tug jerk him over backward and almost cried out in alarm until he realised he was still attached to his parachute that now lay flapping on the ground like some kind of wounded bird. He fumbled at the catch, the gloves on his hands making his fingers clumsy, and eventually felt it release. He pulled away the harness and tried to sit up. His head swam with nausea as he looked around, trying to make his brain obey him and decide what course of action he should take.

The parachute billowed out as the wind hit it and threatened to blow it away. That would never do. He grabbed at the strings, attempted to stagger to his feet, and collapsed in pain again. His leg simply wouldn't hold him. He dragged the parachute toward him, reeling it in, and fought with the wind to roll it up. It was amazingly light, and he managed to do a reasonable job of stuffing it back into its pouch.

Once he had safely stowed the parachute, he sat, clutching it to him, looking around and assessing the situation. The hillside around him was planted with rows of olive trees. Round little trees with feathery leaves. Not much chance of hiding among them. The first real woodland— although now mostly bare at this time of year—was at the top of the hill several hundred yards away, and he had no way of knowing if it was the start of a true forest or merely a thin stretch of trees bordering another farm. Clouds hung down over the hilltops, but as they swirled and parted he noticed beyond the trees a rocky outcropping rising with the ruins of what looked like an old fortress on it. That might be a promising place to hide, at least until he had time to assess his wounds and decide what to do next.

He swivelled around to look down the hill. The rows of olive trees ended in a small depression, and on the other side the ground rose again, this time planted with rows of what looked like vines, although they were dead and brown intertwined sticks at this time of year. Beyond them, on the ridge, ran a row of black cypress trees looking like soldiers standing at attention through the mist that clung to the hillside. *A road,* he thought, remembering a time when he had painted scenes like this. Where the cypress trees ended, the top of the hill was crowned with woodland, and above them he could make out the tiled roofs of a small hill town. A square church tower rose above the roofs, and as he watched he heard a bell tolling six.

He stared at the hill town, wondering what sort of reception he'd get if he headed in that direction. Having lived in Italy he was hopeful that the local people would not be too fond of Germans. But then Germans might be occupying the town. It was a risk he couldn't take—at least not until he knew more.

A sudden awful shriek made him jump before he realised it was a rooster greeting the dawn. A second answered it. A dog barked. The village was coming to life. He needed to move before he was discovered. He started to crawl forward, using his hands and his good leg, dragging his parachute pack beside him. He dared not leave it behind—it would certainly give him away. And besides, a parachute might be useful—a future shelter if it rained or snowed, maybe? He wondered if he'd go faster if he stood up and hopped, steadying himself with tree branches. *A crutch,* he thought. *I need a stick to make a crutch, or maybe a splint would work if the bone is broken.* His going was painfully slow. The olive trees seemed to go on forever. He kept turning to look back to see if anyone was coming. The snort of an animal made him freeze and drop down to the earth. As he scanned the horizon, he spotted a horse and cart leaving the village along that high road. He heard the creak of wheels and the horse snorted again. He watched as it passed between the cypress trees, but it was going away from him, and he heaved a sigh of relief as he returned to his weary task.

A stiff breeze picked up, rustling the olive branches and sighing through the grass, masking faraway sounds. He felt horribly thirsty, his mouth parched and dry, and wished he'd had the sense to bring his canteen with him. Or his flask of brandy—that would have been most welcome. The woods were closer now, but he needed to stop. His strength gave out and he sat, leaning his back against a sturdy olive trunk, out of sight of the village, and closed his eyes. He felt horribly weak and realised he might have lost a lot of blood.

"I don't want to die here," he muttered. He made himself picture home. He was riding up to Langley Hall on a lovely summer day. The horse chestnuts were all in blossom. The air was perfumed with newly mown grass and the scent of roses. He reined in the horse to a trot as a groom came out to meet him.

"Good ride, Mr. Hugo?" he asked as Hugo swung himself down easily from the saddle and handed over the reins.

"Splendid, thanks, Josh."

Up the steps and in through the front door. His father sitting with the newspaper in the breakfast room, looking up with a frown. "Been out riding, have you? In my day, one changed out of riding togs before one came to breakfast."

"Sorry, Father, but I am devilishly hungry. How are you today?"

"Not bad, considering. Still short of breath going up the stairs. Still, it's to be expected, isn't it? If you've been gassed your lungs are bound to be defective."

"Beastly war. Made no sense at all."

"I doubt that war ever does, but we don't seem to learn, do we . . . ?"

Hugo pulled his memory away from that conversation, and from the image of his father's hacking cough and gradual fading away. *Think of your wife, Brenda. Think of your son.* He tried to picture them, but already the images were blurred and indistinct, like old photographs. How many years since he'd seen them? Four. Almost half of Teddy's life. When he'd left, Teddy had been a timid little boy, clinging to Nanny's skirt. Now he'd be nine. Hugo had no idea what he looked like or what he was doing. Letters only arrived every few months, most of them blacked out by

the censor so that they said almost nothing—
"Teddy is doing well and sends his daddy
love"—leaving Hugo to wonder whether Teddy
had been sent away to prep school yet, whether
he liked playing cricket, whether he had turned
into a good rider . . .

He opened his eyes to see someone standing
over him. He sat up with a start, his gloved hand
reaching for his service weapon and realising
that it was not loaded anyway. He remembered
the knife, stowed in the inside of his boot—
again completely useless to him. Why hadn't he
thought ahead, prepared to defend himself?

As his eyes focused he reacted with horror. A
thin, hooded, faceless figure, garbed in black.
The grim reaper. Death come for him. As he
attempted to get up, the figure gave a little gasp
and stepped back. Then Hugo saw that it was a
woman, dressed entirely in black, her head and
shoulders covered in a shawl. She was carrying
a basket that she now held in front of her, as if to
defend herself.

"Are you a German?" she asked in her native
Italian, then added, "*Deutsch*?"

"No. I'm not German. I'm English," he replied
in Italian, grateful that his year studying in
Florence had made him reasonably fluent in the
language. "My plane just—" He searched for the
words "crashed" or "was shot down" and found
neither. They weren't the sort of vocabulary

he'd had to use before the war. "My plane went down." He emphasised this with a gesture of a plane crashing.

The woman nodded. "We heard it," she said. "The explosion. We didn't know what it was. We were afraid the Germans were blowing something up again."

He found her hard to understand. He was afraid that he had forgotten all the Italian he had learned but then realised she was speaking with the strong Tuscan dialect he had heard used among country people. And her hand gestures confirmed what she was saying.

"Are there still Germans in this area?" he asked.

She nodded again, glancing around her as if expecting them to appear at any moment. "Oh yes. They have dug themselves holes in the hills, like rabbits. I do not think it will be easy for your people to drive them out. It is not safe for you to stay here. You must get away to the south. That way." She pointed. "That is where the Allies are advancing. We hear that they are already close to Lucca."

"I can't walk," he said. "I think I've been shot in the leg. I need a place to hide until I can treat the wound and see what needs to be done."

She glanced up again. "I can't take you to my village," she said. "The Germans come through sometimes. They demand lodging and they take

44

our food. You would not be safe. Word would get out, and there are those among us who would willingly sell information for food or cigarettes."

"I wouldn't dream of putting you in any danger," he said. Actually, that was what he'd wanted to say, but he could only produce, "I will not make dangerous for you."

She spread her hands wide. "If it was just me, I would say yes. I would take this risk. But I have my young son and my husband's grandmother living with me. I must protect them."

"Of course. I understand. You must not have danger from me."

She was frowning at him now. "How is it that you speak my language?"

"I lived in Florence once when I was a young man. I was there for a year to study art."

"You are an artist?" she asked.

"I wanted to be a painter before the war. Now I've been flying planes for five years."

"This war has robbed us all of what we loved," she said, and looked away.

He nodded. "If you could just help me up, I'll be on my way," he said. "Any moment I could be discovered and you would be in trouble for talking to me."

"I don't think anybody would come in this direction now." She looked around cautiously as she spoke, as if not quite trusting her words. "The olive harvest is over. I myself came to see if any olives still lie among the trees, or maybe there are mushrooms or chestnuts in the forest. We eat what we can find these days. The Germans take what we have."

The mention of Germans made her face grow pinched and fearful again. She pulled the shawl more tightly around her. "You cannot walk at all?"

"I could try if you would support me. Just as far as the trees up there. Then I would be hidden."

"The monastery," she said with sudden emphasis. "I will take you to the monastery. You will be safe there."

"Monastery?" Hugo reacted with the Protestant's suspicion of all things Catholic, especially monks. "Are you sure that would be a good idea?"

"It is a ruin," she said. "Nobody goes there now. But it would be a place to shelter, if you can make it that far."

"Then let's try. Maybe you could help me up?"

She put down her basket and lifted him under his armpits. She was remarkably strong for her frail appearance. He stood, sweating with pain as his wounded leg tried to take his weight.

"Come," she said. "Put your arm around my shoulder. I will support you."

"Oh no. I couldn't. It's not necessary," he said, seeing his own size compared to hers now that he was standing in front of her.

"Don't be stupid. You can't walk without help. Come on. Do it."

He did as she told him, conscious of her slight, bony shoulders under the shawl and not wanting such a delicate little thing to take his weight.

"That's right," she said. "Lean on me."

He dragged the parachute pack in his other hand as they started forward between the rows of olive trees. The wind buffeted them, unfurling her shawl across their faces. The going was horribly rough—the soil soft and muddy in places, rocky and partly frozen in others. Hugo gritted his teeth and inched forward. At last they made it to the tree line. Some of the trees were now stark and bare, while others still bore leaves—evergreen oaks and among them a few tall, dark pines. Hugo paused and leaned gratefully against a solid tree trunk.

"I need to catch my breath," he tried to say. Actually, he said, "I need to wait and breathe better." His Italian had never progressed enough to be idiomatic.

"Let us move a little further into the woods. Here you may still be seen. We never know where the Germans may be lurking." She urged him forward.

They stumbled between trees, slithering on wet leaves, tripping over roots. Here the air smelled rich and moist and the world was completely still. The woman left him, darting forward to snatch

47

at a dangling branch. "Oh look, chestnuts," she said. "That is good. Usually all the wild chestnuts have been found by this time of year. And I see some mushrooms growing on that trunk. I will pick them on my way home."

"And I see a dead branch lying over there," he said. "If you would pick it up for me, I could try to use it as a crutch."

"Good idea." She lifted the heavy branch, shaking off dead leaves. "If we break it about here"—and she did so, the branch giving a loud crack as it snapped—"it should be just right."

He tucked the thicker end under his armpit. "Yes, I think it might work."

He gave her a hopeful little grin and she returned his smile. "That is good." He noticed the way her whole face lit up as she smiled. Hidden beneath that shawl, she could have been any peasant woman of any age. Now he realised she was little more than a girl with a cheeky smile and dark eyes that sparkled.

"Now comes the difficult part," she said. "I hope it will not be too much for you."

CHAPTER FIVE

JOANNA

April 1973

Miss Honeywell and I parted company amicably. She even invited me to come and have a glass of sherry with her that evening if I was going to be alone in the lodge. I thanked her courteously but part of me was dying to shout out, "You old hypocrite. Do you not remember how foul you were to me?" I had always suspected she resented the fact that my father had a title and so no matter what else was taken from him she still had to call him Sir Hugo. I'm sure it rankled.

I walked slowly back up the drive, conscious of the sweet scent of the hyacinth and narcissus blooming on either side and the smell of newly cut grass that wafted from where the mower had been working. I hesitated outside the front door of the lodge, suddenly not wanting to go in and see what had become of my father's life. I had not come home frequently after I'd left school. Father and I found conversation awkward, and things sometimes devolved into arguments or even shouting matches, so we tended to meet for lunch at a pub somewhere. We could both be cheerful for the time it took to eat a good roast and some apple pie.

I fitted the big key into the lock and turned it. The door swung open with the sort of creak you often heard when someone was entering a haunted house on radio plays. I stepped inside, recoiling at the stale odour that hung in the air—rotting food mingled with cigarette smoke and clothes that needed washing. It was clear that he had left right after breakfast. The remains of a boiled egg, toast in the silver toast rack, an empty teacup, and a milk jug stood on the table. This I actually found reassuring. If he had been meaning to kill himself he would certainly not have had a boiled egg for breakfast first. Neither would he have left the milk out to spoil. My father had always been fastidious. The state of the milk made me realise that it was not this very morning that he had died but at least a day ago, after Miss Honeywell had walked her dog yesterday morning. And this was followed by more worrying thoughts: had he simply keeled over and dropped dead? Had he lain in the grass, calling for help? Could he have been saved if someone had heard him?

"Oh, Daddy," I whispered. "I'm so sorry."

I found myself swallowing back tears. All my life I'd wanted him to love me. I think he did, in his own way, but not like my mum did. I don't remember him ever hugging me. When I was little he had taken me on his knee and read books to me, but that was the extent of our closeness. I don't think he knew how to be a loving parent. Like all upper-class boys he was sent off to boarding school at seven and had learned to lock away his feelings.

"Daddy," I whispered again, as if he could hear me. "I did love you. If only . . ." I let the rest of the sentence hang in the air. Mechanically I picked up the remains of his breakfast, threw the eggshell and toast into the bin, and set about washing up the plate and cup as if keeping busy would hold the feelings at bay. Then I put the toaster away and wiped down the table. When I had finished, the kitchen looked clean and neat, the way it had always been when my mother had been alive. But in those days it had been warm and friendly, with clean curtains fluttering at an open window and always the good smells of her cooking in the air: freshly baked scones and steak and kidney pie and sausage rolls and Victoria sponge . . . my mouth watered now at the thought of them. My mother loved to cook. She adored taking care of my father and me. I blinked back those tears, ashamed of myself and my weakness. After my mother died I had never allowed myself to cry. Whatever mean things those girls did to me at school, however horrible Miss Honeywell was, I had always stared back at them with a look of defiance and contempt. It was only since . . . only recently that I had become so soft and fragile.

The memory of my mother's cooking made me realise I was hungry. I'd had no lunch, and a couple of nibbles of a custard cream biscuit were not exactly filling. I went to the pantry and was horrified at the lack of supplies. A dried-out piece of cheese, some withered potatoes, a few tins of baked beans and soup. It occurred to me that during term time he had taken his main meals with the rest of the staff at school. During the holidays he was literally starving himself. I cut a slice of bread and made myself a grilled cheese sandwich. As I ate I looked around the kitchen. How bleak it looked. No wonder he had sunk into depression.

Feeling a little better with food inside me, I got up and inspected the rest of the house. Apart from the kitchen there was a living room downstairs and a tiny study that was strictly my father's private domain. Upstairs were two little bedrooms and a bathroom. As I walked around, it occurred to me that these things were presumably mine now. I was the only child. I doubted that he had left a will—after all, he had nothing to leave but these few possessions. The title would die with him, unless a third or fourth cousin was lurking somewhere. Not that anyone would want to inherit a title that came with no property, no land, and no money.

It didn't take me long to walk through the rooms. The one thing that struck me more than any other was that there was nothing personal in any of them. If you'd been brought to this house you'd never have been able to guess what kind of person lived there. In my mother's day there had been cut flowers and women's magazines and open recipe books lying on tables. There were photos of me as a baby. A sweater she was knitting lying on the sofa. But now there was not a single photograph or invitation or card. The place might as well have been inhabited by a ghost.

I went through into what had been my bedroom. Again, nothing of me remained. I had taken my few possessions when I moved out. I sank on to the bed, feeling suddenly weary. This room had been my sanctuary. Before my mother died she used to tuck me in every night. After she died I would curl up into a tight ball in this bed with the covers over my head, shutting out the world and the mean girls and the lack of love and the knowledge that nobody would ever tuck me in again.

I looked around the room. Was there anything here I wanted? I didn't think so. And in the rest of the house? I did another quick tour. I could see that my father had rescued a couple of good pieces from Langley Hall: the satinwood bureau in his study with the inlaid marquetry and tiny drawers with their carved bone handles. I'd always admired that. And the grandfather clock that was supposedly over three hundred years old. Certainly not the sagging sofa or well-worn leather armchair he always sat in to watch television. Upstairs there was an elegant bow-fronted chest of drawers in the main bedroom and a gentleman's armoire with drawers down one side and racks for hanging shirts and trousers on the other. It was a fine mahogany piece, but again I was struck by the contrast of the elegant furniture and the pitifully few garments hanging in it. Apart from that, a couple of paintings on the walls: a hunting scene and a framed print of Langley Hall in the eighteenth century with elegant Jane Austen figures strolling in the grounds. *If I'd been born in another century, I might have been making a good match with Mr. Bingley,* I thought, and had to smile.

I supposed that some of these might fetch some money at auction. I certainly had nowhere to put any furniture, and I didn't particularly like the paintings. I'd have to find out when they would become legally mine. I knew a little bit about probate through my own work. If the person left no property or shares or other tangible assets, then probate was not necessary. But I'd need to obtain a death certificate and would have to wait until the coroner released the body. I wondered if he had a solicitor who could direct me. Presumably some law firm had been in charge of the sale of Langley Hall and the payment of death duties. I should go through his desk or, failing that, see if he had a safe-deposit box at the bank—which they wouldn't let me open until I had the death certificate. It all seemed overwhelming and complicated, and I don't think I had ever felt more alone. To realise that one has nobody in the world—that is a sobering thought. I knew that my mother had been an orphan, my father the only son of an only son. I might have had distant cousins somewhere, but I had certainly never met them.

"No good comes from moping around," I told myself. Since I was not yet at liberty to start packing up his things I'd go into the village and see the vicar about a funeral. Maybe he could telephone the coroner and find out when the body would be released.

Having something positive to do, I gave myself a wash and brush-up and walked into the village. As happens so often in April, the sunny day had now clouded over with the promise of rain any moment. A cold wind had sprung up from the west, and I realised my folly of going out without an umbrella. I'd be soaked by the time I reached the village. The mile walk seemed to go on forever. I pressed myself against the hedgerow until suddenly I heard the hum of an approaching motor and almost considered holding out my thumb for a lift. As it happened, I didn't have to. It was a delivery van and it came to a halt beside me. The driver leaned over and opened the passenger door.

"It's never Jo, is it?" he called. "Do you want a lift?"

I took in the big man with his florid face, trying to picture who he might be. When I hesitated, he added, "It's me, Billy. Billy Overton."

I saw then the writing on the side of the van. "Overton's Bakery. Fine Bread and Pastries." I gave him a grateful smile and climbed up beside him.

"Billy Overton," I said. "I didn't recognise you."

He grinned. "Well, I have to admit I've put on a few pounds recently. I was a skinny little kid when we sat next to each other in school, wasn't I?"

"You were. And so shy that you hardly said a word."

He burst out laughing at this. "You're right. I've come out of my shell these days. Had to, really, since I deal with the public all the time."

"You're working for your dad now, then?" I asked as he let out the clutch and we drove on.

"That's right. Went straight into the business after school. We've opened a couple more shops now—one in Whitley, one in Hambledon—doing really nicely since they put in that big housing estate. Now Dad concentrates on the baking and I make sure the retail side is going smoothly."

56

"Good for you," I said.

"How about you?" he asked. "What are you doing with yourself?"

"I'm a lawyer," I said. "At least I will be when I take the bar exam later this year."

"A lawyer. Fancy that." He nodded with approval. "Well, we always thought you'd make something of yourself. You always were the smartest in the class."

"You were pretty smart yourself," I said. "I seem to remember we had a contest going for who was top in the maths test each week."

"I did always have an aptitude with sums, I have to admit," he agreed. "It stands me in good stead now, since I handle all the books. Dad cooks the bread and I cook the books, as my wife says." And he gave another big, hearty laugh.

"You're married, then?"

"Married? I've got a three-year-old and another on the way any day now. How about you? You married, too?"

"No. I haven't found the right man yet," I said.

"Well, I suppose not. You've been busy with your career."

"Did you marry a local girl?" I asked, turning the subject back to him.

"Pauline Hodgkiss," he said. "You remember her?"

"But we always hated her!" I blurted out before I realised this wasn't tactful. "She was so snooty, going on about her dad's nursery and the nice car they had."

"She improved with age," he said, turning to give me a cheeky grin. "And it's useful having the nursery and market garden in the family. We get fresh strawberries for our tarts." He paused, then his face grew solemn. "I suppose you're down here on account of your dad, then? It's true that he's dead, then? We heard the rumour that he'd died, and my mum saw the ambulance going past."

"That's right," I said. "He was found by the headmistress out in the school grounds. She thinks it must have been a heart attack."

"That's terrible," he said. "I'm so sorry for you. Nothing's worse than losing your parents. I remember when you lost your mum and how hard that was on you."

I nodded, scared that if I opened my mouth to speak I'd cry.

"My parents always felt so sorry for your dad," he went on. "They said it wasn't right that he had to sell his home like that, not when it had been in the family for generations—and provided employment for generations of us people in the neighbourhood."

"I suppose it's happening all over," I said. "Nobody can afford to run these big houses anymore. They're like white elephants, aren't they? In constant need of repair and costing too much to heat, and nobody wants to be a servant any longer." I paused, thinking. "At least I suppose I should be glad that I didn't inherit Langley Hall, or I'd have been faced with the death duties and the painful task of selling up."

"So you won't have ties here any longer," he said as we turned into the village high street. "No reason to come down this way again."

This struck me like a punch in the stomach. No ties to the place where I grew up, where my family had lived for so long—nowhere I belonged ever again. I looked away out of the window so that he didn't see the despair in my face.

"So where can I drop you?" he asked.

"The vicarage, please. I'll have to arrange for a funeral."

"If you want cakes or sandwiches for it, just let me know and I'll supply them. On the house." And he smiled.

"Thank you. You're very kind." I heard my voice wobble as I said the words.

He came around to help me out of the van. "Are you staying at the lodge or going back to London?"

"No, I'd better stay here while I sort things out."

"Then let me know if you need a lift back out to Langley. I should be around for an hour or so."

"Thanks, Billy. You always were a good friend."

He actually blushed, making me smile.

As I walked away a car drew up on the other side of the street. A window rolled down and a voice called, "Miss Langley!"

I turned to see Dr. Freeman. I went over to him.

"I'm so sorry about your father," he said. "He was a good man."

"Were you the one who was called to him yesterday morning?"

"I was. Poor chap. He must have been dead for a while when they found him. Massive heart attack, I'm afraid. Nothing that could have been done, even if someone had been with him."

This made me feel a little better. At least he hadn't lain there alone and calling for help.

"Will they be doing an autopsy, do you know?"

"No need," he said. "I've submitted my report that the cause of death was a myocardial infarction—a heart attack. There were no signs of foul play. No reason to submit him to the final indignity."

"Thank you, Doctor. So his body can be released for burial?"

"It can." He got out of his car. "Now if you'll excuse me, I'm already two hours late for lunch and my wife will not be pleased." He gave me a friendly nod and walked toward his front door.

I continued on to St Mary's Church. The church itself was a fine old grey stone building dating from the fourteenth century. The vicarage was less old and less attractive: solid red brick from Victorian times. I was about to walk up the path to the vicarage when on impulse I turned the other way, pushed open the heavy oak door, and went into the church instead. I was immediately enveloped in the cool stillness of the place. It still had that wonderful smell that old churches have: part damp, part old hymn books, and the lingering scent of burned-out candles. I stood there, staring down the nave to the altar window with its original stained glass of the Virgin Mary holding the baby Jesus. I'd always loved that window as a child. The Virgin's robe was the most beautiful blue, and when the sun shone through the glass it sent stripes of blue and white and gold on to the choir stalls in a way that had always seemed magical to me.

I watched it now, trying to recapture that feeling of peace that always came to me in that church, but the Virgin looked out past me, that chubby baby so secure in her arms, her serene smile mocking me. "Look what I've got," she seemed to be saying. "Isn't he perfect?" I closed my eyes and turned away.

I started to walk around, staring at the walls, studying the monuments and plaques to generations of dead Langleys. As I child I'd known them all by heart. Edward Langley, Baronet Josiah Langley. Eleanor Langley, aged twenty-two. And now it was as if I felt their presence. "Don't worry," they were saying. "You'll get through this. You're a Langley. We're strong."

It was all right for you, I thought. *You had a home to go back to.*

A noise behind me made me jump.

"I thought I spotted someone going into the church," the vicar said. "Joanna, my dear. I'm glad to see you seeking comfort from the Lord."

Actually I had been seeking comfort from my ancestors, but I let him pray with me before he led me back to the vicarage, where his wife served me tea and a big slice of fruit cake.

CHAPTER SIX

HUGO

December 1944

They came out of the trees to find the ground rising steeply before them through the mist— first a grassy knoll and then a rocky crag topped with what looked like an old, ruined building. A flight of ancient, worn stone steps had been cut through the grass, then a steeper flight ascended the rock to the remains of some buildings. At least that clearly used to be the case, but part of the rock had been destroyed, and the steps now clung precariously to the side of a sheer drop. At the foot of the flight was a post with the words "*Pericolo. Ingresso Vietato.*" Danger. Entrance Forbidden.

"It doesn't look as if the monks have been here for a long time," Hugo said.

"Two years now."

Hugo had been thinking it was an old ruin. "Two years?"

"It was bombed by the Allies."

He reacted in horror. "We bombed a monastery?"

She nodded. "It was necessary. The Germans

had taken it over and were using it as a lookout point. They brought big guns up here to shoot at passing aeroplanes and to command the road in the valley."

"I see. So the monks had already left?"

"Yes, they were turned out when the Germans arrived. It was a famous chapel, with beautiful pictures. The Germans looted all the artwork, may they burn in hell. The buildings are now beyond repair, and we are forbidden to go here."

"Then leave me now. I don't want to get you into trouble."

"Who will see?" She spread her hands. He had always noticed how expressive Italians were with their hands. "The only reason anyone would come here at this time of the year is to look for mushrooms, like me, or to set a snare for rabbits." She patted his arm. "Don't worry. I will be careful. When the place is swarming with Germans, one learns to move like a shadow. Come. Shall we try to climb these stairs?"

"If you don't mind, I'll go up on all fours, like a baby," he said. "Steadier that way."

"Then give me the stick and your bag."

"It's my parachute," he said.

"Parachute? Good silk." Her eyes lit up. "When you no longer need it, I can use it to make new underclothes. We have had no new clothes for years."

He was amused. "All right. It's a deal."

"You start to go ahead of me," she said. "I will make sure you don't fall."

As if she could catch me, skinny little thing, he thought. He dropped to his knees and started to haul himself up the stairs. He had to put weight on his wounded leg at every step, pain shooting through him. At one stage he thought he was going to vomit, so he paused, breathing hard.

He made it to the top of the first flight. It had begun to rain in earnest now, fat drops pattering onto his leather bomber jacket. Ahead of him the damaged steps rose, impossibly steep, cracked, and dangerous. He dragged himself up, one by one, conscious of the drop beside him. The steps were wet and slippery, and he had a vision of himself sliding off with nothing to grab on to. A metal railing ran up one side, but he was too low down to use it. At last he made it to the top and lay panting on the wet rock.

She came to stand beside him. "Well done, Signor. Come. Only a few more steps and we will find you a place that is dry and safe."

She helped him to his feet and draped his arm over her shoulders again. The incongruity of it crossed his mind—the upright Englishman who kept his distance from women and addressed them with polite frostiness now draped over a strange Italian woman he had just met. They went across the slick pavement of the forecourt, now broken and uneven, one small step at a time. She held on to him firmly, supporting him. Now he could see that the lower buildings to his left were reduced to complete rubble. It was hard to tell what they had been. In fact, they were beginning to look like part of the rock itself. Plants had grown up between the fallen stones, a small tree now sprouted between cracked flagstones, and a vine of some sort—now dead—sprawled over a pile of rubble. But the building immediately ahead of them, to which she was taking him, still had walls standing, although the roof was gone. There were three broad, curved steps leading to what had been a church door, although the door itself now hung at a crazy angle, swinging in the wind. She pushed it aside and stepped into the area beyond.

"Well, it's not very welcoming, but it's better than nothing." She turned back to him. "At least you will be out of the wind here. And we can build you a shelter with some of this fallen wood."

He had dragged himself the last few feet into the former chapel. Amid the utter destruction were still signs that it had once been a house of worship. The walls had been painted with frescoes, now pockmarked and washed away by rain and wind. A headless saint stood in one corner. Small glimpses of the black and white marble floor showed through the piles of dust and rubble. He saw that the wood she had referred to consisted of the great beams of the fallen ceiling. *She is decidedly optimistic,* Hugo thought. He didn't think they could move such beams between them, even if he'd been fit and mobile. But he did notice the pews that lay strewn around and the broken cupboard in one corner. Presumably in time he could build up the fallen blocks of stone, if he was planning to stay here for long. He couldn't see that happening, however. There would be the matter of food, for one thing. But he also couldn't picture himself making his way across country in his current state.

Almost as if she was reading his thoughts, she aided him to a big stone and eased him down on to it. Then she pulled some prickly shells from her pocket. "Here. The chestnuts. Eat them. They are better than nothing. I will try to return with better food for you."

"No, you must not come back. It's too dangerous. I do not want to put your family in danger. You have been very kind and I thank you."

"It is nothing." She gave him a sweet, sad smile. "My husband has been missing for three years. I hope and pray that if he needed help, as you do, someone would do their best for him."

"May I know your name?" he asked.

"It is Sofia. Sofia Bartoli. And yours?"

"I am Hugo. Hugo Langley."

"Ugo? This is an Italian name. You have Italian ancestors?"

"Not that I know of." He winced in pain as he moved.

"Let me see your leg," she said, noticing his grimace. "Let us see how bad it is."

"Oh no. Please don't worry yourself. I can take care of it."

"No, don't be silly. I insist. Where is the wound? Can you roll up your trousers?"

"It's just above my knee. Really, I can take care of it when you are gone. I think there is a first aid kit in my parachute pouch." He hoped she caught the gist of what he wanted to say. He'd spoken haltingly as he fished for unfamiliar words. What he actually said was, "Items for aiding make clean in my sack for parachute."

"*Allora.* Now. Let me see. We must remove the trousers, I think."

He was reluctant to take down his trousers in front of a strange woman, but she was already lifting up his leather jacket and unbuckling his belt.

"Signora, no." He tried to push her hands away.

She laughed. "A typical Englishman. He would rather bleed to death than let a woman see him in his underwear."

"Have you met any other Englishmen?" he asked, amused at this outburst.

68

"No, but one hears that they are cold like fish. Not passionate like our men."

"We are not all cold like fish, I assure you," he said. "But we are brought up to behave correctly at all times."

She looked up at him and smiled. "At this moment I do not imagine that you will have any improper ideas if I see you with no trousers on. Come on, let us get on with it. I must return home soon or they will start to worry that something has happened to me."

She helped him ease down his trousers and then saw the long johns beneath them. At the place above the knee, they were stuck to his skin with dried blood.

"*Gesù Maria*!" she exclaimed. She dropped to her knees beside him and tried to pry away the fabric as gently as she could. He gasped at the sudden pain.

"I'm sorry, but it must be done," she said. "Do you have a knife? We must cut it away, I fear."

He retrieved the knife from his boot and helped cut the underwear free above the wound.

"Water," she said. "I need water to ease the fabric away and then wash your wound so that we can see how bad it is." And before he could answer she had darted out of the sanctuary, leaving him alone. He hobbled to an overturned pew, righted it with much effort, and sat on it with his leg outstretched before him. In the half-darkness it was hard to see just how bad his leg was. He rummaged in the parachute pouch and located the tiny first aid kit in the central pocket. It contained wound dressings, a roll of bandage, a tourniquet, iodine, and, to his great excitement, a vial of morphine and a syringe. He had just opened a wound dressing when Sofia returned.

"I have found water," she said, sounding triumphant. "The rain barrel was overflowing and I collected some in this tin mug I found." When she saw his suspicious face she added, "Don't worry. I washed it out as best I could and wiped it clean with my petticoat." She saw what he had laid out on the bench. "Oh, you have good things there. Now, if you permit, I will try to clean your wound for you."

She started to cleanse the area, gradually peeling away the stuck fabric until it came off. The blood saturated the dressing long before the area was clear. "Your wound still bleeds, I fear. We must apply pressure to stop it."

"But what if the bullet is still in there? Shouldn't we try to locate it first?"

She gave a wonderfully expressive shrug. "A bullet will not matter if you bleed to death first." She took the bandage, unrolled it, made a wad, and pressed it on to his wound. He cried out in pain.

"Of course, I forgot. The bone may be broken. Here, hold this without pushing too hard."

He did as he was told, but said, "I have morphine here. It will help to deaden the pain."

She watched as he injected it, nodding with approval.

"When I return I will bring bandages and a piece of wood for a splint." She looked at him. "Be careful as you pull up your trousers again. That wool fabric would not be good if it sticks to the wound. Perhaps you should not pull them up. Maybe your parachute can help keep you warm. I will try to bring a blanket, too."

He grabbed at her hand. "Signora Bartoli, no. I do not want you to take anything your family might need. And I do not want you to take risks for me. I would certainly appreciate some food and a splint, but then I will try to be on my way. Even if I meet some Germans, I am a pilot. I will be a prisoner of war and treated fairly."

She looked at him, then shook her head and laughed. "You think those animals will treat you fairly? In a village near here they lined up the people and shot them for helping the partisans. All of the people. Babies and children and old women. Bang, bang, bang. All dead. And the Germans are now afraid. They know they are losing. Their line is no longer holding. Every day they are pushed back a little further to the north. You would be a liability to them. No, I do not think they would treat you fairly. We just have to pray that the Allies get here soon."

She put her hand on his shoulder. "Have courage. I will return when I can. You should not try to light a fire. The smoke may be seen."

She paused in the doorway to look back at him. "May God watch over you." And then she was gone.

CHAPTER SEVEN

JOANNA

April 1973

The funeral was held on a rainy Tuesday. The weather had looked promising over the weekend, but on Monday afternoon it clouded over again, and by nightfall the rain had begun. At the time of the funeral it was a bleak and blustery day. I hadn't expected anybody to come but was surprised by the number of local people who filled the pews and later stood around the grave with me while the rain dripped from our umbrellas and on to the coffin. It seemed a fitting send-off for my father that the heavens were weeping for him.

Afterward, the vicar's wife and Billy Overton's bakery had prepared a fine spread in the church hall. One person after another came up to me to express condolences. Some of them I knew, others were complete strangers, but they all had some association to Langley Hall and my family. "And my mother was in service at the Hall when she was a girl, and she always said how kind the old squire was to her when she got scarlet fever." Similar stories over and over, until I realised that everyone present resented the loss of the Hall as much as my father had done. It represented the passing of an old way of life, of the security of knowing one's place. I found it very touching.

As the crowd thinned, a young man came up to me. I had noticed him at the gravesite. He had been wearing a Burberry raincoat, his face hidden under a big black umbrella. Now he was wearing a well-cut black suit. "Miss Langley?" He had red hair and freckles on his nose and looked absurdly young. "I'm Nigel Barton. You know, Barton and Holcroft, your family solicitors?"

"Oh, Mr. Barton." I shook the hand he held out. "How do you do? I'm pleased to meet you. I was wondering whom I should contact about the formal side of things and whether my father left any sort of will."

"We do not possess a will, Miss Langley. Have you been through his papers?"

"I did glance through his desk, but then I felt uncomfortable about going through things when I wasn't sure I had a right to."

"You are his daughter." He smiled at me. "I think that gives you every right. Perhaps you would care to come to the office in Godalming tomorrow and we can see how I might be of help to you?" He handed me his card.

"You look awfully young to be a partner in a law firm," I said, before realising that this wasn't very tactful.

He laughed. "Not a partner yet, I regret to say. The Barton in the firm's name was my great-grandfather. We've been your family lawyers for a couple of hundred years. I've only been qualified for a couple of years, and I'm very much the junior of juniors."

"I am supposed to take my own bar exam this year," I said.

"Of course. I heard that you were reading law. We'll have lots to talk about. Maybe I can take you to lunch tomorrow? The Boar's Head down the street from our offices serves a pretty good meal."

I hesitated. A man inviting me out to lunch? I wasn't sure I was ready for that. "I'm sure that's not necessary, nor is it part of the usual service," I said, and saw his face fall.

"It's not, but it's a really good excuse for me to have a slap-up meal instead of the usual sandwich," he said. He gave me a hopeful smile.

Why not? a voice was whispering in my head. *He looks harmless enough. It's not as if he's inviting you to a nightclub. Not a date. Strictly business.*

I managed my own smile. "Thank you, Mr. Barton. It's very kind of you."

He beamed as if I'd given him a present. "I won't keep you now, then. I'm sure all these people are waiting to talk to you. Around eleven thirty tomorrow, shall we say?"

Billy Overton and Dr. Freeman both offered to drive me home, but Miss Honeywell appeared out of nowhere and I rode home with her.

"It was a very satisfactory funeral," she said as we left the village street and turned into the leafy lane. "You must feel comforted by how many people came and by the reverence in which they hold the Langleys."

"Touched and surprised," I said. "I only wish my father had been alive to hear all the nice things they said."

"I'm sorry I was a little late," she said. "A last-minute phone call with parents who are in the Middle East. I had to reassure them their daughter would be kept safe from gardeners and grooms."

I chuckled. "And did you reassure her?"

"I'm not sure. These foreign girls grow up so sheltered that they hurl themselves at any man." There was an uncomfortable silence. "You'll be going back to London, I take it?"

"Not for a few days," I said. "You asked me to clear out the lodge, and I haven't yet found a will, so I don't feel comfortable disposing of my father's belongings."

"I don't think he left very much, did he?" she said. "I know he kept a few good pieces of furniture from the Hall, but apart from that . . . Oh, and I believe there are still a couple of trunks of personal items that he asked if he could store in the attic. You should take a look at them when you have time. Mainly things like old trophies and photograph albums, I think. And some family portraits. You may want to keep some of them."

"Thank you, yes, I'd like to look through them."

"Come over whenever you like. The front door is open during the day."

"I'm afraid I have no idea how one gets to the attic," I said.

She laughed. "Of course. I always think that you once lived at Langley Hall."

"I was born in the lodge," I said.

"Don't worry. I'll have one of the gardeners bring your father's things over next time I see them."

We had reached the gates to the school. She stopped the car to drop me off at the lodge. "Your employer doesn't mind your taking this time off?" she asked.

"They have been most understanding," I said, not wanting to touch on the truth. I thanked her and let myself in. Again I was struck by the feeling of cold and damp, almost as if the lodge itself was echoing my father's sadness and despair. I told myself that I should make an inventory of everything, but felt suddenly drained after the funeral. I realised I hadn't eaten any of those cucumber sandwiches or sausage rolls or little cakes, and wished now that I had packed some up to eat later. I made myself a cup of tea and a slice of toast, then I decided to call Scarlet. Scarlet was my former college roommate. I was currently occupying the sofa in her flat, having had to move out of my last digs in a hurry. She was completely different from me: for one thing she was a cockney whose father ran a pub. Her name wasn't really Scarlet, either—it was Beryl, which she hated. She felt that Scarlet suited her personality much better. She had embraced everything that the seventies stood for: she wore long tie-dyed skirts, her unruly hair half covered her face, she smoked pot, and she went on protest marches against war and for women's rights. I had always been the good one, the studious one, focused on my degree, not on ending the war in Vietnam. But surprisingly we got on really well. She was kind and easy-going, and she had welcomed me instantly when I'd had nowhere to go. She now worked in the theatre, assistant stage manager at the Royal Court, known for its avant-garde plays.

I wasn't sure I'd find her at home mid-afternoon, but the phone picked up after several rings.

"Yeah? What do you want?" said the grumpy voice. It sounded more like "Waddayouwant?"

"Sorry," I said. "Did I wake you?"

"Oh, Jo, it's you, love. Don't worry about it. I had to wake up anyway in ten minutes. Dress rehearsal tonight. New play. Ten women on a train going to Siberia. Bloody depressing if you ask me. They all end up committing suicide. And talking of depressing, how was the funeral?"

"Very nice as funerals go."

"And how are you coping?"

"Keeping my head above water describes it best. The lodge is about the bloodiest gloomy place you could find. But I've got to go through my father's things and get it cleared out for the next tenant, so I won't be back for a while."

"No problem. I'm not planning to rent out your bed. Not planning to invite anybody into my own, either. I've had enough of men."

"That new actor didn't turn out the way you hoped? I thought he was taking you out to dinner."

"He bloody didn't turn out to be anything. We went out to dinner. I invited him back to the flat, and he started showing me pictures of his partner, Dennis."

I started to laugh. "Oh, Scarlet, do you think we're both doomed?"

"It's too bad we don't fancy each other, isn't it? Do you think someone could learn to become a lesbian?"

"I don't think so." I was still laughing. "It is good to hear your voice. I've had to be polite to people I don't know all day. And tomorrow I have to have lunch with a very earnest young solicitor."

"There you are, then. Someone your type."

"No more lawyers, thank you. Actually, no more men, thank you. I've learned my lesson. From now on I live a quiet life. No men. No sex. Study and books and the occasional lonely meal at a good restaurant."

"And cats. Don't forget the cats."

I laughed then. "I need to get back to London as soon as possible. If the solicitor tells me I can do what I like with the things in the lodge, I'll have an auctioneer come and pick up anything worth selling. Then the rest goes to a charity shop, and goodbye, Langley Hall."

When I put the phone down, I realised what an effort it was to sound bright and cheerful. *Keep busy,* I told myself. That's what I had to do. So I got a large rubbish bag and started filling it with my father's clothes. I wasn't sure if anyone would want handkerchiefs with a monogram on them, but you never know. Then I filled a box with books, setting aside a few that had been my childhood favourites—the ones that my father had read to me. By the end of the day, I had cleaned out the bedroom and the linen closet. Then I went through my father's desk, carefully this time, in case there was a will or some other surprise hidden in a secret drawer. There was a post office savings book with five hundred pounds in it. A receipt for some shares in a building society. A bank book. That was about it.

It seemed my father was probably worth a little over a thousand pounds. Better than nothing.

I opened a tin of soup for my supper. As I stood stirring it at the stove, I was suddenly overcome by a memory of my mother standing at this same stove and stirring a big pot. "Chicken stew and dumplings," she said, beaming at me. "Your father's favourite. This will cheer him up if anything will."

The memory of that warm, friendly kitchen with its good smells and kind words was too much for me. I turned the stove off, left the soup, and went to bed.

CHAPTER EIGHT

JOANNA

April 1973

The next day, I was about to leave to catch the train to Godalming when there was a tap at the door. Two burly men stood there carrying a trunk between them.

"Where do you want it, miss?" one of them asked.

Seeing my surprise, the other added, "It's from the attic. Miss Honeywell told us to bring down your things."

"Oh, I see. Thank you. This way, please," I stammered. I led them through to the sitting room.

"There's some pictures, too. We'll be back," the one who spoke first said.

"I have to leave now to catch a train," I said. "Just put them in the sitting room with the trunk, would you?"

And I left. Barton and Holcroft's offices were in an elegant Georgian building at one end of Godalming High Street. Nigel Barton appeared from an inner office before I could announce myself.

"We'll be back in an hour, Sandra," he said to the receptionist. He ushered me out of the door, down the street, and into The Boar's Head. It was one of those quaint old pubs with leaded panes in the windows and a quiet hum of conversation from the few people standing around the bar. Good smells came from the kitchen. Nigel found us a high-backed oak booth and went to order our drinks. He came back to report that there was roast lamb or fish pie. Normally I would have selected something lighter at lunchtime, but I found I was starving and willingly accepted the roast lamb. As he had predicted, it was excellent. I suddenly realised how long it had been since I'd had good food—not really since my mother had died—and how much I enjoyed it.

When our plates were clean, Nigel stacked them to one side. "Now to business," he said. "I take it you found no will."

I shook my head. "There is a savings book, a receipt from a building society for some shares, and his bank book. But probably not over a thousand pounds in total."

He nodded. "You'll need the death certificate before they'll hand over any of that money. And I'll have to write a solicitor's letter. Apart from that there are no assets?"

"A couple of good pieces of furniture that I might put up for auction. I think I'd like to keep the desk, but I'm not sure where I'd put it."

"I'll have to locate your brother before you do anything," he said.

I didn't think I'd heard right. "My brother? I'm an only child."

"Your half brother. From your father's first marriage." He took in my shocked face. "You didn't know your father had been married before?"

"No. I was never told. I knew that my parents had both married late in life and that I was a complete surprise to them, but I had no idea . . ." I let the rest of the sentence drift away as I tried to come to terms with this news. "When was this?"

"Your father was married before the war and had a son. The marriage was dissolved when he returned at the end of the war. His wife married again and took the child to live in America. Lord knows how I'll trace him now. I believe the stepfather adopted him, but I presume he'd still inherit the title, if he wanted to do such a thing in America."

I was still in shock. How could my father have lived with me all those years and never even mentioned his son? And more to the point, why had his son never been in contact with him since the end of the war?

"I'll get in touch with the American embassy," Nigel said. "But I wouldn't worry. I think it's quite clear that your father would have wanted you to inherit what little he left."

And if it wasn't quite clear? I was thinking. *If the law decided that an oldest son should inherit everything?* A thousand pounds would make all the difference to me now, especially at this uncertain time. If my law firm wouldn't take me back, then I could still survive with that money.

"If his stepfather legally adopted him, then presumably he'd have no claim," I said. "He's no longer a Langley."

"Complicated matter, if American law is involved," he said. "Still, more interesting than most of the cases I'm given. Is your practice more exciting than that of a high-street solicitor?"

"Not at all," I said. "I expect it's pretty much the same. Lots of conveyancing."

"You chose to be a solicitor and not a barrister?" he asked. "You wanted the comfortable, quiet life rather than the excitement?"

I looked down at the worn oak table. "Actually, I'd have very much liked to be a barrister," I said. "I got a good degree, but I had more than one thing against me. Money, for starters. The chambers at which I interviewed were quite keen on me when they heard I was the daughter of Sir Hugo Langley and thought it meant I was part of the county set with good connections. They lost interest when they found out they were wrong and we were penniless. And then there's the fact that I'm a woman. The elderly head of chambers told me outright that I was wasting my time. If I became a barrister, I'd get none of the juicy cases. No solicitor worth his salt would want to put his case in the hands of a woman, when almost all judges are male and most juries are male, and none of them would take a woman seriously."

"That's preposterous," Nigel said.

"But true."

He nodded. "I suppose it is true. Still, there are plenty of interesting things to do once you qualify: corporate law, international law, as well as criminal."

"Yes." I gave him a bright smile. "I haven't quite decided what I'd like to do yet. Pass that wretched exam first, right?"

"I'm sure you'll ace it." His smile seemed a little too friendly for comfort.

"So what's next?" I asked. "For my father's estate, I mean."

"I'll see to the death certificate, try to contact your brother, and, if you like, I could send an appraiser to see if anything you have is worth sending to an auction."

"You're very kind."

"No, my grandfather would kill me if I didn't take proper care of a Langley." He grinned, making him look absurdly young again. A nice, pleasant, harmless young man. And yet Adrian had been all of those things . . . One should learn from one's mistakes.

Nigel escorted me to the station and I took a

taxi back to Langley Hall. I almost fell over the two trunks and large brown paper-wrapped parcel deposited right inside the sitting room. I had to admit to being rather curious. I suppose at the back of my mind was always the thought that the lost Langley jewels might be in one of them! I tore off the brown paper wrapping from the large parcel and found myself looking at my own face. It was so startling that I almost dropped the picture. It was even more startling when I read the inscription: "Joanna Langley. 1749–1823."

My heart was racing so fast that I had to sit down. I examined the portrait again and noticed subtle differences. She had hazel eyes and mine were blue. She also had a mole of some sort on her left cheek and a slightly longer nose. I was looking at an ancestor. But it felt rather special to know I had a namesake who looked like me. It affirmed for the first time that I really was a Langley and that the lovely house down the drive was my birthright.

The rest of the pictures were all portraits of various Langley ancestors. Most of them were dark and gloomy, and I wasn't sure I would want to keep many of them. I supposed I should, given they were my only ties to my past. Someday I'd have a place of my own, when I was a rich corporate lawyer—a flat overlooking the Thames, all glass and modern furniture, and I'd put these pictures on the wall just to impress my clients. But they'd need cleaning first. They were awfully dirty from generations of candle smoke and neglect.

I felt quite cheerful when I opened the first of the trunks to find it contained more pictures, only this time bright, modern ones. I was looking at splashes of Italian sunshine, old stone buildings, black cypresses. I read the signature in the corner of one: Hugo Langley. So my father really had been a painter. What's more, he had been talented. What on earth made him give it up?

I put the pictures aside, intending to show them to Nigel. Maybe they would fetch serious money at an auction, if I could bear to part with them. Then I opened the second trunk. This one held old albums with leather covers and impressive clasps. Photos of long-ago Langleys in long dresses and ridiculous hats, frozen in time as they posed for a camera or standing in groups outside Langley Hall holding tennis racquets or having tea on the lawn. I was witnessing the lifestyle I'd never know. I put the books aside and delved deeper. A silver cup presented to Sir Robert Langley as Master of Hounds. A smaller one to Hugo for winning the high jump during sports day at Eton. Then I came to a small leather box, beautifully tooled and gold embossed. I opened it, anticipating those long-lost jewels, and almost closed it again when I saw that it contained only a tiny carved wooden angel, what looked like a medal of some sort on a ribbon, a cigarette packet, a bird's feather, and a folded-up envelope. Why anybody would keep such trifles in such a lovely box I couldn't imagine. Some Langley from history playing a game of pretend as I had done as a child, maybe.

I took out the cigarette packet to throw it away when I saw that it had been opened. On the inside of the cardboard was a sketch of a beautiful woman. It was only a tiny sketch, hastily done and not in any way finished, but somehow it conveyed the woman's personality. I could see her eyes almost sparkling with amusement as she looked at her sketcher, her mouth about to smile. I smoothed it out and put it down on the table. Then I unfolded the envelope. I recognised my father's elegant handwriting. It had an airmail stamp on it, and it was addressed to a Signora Sofia Bartoli in a place called San Salvatore in Tuscany. The date beside the stamp was April 1945, but it had never been opened. Another stamp beside the address was in Italian, but I got the gist of it. "Not known at this address. Return to sender."

Intrigued now, I tore the envelope carefully open. To my annoyance the letter was in Italian. I managed to read, "*Mia carissima Sofia.*" I stared in disbelief. I couldn't imagine my cold and distant father calling anyone his beloved. He certainly never showed any such outpouring of affection to my mother or me. I tried to read on, but the rest was beyond me. Then I remembered an Italian dictionary among the books I had put in a box to take to the charity shop. I ran to retrieve it, then sat at the kitchen table, frowning in concentration as I tried to make sense of the words. It was lucky I'd had years of Latin and French schooling because that made it easier, and when I had finished I could not quite believe what I had translated. Surely I must have got it wrong. I went through it again.

My darling Sofia,

How I miss you every day. How long the months have seemed since I was with you. All that time in hospital, not knowing if you were safe, wanting to write to you but not daring to do so. But I have good news. If your husband is indeed dead then we are free to marry. When I was finally allowed to return home to England, I learned that my wife had found someone else and left me for a better life in America. As soon as this horrible war is over, and the news indicates this will be very soon, I will come for you, my love. In the meantime, I want you to know that our beautiful boy is safe. He is hidden where only you can find him.

I broke off in amazement. My father—my distant, unemotional father—had a child in Italy. A child with an Italian woman called Sofia. But hidden where only Sofia could find him? A chill came over me. The letter was never delivered. A child hidden away and never found? Of course now, twenty-eight years later, I had to hope that Sofia had recovered the child and all was well.

CHAPTER NINE

JOANNA

April 1973

I don't know how long I sat there staring at the flimsy sheet of airmail paper. Having grown up as an only child, I was shocked to discover in one day that I might have two brothers in other parts of the world. *If this one had survived,* I thought. Perhaps he had been hidden with a kind family in the hills, to be reunited with his mother when hostilities ceased. That is what I tried to believe. But now I was dying to know more. My father never spoke of his wartime experiences, but I knew from my mother that he had been a pilot with the RAF and terribly brave, flying missions over occupied Europe until he was shot down and nearly died. I hadn't even known this happened over Italy. One didn't tend to think of Italy as a scene of bombing missions.

I turned away in frustration. If only I had known about this before he had died, I could have asked him. I could have found out the truth. Now I'd have to fish it out for myself.

I finished going through the two trunks and didn't find anything of value to anyone but a

Langley. Not a single picture of the first wife or my half brother, but there were some small snapshots of a younger, healthy version of my father laughing with friends at a café. Written on the back of one was "Florence, 1935." I put the trunks to one side and went back to emptying linen closets, the pantry, the bathroom cupboard, assembling a big pile to be donated and an equally big pile to be taken out with the rubbish. I found that I felt completely unsentimental about discarding items from my childhood, only anxious to get this task done and set off on my quest.

The next day I was hauling out bags and boxes for the dustman when a car drew up and Nigel got out, accompanied by an older man.

"This is Mr. Aston-Smith," Nigel said. "He's an appraiser. I thought we'd get a jump on things and have the furniture valued." I escorted them inside, apologising for the mess. I showed him the family portraits, the few good pieces of furniture. I was tempted to show Nigel the letter. I needed to show it to somebody, but I couldn't bring myself to do it. Mr. Aston-Smith didn't take long. He walked around making muttering noises and scribbling in a notebook. In a very short time he came back to me.

"Not much here, I'm afraid," he said. "The desk is a fine piece. You'd probably be looking at a good five hundred pounds at auction. The chest upstairs maybe slightly less. The grandfather clock—that might also bring in serious money. The armoire—well, it's good wood, but nobody wants large pieces of furniture like that these days."

"And the pictures?"

"On the wall? Prints. Worth maybe a hundred a piece."

"I meant the other pictures. My father's work."

"They are good, I'll grant you that," he said. "But he doesn't have a name, does he? It all depends on name for modern art at the big auctions. Snob value rather than quality, I'm afraid. Again they'd bring in an amount in the hundreds rather than the thousands."

"And the family portraits?"

"I can't tell you much. They are all in need of a good cleaning, as I'm sure you noticed. If you like, I can take them to an art restorer I work with and we can make a judgment on them after they've been cleaned."

"Would that be very expensive?" I was conscious that the amount I was to inherit was hardly a fortune, especially if I had to share it with a newly discovered brother.

"Not too horrendously so, depending on the amount of restorative work that would need to be done. Just a simple cleaning to begin with, and then we could make a decision about whether to proceed."

I glanced at Nigel. He gave me one of his hopeful smiles. "All right, then," I said. "Please do take them."

As they headed for the front door, I made a decision.

"And I want to keep the desk," I said, "but I've nowhere to put it at the moment."

"Maybe they'll let you store it in the school attic," Nigel suggested, "with any other small bits and pieces you are hanging on to."

"Excellent idea." I smiled at him. "Miss Honeywell should be amenable since I'm rushing to get the place cleared out. I'll ask her."

"How long do you think you'll still be here?" Nigel asked.

"I hope to be gone by the end of the week."

I saw his face fall. "I see. Presumably you need to get back to work."

Of course I needed to get back to work, but I wasn't sure I still had a job. Nevertheless, I smiled and nodded.

"I'll keep you up to date," he said, "and I'll let you know when the funds from the various accounts will pass to you."

I looked at Mr. Aston-Smith. "Perhaps your person should hold off with the restoring work on the paintings until I know that I have legally inherited the money."

"Very well," he said. "I'll take them with me but await your instructions. And presumably I should do the same with the furniture you want to send to auction. We don't want to sell anything you don't have a right to."

"Don't worry," Nigel said. "I'll take care of it. You go back to London. I'll telephone you with any news."

And so they left with my family portraits. I went on with my clearing up. Later, I was about to sit down with a cup of tea when there was another knock at my front door. This time a large, florid man stood there. He frowned when he saw me.

"So what's this with the girl's school?" he asked in a deep voice with a definite transatlantic accent. "When did Langley Hall get sold?"

"Right after the war," I said.

"Too bad. I was hoping to look around the old place. Are you the gatekeeper's daughter?"

"I'm Joanna Langley," I said stiffly. "Daughter of Sir Hugo Langley."

His eyebrows shot up. "No kidding. So the old man married again? What do you know."

It was just dawning on me who this was. I stared at his face and saw no resemblance to my father, who had always had the lean appearance of a Romantic poet. This man was well fed and chubby in a not particularly attractive way.

"You're Hugo's son?" I asked.

"That's right. Teddy Langley, I used to be. Now I'm Teddy Schulz. Of Cleveland, Ohio."

I forced myself to hold out my hand. "I'm pleased to meet you, Teddy. Until a couple of days ago, I had no idea that I had a brother. It came as a big shock."

"Yeah. I just got a shock, too. The old guy's death, I mean. A client came back from England and showed me the newspaper with the obituary in it. 'Any relation of yours?' he said. So I thought I'd better hightail it over the pond, being the son and heir, y'know. I presumed the estate would be coming to me. Isn't that how it works with English law? Oldest son gets the lot?"

I didn't know what to say to this. In truth I was feeling a little like Alice plunging down a rabbit hole that revealed one unpleasant surprise after another. Teddy had been looking around as he spoke. "So who got the dough from the sale of the house?"

"The dough?" I stared at him. "The money from the sale all went to pay off the death duties when my grandfather died and my father inherited. We've been living in the lodge ever since, and my father was the art master at the school."

"No money? That's too bad. I always pictured my pa living in luxury in the big house of my childhood." He glanced at the lodge. "Certainly not like this. So what about the furniture and stuff? All those creepy antiques I remember. I presume I'm entitled to a half share, as his son."

I had taken an instant dislike to him. "You inherit the title, so I'm told. But I expect you'd have to revert to being Teddy Langley."

"Sir Teddy. Well, ain't that a kick! Does it come with an allowance?"

"It comes with nothing." I forced myself to be gracious and British. "I've been clearing out my father's belongings, and you are welcome to look through old photograph albums and see if there are any photos you want. Or any pieces of furniture, for that matter."

"Sure, okay." A gleam had come into his eyes. I led him inside. He looked at the sad piles of stuff waiting for the van from the charity shop. "Is this it?" he asked. "This is how you lived?"

"This is it."

"And no money?"

Again I had to wrestle with myself to be honest. "I think he might have had up to a thousand pounds in his various savings accounts."

He gave me an incredulous stare. "A thousand pounds? That's all? You'd better keep it. I've done pretty well for myself. My old man, Schulz, went into the real estate business after the war, and I joined him right after college. Strip malls, mainly. I make more than that in a week. You clearly need it more than I do."

"Thank you," I said. "Actually I do need it. I don't have anywhere to live right now."

"You're not married?"

"I'm only twenty-five," I said. "I've plenty of time for that when I qualify."

"As what?"

"A solicitor. I'm taking my exams this year."

"An attorney, huh? They make good money."

"When and if I qualify," I said. "Look, would you like a cup of tea? I've just made a pot."

"Sure. Why not?" he said. "A cup of tea. That's what everyone drank all through the war. A bomb was dropped and everyone said, 'It's all right. Have a cup of tea.' " And he laughed.

I served him tea and some slightly stale biscuits. I don't think he enjoyed either.

"I'll give you the name of the solicitor who is handling Father's estate," I said. "He was going to ask the American embassy to help find you. Now you've saved him that task. But he can tell you the particulars about the title."

He stood up, shaking his head. "I can't think what good a title would be to me if it didn't come with the property."

"It might help you sell more real estate," I said sweetly. I had meant it as sarcasm, but he thought I was serious and burst out laughing, clapping his hands together. "You might have something there, Sis. Add a touch of class to the business."

He paused, taking a sip of tea. "Y'know, I'd been planning to come over and surprise the old guy. I was going to bring the wife and kids and let him see how I turned out. He never thought I'd amount to much. Too bad he died not knowing."

I didn't think my father would have been as thrilled as Teddy clearly thought he'd have been. I wasn't quite sure what strip malls were, but they didn't sound too respectable. Teddy fished into his own wallet. "Look, here's my card. If you're ever in the States, come and visit. My ma would be interested to see you, I'm sure. And the kids would get a kick out of an English aunt, speaking the way you do."

"Thank you, you're very kind," I said. He stood up, heading for the door. "And you're sure you don't want any of this before I donate it?" I asked, gesturing around the room.

He was still grinning. "This old stuff? Hell no. You're welcome to the lot."

We parted company then. I watched him get into a car and drive away, wondering what kind of little boy he had been when he had lived at Langley Hall and thinking about how glad I was that my father was dead. I didn't think he'd have been happy to see what Teddy Schulz had become.

By the end of the next day, I was ready to leave. Miss Honeywell had agreed to store the desk and trunk in the attic again. I promised to come for them as soon as I had a new place of my own. And she had generously offered for her own maids to come over and clean up the lodge for the new tenant. She had even shaken my hand warmly. "I wish you nothing but the best, Joanna. I'm sure you'll make a splendid lawyer and do great credit to your family name."

I was standing outside the front door, staring for one last time around what had been my home, when a car drew up and Nigel Barton got out.

"You've caught me just in time," I said. "I was about to leave."

He looked at my two suitcases. "Then let me give you a lift to the station. Or have you called for a cab?"

"No, I was planning to walk, so thank you," I said gratefully.

I glanced back at Langley Hall as we drove away.

"Your brother came to see me," he said. "That was a bit of a surprise."

"It was for me, too," I agreed. "I think he was horribly disappointed in his inheritance."

"Yes, he questioned me for some time. I believe he thought you were hiding something from him, or you didn't quite know the contents of the will. When I reassured him there was nothing but a title, he went away. Not the most pleasant of individuals."

"Daddy would have been horrified," I said.

We pulled up in the station yard. "I'll be in touch," he said. "I think the various sums of money will be released in the next week or so. And the items should go to auction soon."

"Thank you. You've been very kind," I said.

"Not at all. It's been a pleasure." He paused. "Joanna—I may call you Joanna, mayn't I? I do come up to town from time to time. Maybe I could take you to a show or something."

Scarlet had said something about falling off a horse and the best thing to do being to get right back on again. But it had been such a great and damaging fall. I wasn't sure I wanted to ride anymore. *It's only a show,* my inner voice was saying. *Nothing more.*

"Thank you," I said. "I'd like that."

His face lit up.

But we never did go to that show because in a little over a month, I had left for Italy.

CHAPTER TEN

HUGO

December 1944

After Sofia had gone, Hugo sat holding the bandage over his wound for a long while until gradually he felt the morphine starting to work. There was still some water left in the battered tin mug, and he drank it gratefully, then remembered the chestnuts she had left for him. He peeled off the prickly casings and ate their contents. They weren't as satisfying as the roasted chestnuts at home, but they were edible.

The rain was starting to drip on to him, and Hugo realised he would need to concoct some kind of shelter for himself before the rain got any worse. He used the last of the bandages to hold a pad around his wound and pulled his trousers back up, in spite of Sofia's admonition. He wasn't about to be caught by Germans with his trousers down! Then he stood up, reaching for the stick that acted as his crutch. The morphine was working well and he felt only faint stabs of pain as he moved forward cautiously. The first thing he did was relieve himself. After that he felt well enough to fish for the packet of cigarettes and lighter in his bomber jacket. He perched on the broken pew, taking long drags and giving a sigh of contentment. He had nearly a full pack. If he rationed himself he could make them last for several days.

He smoked the cigarette right down to the butt, then stubbed it out. He now felt ready to tackle what needed to be done. He stood in the middle of the chapel assessing the situation. There were certainly plenty of building materials. The whole roof had collapsed, but in the far corner there had been some kind of side chapel built into a nook, with the altar still standing. He hobbled around, dragging pieces of broken wood over to the corner. He placed what must have been a cupboard door on the floor, then leaned several planks against the altar front to make a tepee-like shelter. Then he brought out his parachute. He couldn't decide whether to drape it over the whole thing as a waterproof tent or to use it as a covering around himself inside. He opted for the latter—at least under those planks of wood it wouldn't draw attention to himself—and spread it out on the floor. Then he lowered himself to the ground and eased himself in through the gap, wrapping himself in the parachute.

The floor felt horribly hard, but the fine parachute silk did seem to trap his body heat. He wished he'd taken the time to put on his usual canvas flight suit. He was supposed to wear it over his clothes, but the pilots found them bulky. On missions like this he wasn't even flying high enough or long enough to get really cold. He took out his service revolver and loaded it, retrieved the knife, and made sure they were where he could easily reach them. Then he tucked the pouch that had held his parachute and first aid kit under his head and lay back. Now there was nothing to do but wait.

He must have drifted off to sleep. The morphine was giving him strange dreams. He was on a high mountain, with clouds swirling below it, and angels and devils were wrestling for his soul. The devils had swastikas tattooed on to their foreheads and were trying to drag him down to a place below the clouds. Then one of the angels took him by the arm and lifted him up, and now he was flying.

"Don't let me fall!" he cried out, looking up at the angel.

"Of course I won't. You are safe with me," the angel said, and her face transformed into that of Sofia Bartoli. Hugo opened his eyes and found he was smiling. Then his heart gave a lurch as he spotted a woman's face looking at him through a gap between his piled planks of wood. Not Sofia—a woman with light hair and a crown. He sat up, banging his head against the altar table and swearing. He peered out.

While he had been sleeping, the rain had

stopped, and sunlight was now streaming into the chapel. The rays of slanted winter sun were falling directly on to a fresco on the opposite wall. Parts of the fresco were pockmarked and damaged, but this part was still intact. It showed a picture of the Virgin Mary. He couldn't tell if she had been holding the Child Jesus, as that part of the fresco had been blown away. Just her face smiled down at him, and he found this extremely comforting—a sign almost that heaven was protecting him.

The thirst had returned, and his head felt woozy from the morphine. He looked down at his watch. Only eleven o'clock. He had a long day ahead of him. He eased himself out of his shelter and managed to stand up. The morphine must have been wearing off because the pain shot through him again and he cried out. He started in fear at a loud noise nearby but then saw that it was only a pigeon flapping away from the jagged wall above him. *Pigeons,* he thought. *Future food, if I have to stay here long. But I couldn't cook it up here. Maybe Sofia could take it home, cook it, and . . . Stop,* he told himself. *I can't put her and her family in danger.* She had already told him that a whole village had been executed for helping the partisans. She would undoubtedly suffer the same fate for aiding a British pilot.

I must get away from here, he decided. *Maybe hide out for a few days, just until the wound has healed and I've made a splint. Then I'll go south.*

He took the battered tin mug, then eased himself along the wall to the front door.

He gasped. Before him a vista stretched out in all directions: hill after hill, covered in thick forest, disappearing into blue haze, and in the distance higher mountains, their tops already dusted with snow. No sign of a big town, but some of the hills were crowned, like the one immediately before him, with a fortified village. It stood out now in clear three dimensions, highlighted after the rain, the houses clinging together as if afraid they might slip down the hillside. He stared at it with appreciation, admiring the faded ochre and green shutters of the houses, the graceful bell tower rising above the terra cotta tiles of the roofs, the crumbling walls built to keep out intruders. Smoke curled up from chimneys into the still air.

The hills close by were a mix of cultivation, neat lines of olives or vines cut out of thick woodland. *Wild and tame,* he thought. That summed it up. Then his gaze moved over to the west. Where part of the rock had been blasted away he could see the remnants of a track snaking up the hillside to the monastery. He could pick it out through the trees to where it met a road far below in a valley. As he watched, he saw three army trucks driving northward. He picked out the swastika on one of them.

There is no way I can escape at this moment, he thought. He was glad that the track had been blown away near the top. No German lorry would try to come back to this point. Thus reassured, he stepped through the doorframe and made his way carefully over the cracked and tilted stones of the forecourt. He found Sofia's rain barrel full and overflowing and dared to take a long drink, praying the rain had not stirred up whatever might have been breeding in it. Then he looked around at the piles of rubble, wondering if there might be anything that could be of use.

He was clearly standing beside what used to be a kitchen. Shards of pottery lay strewn about, an occasional cup handle or curve of a basin revealing what the items had once been. But there was nothing whole and intact. In his current condition he didn't dare to go further, to dig and potter among the ruins, but then he spotted a pillow, burned and with the stuffing spilling out of it. It was, naturally, soaking wet, but he carried it back in triumph, hoping it would dry out soon.

Once back inside he was overcome with exhaustion and barely managed to spread out the kapok from the pillow on one of the fallen beams before feeling that he had to sit down or he would pass out. He lowered himself with much grunting and swearing back into his little shelter, lay down, and knew no more.

When he opened his eyes again it was dark—

the sort of absolute darkness you find only far away from civilisation. He couldn't even see his hand in front of his face. *She wouldn't come now,* he thought. There was no way she could find her way up through the woods in this darkness. He felt an absurd sense of disappointment. Of course she couldn't leave her family twice in one day. It would look too suspicious. Then doubts crept in. What if she had been seen? What if someone in the village had binoculars and had been spying on her? What if she had been turned over to the Germans and right now they were on their way to get him?

He broke out into a cold sweat. He had to speak to himself quite sternly to get a grip on his fear. Of course nobody had seen them from the village. When they had come up to the ruins, the clouds had been hanging over the hilltops. He had only just been able to make out the village. Not the sort of day that anyone would take their binoculars and decide to observe the countryside . . . unless you were a German sentry posted as an observer on a hilltop. The fear returned. He knew that he would never feel safe for even a minute, and was overcome with empathy for the inhabitants of that village, never knowing when the Germans would arrive claiming that they had helped a partisan, lining them all up in the village square, and shooting them all.

I should start making myself a splint, he

thought, but could do nothing until it was light again. He certainly wasn't going to use his precious cigarette lighter except for emergencies. And so he lay there, listening to night noises— the creak and crack of branches in the forest below, the hoot of an owl, the distant howl of a dog. It was going to be a long night.

He must have been dozing because he awoke to see a light flickering nearby.

"Signor? Ugo?" He heard the whisper and the fear in her voice.

"Over here, Signora. In the corner."

He watched the light bobbing closer as he sat up and pushed one of the planks aside. She was wrapped as before in a big black shawl, and he could just see her eyes in the light of the candle-lantern she was carrying.

"Oh, you have built yourself a home," she said, smiling at him. "How clever. When I did not see you and you did not hear the first time I called, I was afraid that perhaps you had . . ." She didn't finish the sentence. She let the shawl fall over her shoulders.

"Not quite dead yet," he said, attempting flippancy.

She laughed. "That is good to hear, because I have brought you things to make you strong again."

He hauled himself out of his shelter, grunting with pain as he did so. She came over, put the lantern on a beam, and squatted down beside him. "See, I bring you food."

She opened a cloth bag she had been carrying and brought out what looked like a towel. She unwound it to reveal a basin inside.

"Soup," she said. "I hope it is still hot. It is good. Full of beans and macaroni and vegetables." She handed it to him. The basin was still hot to touch.

"It's very warm. You must have come quickly."

"Oh yes. I did not like to linger in the olive groves alone. You never know who might be there these days. If the partisans are meeting, they would not want to be seen by a woman. I would be in as much danger from them as from the Germans."

"Look, please don't come again," he said. "I really don't want to put you in danger."

"Don't worry. I am careful," she said. "I did not light the lantern until I was well away from the village. Here. You will need this." She handed him a spoon and watched as he ate.

"It's very good," he said. "I should save some for tomorrow, unless you need your basin returned now."

"It will not taste so good when it is cold," she said. "Besides, I have brought you something for the morning. Not much, I am afraid, but it will keep you going." She reached into her bag again. "Some polenta. A little hard cheese. An onion.

Polenta we still have. The Germans do not like cornmeal."

"I can't thank you enough."

"It is nothing." She gave him such a sweet smile. "When the world has gone mad, we must help each other when we can. Most of my neighbours are good and share what little they have. When Benito snared a rabbit, he gave us some of it to make the good broth you are eating. And when I came home this morning, I passed Signora Gucci and she saw the mushrooms I had found.

" '*Funghi di bosco*!' she exclaimed. 'I love *funghi di bosco*. If you can find some for me I will bake bread and biscotti for your family.'

" 'Here, take them now,' I said, and gave her most of them. 'I will go out looking every day to find you more.' " Sofia looked up at Hugo. He saw her eyes, glowing in the light of the lantern. "She is quite rich, and she has a son who brings her things from the black market. If I can find her mushrooms, she may keep us supplied. And . . . and I have an excuse now to come up here. She is a gossip. She will tell everyone how diligently I am hunting for her."

He returned her smile. "But how did you manage to get away tonight? Did your husband's grandmother not want to know where you were going? What time is it, anyway?"

"It's after nine," she said. "The old lady and my

son are asleep. They think I am in my room, but I climb out of the back window where I can't be seen."

"How old is your son?"

"He is three." She paused. "My husband has never seen him. He was called up and sent off to Africa before Renzo was born."

"And you don't know if he is still alive?"

"That's right." She stared down at her hands. "I have never had confirmation that he is dead, so I have to believe that he is in a prison camp somewhere. I have to keep hoping."

He reached out and covered her hand with his, a gesture he would never have done at home. "I am so sorry. It must be awful, not knowing. But then my wife doesn't hear from me often and knows that I fly bombing missions. She must worry, too."

"You have children?"

"One son. I suppose he's nine now, but I haven't seen him since he was five. I try to picture how he looks all grown up, but I can't. All I see is a little boy dragging his teddy bear around with him everywhere. A timid little chap, running back to Nanny."

"Nanny? Your grandmother lives with you?"

"No, his nursemaid."

"A nursemaid? Then you are rich?"

He hesitated. "We have a big house. Not much money, but plenty of land and servants."

"You are a milord?" She was looking at him with wonder now.

"My father is. I shall be when he dies. Not a lord, exactly. A baronet. A sir."

"Sir Ugo. Imagine what they would say in the village if they knew I was speaking with a milord." She said it with great drama, making him laugh.

"That all seems so irrelevant now, doesn't it? Lords and chimney sweeps fight side by side and die side by side, and nobody cares what they once were."

"That is so true. You must miss your poor wife very much."

He hesitated thinking about this. Did he miss her? "I'm not sure how much. We were never very close. But I miss my former life. How easy it was, having someone to cook my meals, wash my clothes, saddle my horse for me. And I took it all for granted. But you clearly miss your husband."

"Oh yes. I miss my Guido terribly. I was only eighteen when I met him. I had been raised in an orphanage in Lucca. Raised without love, you know. And when I was eighteen I was sent to be a servant at a big farm. Guido was working in the fields there as a hired hand. *Gesù Maria*! He was so handsome. And the way he smiled at me—I felt as if I was melting like candle wax. We fell in love instantly, and when his father died we married, and he brought me to his house in San Salvatore. His father had some land—not much, you understand, but enough: the olives we walked through, and pasture for the goats. We had a small flock of them, and we made goat's cheese for the market. But we had only been there for a year when the war came to us and Guido was taken away."

"And you were expecting a child."

"Yes. It was the worst day of my life when I watched him get into the truck with the other men and be driven off. He waved to me and that was the last I ever saw of him."

"I'm so sorry."

She nodded, and he could see her fighting back tears. "Still, I must go on for the sake of my son. It is not easy. We pick the olives, then the Germans come and take most of our olive oil. We grow some vegetables and they come and take those, too."

"And the goats?"

"They were taken long ago. I begged them to leave me one so that I could have milk for my child, who was not well at the time, but they didn't speak Italian and I didn't speak their language, so I had to watch my goats being loaded into a truck." She pulled the shawl more tightly around her against the cold wind that blew in through the door opening. "I should not complain. It is the same for everyone. They take

115

what we have—cows, chickens, even vegetables. All gone."

"I heard a rooster crowing in your village, so someone must still have chickens," he said.

"That is our mayor, Signor Pucci. He pretends to be friendly and helpful and they let him keep a couple of chickens. And one of the farmers still has a few sheep. The Germans do not like the taste of lamb." She gave him a wry smile. "And so we exist. I am luckier than some. I grow corn and vegetables. I dry the beans from the summer crop. I make cornmeal for polenta. We will not starve, and neither will you, as long as I am here."

Hugo had finished the soup. He felt its warmth spreading through his body.

"I can't thank you enough." He handed her back the empty bowl.

"It is nothing. And see, I have brought you other things." She reached for the bag and produced items like a conjurer. "A blanket! It will help to keep off the worst of the cold. And an old sheet— it is clean. You can tear it up to make bandages for your wound." She held up a small bottle. "This is grappa. It will help to keep out the cold. And I found this." She held up what looked like a spoke from the back of a kitchen chair. "This may work as a splint while your bone heals itself."

"You're amazing," Hugo said. "But won't these things be missed?"

"I'll tell you a secret." She put her finger to her

lips even though they were alone in the darkness. "My husband's family has been in their house for many generations. The attic is full of unwanted things. When I have more time, I shall see what else I can find."

"You must go now," he said. "I will be content with food in my belly and a blanket. And tomorrow I may be feeling stronger."

"Let us pray to Our Lady that you will. And I don't know the saint of broken legs or wounds. I must ask Father Filippo. He'll know."

"Father Filippo?"

"Our parish priest. He is very wise. He knows everything."

"Don't tell him about me!" he said, his voice rising.

"I will have to, in confession. But the seal of the confessional is sacred. He may tell no one. He has made this promise to God. So do not worry."

She patted his hand, stowed the basin in her bag, and draped the shawl around her head and shoulders again.

"May *la Madonna* watch over you until I return, Milord Ugo."

He watched her lamplight bobbing across the darkness of the chapel. In the doorway she turned and smiled at him. He had an absurd desire to blow her kiss. Then he heard her footsteps going down the stairs until they were lost in the silence of the night.

CHAPTER ELEVEN

JOANNA

June 1973

It was the beginning of June when I got out of the train in Florence. Back home in England it had been dull and drizzling for days. People had muttered about how late summer was this year, and there had been news reports of early crops being flattened by hail. Here the sky was a brilliant blue—the blue that my father had painted all those years ago. The ochres and terra cottas of the buildings with their bright red tiles glowed in the rich light. I stood looking around me, taking in the people, their faces alive and animated, not trudging with heads down against the wind as they did in London. There was the dome of the cathedral, taller than every other building. And beyond it the hills rose, clothed in forest. It was so lovely it almost took my breath away.

I felt incredibly free, as if I was a butterfly just released from my cocoon. To her credit Scarlet had not thought I was completely mad when I announced that I was going to Italy to find out what had happened to my father during the war.

"Yeah. Good idea. Get right away from all the nastiness and from that bastard Adrian. Give yourself a chance to put it all behind you." She didn't say, "What about your articles? Do you think your solicitor will still allow you to come back? And what about your law exam? When do you propose to sit it now?"

I had asked myself those questions but had silenced the doubting voice. I had always been the good child, trying to please, to succeed, to do the right thing, and look where it had got me. Now I had a little money in my pocket (enough for a down payment on a flat, I had reminded myself), and I was going to do something quite reckless and uncharacteristic. It felt wonderful.

I had met Nigel Barton again in London when he came to tell me that I was free to take the money from my father's bank accounts and that the person who had cleaned the paintings thought they might be worth more than a cursory clean.

"I'll let you know as soon as your items go to auction," Nigel said. "And when we know more about the paintings, you can decide if you want to keep them or send them to auction as well."

"Thank you," I said. "You've been very kind."

"Only doing my job, as my father used to say." He smiled. "So you'll go back to work now, but I'm sure the grieving process will take you a while. It always does."

I felt tears stinging at my eyes. "I didn't

119

think I'd grieve at all," I said. "My father was not an easy man. He was critical and he never encouraged closeness. But now I really miss him, and I wish I'd taken the trouble to get to know him better." I weighed whether to show him the letter and tell him my plans. "Actually, I've just found out that he was in Italy during the war," I said. "I always knew he'd survived a plane crash, but I didn't know where. I thought I'd go over and see the site for myself—see if the villagers remember anything about him."

"Oh, good idea, now you have a little disposable income," he said. "Whereabouts in Italy?"

"Tuscany," I said. "The village was called San Salvatore. I'm not exactly sure where it is."

He frowned. "San Salvatore? No, that's not familiar. I've done the principal tourist sites: Siena, Cortona, Florence, of course. Do you know the area?"

"I've never been abroad before apart from a two-day trip to Paris with the school once," I confessed.

He beamed then, making him look quite attractive. "You'll love it. And the food!"

"The food is good?"

"The food is incredible. All those rich, herby sauces for the pasta. You'll put on weight, I guarantee, although that wouldn't worry you, I'm sure. You are so slender."

"Slender" wasn't really the word—"skinny"

120

was more like it. I had lost weight in the past months. "I look forward to it, then," I said. "My mother was a terrific cook, but since then I don't think I've really enjoyed my food."

"And the local wines," he said. "I wish I had some holiday coming. I'd pop over and join you."

"I expect I'm only going to be a few days," I said hesitantly because he was coming across as too eager again.

"Take your time. Enjoy it," he said.

I had spent the last few weeks in London taking a crash course in Italian. Of course I wasn't fluent yet, but I felt confident that I could get by. I had a small Italian dictionary and phrase book in my purse, just in case, and my father's little box. I had carried that with me everywhere as a kind of talisman.

It was only as I sat jolting and unable to sleep on the night train travelling across France and then through the Alps that doubts started to creep in again. What was I doing? What did I really hope to achieve? The woman to whom my father had written had no longer been at her last known address. That meant she had moved away, or had died. If there had been a child and that child had been hidden away where nobody else could find him, then he too would be long dead. Even if by some miracle I located Sofia, I would only be reawakening a long-ago grief, maybe causing trouble for her if she had a husband or family. The

121

problem was that I had to know. I was naturally curious on my own behalf, but more than that, I felt this was something I had to do for my father. I would be filling in the blank pieces of his life-puzzle. Maybe I would answer the questions of why a brilliant young painter suddenly stopped painting and why for the rest of his life he was a hollow, remote, and depressed man.

By the time the train approached Florence, I had adopted a more positive outlook. I was on a quest. Whatever happened I felt that I was doing the right thing. I had no idea how to find the village of San Salvatore. I had looked for it on a map and couldn't locate it. It was possible it didn't still exist, of course. Places had been bombed into oblivion during the war, I knew that. But I wasn't going to give up. Before I started on the next stage of my journey, I found a bank and changed some pounds into lira. There seemed to be an awful lot of them, and I wondered how I would keep track of all those thousands. Then I treated myself to a cappuccino and a sinful pastry made with honey and almonds at a pavement café before going back into the station to find out how to undertake the next stage of my journey.

Even the man in the travel agency at the station had to look up the village on a map. "San Salvatore," he said. "The name is familiar, but . . ." Then he put his finger on it. "Ah, that's why I couldn't find it. I was looking down in the

Chianti region, but it's actually in the northern part of Tuscany. In the hills above Lucca. See." I peered over his shoulder and nodded. A tiny dot amid lots of green.

"And how do I get there? I suppose there is no train?"

"There is a train for the first part of your journey," he said. He studied the map again. "You would need to take a train to Lucca," he said, "then change to the branch line that would take you up the Serchio Valley to a town called Ponte a Moriano. But after that, perhaps a local bus into the hills, to a village called Orzala?" He broke off and gave a very Italian sort of shrug. Then he added, "It might be simpler to rent a car."

I didn't want to admit that I still didn't have a driver's licence. "I don't think I'd feel comfortable driving on the wrong side of the road," I said, "or on mountain roads." I thanked him, went to buy my ticket, and found my way to the right platform. We left the city behind and passed through a mixture of small towns, industrial sprawl, and arable land before arriving at the old city of Lucca. Here I disembarked and had to find out which train would take me to Ponte a Moriano. Having been told which train I needed, I had to wait an hour on a hot platform. I went outside the station to look around, but all I could see were lawns leading to an impressive city wall, nothing of the city itself except for a tantalising glimpse of towers and red roofs beyond that wall. I was tempted to explore, but it was a long walk and I didn't want to carry around my suitcase on such a warm day.

Eventually the train was announced. I had to fight my way aboard along with many other people. This train looked as if it could do with sprucing up. The seats were wooden, not upholstered. The windows were horribly dirty. And the carriage was crowded with what were clearly country folk. Some of the women wore shawls over their heads. The older women were all in black, their hair hidden under black scarves. One had a live chicken in a basket. Noisy children ran up and down the aisle. Babies cried. A priest in a broad black hat looked at me disapprovingly, almost as if he could read my past sins. I turned away, uncomfortable under his gaze.

The route led us between cultivated fields and old farmhouses. Sometimes I got a glimpse of a wide river. As I looked ahead I could see the first of the forested hills rising on either side of a valley. Now the track ran closer to the river, and I saw that it was fast-flowing, spanned here and there by ancient bridges. We stopped at a couple of little stations that seemed to be in the middle of nowhere. There were vineyards now planted on the hillsides and olive groves. Much sooner than I had expected, we arrived at Ponte a Moriano.

Only one couple beside me got off. They were met by adoring relatives with many hugs and kisses on both cheeks. The station was a simple square building, yellow with green shutters, the paint peeling and pockmarked. I came out of the station to find myself standing in an empty street with no indication where the centre of the town might be. Flies buzzed. It was hot and I was now thirsty and hungry. I went back into the station building, and in my fumbling Italian I asked where I might find the bus to take me to San Salvatore. The man in the ticket booth let out a stream of Italian at me that was quite incomprehensible. Eventually, with gestures, I thought I understood where I would find the bus to take me into the hills. It was on the other side of the river. I picked up my suitcase and set off down a long, tree-lined street. There were houses with gardens on either side. Still, I had no idea where the centre of the town might be. The street ended at a bridge over the river. I asked an old woman dressed all in black and working in her garden where I would find a bus, and she pointed across the bridge. I trudged across, too tired and grumpy to admire the view of the hills rising on either side of the valley. The other side was clearly the centre of the old town. There were shops, all closed for a midday siesta, and old, crumbling buildings. And in a small central square, joy of joys, two buses were parked. A man was leaning against one of them, smoking. In my best Italian I asked where I could find a bus to San Salvatore.

"*Domani,*" he said. "*Domani è sabato.*"

For a moment I didn't think I'd understood him. "Tomorrow?" I asked. "Tomorrow and Saturday?"

He nodded.

So I was faced with the prospect of staying the night in a place where I didn't want to be or finding another way to the village. "And if there is no bus today," I went on in my painstakingly correct Italian. "How do I reach San Salvatore?"

"Why do you wish to go there?" he asked. "Lucca, Pisa, Florence . . . these are what the tourists like. Nothing of beauty in San Salvatore. No historic buildings. No castle."

"I know," I said, fighting back impatience. "I am visiting friends there."

"Ah, friends." He nodded as if this was approved of. "You have friends in Italy. This is good. So—you can take the bus to Orzala and then it is maybe five kilometres and perhaps someone is going that way and can drive you."

"Okay," I said. "And the bus to Orzala goes when?"

"When I start the engine," he said, giving me a grin.

Passengers arrived to join us. We drove out of the little town, and the road started to climb immediately, zigzagging up the hill in a series of switchbacks. At this time of year everything was bright green—the grass beside the road, the leaves on the grapevines and the oak trees in the forest. And dotted among the green were bright splashes of red. Poppies were everywhere—among the lines in the vineyards, between the olive trees. Amid this riot of colour were old farmhouses, either built of rough stone or faded red stucco, their shutters bright green, their roofs tiled. Occasionally I caught a glimpse of a tower, either a church belfry or a castle. We stopped in a small village, then the road climbed again until it was running along a ridge. On either side of us the land fell away into deep valleys and then rose again to even higher peaks. The mountains seemed to go on forever until they faded into the blue distance.

We came to a halt in a village that was little more than a row of houses and a couple of farmyards. The bus driver turned to me and told me this was where I needed to get off. I found myself all alone in the street as a church bell far off tolled midday. Nobody seemed to be about apart from a black cat stretched out on the yellow gravel outside the houses. The sun was now hot and there didn't seem to be a café or any shade. The bell went on tolling and I wondered if it was someone's funeral.

I stood for a while trying to decide what to do.

It seemed I was destined to walk the last five kilometres, but I had no idea which direction to take. I could hear the sound of a radio coming from inside one of the houses, so I took a deep breath and knocked on the door. Another woman in a black dress—clearly the obligatory uniform of women over a certain age—opened the door and glared at me.

"*Buongiorno*," I said in my best Italian. "Where is the way to San Salvatore?"

She took in my foreign appearance, my jeans, the duffel bag on my shoulder. "*A destra*," she said. "To the right. Up the hill." Then she closed the door again.

"Friendly natives," I muttered. Was this what I was about to face? In which case I wasn't likely to learn much about my father. I stood looking around me. I seemed to be on top of the world with views in all directions, but there were higher hills to the north and west covered in thick forest. No sign of any village. I sighed and set off along the road, then spotted a small side road leading up the hill between vineyards before it disappeared into the forest. The hill rose steeply and it seemed a daunting prospect. I had gone about half a kilometre when I heard the sound of an approaching engine. I stopped and did what I had done only once before: I stuck my thumb out.

A van approached, driving fast. When the

driver saw me, he screeched to a halt. I ran up to him. "Are you going to San Salvatore?" I asked.

"I'd be wasting my time on this road if I wasn't," he said. "It doesn't go anywhere else. Jump in."

He was a portly middle-aged man and seemed quite safe. I got in and sat with my bag on my lap because there was nowhere else to put it. The interior of the van was crowded with various sorts of tools. He was either a plumber or a handyman of some sort. He was wearing a not-too-clean overall, and he gave me a friendly grin. "German?" he asked, noting my fair hair and height.

"English," I said.

"Ah, English." He gave a nod of approval. "And you speak Italian."

"Just a little," I replied. "I hope to learn more."

"And why do you go to San Salvatore?" he asked. "Nothing much there. No historic buildings. No towers like San Gimignano."

"My father was there during the war," I said. "I wanted to see for myself."

This made him react with surprise. "In San Salvatore? I always thought it was the Americans who liberated this part of the country. The English were over on the coast."

"His plane crashed, I think."

"Ah." We drove for a while in silence. The road was now little more than a dirt track. At first it climbed through thick forest, then emerged on to a ridge lined with cypress trees. The view was spectacular. Ahead of us I could see a cluster of buildings huddled together at the top of a hill. On all sides vineyards and olive groves fell away into small valleys, only to rise again to meet woodlands. The top of the hill opposite was thick with leafy forest, and a rocky crag rose from it, topped by an old ruin. It was the sort of scene one would have expected from the Romantic painters. All it needed was a few merry peasants coming home with rakes on their shoulders.

We entered the little town and drove up a narrow street lined with old stone buildings, most of them with shutters closed against the midday sun. Down below, shops were open to the street: a butcher or delicatessen with piles of salami in the window, a shoe shop, a wine merchant with casks outside. Impossibly narrow alleys led off from that central street, some hung with laundry, others with casks of wine outside doorways. And everywhere there were bright window boxes full of geraniums. The street was made of cobblestones and we bumped over them. Then we came to a central piazza. On one side was an imposing church built of grey stone. Facing it were what seemed to be municipal buildings with crests above their doors, and on one side was a small trattoria with tables outside. At one of these tables a group of men sat in the shade of a sycamore tree with glasses of red wine and plates of bread and olives in front of them.

My driver stopped. "Behold," he said. "This is San Salvatore. You must descend here. I go to the farmhouse just outside the village."

I thanked him and climbed out. The van drove away and I stood looking around, conscious of the eyes of those men on me. There didn't seem to be anyone else to ask, so I plucked up the courage to ask them if they could tell me where there was a hotel in the village.

This made them look amused.

"No hotel, Signorina. If you want a hotel, there is perhaps a pensione down in the valley at Borgo a Mazzano. Otherwise"—he spread his hands expressively—"there are good hotels in Lucca."

I fought back tiredness and frustration. I had not really slept on the train all night. Now I was really hot and hungry. "Is there nobody who rents rooms to visitors in this town?" I asked.

They looked at each other, muttering and conferring. Then one of them said, "Paola. She fitted out that old animal barn to let to visitors, didn't she?"

"Ah, Paola. Yes. Of course."

They nodded to each other. Then one addressed me. "You should go to Signora Rossini. She may have a room for you."

"Thank you," I said, although the mention of

her old animal barn did not sound too inviting. "And how do I find this Signora Rossini?"

One of the men stood up. For a moment I thought he was going to escort me, maybe offer to carry my bag, which now seemed to weigh a ton. Instead he came around to me, then pointed. "See that archway? Go through the tunnel. Then keep straight ahead, you understand. Always straight. And after the last houses of the village, it is the first place you will come to on the left."

I thanked them again and set off with trepidation. *I'll stay tonight,* I thought, *and then maybe take the bus back to the valley tomorrow and stay at a proper pensione there.*

CHAPTER TWELVE

JOANNA

June 1973

On the side of the piazza, a narrow alley dipped down between a greengrocer's with a wonderful display of fruit and vegetables outside and what looked like a wine shop on the other side. Then it entered a tunnel. I hesitated, wondering if this was some kind of local joke and God knows what I'd find at the other end of that tunnel, or even if it actually led anywhere. Was it a route to a dungeon? A cellar?

But I could still feel their eyes on me, and I was not going to give them the satisfaction of seeing my fear. I stepped forward bravely. The floor was made of large cobblestones, the walls hewn out of the stone of the hillside. And after the tunnel turned a corner, I saw that one side had openings to the view while the other had what looked like wine cellars. I came through the tunnel without incident and followed the path that dipped steeply into the valley. The village came to an abrupt halt after only a couple of rows of houses, and I took the track that led down the hill. It consisted of two rows of rutted dirt made by the wheels of successive carts and tractors. Between the dirt rows poppies poked their heads above the grass. After the houses came to an end, I walked between leafy vines on one side and on the other kitchen gardens with runner beans covered in their red flowers climbing on beanpoles above tomatoes and other vegetables I didn't recognise. I went a way down the hill, and there on the left ahead of me was one of the old farmhouses I had admired on my journey here. It was built of faded pink stone, its terra cotta roof glowing a rich, warm red against a startlingly blue sky. Over its doorway an old and gnarled grapevine created a shady porch, and beside it was a huge clay jar with rosemary spilling over the top. The front door was open. I went up to it and looked for a bell. I knocked tentatively but got no response.

"Hello! *Buongiorno,*" I called. No answer.

From the back of the house I could hear women's voices. I advanced slowly along the tiled passage, which opened up on to a big sunny kitchen from which wonderful smells were emanating—baking bread and herbs that I couldn't quite identify. A row of copper pots hung on hooks. Beside them were braids of garlic and drying herbs. In the centre was a scrubbed wooden table on which various vegetables and herbs had been chopped, and on the right-hand wall was an enormous and ancient open brick oven that could have baked a dozen loaves at once. And at the more modern gas stove beside it a woman was standing with her back to me. My first glimpse of her made me gasp and stand rooted to the spot. It felt as if I had been transported back in time. This was my mother, the same stout build, the same hair twisted up into a bun, stirring something magical on the stove as I came home from school.

Any minute now she'd turn to see me, give me a big smile, and open her arms to embrace me. Instead a dog rose up from under the pine table and came toward me, growling. The woman turned and uttered a little cry of alarm at being startled.

"Quiet, Bruno," the woman said. "Lie down." The dog obeyed, still eyeing me suspiciously.

"*Scusi*, Signora," I said quickly. "I knocked but you didn't hear." Actually, I think I said that I struck the door, not having the word for "to knock" in my scant vocabulary.

"No matter," she said. "You are here now. How can I help you?"

"I need a room for the night," I said. "The men told me you had a place?" I had practised these phrases on the walk down, and they came out quite smoothly.

She nodded, beaming now. "Yes. Of course. My little house in the garden. Once it was for animals. Now it is for people. Good, eh?"

I returned her smile. It was difficult to tell how

old she was—probably in her forties, but her face was remarkably unlined and her hair only showed the faintest streaks of grey. She was wearing a large blue and yellow apron over a white blouse with the sleeves rolled up above the elbows.

She wiped her hands on the apron and came toward me. "I am Paola Rossini," she said. "Welcome."

I shook the outstretched hand. "Pleased to meet you, Signora Rossini. I am Joanna Langley," I said.

"From England?"

"Yes."

She nodded approval. "You look like an English girl. Always tall and elegant. You are a student of Italian?"

"No, I'm here on a visit. I'm looking into places my father visited when he was in Italy."

"Really? And he came to San Salvatore once?"

"I think so," I said, not wanting to broach this matter now.

At that moment there was a loud and piercing cry and I remembered that we were not alone in the room. There had been a conversation going on as I walked down the hall. On a chair in the corner, a young woman sat. Her dark hair spilled over her shoulders, and she was watching me with curiosity. On her lap was a tiny new baby.

"My daughter, Angelina," Signora Rossini said proudly. "And now my granddaughter, Marcella.

She is just three weeks old. She was born early, and for a while we were worried we might lose her, but with good care and her mother's good milk she is now doing well, eh, Angelina?"

The girl in the corner nodded, smiling shyly at me. "Angelina's husband is a steward on a ship," Signora Rossini said. "He is away at sea and has not seen his baby daughter yet. So she comes to her old mother and knows she will be well taken care of."

I couldn't take my eyes off that tiny, perfect human being, nor could I stop my brain from going to places I did not want it to visit. *Three months from now . . . Stop!* I commanded myself.

"My congratulations on your daughter," I said, this being one of the phrases we had learned in the Italian course.

Angelina beamed. "You are married?" she asked. "You have children?"

I tried to keep on smiling. "Not yet," I said. "I am studying to be a lawyer."

"Oh, studying to be a lawyer." They looked at each other and nodded, impressed.

Paola sniffed and realised she had left what she had been cooking on the stove. "*Un momento,*" she said and rushed back to it, giving it a hearty stir.

"What are you cooking?" I asked. "It smells wonderful."

She turned back to me, shrugging modestly. "It

is nothing special. Just a simple lunch that we Tuscans like to eat. We call it *pappa al pomodoro*. You are welcome to join us. There is plenty."

"I would love to, if you are sure it's all right."

"Of course." She turned back to her daughter. "Put the baby down for her sleep, Angelina, and give this another stir while I show the young English lady to her room. I am sure she would like to wash before her meal."

Angelina got up and placed the tiny bundle in a cradle by the wall. The baby let out a complaining wail.

"Let her cry," Paola said. "It is good for the lungs." She turned back to me. "Come. I will show you."

I picked up the bag I had put down on the floor and followed her out of the back door. Bruno the dog trotted beside me, having decided if his mistress liked me then I must be all right. A flagstone path led down the hill through a garden that was a riot of flowers and vegetables. Roses grew between beanpoles and tomatoes. There were bushes of lavender and rosemary that smelled heavenly as I brushed against them. Amid the plants were various ancient fruit trees, cherries and apricots looking almost ready to pick and apples still small green buds. The path ended in an old stone outbuilding with bars at the window. Not exactly prepossessing. Paola went around to the side, took a large key, and opened the door.

"Pass, please," she said, standing back for me to go in first. The room was simple in the extreme: an iron bedstead, a white chest of drawers, a row of hooks on the wall for clothes, and a little table under the window. The floor was made of the same red tiles as the kitchen and passage. There were fresh white net curtains at the window, and the bed was made up with white linens topped with a homemade quilt.

"*Va bene*?" she asked. "It's all right?"

"*Si.*" I nodded enthusiastically. "And to wash?"

"Ah," she said, and opened an ancient door into a tiny bathroom. "You have your own water. It's from the well outside, so it's not a good idea to drink this. But there is a heater for the shower. See, it turns on like this. One must make sure the handle is lifted so." And she demonstrated. "Be careful. It can make the water very hot."

I noted the rather alarming-looking contraption on the wall and decided to heed the warning. The bathroom had a sink, a toilet, and a very small shower. But again it was spotlessly clean. If cows had once been housed here, there was no lingering odour. In fact, the bathroom window was open and the scent of honeysuckle wafted in from the ancient wall outside. I felt instantly that this was a place where I could feel at home.

"Thank you. It's good," I said. "How much money will it cost?"

She named a price. I did a rapid calculation

from thousands of lira into pounds and pence. It was very reasonable.

"And you will eat breakfast with us in the big house," she said. "Also if you want to have an evening meal with us, then it will just be a little more. You tell me in the morning, and I will make something special for our dinner."

"Thank you. I would certainly like to join you for dinner if that is all right." Suddenly I felt rather overwhelmed, as if this kindness was all too much after several months of feeling so alone.

"So I will leave you to settle in," she said. "And I will prepare the meal. Come up when you are ready."

She left the door open, letting in a scented breeze. I was tempted to try out the scary-looking shower after my night on the train, but I didn't want to keep Paola waiting too long. I unpacked a few items, washed my face and hands, put on a fresh blouse, and brushed my hair. Then I closed the door and went back up the path. The table was now laid with brightly painted ceramic dishes and bowls. In the middle was a big platter with tomatoes, a slab of white cheese, a couple of sticks of salami, a bowl of olives, and a big loaf of crusty bread. Paola motioned for me to sit, then served me a bowl of the soup. It was almost too thick to be called a soup, and it smelled of garlic and herbs that I didn't recognise. I took a tentative sip and felt the explosion of taste in my mouth. How could anyone take simple tomatoes and onions and make them taste like this?

"It is delicious," I said, hoping that "*delizioso*" was a word. "Very good."

Paola hovered behind me, then pulled out a chair at the head of the table. Angelina came to join us. She had picked up the baby again, and to my shock she opened her blouse and put the baby to a large round breast before picking up her own spoon.

"So everybody gets to eat," Paola said with satisfaction.

"How do you make this soup?" I asked.

She laughed. "So simple. It is what we call part of our *cucina povera*—simple food for the peasants. And a good way to use up yesterday's stale bread. It is simply stale bread soaked in broth, and then we cook the garlic, tomatoes, some carrot, and celery and add these to it, then serve with olive oil. That's all."

I ate until I had scraped my bowl clean with today's still-warm bread. Paola picked up a jug and asked if she could pour into my glass. I nodded agreement and was startled to find it was red wine she was pouring, not water as I had expected.

"Not too much wine for me," I said. "I am not used to drinking in the middle of the day."

"But this is an ordinary wine. No strength at all.

We give it to our children. Makes them strong. And if you wish, you can mix it with some water." She handed me a carafe of water, and I poured in a little.

I was now told to help myself to the items on the board. I tried some of the salami and cheese, and the tomatoes were sweeter than any I had tasted before.

"What is the name of this cheese?" I asked. "It is very different from any cheese I have tasted."

"Ah, that is because it is cheese from the sheep and not from the cow, such as you have in your country. It is the cheese that my husband and I used to make once. Pecorino, we call it. It is good, no? Sharp and full of flavour."

"It is." I nodded.

"Have more. And try this prosciutto." She put more food on my plate, and while I ate, Paola questioned me. Where did I live? What about my parents?

I told her I lived in London and my parents were both dead. She nodded sadly. "It is tragic to lose a loved one. A wound one never recovers from, I fear. My own dear Gianfranco died last year."

"I'm very sorry," I said. "Was he ill?"

She shook her head angrily. "No. His truck went off the road and rolled over on the way to the market. It was bad weather. Much rain and wind. But Gianfranco was a good driver. Sometimes I wonder—"

"Mamma, you must not say these things," Angelina interrupted. I looked at her enquiringly. "My mother thinks that maybe there are men who did not like my father. He was too honest. He would not pay protection money, and he would not sell his land."

"It's true. I do wonder, often. All I know is my husband was taken from me. Too young. Too young."

"So now you have to run the farm on your own?" I asked.

"It was too much for a woman alone," she said. "We used to have sheep and goats for the cheese, but they are gone now. I had to sell them, and you have their little house. My vineyard is rented out to others. I keep a few olive trees for the oil, and I grow vegetables in my garden, as you can see. I take them up to the market once a week, and I make preserves with the fruit. It is enough to get by."

We ate for a while in silence. I felt the wine in my head, and the heat of the afternoon was making me sleepy. "If you don't mind, I'd like to take a little sleep," I said. "I was up all night on the train."

"Of course." Paola got up, too.

"And maybe later you could show me how to cook some of your recipes?" I said.

"It will be a pleasure. You like to cook?"

"I'd like to learn," I said. "My mother was a

good cook, but I have never learned to cook anything more than a fried egg."

"She never taught you?" Paola asked.

"No. She died when I was eleven."

Paola came up to me, her arms open, and took me into an embrace. I smelled garlic and sweat and a faint rosewater type of perfume, but the mixture was not unpleasant. "No young girl should have to grow up without a mother," she said.

I fought back tears.

The combination of wine and tiredness meant that I slept for over an hour. I awoke with my head groggy and had to splash water on my face to make myself feel vaguely normal. When I came back to the kitchen, I saw Paola was working at the big table. She greeted me with a smile. "Ah, the little one who wants to cook. You came at the right moment. See, I am making pici. It is a pasta of this region, made with only flour and water. No eggs. Do you want to join me?"

"Oh yes, thank you. I'd love to," I said. I washed my hands in the sink, then she showed me her process. "You see, we start with a mound of two types of flour. I like to use semolina as well as the flour we call *tipo* 00. Very fine, no? And then we make a little well in the middle, and we start to pour in the water, little by little, gently, and we mix. And we start to knead."

I tried to follow along with my pile of flour. It wasn't as easy as she made it look. Flour stuck to my fingers. It became a sticky mess.

"More flour, I think," Paola said kindly, taking over until I had a smooth dough in front of me. "Now comes the real work. We knead and we knead. At least ten minutes."

Again I followed along. It was an effort, but it felt good to have my hands working, to be creating something. I found myself relaxing—smiling. I looked around the kitchen as I worked. Bunches of herbs were drying in a corner, tied to a rack, and along one wall were large terra cotta jars full of olive oil and other things I couldn't identify from where I was standing.

"Now we must let it rest," Paola said. "Come, we will have a coffee and biscotti while we wait."

She poured two cups of thick black coffee and pushed a plate of hard biscuits in front of me. I sat with her and nibbled at them. "Good, no?" she said. "And the biscotti are better when you dip them in the Vin Santo. I will show you later."

"It's very good just like this," I said, although I wasn't used to such strong coffee, which hit me with a jolt to the system.

"And now we finish the pici." Paola got up and took the cloth from the top of our dough. "Let me show you how we roll it."

She broke off a piece and put it onto the floured table. Then she rolled it with her hands the way we used to make snakes with modelling clay when I was a little girl. Back and forth she rolled until it was a uniformly thin, long strand. Then she handed me a piece. My strand was not as uniform and even, but I certainly enjoyed the process.

"We will have it tonight with a rabbit ragu," Paola said as we worked. "Those rabbits have become a pest to my vegetables, so I invite the boys from the village to come and shoot them for me. They like to shoot, and I like to eat rabbit. I give them one to take home to their mother, and everyone is happy."

I had to concentrate really hard to understand this, not having learned the word for "rabbit," but once she mentioned eating her vegetables in her garden, I managed to guess what she meant. "How do you make a rabbit ragu?"

"Also not hard. You start with pancetta and onions and sage and rosemary, and tomatoes and garlic of course, and it cooks gently for a long while. I made it early this morning."

I decided the time was right to mention my father. "Signora Rossini, I told you I came here because my father had been in this place during the war." I paused. "He was a British airman. His plane was shot down. Do you remember any of that? A British airman? A plane that crashed nearby?"

She gave me an apologetic smile. "I was not

146

here in the war," she said. "My mother sent me to my aunt up in the hills, on account of the Germans. I was a young girl and the Germans . . . they thought it was their right to take any young girl they fancied. Just as they thought it was their right to kill whenever they wanted. They were animals. I cannot tell you how much we suffered."

I nodded with understanding. Then I asked, "Do you remember a woman called Sofia Bartoli from this village?"

"Sofia Bartoli? Oh yes, of course I remember her. I remember when her husband Guido brought her home right before the war. She was not from here, you know, so the people of this town did not look upon her favourably. They do not like outsiders. And she was an orphan, I remember, with no family. I was only a little girl, but I thought she was very pretty, and kind, too. I heard she lost her husband in the North African conflict."

"And do you know what happened to her?"

"When I returned to the village when the war was over, she was gone. Nobody said much about it, but it wasn't good. She went away, leaving her baby son."

CHAPTER THIRTEEN

HUGO

December 1944

Hugo had a cold and uncomfortable night. His leg throbbed and sent pain shooting through him every time he tried to move, and the blanket did little to shield him from the damp cold that rose up from the stone floor. He took a small sip of the grappa, and it spread like fire through his veins for a while. He felt in his breast pocket and retrieved his cigarettes and lighter, then lay back smoking one, conscious that the tiny circle of glowing tobacco did nothing to dispel the darkness around him. But at least the inhaled smoke calmed his nerves. He was glad to see the first streaks of daylight and to hear that distant rooster welcoming the dawn. He nibbled a little of the polenta and cheese, leaving the onion for later, then forced himself to go outside and find a place to heed the call of nature. It was a clear, crisp day with occasional white clouds racing across the sky from the west. He managed to hobble out to the rain barrel, wincing with every step, where he drank some water and washed his face and hands. He carried more water back in the tin mug. He also retrieved more stuffing from the pillow and found a spoon lying amid the rubble. That small victory cheered him up. When he felt a bit stronger, he would do more searching. Maybe there was a mattress under some of those fallen roof tiles.

He managed to get the mug of water back to the chapel without spilling too much, then he took down his trousers and tore off some of Sofia's sheet to clean the wound again. It still looked pretty repulsive, with oozing dark blood, but he dripped iodine on to his homemade rag and tried to wipe away as much of the blood as possible. It stung horribly and he cursed under his breath, conscious of the Virgin and a few damaged saints looking down at him. Then he bound up the wound and used Sofia's piece of wood to make a splint. He wasn't sure it was helping. It certainly didn't support him enough for him to put weight on that leg. There was no way he could make his escape southward. *I'll just have to be patient,* he told himself, and was ashamed to find that he felt a small bubble of happiness that he would be seeing Sofia again for at least a few more days.

She came again that afternoon.

"I am in luck," she said, throwing off the shawl from her head as she stepped into the chapel. "Signora Gucci has told everyone that I brought her *funghi di bosco* yesterday and have promised to find more mushrooms for her. What a sweet and kind young lady I am. So now when they see me going up the hill to the woods, they say, 'Ah, Sofia. She goes to hunt the mushrooms. What a good woman.' "

"I hope you find some, or she will become suspicious."

"I hope so, too. But it has been wet recently. Good weather for mushrooms. And I think I saw more chestnuts. That is good, too. We use chestnut flour for baking in this region, especially when there is no more real flour." She had her big basket on her arm today. "But see what I have brought you: it is *fagioli al fiasco sotto la cenere*." She handed him a bowl of what looked like white paste.

He didn't understand the Italian words in her dialect, except that "*fagioli*" was beans, and this did not look like beans—more like oatmeal. He didn't think he'd ever seen an oat when he was in Florence, and certainly nobody ate oatmeal for breakfast.

"What is this?" he asked.

"It is made of white beans cooked in water and then cooked again with olive oil, rosemary, sage, and garlic in the coals of the fire all night. We put it in a Chianti bottle and cook it slowly in the embers. Then we mash it. It is very good and nourishing. We eat it all the time these days when there is no meat or eggs to be had." She reached into the basket again. "And some bread this time. Signora Gucci already baked us a loaf."

He took the crusty knob that she handed him and used it to scoop up the bean puree. The *fagioli* was good—so smooth he thought that milk or cream must have been added to it. She watched him eating, her face like that of a mother who knows she has provided the best nutrition for her child. When he was done she nodded in satisfaction. "That will keep you going for a while. And I brought you other things. Here— this is one of Guido's shirts that he used to wear to work in the fields in winter. It is made of wool and will keep you warm."

"I couldn't take Guido's shirt," he said, not wanting to accept it from her outstretched hand.

"Take it, please. He is not here to wear it and, who knows, maybe the moths will get at it and then it will be useless. And if he returns to me, I will be happy to make him a new shirt from the best cloth at the market."

"Thank you." He took it with reverence.

"And also I think it must be hard to be here in darkness at night. So I've brought you a candle. Please try to make it last. I do not have many and we often lose electricity these days. Do you need matches?"

"I have my cigarette lighter." He patted his pocket.

"You have cigarettes?"

"Yes. Would you like one?" He fished for the packet.

She shook her head. "I do not smoke, thank you. But it is a pity I cannot let anyone know about you. Cigarettes are the best things to barter with. The men around here would find me a pheasant or a rabbit for a pack of cigarettes." She paused, then shook her head. "But alas, English cigarettes would not be a wise thing to show anybody."

"You should go and look for your mushrooms," he said.

She stood up. "You are right. I cannot stay away too long. My son was in tears this morning because he wanted to come with me to help find mushrooms. But I had to tell him it was too far for him to walk. He is afraid every time I leave, poor little one. He has seen men taken from our village. And he thinks about the father he has never seen."

"Please be careful, Sofia," he said. He didn't realise immediately that he had called her by her first name.

Their eyes met. "Don't worry about me. I am always careful."

"Are there Germans in your village now?"

She shook her head. There was a long pause and then she said, "A German staff car came early this morning because someone had reported seeing an aeroplane crash. We told them we heard

152

the noise of a crash but it was the middle of the night and we saw nothing. Then they went away again."

Hugo let out a sigh of relief. "Are they often in your village?"

She shook her head. "They do not come much these days because they have taken most of what we have. And we are too far from a good road. But we never know. I pray every night to *la Madonna* that the Americans will come and make them flee north. *Arrivederci*, Ugo. May God be with you."

In the doorway she paused, adjusted the shawl around her head and shoulders, looked back at him, and smiled. He sat still as a statue, watching her go. *She is still a child,* he thought. If she had married at eighteen, then she was still in her early twenties, and yet she bore this worry and deprivation with such grace and fortitude. No blaming God or weeping about her lost husband. Just getting on with it, the way that Hugo had been brought up to do.

"Just a child," he reminded himself. Far too young to touch the heart of a man of thirty-five.

The pigeons startled him, fluttering to land on one of the fallen beams. *A snare,* he thought. *I should try to build a snare.* And he thought back to his childhood. In those days there had been poachers in the Langley woods. The gamekeeper played a never-ending game of cat and mouse with them. A waste of time, really, Hugo had thought, because mostly they were only after rabbits. But the squire's pheasants had to be protected for the shoot. Hugo remembered going around the property with Ellison, the sour old gamekeeper, while the old man grumbled ceaselessly about the louts and layabouts and what he'd like to do to them, only stopping to destroy any traps he found. Some of them were vicious steel-toothed devices, strong enough to dig deep into an animal's foot. Others, probably made by local lads, were simple snares—wire hoops that would pull tight when an animal triggered them. Hugo tried to remember what they looked like and how they worked. No point, really, as he had no wire, but it was something to occupy his mind. He thought how pleased Sofia would be if he presented her with a brace of pigeons.

He got to his feet, which was harder to do now with the splint in place, retrieved his makeshift crutch, and hobbled to the door. The light clouds of morning had been replaced by heavy grey ones, and a thick bank of them was moving in from the west. The wind had picked up, too, buffeting him as he tried to walk. It would rain before long; that was certain. He drank again from the rain barrel and tried to do more foraging among the rubble, but he was unable to climb over the loose stones and bricks and couldn't bend to lift any of the debris and see what lay beneath. He didn't find any wire or string, but he did manage to extricate an old kitchen drawer. *That might just work,* he thought, and began to carry it back, just as the first raindrops pattered on to the rock.

He was only halfway to his shelter when the storm broke with force. It was as if the heavens had opened. Raindrops bounced off his leather jacket. He tried to move more quickly and felt himself slipping. He grasped at one of the beams and stopped himself from falling, sweat mixing with the rain on his face. By the time he had lowered himself into his shelter and pulled the parachute over him, he was soaked through. He lay there shivering as the wind blew raindrops through the gaps between his planks. The parachute silk wasn't as waterproof as he had hoped. It clung to him, sodden. Then came a great flash of lightning, followed almost instantly by a clap of thunder. His first thought was of Sofia. Had she reached the safety of the village? He lay there huddled under his parachute, worrying about her getting struck by lightning or at the very least catching a cold from a drenching. And he cursed his own impotence. He was the man. He should be saving her, taking her and her son to a safe place far from this conflict.

"Damn and blast this leg," he said out loud.

The storm raged on for most of the day. By evening there were periods of calm between bouts of heavy rain. Hugo didn't want to waste his candle. In the last of the daylight, he spread out his parachute to dry, draping it over the outside of his shelter. As he did so he remembered the parachute lines. "Idiot," he told himself. "You have all the string that you want to make a snare." Tomorrow he would rig up a perfect trap and catch a pigeon.

He ate the last of his bread with the onion, which tasted surprisingly good, then settled himself for the long night ahead. The blanket was not too damp and he wrapped himself in it. *Tomorrow I will get to work,* he told himself.

He had no idea how dramatically things would have changed by morning.

CHAPTER FOURTEEN

JOANNA

June 1973

My heart beat faster. She'd left a baby son behind. The beautiful boy. He might still be here.

I took a deep breath and formed the sentence in my head before I asked, "So this son of Sofia, is he still in the village?"

Paola nodded, smiling. "Yes, of course. He was taken in by Cosimo and raised as his own son."

"Cosimo?"

The smile faded from her face. "Cosimo di Georgio, the richest man in our community. He owns much land around here. He would like to buy my olive grove. His aim is to control all the olive trees, but I do not wish to sell. But here he is respected as well as feared. In the war he was a hero, a partisan fighter—the only one to survive a massacre by the Germans. He had to lie there among the bodies, pretending to be dead, while the soldiers went around with bayonets. Can you imagine that?"

"So he adopted Sofia's child?" I asked.

She nodded. "Yes, and lucky for the boy that was. Guido and Sofia, they were poor like the

157

rest of us, but now Renzo is the heir to Cosimo. He will be rich one day. Rich and powerful."

Again I phrased what I wanted to say very carefully. "If I wanted to meet this man, Renzo, how would I do so?"

"If you go up to the village around six or seven, you will find most of the men sitting together in the piazza. They meet in the evenings while their wives prepare their meals. I am sure they will know where to find Cosimo and Renzo. Cosimo had a stroke a few years ago, I'm afraid."

"A stroke?" This Italian word meant nothing to me.

"When the blood is blocked and the left side no longer works well," she explained. "Now he walks with a cane and Renzo stays by his father's side to help him."

She reached for a towel and covered the bowl, wiping her hands on her apron.

"Are we finished with the pici?" I asked. "Do you need more help?"

"Until we cook it. Go and enjoy yourself, young lady."

I smiled and nodded. "So maybe I should go for a walk and explore the town. I'd like to see Sofia Bartoli's house."

"You can see it for yourself. As you walk up the street, you turn into the last little alley on the right. Sofia's house is at the end."

"Does her family still live in it?"

"Oh no. Her husband did not return from the war in Africa, you know. There was only an old grandmother, and she died soon after I returned to San Salvatore."

I nodded, understanding this. "And I also want to see if I can talk to the men in the piazza," I said. "I don't know if they can tell me anything, but perhaps they met my father."

"Perhaps." She didn't sound too hopeful.

"And then, if I may, I'll come back to join you for dinner. I'm really looking forward to trying the pici and the rabbit."

"Good." She nodded approval. "Of course you are welcome to join us. It will be nice for Angelina to have a young person to talk to. She is bored with just her old mother. She would like to know about English fashions, I am sure. And music. She is still a teenager at heart!" She chuckled.

"How old is she?" I asked.

"Almost twenty now," Paola said. "Time to settle down and be serious as a mother and wife, not listening to popular music and wanting to dance."

Almost twenty, I thought. *And here I am at twenty-five still thinking I am young and have plenty of time to decide what to do with my life.*

I went back to my room and collected my camera and purse. I also put on a hat as the late-afternoon sun was fierce. Then I set off back up the path to the little town. The tunnel and the alleyway were pleasantly cool after the walk uphill with the sun on my back. I stood in the tunnel, looking out through the opening at the landscape beyond. Everywhere I looked there were olive trees. If this Cosimo owned them all, he must be a rich man indeed. And that old ruin I could see beyond the trees—was that a castle, perhaps? I thought it might be worth exploring if I didn't mind the trek up through the olive groves. This made me stop and think: How long was I planning to stay here? If nobody in the town knew anything of my father, what would be the point of staying on? But I thought of Paola and her bright, warm kitchen, and it struck me that this was a place where I might be able to begin to heal.

The piazza was deserted at this time of the afternoon, the sun beating down on the cobblestones and reflecting off the faded yellow stucco of the municipal buildings. The sycamore trees looked dusty and drooped in the heat. I went up the steps and into the church. The smell of incense hung heavy in the air, and dust motes danced in the shafts of sunlight that came in through high, narrow windows. Around the walls were old paintings and statues of saints. I recoiled as I came upon an altar and beneath it a glass-fronted case containing a skeleton clothed in bishop's robes and with a crown on its skull.

Was this a local saint? As one raised with only the minimum of Anglican exposure, I always found Catholic churches to be frightening places—one step away from black magic. When a priest appeared from behind the high altar, I made a hasty exit.

I followed the one road up from the piazza. There were a few more shops and a jumble of houses clinging to one another against the hillside. Here and there an alley led off, some of them so small that I could stretch out my arms and touch both sides. Shutters were closed against the afternoon heat. Some houses had wooden balconies decorated with more geraniums. Others had big clay pots and jars like the one outside Paola's house, all with flowers and herbs spilling over the sides. An occasional cat basked in the sun. Other than that the street was deserted. From inside the houses came the sounds of pots and pans clanging as the evening meal was being prepared, babies crying, a radio blaring out a plaintive song.

Ahead of me I could see sky and greenery as the houses came to an end. I turned into the last alleyway on the right and found myself staring at Sofia's house. It was bigger than the houses around it and painted yellow, its paint faded and peeling. Two storeys high with a balcony at the front, it must have had a fine view over the surrounding countryside at the back. I wondered who lived in it now, but it had a deserted feel to it. No geraniums, no window boxes. A sad house, I felt, and turned away.

As I came to the highest point of San Salvatore, the road abruptly ended in a little park with a couple of large old trees and benches beneath them. An elderly couple sat on one of the benches in the shade. She was dressed head to toe in black like the other old woman on the train. He was rather smart in a starched white shirt, and he had a big nicotine-stained moustache. I was touched to see that they were holding hands. They looked at me with interest. I nodded and said, "*Buongiorno.*"

"*Buonasera,*" they replied, a gentle rebuke that the day had now officially passed into evening.

I continued to where a wall ran around the parapet, and next to the wall a big cross had been erected. I read the inscription: "To Our Brave Sons Lost in the War of 1939–45." Beyond was a glorious view: range after range of forested hills, some crowned with villages such as this one. Directly below the wall the land plunged away into a deep valley where I could see a road. But there was no way down from the village to join it. Clearly this was a place built for defence in the old days!

I stood there taking photos of the view. When I looked back the old couple had gone, making me wonder if I had only imagined them. In truth this whole town had a tinge of unreality for me, like being in a beautiful but unsettling dream. Was it only yesterday that I had been in rainy London? Was it only a year ago that I had moved in with Adrian? And my father had let me know in no uncertain terms how much he disapproved . . . And then . . . I closed my eyes as if trying to shut out the painful memories. *How much can happen in so short a time,* I thought. How quickly life can change. Well, maybe it was time that it changed again. I was in a beautiful place, staying with a kind woman, and I was going to enjoy myself, whatever the outcome was.

Having made that decision, I started to walk back through the town. In just half an hour or so, things had changed. The world was coming to life. Small boys were playing football in the street while a little girl sat on a step watching them. The greengrocer was carrying in crates of vegetables, ready to shut up shop for the night. A group of women stood talking together, waving their hands expressively as only Italians do. From open front doors came enticing aromas and the sounds of radios or televisions playing. And when I arrived back in the piazza, it was now bathed in deep shadow and pleasantly cool. I saw that the men had returned to their table outside the trattoria and were arguing so loudly and violently that I was afraid a fight might break out at any moment.

I shrank back into the shadows of the side street, not wanting them to know I was there at such a crucial time. Then one of them threw up his hands in a gesture of futility, another laughed, and the moment was diffused. Wine was poured from a carafe on the table, and it appeared that everyone was contented again. All the way through the town I had rehearsed my lines for my upcoming speech. I had actually written some of them on the train, to be memorised in case my fledgling Italian deserted me in a moment of stress.

It took me a few seconds of deep breathing to pluck up the courage to walk across the piazza to them. They looked up at the sound of my approaching footsteps.

"Ah, the signorina," one said. "Did you find Paola? Do you stay in her animal house?"

"Yes, thank you," I said. "It's very nice and she is kind."

"Paola is a good woman," one of the men agreed. "She will feed you well. You need feeding up. No flesh on your bones."

I didn't quite understand this but saw them examining me critically. Not plump enough to be an Italian girl.

"I have come to find out about my father," I said. "He was a British airman. His plane crashed near this town in the war, but he survived. I wondered if any of you knew about him or met him."

They were all middle-aged, or even elderly.

Some of them must have been in the village at that time. But I was met with blank looks.

Then an older, wizened man said, "There was a plane that crashed down in Paolo's fields, remember? The Germans came and asked us about it, but we knew nothing."

"I remember that Marco was angry because the plane burned two good olive trees," another man agreed. "But of that plane there were no survivors, I am sure. It was burned completely."

It occurred to me that they were not talking about my father's plane. Perhaps his plane had not crashed exactly in this area, and he had been making his way south to escape from German-held territory when he came to San Salvatore. Clearly none of these men knew anything of a British pilot in their town. I decided to change the subject. "Do any of you remember a woman called Sofia Bartoli?"

That produced an immediate reaction. I was met with hostile stares. One of the men turned and spat on the ground.

"Did this woman do something bad?" I asked.

"She ran off with a German," one of the men said finally. "Just before the Allies were driving the filthy Germans north. She was seen going off with him in the middle of the night, escaping in an army vehicle."

"Going willingly with him?" I asked. "Are you sure of that?"

"Of course. It was the one who had been staying in her house. A good-looking man. An officer. My wife was told by Sofia's grandmother that she knew she was sweet on a man. Well, you can tell, can't you, when a woman has feelings for a man."

"She obviously thought she'd have a better life in Germany than staying here, working day after day in the fields," a man at the end of the table muttered. "Especially if her husband was already dead." There were more mutters of agreement.

"She left behind a child?" I asked. "A baby boy?"

There were nods around the table. "Yes, Renzo. Her son. She abandoned him."

"And Renzo still lives in this town?"

One of them looked up. "Here he comes now, with his father."

CHAPTER FIFTEEN

JOANNA

June 1973

Two men were walking together into the piazza. One was a big bull of a middle-aged man, powerfully built with the grey curly hair and profile of the Roman Caesars. Yet in spite of his powerful appearance, he walked with a stick. The other was tall, muscular, and remarkably good-looking. He had the same strong chin, dark eyes, and mass of unruly, dark curls. He was wearing a white shirt, opened several buttons down to reveal a tanned chest, and dark, form-fitting trousers. The effect was of a Romantic poet, although rather more healthy-looking. A fleeting thought crossed my mind that it would be highly unfair if the most attractive man I had ever seen turned out to be my brother—until I reminded myself that I had sworn off men.

I kept staring at him, trying to see any hint of my father in him. But he was nothing like my slim and fair-haired father.

I was wondering what to say to them when one of the men called out, "This young English lady is asking about Sofia Bartoli's son."

The younger man, who I presumed was Renzo, gave me a cold stare. "I have the misfortune to be that woman's son," he said in remarkably good English. "But I remember nothing of her. What do you wish to know?"

"You speak English?" I was surprised and impressed.

The man nodded. "I spent a year working in London. In a restaurant."

"Were you a waiter?" I was hoping to break down the obvious hostility that I could feel.

"I was studying to be a chef," he said. "But then my father had a stroke. I had to return home to help him run his lands and his businesses." He turned to give a deferential nod to the older man.

One of the men had risen and pulled out a chair for him. "Here, Cosimo. Take my seat," he said.

"Not necessary," the older man said. "We go inside to eat. Our table awaits us." So that was Cosimo, the richest man in the town, the one who owned all the olive groves except for Paola's.

He touched Renzo's arm and let out a rapid fire of words in Italian.

Renzo turned back to me. "My father wishes to know what your interest is in Sofia Bartoli."

I hesitated. "I believe that my father once knew her."

Again the older man said something in rapid Italian and the men grinned. Renzo looked quite uncomfortable as he said, "My father thinks that maybe quite a few men knew her."

The older man was continuing to stare at me. "You are German, I think," he said in accented English.

"No, I'm English."

"I think German," he repeated. "I think you are Sofia Bartoli's child with that German scum and now you have come to reclaim her land and her olive grove."

"Absolutely not," I said angrily. "My father was a British pilot. His plane was shot down. He was badly injured."

I was still watching Renzo, wondering if he could have been the beautiful boy who was hidden away where only Sofia and my father could find him. But my father had written "our beautiful boy," not "your." That implied the child was theirs, not hers. Perhaps he had developed a real attachment to the little boy. "Tell me," I said, "were you ever hidden away during the war?"

"Hidden? How do you mean?"

"Hidden away where nobody could find you, to keep you safe?"

"From the Germans?" He frowned, then shook his head. "I have no such memory. In fact, that cannot be. I remember we had a German officer staying in our house. He was kind to me, I do not have a bad memory of him. He gave me sweets."

"How old are you?" I asked, realising that I was probably sounding very rude.

"You ask many questions for a woman and a stranger to this place," Renzo said. "I don't see what this has to do with you, but I am thirty-two. And in case you wish to know, I am not married. Are you?"

I felt myself blushing now. "I'm not married, either." So he was too old to be my father's child. I knew that my father had crashed and been wounded toward the end of the war, and this man had been born in 1940 or '41.

"And did you ever have a little brother?" I asked.

"This was not possible." He gave me a scathing look. "My real father was sent to Africa before I was born, and he never returned. If it had not been for Cosimo, I would have been a destitute orphan. I owe everything to him." He put a hand on Cosimo's arm. "Now, if you will excuse me, my father wishes to have a drink at his favourite table."

And they walked together into the trattoria. Once they were inside, the man sitting closest to me said in a low voice, "That man is Cosimo. It is not good to cross him. He is powerful. He owns much land around here, and the olive press, too."

A younger man got up and motioned for me to sit at the table. "Come. Join us for a drink," he said. "Sit. Get her a glass, Massimo. And try some of our local olives. They are the best."

I hesitated, wondering how to refuse and whether it was possible that I would learn anything more from them. The man insisted, and I sat. A glass was put in front of me and filled with dark red wine. A bowl of olives was pushed down the table along with a loaf of coarse bread and a jug of olive oil. The man who had invited me, a skinny individual with slicked-back hair and a slightly racy look, tore off some bread for me and poured a little of the oil on to my plate.

"This is oil from our olive trees," he said. "Good Tuscan oil. Extra virgin, eh? Good to be extra virgin."

The way he said the word "virgin" combined with the way he looked at me made me uneasy, but then he laughed and I decided he was only teasing.

"You see the colour of our olive oil?" a broad-shouldered man sitting opposite me asked. "Bright green. The green of springtime. That is the colour of Tuscan olive oil. The best. Of course it has to come from my trees."

"Your trees?" one of the men at the far end of the table demanded. "You sold most of your trees to Cosimo. Now it comes from his trees."

"Not true. I kept the best trees for myself."

"I heard he made you an offer too good to refuse. Or he had something on you."

171

"Not true. You lie!"

Voices were raised again and I thought they might well break into a fist fight. But then an older man said, "The signorina will think she has arrived among wild animals. Behave. Now eat, Signorina. Eat. Drink. Enjoy yourself."

They all watched as I dipped the bread in the oil and then ate with an expression of satisfaction.

"Good, no?" they asked. "The best olives in the region."

"And could be even better," the young, racy one said, giving a look I couldn't quite interpret.

One of the men put a finger to his lips. "It's not wise to say such things, Gianni. Especially when someone might be able to overhear us. Watch your mouth or you will be sorry."

The distinguished old man with a shock of white hair took over the conversation. "So tell us, Signorina. Your father, the British pilot, he is still alive? He sent you here to find Sofia Bartoli?"

"No, Signor," I said. "He died a month ago. I came here because I found her name mentioned among his belongings. He never spoke of her to me or my mother, but I was curious. Now I see I was wrong to delve into the past. My father would not be happy to learn of her actions. But at least I have seen this beautiful region, and I am glad I came."

"You will now go back to England?" the older man asked.

"I may stay for a few days. I am happy in the little room at Signora Rossini's house. I will take walks and enjoy your beautiful countryside."

This was generally approved of. "You must let me show you my sheep," the amorous one said. "I keep them up at the top of the mountain where the grass is the best. And I make my pecorino cheese up there. I will show you how I make my cheese, too."

"You want to watch that one, Signorina," the distinguished one said. "He has a reputation with the ladies. You can't trust him further than you can throw him."

"What, me?" the man who I now remembered was called Gianni asked, putting his hand to his heart. "I am merely showing hospitality to a young stranger. I am a safely married man."

"Married yes, safe no," one at the far end commented, causing loud laughter.

Gianni looked sheepish. "We should feed the young lady. Bread and olives is not enough. Let's call for bruschetta."

"Oh no, it's not necessary." I held up my hand. "I go back to eat at Signora Rossini's."

"She won't serve dinner for hours," Gianni said. "Not until the sun is well and truly set. You will faint from hunger before that." He got up and went into the darkness of the trattoria. Then he came back, looking self-satisfied. "They will bring a tray for us. Very good here, you will see."

I had no idea what bruschetta was. My knowledge of Italian food was limited to spaghetti Bolognese or ravioli of the sort one bought in a tin. Soon a platter was carried out to our table by a skinny young man wearing an apron. On it were thick slices of toasted bread with different toppings. Gianni looked at me with intense interest and said something under his breath to one of the men. The man replied. They exchanged a smile. A translation was not offered to me.

"So now you try the bruschetta," the distinguished older man said. "Each one is crowned with different flavours that we like in these parts. This one has chicken liver mixed with anchovy, this one tapenade, and this slices of fennel with goat cheese. Eat. They are all good."

I was all too aware that I was going back to Paola to eat what would undoubtedly be a large meal, but I could hardly refuse. They insisted that I try every flavour, watching my face with expressions of anticipation so that I had to smile broadly and nod satisfaction after each bite. This was not hard to do as each of the flavours was exquisite. I had grown up with simple English cooking—steak and kidney pie, shepherd's pie, fish and chips, lamb chops—and then as a student my daring experiments in the culinary line were limited by my budget and included Chinese and Indian (or rather the English versions of Chinese and Indian). Therefore I was not familiar with garlic or basil or any of the other tastes I was experiencing. At last, full of food and wine, I was able to plead that Paola would be waiting for me and it would be very rude to be late for dinner.

Gianni, who had volunteered to show me his sheep farm and had insisted on the bruschetta, immediately got to his feet. "I shall have the honour of escorting the young lady home," he said.

"Oh no, thank you. It is not far and I know the way, and it is still not quite dark," I said, having trouble with finding Italian words after too much wine.

"It is no trouble," Gianni said. "I, too, must go home through the tunnel. Come."

He put a hand on my elbow and assisted me to my feet. I wasn't too keen to go through a long, dark tunnel with him, even though I didn't think he'd try anything within shouting distance of the men at the table. Luckily this was decided for me before I could find a way to refuse him.

"Never mind, Gianni," a voice at the end of the table said. I looked across at a big man in a well-worn undershirt. "I must pass Paola's house, and it is time for me to leave if I do not want a lashing from my wife's tongue. Come, Signorina, you will be quite safe with me. I have ten children and a terrifying wife to keep me in line."

There was good-natured laughter around

the table, but the white-haired one said, "Yes, Signorina, you will be quite safe with Alberto."

I thanked them profusely for their hospitality and remembered to comment again on the quality of their olive oil. This was met with broad smiles all around. At least I had done something right.

"So tomorrow, Signorina." Gianni still hovered beside me. "Any time you want to see my sheep and my cheese making, you come and find me, okay? I can tell you lots of interesting things, also about the wartime."

"What do you know of the war?" one of them bellowed. "You were just a child. We were off fighting. We can tell her what the war was like."

"I was a child, yes, but I ran errands. I took messages for the partisans. I saw much," Gianni said. "You would be interested, I think, Signorina."

"You and your tall tales." Alberto shoved him aside and took my arm to lead me away from the group.

"That Gianni, he is full of hot air," Alberto said to me. "You must take anything he says with a pinch of salt, Signorina. In the wartime he ran messages, but they were more likely to be for the black market dealers than the partisans. No partisan would have trusted him with an important message. He'd have blabbed about it to the wrong people and squealed to the Germans if they had questioned him."

We walked then in silence across the piazza and through the tunnel. I suspected that he was now tongue-tied and perhaps was already wondering what the shrewish wife would say about being seen with a young lady. On the other side of the tunnel we emerged into the last of the pink twilight. Bats were flitting and swooping silently across our path, attacking the mosquitoes that now hummed around us. We reached the path to Paola's front door.

"Here we are, Signorina," Alberto said. "May I wish you a good appetite for your evening meal and a good sleep." He gave a quaintly old-fashioned bow and then strode off down the path that led to the valley.

CHAPTER SIXTEEN

HUGO

December 1944

In the middle of the night Hugo awoke with teeth chattering. His whole body was shivering and shaking. He sat up and felt around for Guido's shirt that he had stuffed into the parachute bag under his head. It took him a while to extricate it, take off his bomber jacket, then put the shirt on. It smelled of damp sheep but was actually nicely dry. By the time he got the jacket on again he could not control the shaking. He tried to huddle himself into a ball, but it was impossible with his splinted leg.

The shaking finally ceased, leaving him exhausted and drenched with sweat. It was all he could do to stop himself from tearing off his leather jacket. He passed into black dreams. He was flying and was surrounded by mosquitoes trying to bite him. Then the mosquitoes turned into German planes, tiny vicious planes zooming around his head as he batted at them ineffectively.

"Go away!" he shouted into the darkness. "Leave me alone."

Then the planes turned into fluid, flying

creatures and they left him, swooping across a red sky to where Sofia was walking through the olive groves. And they descended on her, grabbing at her shawl and her dress, trying to lift her up.

"No! Not Sofia!" He was screaming now, struggling to stand up and run to her. But his legs had turned to jelly and collapsed under him. He watched helplessly as they lifted her up and bore her away into the darkness.

"Sofia!" he cried out in despair. "Don't go. Don't leave me."

"*Sono qui.* I am here," said a quiet voice beside him. Someone was stroking his hair.

He opened his eyes with difficulty. It was day, and a watery sun was peeping over the jagged edge of the chapel wall. His head was still pounding and he had difficulty focusing, but gradually he could make out Sofia's sweet little elfin face looking down at him with concern.

"You were shouting," she said.

"Was I? I was dreaming, I think."

She knelt beside him. "And your forehead is so hot. You have a bad fever. I am afraid your wound has become infected. Let me see."

He was too weak to stop her as she unbuckled his belt and eased down his trousers.

"Your clothing is wet with sweat," she said, shaking her head. Carefully she inched off his makeshift bandage, then shook her head some more. "You need a doctor. This looks very bad."

She stared at his leg, chewing on her lip like a nervous child, trying to make up her mind.

"I think Dr. Martini is a good man . . . He was good to Renzo when he caught measles."

"No doctor," Hugo said. "It is a risk we should not take. At the very least he would be seen coming up here."

"That is true." She nodded. "But if we do not bring a doctor, I think you might die."

"So be it," he said. "I would rather die than risk your life any more."

She took his hand. "You are a brave man, Ugo. I hope your wife appreciates what a good and kind man you are."

Even in his fever this made him smile. He didn't think that Brenda would ever describe him as brave, good, or kind. But then at home he had been a different person: arrogant, selfish, playing at the lord of the manor.

"I will do my best for you," she said. "Let us try this and see if it can disinfect the wound." She took the small bottle of grappa. "Good. You have not drunk it all."

She ripped a strip from the old sheet, then soaked it in the grappa. He screamed in pain as she washed the wound, then was ashamed of himself and bit into his lip to stop from screaming again.

"I have done my best," she said. "It seems to be clean. Of course I do not know what it is like

180

inside or if the bullet has damaged some blood vessel. We can only hope."

He watched as she made a pad of clean linen then bound it to his leg.

"You have no more morphine?" she asked.

"I'm afraid not. Just the one syringe, and I used that."

"No more medicines?"

He examined the first aid kit. There were a couple of small sticking plasters, big enough for a cut on the finger, and a strip of aspirins.

"I have these."

"Aspirin. They will help take your fever down. That is good. But you should not become too cold." She reached up inside his jacket. "Your shirt is quite wet, too, but I do not think we should try to remove it. Let us pull up your trousers quickly and then I will wrap you in your blanket and the parachute."

She eased his trousers over the wound with great care, then up over his hips in a businesslike manner. Then she went to get water and held his head as he sipped it and swallowed four aspirin.

"And I have brought you more of the bean soup," she said. "You need nourishment. Can you eat a little?"

She took the covering from the basin and held him propped up against her as she fed him. He tried a few mouthfuls, then fell back against her, exhausted.

"You must eat. You must stay strong," she said.
"I can't. I'm sorry."

She got up then, easing him back against his pillow. "I will go back to the village and see what medicines they have at the pharmacy that I can ask for without causing suspicion. Alcohol for your wound, that will be no problem. I have used all the grappa. I do not think they will give me a sulpha drug without a prescription, but I can try. I'll tell them that Renzo has a sore throat. It is true that he does, but only with a cold. Nothing serious. Then I will try to come back tonight."

"You are so good to me," he said. "If this stupid war is ever over and I reach my home, I will try to make it up to you. I will send your son to a good school. Buy you more goats. Whatever you want."

"Let us not talk of the future," she said, giving him a sad smile. "Who knows what it may bring. We are all in the hands of God and the holy saints."

Then she tucked him in as if he was a little child, wrapping the parachute around him. "Rest now." She stood up. "See. I leave you water to drink, and the rest of the soup, if you can try to eat it. I think you should try." She wagged a finger at him, making him smile.

"Very well. I will try."

As she walked away, he wondered if it would be the last time he would see her.

CHAPTER SEVENTEEN

JOANNA

June 1973

Paola had clearly been waiting for me. She looked relieved when she opened the front door. "Oh, Signorina Langley, *mia cara*. There you are. I was worried that something had happened to you. I said to Angelina that you surely would not want to be out alone in the dark. What would you be doing?"

"I am so sorry, Signora," I said. "I talked to the men who sit in the piazza, and they insisted that I join them for a glass of wine. Then they ordered bruschetta and it would have been rude to refuse. I told them I was eating dinner at your house, but they said you would not eat until very late."

Paola laughed. "It is no problem, my little one. I was merely concerned for your safety. Not that I think you run the risk of being unsafe in this village, but there are dark alleyways where you can trip and hurt yourself. Now come, sit. The dinner awaits us."

I followed her down the hall and was ushered into a dining room, this time with a table elegantly set with candles on it. Angelina was already there. The baby slept in its cradle at her feet.

"You see, Mamma, I told you she would be safe," Angelina said. "She is a girl from London, from a big city. She knows how to take care of herself and watch out for danger."

I laughed. "I did have to say no when the man called Gianni offered to take me home," I said. "I thought he was a little too friendly."

Paola shrugged. "He is all talk, that one. No real harm in him, at least not to the ladies. If you had become amorous, he would have run a mile."

Angelina laughed, too. "But in his business dealings, well, sometimes he does like to play with fire," she said.

"We don't know that," Paola said. "It is only rumours."

"It is what they say in the village," Angelina replied. "They say he is friendly with those who might be *Mafiosi*. They say he might trade in stolen goods. And then there is the olive press . . ."

"Olive press?" I asked.

Angelina nodded. "The only olive press for the whole community is owned by Cosimo. Did you meet Cosimo?"

"I did. He looked rather . . ." I didn't have the Italian word for "imposing."

"He is powerful," Paola said. "Rich and powerful. A dangerous man to cross. He owns the only olive press, and he lets those he likes or to whom he owes favours get the best times to press their olives. If he does not like you—if you refuse to sell your trees to him, like me—then you find that your time to press olives is at two o'clock in the morning."

"Does the press run day and night?"

"It does. In the picking season, the sooner the olives are pressed, the better. So each person wants time at Cosimo's press."

"So what was Gianni doing that might anger Cosimo?" I asked.

"He still has olive trees, over beyond the old monastery. Cosimo has never liked him, and he always gives Gianni the worst times. Sometimes he makes him wait for days. So Gianni was trying to get together with some of the local farmers to set up a co-op and build their own olive press. I don't know how far he has come with this idea, but of course Cosimo would be angry if anyone tried to go against him."

"Gianni is a fool," Angelina said. "He likes to talk big. But if it came to a showdown with Cosimo, he would run away with his tail between his legs."

While we talked Paola carried in dishes and placed them in front of us. "Asparagus from the garden," she said. "It is asparagus season. Such a short time that we make the most of it and eat asparagus at almost every meal."

She placed a dish of white stalks in front of me, then drizzled them with olive oil and grated Parmesan cheese over them from a big block. I had eaten asparagus before—certainly not often, as it was a delicacy in England—but it had tasted nothing like this. Each mouthful was heavenly, the sharpness of the cheese contrasting with the sweetness of the vegetable.

After we had finished this course, Angelina cleared away the plates and returned carrying a big tureen. When Paola took off the lid, the herby aroma filled the room. She served me a generous portion, much bigger than I would have liked, but it would have been rude to refuse. "Here we are—the pici you and I made this afternoon and the rabbit ragu. Enjoy."

And I did enjoy. Somehow I seemed to find room to clear my plate. There was just enough of the rabbit in the sauce to flavour it, but it was the herbs and tomatoes that made it so delicious. I resolved to learn about herbs from Paola before I departed, and if ever I had a garden, I'd grow them myself.

After the main course had been cleared, biscotti were put on the table along with small glasses of a rich amber liquid. "This is the Vin Santo I told you about," Paola said. "The holy wine."

I looked surprised. "This is really holy wine from the church?"

She laughed. "This is what we call it. No, it

doesn't come from the church now. There are many stories about the name. Some say it was the style of wine from dried grapes favoured for Mass. But others say there was a holy friar who used the leftover wine from the Eucharist to go around and cure the sick. These days it just tastes good for dessert. This is how you eat the biscotti. You dip and then you eat."

Angelina got up. "I'm going to bed, Mamma. I am tired. The little one kept me up most of last night. Please God she sleeps for a while now."

Paola gave her a big hug and kisses on both cheeks. Angelina shook my hand, giving me a shy smile. "Tomorrow you must tell me about life in London," she said, "about the fashions and the music and the movie stars. I want to know everything."

"All right." I returned her smile.

She picked up the little cradle and carried it from the room. After she had gone Paola leaned closer to me. "It is good to see her animated again," she said. "For a while after the baby she showed no interest in anything. She was very ill, you know. They had to take the baby early, or she would have died. I thought I would lose her, my only child. But now, thank God and the Blessed Virgin, she is on the road to recovery."

She put a hand on my shoulder. "You lost your poor mamma, so you know what it feels like to lose someone you love. After my dear man it

187

would have been more than I could have borne. It's the very worst thing in the world for a mother to lose her child."

I felt tears welling up in my eyes and tried to swallow back a sob. The wine had worn at my defences. I wanted to tell her. I wanted to tell somebody and have her arms around me, telling me softly that she understood. But I stopped myself at the last moment. I couldn't tell even this sweet and kind woman how it felt to have lost my baby.

"Don't look so sad," she said, touching my cheek. "All is well. We are tested and we survive, and life will be good again."

With those comforting words I bid her good-night and went to bed.

It was only when I was curled up in bed feeling the cool touch of those soft sheets against my cheek that I allowed the tears to come. I might have held them back until now, but I couldn't any longer. I relived every moment. I remembered my surprise when the doctor told me that I was pregnant. My initial fear was replaced with reassurance. The pregnancy was not planned, and had come sooner than we'd hoped, but Adrian would do the right thing and marry me. I'd put my clerkship with the solicitor on hold, that's all. But that wasn't what happened. Adrian had looked scared, then annoyed. "Are you sure? It couldn't have come at a more inconvenient time, could it? We're both so close to taking our bar exams. Certainly in no position to settle down and start a family." He paused, a frown spoiling that smoothly handsome face. Then he relaxed again, and gave me a little smile. "Don't worry," he said. "It will be all right. I know someone who can take care of it."

It took me a while to realise that he wanted me to have an abortion. Shock, horror, revulsion.

"An abortion? Is that what you are suggesting?"

Adrian remained so calm. "He's a good chap. Knows what he's doing."

"Adrian, it's our baby. How can you be like that?"

"Oh, come on, Joanna. It's the nineteen seventies. Women have abortions all the time. It's no big thing anymore."

"It is for the baby," I said. "And it would be for me. My father would never forgive me if he found out."

"Your father has hardly been the most supportive man in the universe, has he?" Adrian demanded. "And hopelessly old-fashioned. He can't even accept our living together, for God's sake."

"All right," I said, taking a deep breath, "I could never forgive myself. There. I've said it. And if you care so little about me . . ."

"Of course I care about you," Adrian said. "It's

just that I'm not prepared to wreck two lives for the sake of a baby neither of us wants." He put a hand on my shoulder then. "You're still in shock. Think about it and I'm sure you'll come to see that my way is best."

I did think about it. I told myself that in truth there was no other solution. Adrian would keep pressuring me if I stayed with him. He certainly wouldn't want to share his flat with an unwanted baby that might ruin his precious reputation. And if I moved out? I had no guarantee my father would take me in, and apart from him I had no one. I think the biggest shock was realising that Adrian, my Adrian, who I had thought was my soulmate, my lover, my best friend, was none of the above. He was someone I could no longer rely on. I told myself he was right. We were in no position to start a family. It was only a bit of tissue at this stage, not a baby. But I simply couldn't do it.

Strangely enough, it was liberal free spirit Scarlet who was on my side. "Don't do it if you don't feel it's right," she said. "And don't stay with that creep Adrian if that's the way he treats you. You've got me. I'll help you get through it. And I bet your dad will, too, once he gets used to it. Go and see him and tell him. He'll rant and rave a bit, but then he'll come around."

"I don't know," I said. "You know what a fuss he made when I moved in with Adrian."

"But it's his only daughter in trouble. It's my betting he won't let you down. He'll want to look after you."

I agonised over this. Even if my father forgave me, I could never go and live with him. I imagined Miss Honeywell's horrified looks and the schoolgirls' giggles. There didn't seem to be any way out. I almost relented and went to tell Adrian he was right. Except that I couldn't.

I wandered aimlessly around London, debating whether to go down to Surrey and see my father or not, trying to come up with some kind of solution . . . And I didn't see the taxi come speeding around the corner as I stepped out to cross King's Road in Chelsea. I remember the sensation of flying, then of lying on the pavement with faces staring down at me, and a kind man covering me with his jacket, and an ambulance. Then nothing much for a couple of days. Scarlet came to see me in hospital. She asked if she should telephone my father, but I didn't want her to. I felt too weak to face him. It wasn't until a few days later that I learned that among my other injuries—broken ribs, broken collarbone, a severe concussion—I'd had a miscarriage and lost the baby. I should have been relieved, but instead I wept.

Adrian came to see me, too, and sat on the side of my bed, holding my hand awkwardly and muttering pleasantries that it was all for the best, wasn't it, and I'd be as good as new in no time. Actually, it took quite a while for me to heal. I had dizzy spells. Terrible headaches. It hurt me to breathe. Adrian came to see me daily at first, then less frequently. When I was due to come out of hospital, he came and sat at my bedside and said he thought it would be better if I went home to my father to recuperate. He had something he'd wanted to tell me for some time, but he'd waited until I was strong enough. He had fallen in love with someone else. He was going to get married—to the daughter of the senior partner at his law firm.

And that was that. I collected my things and fled to the only safe haven I could think of: Scarlet's flat. She, bless her heart, welcomed me with open arms. She let me curl up on her sofa and recover. But I was still too fragile to go back to work. My solicitors were understanding to start with. They realised I'd had a bad accident and wished me well. But lately they'd made it clear that they wouldn't wait forever.

The physical wounds were healed, but there was still a big, empty void inside me. It felt as if I had been going around like a shadow of my former self, like a hollow person with no clear purpose and frankly not much hope. What I wanted was my mother. I suppose my father had never allowed me to grieve properly when she died. We had to make the best of things and soldier on, to be a credit to the family. That was what I'd been told, and it was only now that I was grieving for her. I wanted someone like Paola to love me.

Eventually I cried myself to sleep. I awoke the next morning to the sounds of the countryside: a rooster crowing, a dawn chorus of birdsong. Sunlight was streaming in through slatted blinds. I got up feeling strangely energised and refreshed, looked at myself in the bathroom mirror, and was horrified at the puffy, misshapen face I saw staring back at me. I'd definitely need a shower before I allowed Paola to see me.

I pulled on the shower handle. A small trickle of water came out and then stopped altogether. I thought maybe I'd got the mechanism wrong, and tried turning it in the other direction. Whatever I did I could get no water.

Frustrated now, I put on yesterday's clothes, brushed my hair, tried to cover my blotchy face with powder, and went to look at the well. Had the pump somehow ceased to function? The well was housed inside a wooden structure, the lid of it held in place with a large stone. I removed the stone, then tried to raise the lid. It was too heavy for one person to lift, or at least for me to do so. I tried several times, then gave up, admitted defeat, and went up to the farmhouse. I wondered if Paola would be awake this early, but as I approached the kitchen, I heard her singing. Through the open window I watched her kneading dough at the table. Such a warm and comforting scene. I tapped on the back door so that she wasn't startled, then entered. She turned to me, a big, welcoming smile on her face. "Ah, my little one, you are awake with the sun. Did you sleep well last night?"

If she noticed my face was not looking its best, she did not betray the fact.

"I'm sorry to bother you," I said, "but the shower. It gives no water. I have turned the handle this way and that way and still no water. I tried to see if there is a fault with the well, but I cannot lift the cover alone."

She looked puzzled. "That is strange. Maybe there is something wrong with the pump in the well, but it was working perfectly when I tested it a few days ago. Come, we shall see."

I followed her through the garden to a small shelter behind my little house. "Come, we shall lift the cover together," she said. I took one side and she the other and we lifted it.

"Now, let us see what is the matter," she said.

We peered inside. I'm not sure which of us screamed. I heard the sound piercing through my head, and I know my own mouth was open. A man's body had been jammed into the top of the well.

CHAPTER EIGHTEEN

HUGO

December 1944

Miraculously, the aspirin did seem to bring down Hugo's fever a little. He felt like a limp rag, but remembering Sofia's stern admonition, he forced himself to sip at the soup. Then he lay back, gasping, his forehead beaded with sweat. *What will happen now?* he worried. What if gangrene had set in and his leg had to be amputated? It was obvious he'd never make it past the Germans to the Allies, and Sofia had been right—if the Germans came upon him in this condition, they would see him as a hindrance and a liability and would dispatch him instantly. He realised there was little hope of surviving. He wondered if he should do the right thing and try to make his way down to that road below and await his fate rather than risk any more visits from Sofia.

When he tried to get up, nausea and dizziness overwhelmed him. He realised he could not go anywhere in this state. That was when he took out his service revolver and examined it, turning it over in his hand. He could end his life now. That would be the best thing to do, the noble way out.

He felt the heaviness of the revolver, pictured how he'd point it at his temple, hold it steady, and click. All over. But he hesitated. Not from fear of ending his life, but because he didn't want Sofia to find his head blown away. He didn't want to leave without saying goodbye.

"If the leg gets worse," he told himself, "if gangrene really sets in, then I'll do it. But I'll tell her what I'm going to do and why it is the only solution."

Then he lay back and fell into a restless, fevered sleep.

He wasn't sure how many days passed this way. He was vaguely aware that she came again, that she cleaned his wound with something that stung so badly he had screamed. He remembered she had held his head, made him swallow some kind of medicine, wiped the sweat from his brow, and tried to make him take some warm soup. But he remembered these things as part of unquiet dreams, not sure they had actually happened.

So it was a surprise for him to open his eyes one bright morning and find that he felt comfortably warm and the fever had departed. As he came back to full consciousness, he realised he had a real pillow under his head, a sheepskin over him, and something tied to his wrist. He held up his arm and saw it was a medal. A religious medal to some kind of saint. *Whoever it is, it certainly worked,* he thought.

He attempted to extricate himself from the cocoon that had been wound around him. Even that small task was beyond him, and he lay back before attempting again. This time he succeeded. He freed himself, wriggled out of his shelter, and felt the coldness of the stone floor against his body. He tried to stand but gave up when the room swung around him and he felt horribly nauseous. He sipped a little water and took a few bites of the bread that had been left on the bench beside him. When he plucked up the courage to examine his wound, he went to take down his trousers and was astounded to see that they were not his own. They were made of coarse black wool. And he was wearing different underpants, too. She had changed his clothes for him while he'd slept like a baby. He turned his face toward the wall, his cheeks burning, feeling horribly embarrassed and ashamed, even though he'd had no part in this.

Carefully he pulled back the trouser leg until he came to the bandage. It was no longer soaked in blood, which was a good sign. And the wound didn't smell bad, which was even better. He unwound the bandage and peeled back the pad from the wound. It wasn't a pretty sight, with part of his flesh blown away, but it wasn't too awful, either. It was clearly healing. He washed it with the remains of the water, then applied a clean pad and reapplied the bandage.

Then he rearranged himself in his hiding place and waited for Sofia to come. He glanced at his watch but it had stopped. Of course, he hadn't wound it for days. From the position of the shadows on the wall, he could tell it was still early morning.

In the distance he heard a church bell ringing, followed almost immediately by one closer by. More than the tolling of the hour this time. The bells went on and on until the air echoed with the sound. *Sunday,* he thought, *it must be Sunday,* and felt comforted that all around him people were going to church to pray. He had never been much for God himself. Members of the British aristocracy went to church as a display of solidarity with the lower classes around them but didn't actually believe. At least his father didn't. He had once said to Hugo, "When you have been in the trenches and watched men blown apart or drowning in mud, you can't believe that any God would let those things happen and not interfere."

And yet Sofia had tied the saint's medal to his wrist and it seemed to have worked. He tried a tentative prayer. "Dear God, if you're there and you can hear me, keep her safe. Let me get home somehow. Protect Langley Hall and those in it. And, dear God, protect Sofia and her family." He was going to add, "Let her husband still be alive and come back to her," but he couldn't say the words.

The bells died away to silence. He fished for his packet of cigarettes. There were twelve left from the twenty. He lit one, lay back, and smoked it, watching the vapour hanging in the frigid air. The day was quite still. No birdsong, no wind, no dogs barking. Utter stillness. It felt as if he was the only person in the world.

He wondered when she would come. He suspected she wouldn't go out looking for mushrooms on a Sunday. He remembered from his own time in Italy that Sundays had been times for church and big family meals. Not that she had much food or much of a family, but she'd be obliged to stay with them. He felt empty and hungry, so he finished the bread that was already becoming stale. A pigeon flapped and fluttered across the top of the wall, and he wished he had the strength to get up and set that trap. But he hadn't.

A watery sun rose higher in the sky. The day passed. The sun sank again and still she didn't come. He fought with disappointment. Of course she couldn't come on a Sunday. He'd already realised that. Maybe she'd slip away in the dark again, although he didn't like the idea of her walking alone through the olive groves when there might be Germans or partisans or black-marketeers prowling around. He lit his candle but eventually blew it out, afraid of wasting it. He lay awake, listening to the night sounds, the hoot of an owl, the sigh of the wind. *She won't come now,* he told himself. And then the worries crept in. Had something happened to her? Someone had seen her coming through the olive groves and betrayed her . . . He tried to shut out the dark thoughts, but they would not subside.

He must have drifted off into dreams because he awoke with a start at a loud sound close by and reached for his weapon.

"It is only me, Ugo," said a gentle voice. "Do not be afraid." And he watched her lantern bobbing toward him across the floor.

She placed the lantern on the bench and dropped to her knees beside him, her face glowing with joy in the candlelight. "You are awake and sitting up. That is such good news. I was so worried. Each time I came back I expected to find you dead. But I entrusted you to the care of Saint Rita."

"Saint Rita? Who is she?"

"She is the patron saint of wounds."

"This is the medal you tied to my wrist?"

"Of course," she said. "She did well for you, did she not?"

"I'm feeling much better," he said. "The fever has gone and the wound is beginning to heal. I can't thank you enough, Sofia. You have taken such good care of me. You have even changed my clothes, like an infant."

She smiled. "I could not let you lie there in such a state. I took your own clothes away and have cleaned them. I will bring them back next time."

"And what I am wearing now belongs to Guido?"

"Of course. He is not here to use them. Rather you than the moths."

He took her hand. "I will make all this up to you, I promise. When I am home I will send you money for new clothes, good clothes. Good soft wool."

"Let us not talk of such things," she said. "Who knows what tomorrow will bring? Nothing good, I feel. But eat. I've brought you soup. You must be hungry."

She unwrapped the bowl and he ate it eagerly. It wasn't much of a soup, really. Some cabbage and carrot leaves and a few beans. As if reading his thoughts, she said, "I know it is not much. We haven't had any meat for days now. But it is warm."

"You are too good to share what little you have with me," he said.

She turned away. "I do not know how long I can keep on coming here," she said. "The Germans were in my village today. You heard the church bells?"

"I thought it was Sunday."

"No, each village rings the bell when Germans

approach. That way the young men in the village know to go and hide in the woods, and the young women hide wherever they can. I was up in my attic all day hidden in an old wardrobe." She paused, her eyes holding his, begging him to understand her. "These men are animals, Ugo," she said. "The war has turned them into animals. We women fear for our honour every time they come near. They took the baker's daughter once—a young girl of fifteen—and they violated her, one after the other. She has never been the same since. Her mind snapped at the horror of it."

"How terrible. I'm so very sorry. I can assure you that British soldiers would not behave in that way."

She gave a wonderfully Italian shrug. "Who can say? Some of these men were undoubtedly good boys at home. They helped the family in the fields, or they worked in banks and took girls dancing. But the war has changed them, ruined them."

"Are the Germans still there?"

She shook her head. "No, saints be praised. They came to see if our village was a good place to wait out the winter. Their army has established a line just north of here, and they are looking for places where they can defend the roads from the south, from where the Allies will come. But I am glad to say that the views from our village did not

202

meet their liking, and as we have nothing worth taking anymore, they left. Actually, that is not true. They took the mayor's remaining chickens . . . may their souls rot in hell."

A gust of wind swept in, making the candle in her lantern flicker and sending shadows dancing. "So you are safe for a while?"

"Maybe. We hope that they will have news of the Allies advancing and they will flee back to Germany and leave us in peace. But some say the Allies will not advance until the spring now. The snows will come and the roads will be impassable in the mountains."

"That means I will be trapped here until the spring, too?"

"We do not often get snow. Our hills are not so high. But there are very high mountains between here and the coast. Maybe when your leg is strong enough we can find a way to get you to the south. We have no motorcars and no petrol, but there are farm carts, and those who grow produce take them to market."

"What produce do they grow in the winter?" he asked.

"Root vegetables. Turnips. Potatoes. Cauli-flower. Cabbage—although the Germans have helped themselves to all our cabbages. They love cabbage for some reason. I have some turnips and parsnips almost ready for harvest on my small plot of land."

"That's good. And how is the search for mushrooms going?"

She sighed. "I fear I cannot use that excuse any longer. There will be no more mushrooms now, and I think I have found every single one. I will have to sneak out in the middle of the night as I have just done."

"I am feeling better now. Really, Sofia, you do not need to come so often. If you could come once in a while and leave me a little something to eat, I will get by."

"Don't be silly. How will you get well and strong if you don't eat? There is a new moon in the sky. Soon it will be easy to walk without a lantern, and I wear dark clothes. Nobody will see me, don't worry."

"What time is it, anyway?"

"After one. I could not leave before I was sure all the Germans had gone. They found some bottles of wine in the mayor's cellar, and they stayed late, singing their stupid songs."

"But you will get no sleep. You will make yourself ill."

She patted his hand. "Don't worry. Most nights the village is asleep by nine. It is only women and children. The men who remain go off with the partisans to do what harm they can to the Germans by night."

"Are all the men part of the resistance?"

"Who knows? We do not ask and they do not

tell us. Better that way if the Germans question anyone. All I can tell you is that partisans are active nearby and it is possible that our local men are involved. Not that there are many men in the village any longer. The few that are here were with the army in the south, fighting beside the Germans until we changed sides. Then they slipped away before the Germans could conscript them or send them to prison camps. They are brave boys, I am sure, although I am glad that they are off doing their destructive work. That Cosimo is a little too interested in me."

"Cosimo?" His voice was harsh.

She nodded. "Some whisper that he is a leader in the partisans. No doubt a brave fellow. Not bad-looking. A powerful man. But I told him until my husband is declared dead, I am still married to him. All the same he has been hanging around lately. He brings us an occasional egg or flask of wine, and we don't ask where he got it. But I think they are an excuse to visit me. So I am glad that he is away for days at a time."

"He would not try . . ." Hugo forced out the words.

"Oh no. Nothing like that. He is an honourable man, I am sure. He is kind to my son. But I do not wish to be courted by him."

"When I escape, you must come with me," Hugo said.

She smiled sadly. "But what if Guido returned

home to find I was not there? And I cannot leave his grandmother. I promised him when he went away that I would take care of her."

He wanted to say something more, but every thought seemed so hopeless. So he asked, "Is there a saint for everything?"

"Oh yes," she said simply. "Saint Anne for those wishing to have a child. Saint Blaise for throats. A saint for rheumatism, for chilblains . . ."

He laughed, then asked, "And one to protect women and children?"

"We ask *la Madonna* for that," she answered. "She lost her own son. She saw him die. She knows how we feel."

"Do you wear a medal of *la Madonna*?"

"I gave mine to Guido when he went away," she said. "I only pray that it kept him safe and that he is still alive. But I fear it is not so. My heart tells me that he is dead."

Hugo took her hand. She gripped his fiercely, and they sat close together in the small circle of flickering light, sharing their worry.

CHAPTER NINETEEN

JOANNA

June 1973

Angelina was woken up and sent to fetch the Carabinieri. Two men in impressive military-style uniforms arrived, red-faced from running down the hill. It took them some time to extract the body, so firmly was it jammed into the well. When they laid it out on the gravel path, I gave a little gasp of horror. It was Gianni, the man who had offered to escort me home last night, only to be pushed aside in favour of the more reliable Alberto.

The two Carabinieri agents recognised him instantly. "But surely this is Gianni," one said. And they exchanged a look I couldn't quite understand. A doctor was summoned and pronounced that Gianni had been struck on the back of the head with a blunt object. He had then been pushed into the well with his head under the water. The cause of death was drowning.

I found I couldn't stop shivering. It was too horrible to contemplate. Paola took one look at me and put an arm around my shoulder. "The poor young lady is in shock. And she has not even had her breakfast yet. Come, my dear, let me pour you some coffee and you will feel better."

"And who is this young lady?" one of the policemen asked.

"She is a visitor from England," Paola said. "She is newly arrived here and stays at my guest house."

"This is the guest house?" the officer asked, pointing at my open door.

"It is," Paola confirmed.

"So close to the well," said the officer, a rather unpleasant-looking, pudgy individual with little piggy eyes, staring at me. "You sleep there, Signorina? And yet you heard nothing when this man was murdered?"

"I heard nothing," I said.

He asked another question. This time the Italian was beyond me. "I'm sorry. I only speak a little of your language," I said. "I will understand if you speak slowly."

"I asked who found the body," he repeated.

My brain was refusing to function properly. I couldn't think clearly in English, let alone form sentences in Italian. "The signora and I found it," I stammered, waving my arms as one does when speaking a foreign language and lacking the vocabulary. "I wanted to take a shower. There was no water. I went to the well, but . . ." It took me long enough to say these words, then my Italian failed me.

"She was not strong enough to remove the cover alone, so she came for me and together we lifted the cover," Paola said. "We both saw the body at the same time, and I think we both screamed. We were certainly both alarmed."

"Do you know this man?" the other officer asked.

"I know him," Paola said, "as well as you do. He has lived in San Salvatore all his life. But this young lady does not. I told you, she is newly arrived here."

"And do you have any idea why Gianni may have chosen to hang around your house at night?" There was a sneer to the voice of the unpleasant Carabinieri.

"Certainly not to court me," Paola said hotly. "Of course we know no reason. Signorina Langley and my daughter Angelina and I were enjoying our dinner together and then we went to bed. That is the story of our evening. As to how this man wound up in my well, I would say it is likely that he was knocked out on the path on his way out of town and that my well appealed to his attackers as a good place to hide his body because my house was closest to the path."

"We can make no assumptions yet," one of them said. "You will both be required to come up to our headquarters in the town and make an official statement. Later there will be further enquiries. It may be that the inspector from the municipal decides to come from Lucca, since this is clearly a murder investigation. You are not to leave this place without permission, is that clear?"

I hadn't managed to follow this, but I understood more when Paola said, "I have no intention of going anywhere, but this young lady, she may have to return to her homeland quite soon. She is not to be held up by a murder investigation about which she knows nothing."

"As for that, we shall see when we have made further enquiries," the fat one said. "For the time being she is to remain here. Understood?"

I nodded. The full implications of this were just sinking in. The men at that table would undoubtedly be questioned. They would say that Gianni wanted to walk me home but I refused. They might say that Gianni flirted with me. I could see that a warped imagination might read several scenarios into that. Perhaps they would all like to be able to pin a murder on an outsider. I felt sick.

Paola didn't seem at all perturbed. "I'll leave you men to go about your business and have this man's body removed from my premises," she said. "As for my well, I suppose my water is now contaminated. Poor Signorina Langley certainly won't want to take her shower until it has been treated. Come, my dear, you shall use the bathroom at the farmhouse and have a good long soak in my tub. Our water comes from the mains."

With that she put an arm firmly around my shoulder and led me away from the crime scene.

"Don't let them upset you," she said as she closed the kitchen door behind us. "Those men are bullies. They are not from around here. The Carabinieri are only country policemen, always chosen from among the uncouth and the loutish. Many of them come from Sicily, and we know what kind of people live down there, don't we? Gangsters. *Mafiosi.* Still, they are not permitted by law to investigate major crimes. With luck a senior inspector from Lucca will be sent and all will be well. But first let me pour you coffee, and you should have a good breakfast before you take your bath."

Angelina had been standing just outside the kitchen door, watching from a distance with the baby in her arms. As we approached, the baby started to cry. Angelina rocked her back and forth. "Have those horrible men gone yet, Mamma?" she asked. "Is it true that someone was murdered? I did not like to come closer in case the shock curdled my milk and I could not feed the little one."

"It is true, *mia cara*," Paola said. "The poor man who lost his life was Gianni."

"Oh, Gianni." Angelina nodded thoughtfully

211

as she put the baby to her shoulder and patted its back. "Well, I suppose that is not a complete shock, is it?"

"It is always a shock when someone dies before their time," Paola said. "Go put the little one down and we will have our breakfast. This poor young lady is shivering as if she has been out in the snow."

She sat me at the table as if I was a helpless child, put a cup of milky coffee in front of me, and then placed bread and jam and cheese on the table. "Eat. You will feel better."

My stomach felt as if it had tied itself into knots, and I didn't think I could eat anything, but with Paola hovering over and watching me, I had to at least take some sips of hot coffee and then spread some apricot jam on a slice of bread. The bread must have been baked that morning. It was still warm, and the butter and fresh apricot jam melted together so that I almost sighed with pleasure at the combination of textures and flavours. Who could have thought that bread and jam could have such an effect? I had a second slice, then some sharp cheese, and by that time I was feeling almost human again and strong enough to tackle even the most boorish Carabinieri.

Angelina came to join us, cutting herself a big hunk of bread and topping it with lashings of butter.

"Why did you say you were not shocked that Gianni was killed?" I asked her.

She shrugged. "It is said that sometimes Gianni makes deals, not quite legal ones, you know? Maybe cigarettes from a boat that comes to the coast. That sort of thing."

"We don't know that," Paola said. "It is all hearsay. It is true he is not liked in town. Not trusted. And now this business with the olive press."

"He wanted to get men together to build his own olive press, is that right?" I asked.

She nodded. "And of course Cosimo would not be happy if that came to pass. But I don't think it would ever have happened. The other men would not have wanted to risk defying Cosimo. I think Gianni stuck his neck out for nothing."

I tried to make sense of this, not just their Italian words but the implications of them. Gianni was involved in things that were not quite legal. And shoving someone down a well to drown would be the sort of thing that gangsters would do to teach someone a lesson. But he had also dared to cross Cosimo. I pictured that man's face—so powerful, and his eyes so cold when he stared at me and said, "You are German, I think." No, I would not have wanted to cross him.

But he'd had a stroke, which had clearly left him partly paralysed—certainly not able to lift that extremely heavy top from the well and

213

shove a body down into it. But then someone as powerful as Cosimo presumably had minions who would obey his commands. And he had an adopted son who was big and muscular. I had to remember that!

"Tomorrow is Saturday," Paola said. "Market day in San Salvatore. You shall both help me see which vegetables and fruits are ready to be picked and brought to market."

"Don't we have to go up to the town and make our statements at the police station?" I said.

Paola gave a dismissive gesture. "Pah. Let those men wait. We know nothing about Gianni's activities that might have led to his untimely death. It will be good for us to have something to do, and working out in God's nature is always soothing for the soul." She put a hand on my shoulder. "Why don't we do that right now, before the sun is too hot, and then you can take your bath at your leisure?"

I would have liked to bathe first, having hastily pulled on yesterday's clothes, but I wasn't going to argue with Paola when she was being so kind to me. I followed her out to the garden. "Let us see," she said. "These tomatoes—yes, we shall find enough ripe ones here, but we will not pick them until the last minute tomorrow. And these broad beans. They must be eaten young like this. The pole beans—they will take another couple of weeks." She paused, bending to a feathery plant.

"The asparagus? We want to keep enough for ourselves, but the plant has been generous this year. Good."

She continued onward, moving with speed and grace for a large woman. "Ah, look, Angelina. The zucchini blossoms. Perfect."

I saw her examine a yellow flower. "What do you do with those?" I asked. "Can you eat flowers?"

"Oh, but yes! Zucchini blossoms. We stuff them. So delicious. I will make some for us tonight, if you like. And then this plant will keep rewarding us with zucchini all season long."

I had just seen something else I hadn't expected to find in this well-cultivated plot. It looked like a giant thistle. "But surely one cannot eat this?" I asked, pointing at it.

Paola looked surprised. "You do not have artichokes in your country?"

"I've never seen anything like this before."

"Then I will fry some tonight as an antipasto. Oh, but they are good. You will enjoy."

We walked on. We found that there were ripe cherries and even some apricots, but that the peaches would not be ready for a while. "We will pick the fruit tonight after the sun goes down, and the asparagus can be cut, too, but the tomatoes, the blossoms . . . those we will wait until the last minute to pick." She gave us a satisfied smile. "Good. We will have a fine offering at the market tomorrow." And we followed her back to the house.

I went back to my room to collect my sponge bag and towel, looking forward to a long soak in a tub. As I rummaged in my bag for clean underwear, I noticed a piece of paper sticking out from between the slats of the shutter on my window. It certainly hadn't been in the room yesterday. I went over and pulled it free with some difficulty. It was an envelope. I sat on my bed and opened it. As I took out a letter, three objects fell on to the quilt. I examined them one by one. One was a little lapel pin in the shape of a many-pointed star. Another was a scrap of brown cloth, stiff with something like paint. And the third was a small banknote. It said "Reichsmark." A German banknote from the time of the war.

I put them back on to the quilt and tried to read the letter. The handwriting was not easy to read, and my knowledge of written Italian was not great. I went for my dictionary and started to translate slowly and laboriously.

I want to tell you the truth about Sofia. I know. I kept silent until now, for fear of my life, but you are an outsider. I will take you to my sheep and there I will tell you, where nobody can hear us.

It wasn't signed but it had to be from Gianni. He had invited me to visit his sheep last night. I found that my hand that held the letter was shaking. I looked at the objects on my bed. I had no idea what any of it meant, but I was frightened. Had Gianni been killed because he was going to tell me the truth about what happened during the war?

CHAPTER TWENTY

JOANNA

June 1973

I picked up the three objects from my bed,
examining them in my hand and wondering what
they could mean. The German banknote was easy
enough to understand. German money. Someone
had been paid German money. But the other
two? I stared at the piece of stiffened cloth. It
was dark brown. I lifted it up and sniffed for the
smell of paint, then recoiled. It was not paint. It
had a faintly metallic smell. Surely it was blood.
Hastily I scooped up the three things and shoved
them into the toe of one of my spare shoes, where
they would be safely hidden. Then I folded the
letter and put it back inside the envelope, which
I carefully placed between the pages of my
dictionary, just in case.

I could tell nobody—that was clear. Not even
Paola. She must not be put in danger. I realised
now that Gianni had been trying to get me alone
last night not for an amorous encounter but
because he wanted to tell me something. He knew
the truth about Sofia. He must have known about
my father. And this was enough to get him killed.

I stared through the bars on my window out into the blindingly bright sunshine. Had he been followed here last night? Had someone seen him push the envelope through the bars and shutters of my window and then hit him over the head? In which case I was in danger. It occurred to me that I should have just left the envelope where I had found it so that anyone who came to search would realise that I was completely unaware of its contents. But it was too late for that now.

The most sensible thing for me to do would be to go back to Florence and take the next train home. Once I was out of the country, I would be safe. But the two policemen had said I was not allowed to leave the area until I was given permission. There was no bus I could take, and anyone who gave me a lift could get into trouble for abetting my escape. I was trapped here. I would have to make sure I stayed close to Paola. She would not let anything happen to me.

I collected my sponge bag and towel and almost ran back to the house.

"You are indeed eager for your bath," Paola commented, noting I was breathing hard. "Relax, my little one. Forget about what you have seen. Forget about those men. Gianni and his mistakes are nothing to do with us. May God have mercy on his soul, and also on his poor wife, who is now left alone. She will now be like me, unable to take care of the sheep and make cheese. I must

219

go and offer her comfort, but not today. She may not even know the truth yet, poor soul."

Paola took me through a long tiled hallway and ushered me into an enormous bathroom with a big claw-foot tub against one wall. She turned on the water and ran it until it reached the correct temperature. Then she nodded with satisfaction. "Good," she said. "Take your time. Enjoy it. Let your cares be washed away."

While the bath was filling, I cleaned my teeth. I certainly wasn't going to use the water from that well for anything other than flushing the toilet! I lowered myself into the warm water, lay back, and stared at the high ceiling, but I couldn't relax. I was glad to see that there were also bars on this window. I was safe for a while at least. After I had bathed I was relieved to find that Paola and Angelina were working in the garden, picking the broad beans. They were within hailing distance if I needed them. They could also see anyone coming down the path from the town. I dressed, put my dictionary into my purse, and came out to see if I could help with the picking.

"The rest we will leave until it is cool this evening," Paola said. "Now I suppose we must go up to the town, or those brutes will come looking for us. Let us get it over with."

I followed them into the house. Paola took off her apron and put on her hat before we set off up the hill. As we came into the piazza, we found it abuzz with people. We were besieged the moment we were spotted. Most of the Italian was too fast for me to understand and spoken in the local Tuscan dialect, but I got the meaning. Was it true that Gianni had been murdered? Found in Paola's well? And she heard nothing? No cries for help? Who could have done such a thing?

At this last question looks were exchanged. "Well, that Gianni," a woman said, leaning in closer as if she didn't want her words to be heard beyond our little group. "He was maybe asking for trouble. My husband warned him when that man showed up looking for him. Remember I told you?"

There were nods all around. "And that time he had that grappa for sale? Who knows where that came from? Certainly not from around here."

I could see relief in all those faces. Not from around here. His death had nothing to do with anyone in San Salvatore.

"We have to go to the Carabinieri and make a statement," Paola said.

"Good luck with that," one of the men who had been loitering at the edge of our circle said. "You go in that place and you're lucky to come out again."

They chuckled, but I could see they also glanced over at the yellow building.

"Don't say that in front of the English

signorina," one of them said. "She will not believe you're joking."

"Tell her she will be fine as long as she leaves a good bribe," the man said.

"Don't talk like that." A woman in black turned and gave him a hefty shove. "Shouldn't you be minding your shop, not meddling where you are not wanted?"

The man shuffled away. Paola took my arm and marched me toward the open door of the Carabinieri building. "Pay no attention. That man is a troublemaker," she said. "He is as bad as Gianni was. He sold some of the illegal grappa at his shop, didn't he? Claims he didn't know there was anything wrong with it."

We went up three steps and into the cool darkness beyond. It smelled of stale smoke in there. The room we went into was lit only by a small, high window with bars on it. I felt as though I had stepped into a prison cell. I glanced nervously at Paola. She didn't seem at all worried.

"So we have come to make our statements. Let us get it over with. I have much work to do with market day tomorrow," she said.

One of the officers we had seen this morning was seated at a desk.

"Ah, you came. Good. Just tell the truth and all will be well," he said.

"Of course we will tell the truth because we

have nothing to tell," Paola said. "It is not my fault that some man chooses to meet his end on my property. So, where is some paper? Where is a pen? We do not have time to waste."

A sheet of paper was produced, and the officer pointed to a chair for Paola to sit. When he tried to give me a sheet of paper, I shook my head.

"I can't write in Italian," I said. "I don't speak it well, either." I thought at this moment it might be better if they thought of me as a stranger who understood little and therefore could have no connection with what went on in San Salvatore.

"All right." The officer picked up a pen and looked up at me. "How long have you been in San Salvatore?"

"I only arrived yesterday," I told him. "No, I have never been here before. I have never been to Italy before. I know nobody in the town. I was told that Signora Rossini had a room to rent. That is why I am staying there."

"And why did you come to San Salvatore?" he asked, frowning at me. "We have no antiquities here. No famous church. We are not Siena or Florence."

I tried to think of a reason for coming that would not involve my father or the war—an innocent reason. I was a student of agriculture and writing a paper on olive trees? But then I realised that someone would have told them that I was asking questions about Sofia Bartoli and my father. It was better to tell the truth. I had nothing to hide, except for a letter concealed in my dictionary.

"My father was a British airman," I said, those words now coming easily to me as I had said them several times. "His plane was shot down near this town. I wanted to see it for myself because he died recently."

"Ah." That seemed to satisfy him. "I understand. And this man who was killed. You did not know him?"

"I only came here yesterday," I said. "I think he was among the men who were kind to me when I asked about my father. They bought me a glass of wine here in the piazza. Then I went home to dinner with Signora Rossini, and after dinner I was very tired. I fell asleep early. This morning I wanted to wash but there was no water. That was when I asked the signora and she helped me lift the lid on the well and we saw the body. That is all I know."

"Very good, Signorina," he said. I could see that his expression was now relaxed. I was not a suspect.

"Am I free to go if I wish?" I asked.

He shook his head. "We have had to report this to the detectives in Lucca. They will send an inspector, and he will want to confirm what you have told me. A mere formality, you understand, but until he comes you must remain here."

"And when might he come?" I asked. "I have to go back to England."

He gave an expressive shrug. "It is Saturday tomorrow, is it not? Perhaps he will come then, or perhaps he will wait until Monday. We have to see."

I tried to tell myself there was no harm in my waiting around for two more days. I'd be with Paola. I'd be safe. Then my hand tightened around the purse I was carrying. Had someone observed Gianni push the envelope through the bars? In which case what lengths would they go to in order to recover it from me? *I should have resealed it and left it in my room,* I thought. But then I decided that nobody could get into that room unless they managed to break down the heavy door.

I followed Paola out into the dazzling sunshine. "That is finished, thank *la Madonna*," she said. "Now to more important matters. I think we should go to the butcher's and buy some veal for tonight's dinner. You like veal?"

"I don't think I've ever had it," I said, not even knowing what the word meant.

"What do you eat in England?" she asked. "Always roast beef?"

"No, we eat lamb, sausages, fish. And potatoes. Always potatoes, not pasta."

She gave me a look of intense pity. "That is why you are all skin and bones," she said. "You must stay with me long enough for me to fatten you up. Who will want to marry a girl with no meat on her?"

"I wasn't always skin and bones," I said. "I have been sick this year."

"Ah. That explains why you look like a walking statue. You stay here, my dear, and you will see what sunshine and good food can do for you."

It was a very tempting offer. At this moment I could think of nothing better than staying with Paola, learning to cook, being mothered by her. Except that a man had been killed and it may have been because I was in San Salvatore. He had written that he knew the truth about Sofia. Did that mean that someone else in the village knew the truth and wanted it to remain hidden? I looked around the piazza. At this hour of the morning the tables outside the trattoria were empty. The only people around were housewives doing their shopping with baskets over their arms and some small children chasing the pigeons that wheeled and flapped and settled again.

On the church tower above, the bell started tolling. I thought it was for the hour but it went on ringing. Paola crossed herself. "The *angelus*. It is midday. Come, we must hurry before the shops shut for lunch. And that lazy butcher will not open again until at least four."

She set off at a great pace. I almost had to run to keep up. We bought some pale little chops of

226

what I had now worked out must be veal. Then in the delicatessen next door she chose several salamis from among the hundreds arranged on the shelf and some white cheese.

"Now we go home to eat," she said, nodding in satisfaction. "You shall help me stuff the zucchini blossoms."

We arrived back at her house. "First we pick and then we stuff," she said.

"I'll go and put my purse away," I said. "Then I'll help you."

I took the key and wended my way through the market garden to my little house. The door was still locked and untouched. I heaved a sigh of relief. I let myself in and checked that the three objects were still in my shoe. I left my purse and locked the door behind me. As I glanced over at the window, I noticed the imprint of a big boot in the soft earth. Had that been there this morning? I didn't think so, but I wasn't sure I would have noticed. Was it maybe Gianni's print from last night? But I remembered he had been quite slickly dressed—light blue shirt open at the neck and tight black trousers. Certainly no workman's or labourer's boots. That meant that someone had been trying to see in through that window while we had been away.

CHAPTER TWENTY-ONE
HUGO

December 1944

Hugo's leg was definitely on the mend. He still couldn't put any weight on it, but at least it didn't throb violently all the time and the fever had not returned. In the morning he made himself get up and practice walking with the stick. The sun had been streaming in through the broken masonry, but when he came outside he stopped and gasped in surprise. Below him the world lay in a sea of white fog. Only the very tip of the church bell tower rose above it, and in the distance were the crests of other hills. This seemed like a perfect moment to try and explore, knowing he couldn't be seen from below. The ground was frosty, and he moved cautiously, hopping around the ruined buildings, looking for anything that might be useful. He found a cooking pot, another spoon, and, to his delight, a tin of something. He couldn't tell what, because the label had been destroyed, but that encouraged him to keep looking. He tucked his finds inside his jacket and ventured further. He spotted a boot sticking out from under a chunk of masonry. The other of the pair might be nearby. It would be a useful commodity for Sofia to trade. He used all his strength to move the piece of stone aside, then recoiled in horror when he saw that the boot was still attached to a leg. He had forgotten that the Allies had bombed a German gun position. There would certainly be other bodies buried here. This knowledge took away the childish excitement he had felt at making discoveries.

He carried his new treasures back to his lair and set about making a snare to catch a pigeon. His plan was simple enough: a stick to prop up the drawer he had salvaged from the rubble, a length of parachute cord tied to it to be jerked away when the pigeon went inside to peck at the crumbs he would leave. He cut away the parachute cord and then, having his knife handy, remembered that Sofia had expressed a desire for some of the silk to make underwear. He no longer needed the parachute now that she had brought him bedding, so he cut it up into useable pieces, smiling with anticipation at the thought of her face when she saw it.

He set up his trap and sprinkled the ground with breadcrumbs, then retreated into his hiding place. Now all he had to do was wait. The morning passed. He tried not to move or make a noise. Twice a pigeon flapped about, and once it landed on a beam but then flew off again. Finally it landed close to the trap. It walked forward, cooing throatily. For a moment he admired the iridescence of its feathers and was loath to kill it, but he forced these thoughts from his mind. Sofia needed meat. He could provide it. The pigeon waddled under the drawer and started to peck at the crumbs. He jerked at the chord. The stick flew out. The drawer landed with a resounding crash, trapping the pigeon. It had worked exactly as he had hoped.

He half crawled, half slithered over to it, lifted the drawer enough to slide his hand in, and grabbed the pigeon. It fluttered and struggled as he brought it out, but he wrung its neck and it lay still. He stared at it, realising it was the first time he had killed anything with his bare hands. As a boy at home he had known that pigs and chickens were killed on the farms around him. As a bomber pilot he had certainly killed when he dropped bombs on convoys and rail yards, but that was remote and impersonal. This was different. He was appalled at how easy it was to take a life. But that thought was displaced by the thought of Sofia's face when she saw what he had for her. It was the first time he had been able to give her anything in return.

This thought made him remember her excitement about the parachute silk. A double gift. It made him absurdly happy. He lay back, exhausted, and tried to remember presents he had given Brenda. Had she been thrilled with them?

In the early days, when they were in love, he had painted her portrait. She had liked that. But later? And he realised with a nagging sense of shame that his gifts had been routine, without much thought to them: expensive perfume, a pair of silk stockings. If they had grown apart, it was his fault as much as hers.

After the war I will make it up to her. And to little Teddy, he thought. *And Sofia?* The words whispered somewhere in his head. *Never to see her again? Rubbish,* he told himself. *You can't be in love with Sofia. She has been wonderfully kind when you needed help, but you've known her only a couple of weeks at the most. And you are weak and ill. It's quite common for men to fall in love with their nurses . . .*

He pushed the thought aside until she came to him that night. Sofia's face, when he handed her his two gifts, was so alight with joy that he felt his heart melting—as if it had been frozen in ice for too long and had now returned to the heart of a young Hugo, heading out into the world amazed by beauty, hopeful for the future.

"A pigeon," she said. "How did you manage to catch a pigeon?"

"Simple, really. I set up a trap. The pigeon came and took the bait." He grinned. "Let us hope he has brothers and sisters."

"I can make a good stew with this. Good broth," she said. "My son Renzo is looking so

231

frail lately. His sore throat and coughing do not go away. This will do him good. And you, too."

"No," he insisted. "Keep it for Renzo, and the grandmother, and yourself. It's a gift."

"Nonsense," she said. "We'll all share in the bounty."

Then she fingered the pieces of parachute. "So soft. So luxurious," she said. "I will make the best petticoat and drawers with this." She held it up to her face, smiling at him. "It is too bad it will not be seemly to show you when I have finished the garments." Her look was definitely flirtatious.

"Not to mention too cold," he pointed out, and she laughed.

"That too." Then she grew thoughtful. "Maybe I can use some of this silk to barter for things that we need, like more olive oil. I know that the Bernardinis have jars hidden in their basement. Gina Bernardini loves nice things . . ." She paused, looking up at him. "What do you think?"

"They would know that the silk came from a parachute, therefore they would know that I am here."

"But if I said that I found the parachute up in the forest?"

"They would know that a man escaped and was in the area, and someone would tell the Germans and they would come looking for me."

She sighed. "You are right. It is a risk I cannot

take." Then she brightened up again. "But when the Germans finally go and the Allies come, we shall still be bartering and I will still keep some silk, just in case."

Hugo finished the polenta and olive spread she had brought for him and handed her back the cloth they had been wrapped in. She folded it, then looked up and said, "Do you think of your wife all the time, the way I think of my Guido?"

"No," he said. "I'm afraid I don't. Not often. Not often enough."

"You are not happy in your marriage?"

"Not really. We're too different, I suppose. We met when we were both students in Florence. In England I'd probably never have met her. I come from a noble family and hers was, well, lower middle class, I suppose you could say. Her father worked in a bank. A bank clerk. Nothing wrong with it, but we would never have met. But we both shared a passion for art. And she was nice-looking. Good legs. She loved to have fun, to go out dancing and drinking wine. I suppose we were two foreigners drawn together more because we were in a strange land." He paused, looking at her, wanting her to understand. "I expect at the end of our year in Florence we would eventually have parted and gone our separate ways, but we were young and inexperienced. When Brenda announced that she was expecting a child, I did the right thing—I married her. We lived in

London for a while. I painted. I worked in an art gallery. The baby was born. Things were fine."

"And then?" she asked. "Something went wrong?"

"And then my father's health declined. He had been gassed in the Great War, you know. He called me home and said he needed me at Langley Hall because he could no longer run the estate. So I brought Brenda and the child to live in the country in a great big house. She never liked it. Too far from the bright lights and city life and fun. And she never really got along with my father."

"So what will happen when you go home?"

"I don't know," he said. "We'll just have to see."

"At least she likes art. That is a good thing," Sofia said. "Tell me about your art and your studies. I would love to know more."

"Not now. You need your sleep. Go home," he said.

"Oh, but I love to hear about art," she said. "We live in an area of great art, you know. Michelangelo, Leonardo, Fra Angelico, Botticelli."

He was surprised. He wondered what farm girl in England could reel off the names of English painters.

"You know about art?"

She shrugged. "Their paintings are in our

churches. I went to Florence once on a school trip before the war. I couldn't believe that anyone could paint such lovely things. And sculpture? Have you seen Michelangelo's *David*? The nuns said we weren't to look because he was naked. But he was beautiful, was he not?"

"So you looked?" He laughed.

She gave an embarrassed smile. "I was only studying great art. That is not a sin. Do you paint naked bodies?"

He laughed again. "I'm afraid I don't. The people in my landscapes were fully clothed."

"I wish I could see your paintings," she said. "If I could find you some paints and paper, you could paint the landscape here. It is very beautiful, is it not?"

"It is," he agreed. "But paints and paper are the least of our worries." He took her hand and she let him. "You really should go," he said. "You will be ill if you don't get enough sleep."

"Nonna told me I was becoming lazy because I did not wake until seven," she said. "She is always up at five. That is how it was in the old days. She is eighty-one and still expects to help in the fields. She has been urging me to harvest the turnips, saying she feels useless stuck indoors with nothing to do."

"Are the turnips ready for harvest?"

"Soon. Before Christmas. That will be good. Maybe I can trade for things that we need for the holiday. It is so strange. In past years we would all be baking at this moment. Now it will be only chestnut cake if we are lucky. No dried fruit, no cream, no butter. And probably no meat. A poor feast."

"Let us hope it will be the last poor feast before the Germans are finally defeated."

Sofia crossed herself. "From your lips to God's ears," she said.

CHAPTER TWENTY-TWO

JOANNA

June 1973

It's easy enough to explain that boot print, I thought. *The two Carabinieri agents would obviously want to search the crime scene for clues. They may have dusted my window for fingerprints. But then if it wasn't an official search, someone was watching the house and saw me leave.* I glanced around and was relieved when I heard Paola's voice calling for Angelina to bring a bowl. I hurried to join her, and soon she was showing me how to choose the zucchini blossoms and how to pick them, making sure that the stem was intact. After that she cut a few artichokes, dug up some radishes, and chose a couple of ripe tomatoes. Then she stopped by the herb garden and picked various leaves that I couldn't identify, but their scent was pungent when she gave them to me to hold. Finally we walked back to the house. I found myself looking around to see if we were being watched. Paola chatted away as we walked, telling Angelina about our encounter with the Carabinieri and what the townspeople had been saying.

"You see, I was right," Angelina said. "I told you that it was because Gianni kept bad company. He liked to flirt with danger. That's why he was killed."

"But why choose my well? That's what I'd like to know," Paola said. "Why not kill him on his own property? It is more remote, less likely to be seen among those trees. Why not just follow him there?"

"Perhaps he saw he was being followed. Perhaps he fought back and had to be killed in a hurry." Angelina shrugged. "Let's get on with the meal, Mamma. I am hungry and I am sure Signorina Joanna is, too."

"Then lay the table and slice the bread," Paola said, going ahead of us into the cool kitchen. "And put out the salami and the cheese and wash those radishes." She turned to me. "Now pay attention if you want to see how we stuff the zucchini blossoms, Joanna."

She put some of the white cheese into a bowl, chopped up and added some of the herb I had now decided was mint, then grated some lemon zest on to it. Then she took a spoon and carefully stuffed this mixture into each of the blossoms.

She dipped a scoop into the big jar of olive oil and lit the gas under a pan.

"Now the batter," she said. She broke an egg into flour, whisked the mixture, and added water. Then she took a zucchini blossom and dipped it into the batter. When the oil was sizzling, she dropped the blossom in and repeated the same process with the others, one by one, turning them and then removing them when they were crisp.

"Tonight we do the same with the artichokes," she said. "We need to eat these while they are good and hot."

We sat at the table. Bread was passed to me along with sliced tomatoes with rich, sweet vinegar poured over them. I took my first bite of the zucchini blossom.

"Very delicious," I said, wishing my Italian vocabulary of praise was more extensive.

We ate for a while in silence until the baby's cries made Angelina jump up to fetch her. "She went three hours between feeds this time. That is good news, eh, Mamma?"

"Yes, she is certainly growing stronger," Paola said. "I think now we can safely say that she has come to stay."

We finished our meal with apricots.

"Now a little siesta before we pick the vegetables and load up the cart for tomorrow," Paola said. "I expect you are tired, too, *mia cara*."

I didn't like the thought of Paola and Angelina going off to sleep and leaving me alone.

"Not really," I said. "I think I will sit in the shade of the front porch and read my book."

"As you wish. Myself, I need to sleep."

• • •

I went to the front porch and sat on the bench in the shade. It was cool and peaceful. Bees were buzzing around jasmine. Sparrows chirped as they hopped around in the dust. In the distance I heard a donkey braying. But I could not read or relax. I found myself glancing up from the book, my eyes on the path that led down from the village. I tried to make sense of what had happened. Nobody in San Salvatore seemed to have met my father, or even knew of him. And yet Gianni had tried his best to get me alone and tell me something important, something he had kept hidden until now for fear of his life.

And then there was the beautiful boy, the boy my father had hidden where only he and Sofia could find him. But the only boy was Renzo, and he did not remember being hidden away, nor did he remember my father. And he was too old to be a child of my father. I found myself wondering if Sofia had concealed a pregnancy. Would that be possible in a village of this size with nosy neighbours? Renzo, being only three at the time, might not have noticed if his mother put on weight. But other women would. And then the biggest question of all: If my father had been in the area long enough to fall in love and maybe father a child, where on earth had he been hiding? In Sofia's house? But then Renzo had said that a German soldier had been billeted with them.

And surely someone else would have seen him. It didn't make sense. In fact, the most logical thing to do was to leave this place as soon as possible. If Sofia Bartoli had run off with a German and thus broken my father's heart, then I didn't want to know more about her.

The afternoon passed without incident. Paola awoke from her nap and we went into the garden to pick vegetables. By the time the sun set we had a flat cart loaded with wooden trays ready to take to market in the morning. I looked at the cart and wondered if we'd have to pull it up the hill. It looked like really heavy work. Paola left it in the shade at the side of the house. "In the morning Carlo will come for it," she said. "Now we go and eat."

This evening's meal started with round white and shiny balls of a cheese called mozzarella, along with tomato slices and fresh green basil. Then came the fried artichokes. I found these a little chewy and not as good as the zucchini blossoms had been. But the main course of the veal chops in a rich wine sauce—well, that was heavenly.

Afterward we sat talking until I could pluck up the courage to go back to my room. I didn't like to ask Paola to accompany me, but I did say, "You don't think we are in any danger, do you? I mean, a man was killed right next to my room."

Paola shook her head, smiling. "You are in

no danger, my little one. You have had nothing to do with this man and neither have I. He has met a sad end, but most likely he brought it upon himself. Don't worry." Then she put an arm around my shoulder and walked with me to the little house. I went in and locked the door from the inside. Even so I found it hard to sleep. I pictured someone finding a way to prize off the bars at the window, or even putting through a hand holding a pistol and shooting me as I slept. I closed the shutters and the window even though it was hot and stuffy and finally fell asleep in an airless room.

I awoke to shouts and leapt up, my heart thudding. It was not quite light, and my head throbbed as if I had drunk too much wine. I opened my door and saw that the cause of the commotion was that a man had arrived with a tractor and was hooking it up to Paola's cart of vegetables while she yelled instructions with much arm waving. I dressed hurriedly and went to join them.

"Did we wake you, little one?" she said. "I am sorry. I would have let you sleep on and join me later. I have to go up to the village now to set up my stall, but I have left coffee and bread for you on the table. If you would like to join me, come up at your leisure. The bathroom is at your disposal, and Angelina will soon be awake if you need anything."

I realised I had not locked my door behind me when I ran out, so I rushed back. Nothing had been touched. I took my toilet bag, towel, and clean clothes for the day and locked the door carefully this time before I went over to the farmhouse, had a bath, and then had breakfast. Angelina appeared while I was still eating, rubbing her eyes sleepily.

"It is not easy to be a mother," she said. "The baby, she cries and wants to eat every two hours, all night. You are wise to concentrate on your career and not marry. I wish I had studied harder and not let Mario sweep me off my feet." She paused, and a wistful smile came over her face. "But he is very handsome."

"You must miss him very much while he is away."

She nodded. "Of course. But he does this for us so that we can save money and maybe open a little business. I pray for that day."

"You are lucky to have your mother to help you."

"Yes, although she can be bossy and tells me how to look after my child. Her ways are old-fashioned, you understand. But she won't listen to new ways that I have read about in books."

"At least she is here," I said. "I still miss my mother. She was a kind person like yours is. She took good care of my father and me."

"You had no brother or sister?"

I shook my head. "My mother was over forty years old when I was born. It was a late marriage for both my parents. She never thought she could have a child and was surprised when I came along. She told me I was her little miracle."

"I had a brother," Angelina said. "But he died when he was a baby. He caught that disease called polio, you know? So sad. Life is full of sadness, is it not? My mother, she still weeps for my father."

"Yes," I agreed. "Life is full of sadness. But you have a new baby to make you happy."

"If she doesn't want to eat the whole night long," Angelina said, and we both laughed.

"I promised your mother I would come up to the piazza and help her," I said. Soon after, I set off up the hill. It was a cool morning with a few white clouds racing in from the west. Maybe the weather was going to break. I passed nobody on the path and have to confess that I almost ran through the tunnel, but when I reached the village piazza it was full of activity at this early hour. Paola was already doing a lively trade and looked as if she was glad to see me.

"Ah, you came," she said. "I will put you to work. The basket of apricots needs to be filled again. And the tomatoes. And make sure the basil is not in the sun or it will wilt."

I did as she asked.

"And I promised to bring parsley to the trattoria," she said.

"I'll take it over for you," I volunteered.

She shook her head. "No, I had better go myself. I need to know what they might need for the festival tomorrow."

"A festival?"

She smiled. "It is a holy day. Corpus Christi. We have a big procession and then a feast in the piazza here. Everyone brings food to share. You will enjoy it, I am sure."

So off she went. I was a little nervous that I wouldn't be able to understand her customers, but nobody came for several minutes. I was moving the tray of tomatoes out of the direct sun when I saw the shadow of someone approaching. I looked up and it was Renzo.

"Oh, it is you," he said in English. "Why are you still here?"

"I'm not allowed to leave yet," I said.

"Is this not Paola's stall?" he asked, looking around. "Where is she?"

"She went to take parsley to the trattoria," I said. "May I help you?"

"Yes, I suppose so. I need all your tomatoes, and your basil and onions, and do you have garlic? I need a lot of garlic."

"You must be very hungry," I said, trying to be flippant.

"It is the feast day tomorrow," he said, not

smiling. "My father feeds all of his workers. He will roast lambs on a spit, and I am instructed to organise the salads and pasta to go with them."

"He has many workers?" I asked.

"He has much land," Renzo said. "Olive groves, vineyards, the olive press. He is a wealthy man."

"And you will inherit it all one day?" I said. "You have no brothers or sisters?"

"My father never married," he said. "He told me that the girl he loved did not love him, and he wanted no other. Such true love should be applauded, don't you think?"

"Yes, I suppose so," I said, hesitating. "But I don't think I'd choose to be alone for my whole life if I couldn't have the person I wanted." I was surprised to hear myself say those words. Did that mean I was ready to move on from Adrian and there was a light at the end of that tunnel? I glanced up at Renzo. "So when you want to get married, you'll have to choose a girl who will be willing to live here or Cosimo will be alone."

There was something I couldn't quite read in his face. "Yes," he said. "Any future wife would have to be willing to be part of my life here. That may not be so easy. Who would want to shut themselves away in the middle of the countryside?"

"It's very beautiful here," I said.

"Maybe."

"But you had dreams of being a chef," I said.

"You gave them up to take care of your adopted father. That is commendable. I regret that I left my father alone so much."

"Your father is now dead?"

"Yes. He died a month ago. That is why I am here, because I wanted to know what happened to him in the war."

"Then I am sorry we can't help you," he said in a more civil tone.

We stopped talking as a man approached the table. "Excuse me," I said to Renzo. "I must take care of this customer for Paola. I just hope I can understand him. The local dialect is hard for me."

The man was wearing a light suit and had an impressive black moustache. "You are Signorina Langley?" he asked.

"*Si*, Signor."

"You will please come with me. I am Inspector Dotelli of the criminal investigation department in Lucca. I need to ask you questions concerning the death of Gianni Martinelli."

CHAPTER TWENTY-THREE

JOANNA

June 1973

I tried not to let alarm show on my face. "But I made a statement," I said. Actually, with my Italian being quite basic still, I said, "I told the man what I had seen."

The inspector spread his hands. "A mere formality," he said. "You will come with me to the police station."

"I am watching this stall for Signora Rossini," I said. "I cannot leave until she returns."

"This man can watch for you," he said, waving dismissively at Renzo.

"This man is an important customer. He was buying vegetables for the festival tomorrow," I said, feeling my face turning bright red with embarrassment. "I could not ask him to spend more time." I was stumbling over the Italian words now, flustered. "I do not know how to answer your questions," I added. "I speak only a little Italian. I am a visitor from England."

"But you were speaking with this man. I saw you." The inspector wagged an accusing finger. He certainly used his hands a lot in his speech.

"That was because we were speaking in English," I said. "This man worked in London."

"Then he shall come with you to be your translator," the inspector said.

"I have business that needs to be taken care of," Renzo said coldly. "I don't have time."

"I am not requesting," the inspector said. "This is a command from the police. It should not take long." He looked up. "Ah, here comes the lady now, returning to her vegetables. Good. Come with me."

Paola was rushing toward us, her face ready to do battle. "What is this? What is going on?" she demanded.

"The inspector from Lucca," I said, nodding at him. "He wishes to ask me questions."

"We have told the Carabinieri all that we know," Paola said. "This young lady is a stranger here. She cannot help you and I do not wish her to be upset."

"She will not be upset if she answers my questions and tells me the truth. Come, follow me now. It is Saturday, and I wish to get this matter sorted out as quickly as you do."

With that he put a hand on my elbow and literally steered me across the piazza to the municipal building. I glanced back at Renzo. He was speaking with Paola, presumably reserving the items that he wanted. He was still giving her instructions as he followed us toward the dark doorway. The young Carabinieri agent was turned out of his desk with a mere wave of the hand. The inspector took his place.

"You will stay and take notes," the inspector said to the agent who was about to sneak from the room. "Bring a chair for the young lady and you may sit at the desk beside me."

The young man returned with a chair and then took his place beside the inspector, looking extremely uncomfortable. There was no chair for Renzo. He stood behind me. I was not only embarrassed now, I was scared. I had seen the contempt for me in Renzo's face. What if he mistranslated my answers to make me seem guilty of Gianni's murder? My heart was thudding in my chest.

"Now," the inspector said. "Your name, your address, and your reason for your visit."

I looked up at Renzo, wanting to give the impression that I didn't even understand these simple commands. I slowly gave my name and address. "I came here because my father was a British pilot. His plane was shot down near here in the war and I wanted to see the spot for myself."

Renzo translated this. The inspector nodded.

"You arrived in this town when?"

"Only two days ago." It felt much longer.

"And you were the one who found the body of Gianni Martinelli?"

"Signora Rossini and I found the body together," I said. "I sleep in the little house at the bottom of her garden. The water comes from the well behind my room. I wanted to take a shower but there was no water. I went to find the signora and told her. Together we lifted the heavy lid from the well and saw the body. We both screamed and were very upset."

The inspector listened to the translation, then watched the young policeman writing down notes. He looked up at me. "What did you do then?"

"We sent the signora's daughter to fetch the Carabinieri. They came and removed the body from the well. It wasn't easy. Someone had stuffed him in head first so that his head was in the water. It was horrible."

"Did you recognise the man when they brought him out?"

"I did," I said. "I had seen him the night before."

"Ah. So you knew him?"

"I didn't know him. He was one of the men who were sitting around the table in the piazza. I asked them if they remembered my father, but none of them did."

"That is all?"

"Yes," I said. "That was the only time I ever saw this man."

There was an unpleasant smirk on the

inspector's face now. "This is not what I hear," he said. "I heard that Gianni was most interested in you. He flirted with you. He offered to show you his farm."

Renzo's face was now also showing embarrassment as he translated.

"He was only being friendly," I said. "I told the men that I would like to see the neighbourhood and this man, Gianni, offered to show me how he made cheese."

"How he made cheese? Is that what they call it now?" The inspector looked at the young agent and chuckled.

My uneasiness was displaying itself as anger now. "Inspector, I was sitting at a table with other men. They laughed and said that I should watch out for Gianni, so I was aware that he was perhaps not to be trusted. So when he offered to walk me home, I refused. And luckily another man called Alberto said he would escort me as he had to go past Paola's farm on his way home."

"So that was the last time you saw Gianni?"

"The only time."

There was a long pause while the inspector stared at me. "So tell me, Signorina Langley. Is it normal in your country for a girl to approach a table full of men alone, to accept a glass of wine from them? This is accepted behaviour?"

"First, I am not a girl. I am a woman of twenty-five and I am about to take the exam to become a lawyer," I said. I thought I detected a flicker of reaction at the word "lawyer." "And second," I went on, "I wanted to find out about my father and I felt quite safe approaching people in the town piazza. I accepted a glass of wine because it would have been rude to refuse."

"And then?"

"Then I walked home. I already told you a man called Alberto offered to escort me since he had to pass the farmhouse where I am staying. I accepted his offer as it was getting dark. He escorted me to the front door. I thanked him and went in to have dinner with Signora Rossini and her daughter. Then I went to bed. That's all I can tell you."

"You heard nothing after that? A man was killed and pushed into a well and you heard nothing? I find this strange. Unbelievable almost."

"I drank wine," I said. "I am not used to it, and it must have made me sleep extra soundly."

He made a sound half between a cough and a laugh. "You know what I think?" the inspector said. "I think that Gianni was attracted to you. A young lady from a distant city, maybe with different standards from our local girls. He has heard about London girls and their loose ways. He wanted to make a conquest. He came to your room to see you later that night. Maybe he tried to force himself on you. You resisted. You hit him

253

with a rock and knocked him out, then, frightened by what you had done, you hid his body in the well."

"That is absurd," I said, looking up at Renzo to translate for me. "For one thing I would not have been strong enough to hit a man like Gianni over the head if he was already attacking me."

"Very well, let us say that you pushed him away. A commendable action for an upright young woman. He tripped, fell backward, and struck his head against a rock. Not murder at all, but self-defence. Understandable. Any jury would see that you were defending your honour." He paused again.

"But not true," I said. "And how could I have put his body into the well? I told you I was not strong enough to lift the lid alone."

"So you got the signora to help you." He wagged his finger at me again. "Together you pushed this poor man into the well, where he drowned."

I took a deep breath, fighting to remain calm and in control as Renzo translated. "If I had done as you say and stuffed his body into the well, would I have alerted the signora in the morning that I had no water for my shower? Would we have removed the cover, found the body, and then called the Carabinieri? No, I would have kept quiet about the body. I would have left the town, caught the first train back to England, and by the time anybody discovered the body I would have been gone."

The inspector listened to this as it was translated into Italian. I realised I was waving my arms as I spoke, in true Italian fashion. I noticed a strange expression crossing Renzo's face. Then he said, "I can waste no more time on this, Inspector. I have business to attend to. You will please excuse me. It is quite obvious that this young woman did not kill Gianni."

"Then why," the inspector said, "were her fingerprints on a big stone found beside the well? Answer me that one."

"I can answer," I said, not waiting for Renzo to translate. "That stone was on top of the lid. I lifted it down first when I attempted to open the lid."

"Ah, so you do speak Italian," the inspector said.

"Not well enough to say what I want to," I answered. "And I don't understand when people speak rapidly."

"We will leave this matter until next week," the inspector said. "I am not convinced that she is innocent. I will need to question this Signora Rossini as well. She may have been a partner in crime. But I will get a confession out of her if she is guilty. We need to do more tests, question more witnesses. The whole place will be searched for clues and fingerprints. But I will be kind to you,

Signorina. I will not take you to the jail in Lucca. I will permit you to stay here in this town until we get to the bottom of this crime. You are not permitted to leave, do you understand?"

I nodded.

"Very well. You may go for now." He waved us out of the room.

As I came out of the darkness into the bright daylight, my wrist was grabbed. I gasped, struggled, and looked up at my attacker. It was Renzo. He was glaring at me, a look of fury on his face.

"Where did you get that ring?" he demanded. "Have you robbed my house?"

I looked down at my hand. "It is my signet ring," I said. "My family crest. My father gave it to me for my twenty-first birthday."

"But no, you are wrong," Renzo said. "It is *my* family crest. My family. Your father must have stolen it while he was here."

"Absolute rubbish!" I shouted the words, fear and anger now combining. "See the crest on it. It is the griffin. The same crest is carved over the front entrance of Langley Hall. It has been in our family since 1600."

I saw uncertainty on his face now. "But I have an identical ring at home," he said. "It is a man's ring and was found among my mother's possessions. Cosimo told me that it came from my real father's family. From the Bartolis. He said I should be proud that we were once nobility."

"Then Cosimo was wrong," I said, realising as I said it that Cosimo hadn't known the truth. He had not known about my father. But I was feeling excited now. This was absolute proof that my father had been here—that he had known Sofia. I looked up at Renzo's face, now frowning with confusion. "I think my father must have given this to your mother as a token of his love. Now we know he was here in this place and he did know your mother. Are you sure you do not remember him? An Englishman with light brown hair and blue eyes, slender in build like me?"

He shook his head. "I never saw him," he said. "What makes you think that he knew my mother? What brought you here?"

"Well, the ring is proof, isn't it? And I have a letter that he wrote to her," I said. "A love letter. He told her that as soon as the war was over, he was coming back for her. He was going to marry her." I paused, feeling the intense emotion in what I was saying. "But the letter was returned unopened. The stamp on it said, 'Not known at this address.' He kept it locked away in a little box all these years."

"She had gone with the German," he said. "She chose not to wait for your father."

I nodded, feeling close to tears. We stood there in the bright sunlight, staring at each other.

"Then your father and I were both abandoned," he said.

CHAPTER TWENTY-FOUR

JOANNA

June 1973

We looked up as we heard Paola calling.

"Your tomatoes, Signor Bartoli. Do you have a cart to transport them?"

"I will send one of the men up later on," Renzo said. "But I will pay you now. Keep them out of the sun, please."

He took out a wallet and handed over several notes. Paola beamed. "You are most generous."

I turned to Renzo. "Thank you for translating for me. I could not have got through that interview without you."

"Don't worry," he said. "I am sure the inspector realises that you are completely innocent of this crime. Sometimes these men enjoy wielding their power. Or maybe he is just lazy. He goes for the most obvious suspect. But I will speak with Cosimo and he will make sure that you are released. My father has great influence in these parts."

"Why do you think this man was killed?" I couldn't resist asking.

Renzo shrugged. "I can think of several reasons. He mixed with the wrong type of people. He poked his nose where it wasn't wanted. Maybe he overheard things he should not have heard. Maybe he even resorted to blackmail. I wouldn't have put it past him."

I told myself to shut up, but I went on. "I understand he also wanted to build his own olive press. Might someone have wanted to stop him from doing that?"

Renzo shook his head. "Just one of Gianni's big ideas. It would never have happened. Everyone knows that Cosimo's olive press is the most modern and efficient in this area. Why should anyone build another one? Especially a man like Gianni who would undoubtedly have cut corners and constructed a shoddy product. It would constantly have broken down, even if anyone would have lent him the capital in the first place." He gave me a curt little bow. "I must get back to my business. I'm already late. Maybe I will see you at the festival tomorrow? You should come. I think you would enjoy it. Very un-British!" And he smiled as he turned away.

I watched him go. *Such an attractive man,* I thought. Then I reminded myself that he was Cosimo's adopted son. It was quite possible that he knew who killed Gianni. If Cosimo wanted to stop the olive press from being constructed, he had plenty of men to do his bidding . . . including a son. *I must not forget that Renzo might have had a hand in the murder,* I thought.

I went to join Paola at her stall as Renzo stopped to talk with some men on the far side of the piazza. *Gianni's death probably had nothing to do with the olive press,* I reasoned to myself. He had tried to speak with me alone. He wanted to tell me the truth about the war, about Sofia. He had put the envelope through my window. And someone had followed him and killed him. Something had happened in the wartime here. Something to do with blood and German money.

I manned the stall with Paola all day, then helped her pack up the crates and few remaining vegetables. She looked pleased. "Almost everything sold, thanks to Cosimo and Renzo. Now we will not have to eat vegetable soup for a week!"

We walked home together. It was strange, but it actually did feel like walking home.

"That stupid man, that inspector," she said. "But that is how the police are in these parts sometimes. They don't want to delve into anything that might be too dark and complicated, so they try to pin a crime on the most innocent of people. He probably has a good idea that Gianni was mixed up in criminal activities, but doubtless he wants to steer clear of any gangs. But don't worry," she added. "Nothing will come of this. You will soon be allowed to leave, I promise you. And in the meantime I shall teach you to cook good Italian food so that when you have a husband you keep him satisfied."

In spite of everything, this made me laugh.

"Tell me about the war," I said carefully. "Were there any scandals around here? Any people who worked with the Germans?"

"I told you, I was not here," she said. "I only returned after the Germans had left. One heard plenty of tales of horror, of course. Of young girls violated. Of whole villages massacred because the Germans believed they had aided the partisans."

"Who were the partisans exactly?" I asked.

"Brave groups of men who worked against the occupiers," she said. "It was no true organisation, just small independent groups acting in the areas where they lived. Some were fascist, some were communist, some were ex-soldiers, some were just good men who wanted to help win the war. They destroyed trucks and blew up rail lines. They did many courageous things, and many paid with their lives."

"There was a group in this area, then?"

"There was. Until someone betrayed them. The Germans mowed them down. Cosimo was only a young man then. He was one of them. He was fortunate. The German bullet only grazed him. But he had to lie among the bodies, pretending to be dead, as the Germans went among them with bayonets. He was half-mad with grief and covered in blood when he managed to stumble home the next day. The people of San Salvatore were lucky that they were not all executed in reprisal as happened with other towns."

"Would the people of San Salvatore have known who the partisans were?" I asked. "Wouldn't the men have kept their identities secret?"

"Of course. But people always knew. They relied on the farmers to hide them when they were being pursued. They relied on others to feed them when they were away from their homes. And they sometimes wore a little star so that people knew they were who they claimed to be. So yes, people knew."

People knew, I thought. And one of those people had betrayed the local boys to the Germans. Why? Who had prospered from it? Or maybe it was a case of who had been released from German custody by giving this information. I thought of those men sitting around the table and wondered how I could ever find out what they might know.

We reached the farmhouse and stacked the crates, and Paola went for her afternoon snooze. I, too, would have liked a sleep, but I was too tense. So I sat with Angelina as she took care of the baby.

"Would you like to hold her?" she asked suddenly. "Here."

And the child was in my arms. I felt the tiny, warm body, surprisingly heavy for its size. *So perfect,* I thought. A perfect little person. Little dark eyes looked up at me, staring at me with interest.

"Hello," I said. "You don't know me, do you?"

And I thought I detected the glimmer of a smile.

"She is beautiful," I said.

"Yes, isn't she? The most perfect baby ever," Angelina said. "When she was born early, they said she might not live. But I prayed. I prayed to Saint Anne and to the Blessed Mother, and they heard me. And now look at her. Getting fatter every day thanks to my good milk. When Mario comes home he will be so delighted to see her."

I looked down at the tiny mite in my arms, her eyes already fluttering back into sleep. *I couldn't have done this alone,* I thought. To rear a child one needs a Mario who will come home and be delighted. And a grandma who takes care of mother and baby.

That evening, Paola said she was tired and we would have a simple meal. She whipped up eggs and made a frittata with the few vegetables we had brought home: onions and zucchini and beans. It was surprisingly good.

"An early night, I think," she said after we had finished our meal with cheese and fruit.

"Tomorrow is a big day. First the Mass at eight o'clock, then the procession and then the feast. Will you come?"

"Oh yes. Of course. I'd like to see it."

"You are not of our faith, I think," she said.

I didn't like to say I wasn't really of any faith. "I was raised in the Church of England," I said. "It is similar, I think."

"I hear that in England there is no devotion to religion. You do not honour the saints, is that right? You do not pray to them."

"That's true," I said.

She made a dismissive noise. "Then how can prayers be answered if you do not call upon the saints to help? God is obviously too busy to do everything alone."

I thought how sweet and simple this was. But then I remembered the little medal on a ribbon that had been in my father's box. Someone had given that to him, probably Sofia. I wondered which saint was represented on it. It seemed so unlikely for my cold and typically English father to have worn a medal on a ribbon. *He must have loved her very much,* I thought. I remembered the paintings done before the war, so bright and full of life. And it came to me as a shock that his life essentially ended when that letter was returned to him unopened. I wondered how many further attempts he made to trace her until he gave up and married my solid and dependable mother.

CHAPTER TWENTY-FIVE

HUGO

December 1944

The weather turned freezing wet and miserable. Hugo huddled in his shelter for several days while rain and sleet splashed around him. Sofia came at night, her hair plastered to her forehead and her clothing sodden.

"Don't come when it's raining like this. I can survive, I assure you, and you'll catch pneumonia if you get so cold and wet," he begged.

"I am strong, Ugo. I am used to a hard life. Don't worry about me," she said.

"But how will you explain your wet clothes? Your grandmother will be suspicious."

"Nonna can no longer climb the stairs. I dry my things in the linen closet." She gave him a mischievous smile. "Don't worry."

But he couldn't help worrying. One night the storm was so bad that Sofia didn't come. Thunder crashed overhead. Lightning lit up the sky above. Hugo sat up, relatively dry under the part of the parachute he had kept, worrying about her. What if she had tried to come and was struck by lightning? What if a tree branch had fallen on her? He also felt the gnawing of hunger. As he was growing stronger, so his need for food had increased. He faced the sobering reality that if something happened to Sofia he would starve unless he managed to trap more birds. But the thought of eating a bird raw was so repugnant that he brushed it aside.

I must practice walking, he thought. *I must get used to using this leg. In the morning I will try.*

But in the morning the rain continued in a solid sheet until the floor around him resembled a small lake. He huddled miserably in his corner while the rain drummed on the altar above him, and his spirits sank lower and lower. *Let's face it,* he thought. *My chances of escaping are pretty much nil. The Germans are still all over the place. The Allies won't try pushing north into the mountains until spring. And even if I could make my way down the mountain to the road, I'd never be able to run and hide if the Germans spotted me.*

But he couldn't just give up and give in. It was his duty as a British officer to do whatever he could to rejoin his squadron. And as long as there was hope of seeing Sofia again, then that spark would keep him going. By mid-afternoon the rain stopped. The sun came out and the lake on the floor steamed. Hugo emerged from his hiding place and spread the parachute out to dry. The sheepskin and blanket were miraculously not too damp. Then he made his way carefully around the edge of the pool on the floor and stood outside, enjoying the feel of sunlight on his face. Clouds still clung to some of the hilltops, and he noticed that snow now covered more of the mountain peaks.

Once outside on the wet forecourt, he tried to make himself walk, putting weight on his leg. He cried out in pain, and it would have buckled if he had not been wearing the splint. So much for that thought. He tucked the crutch-branch under his armpit and hobbled the rest of the way to the rain barrel, where he had a long drink and washed his face. *A bath,* he thought. *A long hot bath.* And he pictured the bathroom at Langley Hall with its big claw-foot tub and the steaming water. *I will never take anything for granted again,* he decided.

His musing was interrupted by the sound of an engine coming from the road below. Several army vehicles, small as a child's toy cars, were making their way north. Instinctively he ducked behind a section of wall. Then his ears picked up another sound—the deep, throbbing hum of a plane engine. Not a German plane. Not British, either. Then he saw it coming out of the south. An American light bomber, he surmised. It came lower until he could see the sun shining on the American star. It was right over the German convoy, and then a bomb fell, then another. He felt the reverberation even up on his hilltop. Then there were secondary explosions as fuel tanks blew up. The smoke from the fireball reached his nostrils. The plane flew on, and all that remained of the convoy was flickering flames. It was a sobering thought that even here war was never far away, but at the same time he took heart in the knowledge that the Allies were hunting out the Germans, destroying them as they fled northward. Perhaps the war really was going to end soon.

On his way back to his hiding place, he noticed a feather on the floor from the pigeon he had killed. He bent to pick it up. It was a beautiful blueish grey with iridescence at the edges. Again he felt a pang of regret that he had killed something so beautiful and so harmless. He tucked the feather into his breast pocket and hobbled back across the chapel.

That night he rearranged his bed and wondered if Sofia would come. His hunger by now was so intense that he could think of little else. He fantasised about roast beef and Yorkshire pudding, lamb chops, steak and kidney pie. He retrieved the tin he had found among the rubble and wondered if he could open it with his knife. He had meant to give it to Sofia, but she had been so excited with the pigeon and the parachute silk that he had saved the surprise for later. He turned it over in his hand, then put it down—he would only risk damaging the blade of his knife. And what if it was something that was inedible until cooked—tomato paste, for example? She would surely come tonight and maybe bring some of that pigeon stew with her.

But she didn't come. He sat up most of the night listening for any sound, but nothing stirred except the gentle sigh of the wind in the trees and grass. Two nights without her. Something must have happened. He let his mind wander through scenarios: The Germans had returned and taken her. She had been struck by lightning in the storm. She had been taken sick and was now lying there, deathly ill. And he found himself praying as he had never prayed before. "I don't care what happens to me, God, only keep her safe." And then he added a similar prayer to the Virgin Mary, just in case.

He must have drifted off to sleep because he heard his name being called as if from far off. He opened his eyes to see her standing in the doorway, silhouetted against bright sunlight. "*Gesù Maria!*" she exclaimed. "Look at all this water. You are lucky you didn't drown."

And she came toward him. "My poor, poor Ugo," she said. "I am so sorry that I left you alone for so long. The night of the storm—when I wanted to slip away it was impossible."

"I understand that," Hugo said. "I did not want you to risk coming out in such a storm."

270

"I would have come," she said, "but my son is sick. He had a high fever. He wanted to sleep with his mamma, and he is afraid of thunder. He was awake and clinging to me all night. And yesterday his fever was worse. We had to call the doctor. The doctor says he has tonsillitis and really should have his tonsils removed."

The words were unfamiliar to Hugo until she gestured to her throat.

"Ah yes. Tonsils," he said.

"But of course we cannot get to the nearest hospital. There is no transportation. So the doctor gave him some of those sulpha drugs and hoped he would get better."

"And is there any improvement?"

She nodded. "He cuddled against me all night—the poor child was soaked in sweat. This morning he is weak but the fever is down, saints be praised."

"No doubt you had a talk with Saint Blaise?" Hugo said, trying to make her smile, but she frowned at him.

"Never mock the power of the saints, Ugo. They are the ones who intercede for us with God. And yes, I did pray to Saint Blaise."

"I'm sorry. I was not mocking. I just wanted to make you smile," he said. "But you should not have come in daylight. There were Germans on the road below yesterday."

"We saw. The Americans bombed them. That

271

was good, no? And our partisans, they also ambushed a vehicle full of Germans and slit their throats."

"Aren't you worried that the Germans will retaliate for such actions?" he asked.

"How would they find out which village the partisans come from? For all they know, it could be English or American soldiers creeping through the dark."

"All the same, you shouldn't risk coming here in daylight. What if you were seen?"

"I was seen," she said. "Benito said that he had found new mushrooms after the rain. *Funghi di bosco*—our favourites. I said I will go out immediately and look for some myself, so I took my basket and off I went. Nonna is sitting with Renzo, who now sleeps peacefully. If I find new mushrooms, what a joy that would be. It would mean I could come out in the daylight again with just cause. It is another small miracle. Usually there are no mushrooms this late in December. But the rains have not been too cold and there has been no frost here yet. Now if I can only find some, I will return the heroine. And I will make us a mushroom soup next time I come. But first . . ." She reached into the basket and placed the bowl, covered in a thick cloth, on the bench in front of him. "See what I have for you today! I made such a good soup with our part of the pigeon."

"Part? You divided a pigeon?" He stared at her incredulously, thinking how light the dead bird had been in his hands.

"I kept enough to make the broth, and I gave some to Signora Gucci in exchange for some oil and flour. Now I shall be able to make pasta. Not good pasta with eggs, but pici with just flour and water and oil. But better than nothing, eh? We Italians cannot live for long without our pasta."

She laughed. Hugo remembered the tin.

"And I have another little treasure for you." He fished out the can. "I found this among the rubble. I don't know what it is, but at least it will be some kind of food."

She took it reverently, as if he was bestowing a great honour on her. "Thank you, Ugo. We shall have a surprise when we open it!"

"I'll go and look, perhaps there are more," he said. "It's just not that easy for me to move around out there."

"Of course not. You must take care you do not fall and injure yourself again. In the new year maybe you will be healed enough to make your escape and to meet the Allies as they come north."

"I hope so."

She was looking at him with wistful eyes, and he sensed that she didn't want him to leave her any more than he wanted to be parted from her.

273

"I would like to paint your portrait," he said suddenly.

She gave him an embarrassed smile. "Me?"

"Yes. Alas, I have no paints and no canvas. But I will do a sketch so that when I get home I remember every detail."

"Do you have paper?" she asked.

"I have my empty cigarette packet. I can open it out and draw on the inside."

"Oh, you have finished your cigarettes. I'm so sorry."

"I should learn to give them up. They do me no good. Now sit there, on the bench."

She did as he told her, glancing up at him shyly. He took out his pen and sketched her. She was clearly embarrassed, but at the same time her eyes were flirting, pleased with the attention he was giving her and the strange honour of being sketched.

"Tell me about the great painters. Tell me all about art," she said. "I should like to know more."

"You tell me about the ones you saw when you went to Florence that time."

She frowned, thinking. "There was Michelangelo, of course. The master. Both for his sculpture and his painting, no? His *David*—he was like a real person. You expected him to move at any moment. And Leonardo. His *Madonna*—the light and the beauty . . ."

"You are fortunate to live here," Hugo said. "In Tuscany and Umbria you can find paintings by the great masters in ordinary churches. In Arezzo and Cortona and Siena and even in small towns. Works by il Perugino and Giotto. Every one a masterpiece."

He was surprised by the look of despair that came over her face. "If they are still here," she said. "We hear that the Germans have looted everything that they can. They would even take the frescoes if they could find a way to peel away the walls."

"We will win and make them return everything," Hugo said with more confidence than he felt. He finished the sketch and went to tuck it into his breast pocket.

"Let me see it," she said.

"No, it's only a rough sketch."

"But I want to see it." She made a grab for it. He held her wrist at bay. They were both laughing. "You are so mean," she said. "You do not afford me this one little pleasure."

Their wrestling had aroused him. *One little pleasure,* he thought, and an image of Sofia in his arms flashed into his head. Hastily he dismissed it.

"Oh, very well. If you insist."

She took the cigarette packet from him and examined the drawing critically. "I look like that?" she asked.

"You do."

"But you have made me quite pretty."

"No," he said, and watched her face fall. "I have made you beautiful. That is how I see you."

CHAPTER TWENTY-SIX

JOANNA

June 1973

The next day I was awoken by the loud and incessant tolling of bells from the church nearby, echoed by distant peals from other villages. It was the feast day—one of the most holy of the year, Paola had told me. Corpus Christi. The body and blood of the Lord Jesus Christ. The day on which children take their first Communion. I got up and prepared to go over to the farmhouse to bathe and to clean my teeth. I checked around the door and window, but there were no more footprints. It was possible that Gianni's attackers hadn't realised he had pushed an envelope through the bars into my room. It would be well known around the village by now that I had presented myself as an outsider who knew nothing. I would go home again as soon as I was given permission, and all would be well.

At least this was what I hoped. I was still going to stay close to Paola all day at the festival. I bathed, dressed in my most presentable frock—which could have done with an iron by now—then took out the little medal and tied the ribbon around my wrist. Then I went into the kitchen looking for breakfast, but it was bare. No sign of Paola. Now I was alarmed. She knew it was a big day and she would have risen early. Had something happened to her? I had no idea where her bedroom was. I had never been upstairs at the house. I hesitated now, wondering if I dared check on her.

I was halfway up the stairs when she appeared, definitely wearing her Sunday best. She wore a red skirt, a white lace blouse, and a black fringed shawl over her shoulders. She looked startled when she saw me. "You needed something, my little one?"

"I was just wondering if you were all right or if you had overslept," I said.

"No, of course not. Not on a day like this. I just take more time with my preparations. This is the costume of our region, you know. It is fitting to wear it on such a day. These items belonged to my mother."

I told her she looked very nice.

She smiled. "So, are you ready for church?"

How could I ask about breakfast? My stomach was growling. "Do we not have coffee first?" I asked.

"Before Mass? Oh no. We must fast before receiving the Blessed Sacrament. Fast from midnight onward. Do they not do this in your church?"

"I don't think so," I said, my spirits falling at the thought of there being no food for quite a while.

Paola shook her head in disgust. "Angelina. Make haste!" she yelled up the stairs. "We do not want to find ourselves sitting in the back pews where we can see nothing of what is going on."

Angelina appeared, also looking very pretty in a simple flowery dress with a shawl around her shoulders. In one arm she carried the baby, in the other a large bag. The baby was in a white robe trimmed with lace and had a dainty little lace bonnet on her head. She was sleeping and looked like an adorable china doll.

"Here, let me take that for you," I said, retrieving the bag from her.

"Thank you." She beamed at me. "So many things are required for such a small person. A shawl if it grows cold. Another dress if she spits up over this one. And nappies. So many nappies."

We set off, walking side by side up the dusty track. The morning was windy and brisk. Paola had to hold her shawl firmly around her shoulders. "I do not like the look of the sky," she said. "I hope it does not bring rain later. The weatherman on the wireless was saying it would rain later today, but what does he know? He is in a little room in Florence. We will pray to Saint Clara that the weather remains fine. She is always helpful about the weather."

"So tell me, Signora Rossini," I said, holding up my wrist. "What saint is on this medal?"

She held up my wrist to see the medal better. "I believe that is Saint Rita," she said. "She is good at healing, especially wounds. Where did you come by this?"

"It was among my father's things," I said.

"Then your father was wounded?"

"Badly," I said. "His plane was shot down. He managed to parachute out, but his leg was damaged. He always walked with a bit of a limp." I had to mime this last part, not knowing the word.

"Then this saint cured him." Paola looked pleased. "And your father was a believer in the true faith, then."

"I don't think so. I believe someone must have given him the medal."

She looked at me long and hard. "You believe it was Sofia Bartoli who gave it to him?"

"Yes," I said. "That is what I believe."

"She was a kind and good woman, that is how I remember her," she said. "Such a shame it ended so badly—betraying her village by running off with a German."

What if she didn't go willingly? I thought. But one of the men said she had been seen getting into an army vehicle with a German in the dead of night. Just the two of them. No armed escort to make sure she didn't escape.

As we reached the town piazza, I saw that long trestle tables had been set up. Flags draped the buildings, and lines of smaller ones fluttered from the church. The bells were still ringing loudly enough to make speech impossible. From all sides people were streaming toward the open church doors. The men looked uncomfortable in their dark suits with stiff white collars. The women were dressed beautifully, some in similar costumes to Paola's, but all in what was clearly their best finery, their dark, glossy hair piled on their heads. Children in their best clothes skipped beside adults who did their best to restrain them by the hand.

Just as we reached the church door, a collective murmur went up from the crowd. "Father Filippo! Father Filippo!"

We stopped and looked back. A frail old man in a black priest's cassock was being assisted up the steps by two strapping men.

"Good to see you, Father. God bless you, Father," people greeted him as the crowd stood back to let him pass.

Paola was smiling and nodding. "Our former priest," she said. "He was our strength and spiritual guide throughout the war years. They say he stood up to the Germans and kept the town safe. A spiritual giant when he is such a small man."

"Has he retired now?" I asked.

"Oh yes. Years ago he had bad health problems, and now he lives in a home for retired priests not far away. So good that he can still join us for the feast day. It wouldn't be the same without him."

We were swept up with the crowd into the dark interior of the church. As we neared the doorway, Paola produced a mantilla and put it on. I saw all the other women had covered their heads, and felt horribly visible. I was glad that we were off to one side and I was behind a pillar! When all were seated a procession entered: little boys in dark suits and little girls in white dresses and veils, looking like miniature brides.

"The first communicants," Paola whispered. "Don't they look like little angels? I can't wait until Marcella is old enough to make her first Communion."

At the end of the procession came the altar boys, then several priests, all in rich brocade vestments. The Mass began. Everyone in the church sang the hymns and chanted the responses. A great wave of sound enveloped the church. I thought how different it was from the sparsely attended and anaemic services at home. There were prayers, there was a sermon. Then came the solemn part of the Mass. Incense was lit and the herby smoke waved over the congregation. The priest chanted in a low voice. Bells were rung. Then one by one the children came up to receive their first Communion. After they had done so, the rest of the congregation followed, one by one, up to the altar steps. It seemed to go on forever. I was feeling sick with hunger. *At least these people are getting a wafer to eat,* I thought.

Just when I began to hope it was over, the children were invited back to the altar steps to be introduced to the congregation. Then Father Filippo was assisted to the steps to give his blessing to the children and then to the congregation. Another hymn was sung lustily. The priests, altar boys, and first communicants processed out, and at last we were allowed to follow. I was delighted to see that coffee and sweet rolls had been placed on the tables beside the church. I waited my turn patiently as Paola chatted with other women, introducing me.

"Will Father Filippo stay or will he go back to his residence?" I asked.

"He will stay, at least for the procession," she said. "See, a chair is being brought for him now."

An idea had come to me during the long moments when the sermon was being given in language that I didn't understand. Father Filippo had been the parish priest during the war, and priests heard confessions. Maybe Sofia had told him about the British airman. I had to work out how I could manage to have a word with him.

But as soon as we had downed a cup of coffee and eaten a roll, the town band arrived. They were dressed in medieval costume and marched

283

proudly into the piazza, preceded by flag-bearers waving giant banners. There was a collective "Ah" from the crowd. People hastily finished eating and straightened their attire, eager to join the procession. The band finished the march it was playing and stood ready, with just the row of drummers keeping up the beat. *Dum diddy dum diddy dum dum dum.* The sound echoed back from the high buildings. The first Communion children left their families and were ushered into two lines, boys and girls side by side, which clearly wasn't to the liking of some of the little boys. They stood waiting patiently behind the band.

Now the air was full of expectation. The buglers put their instruments to their lips. A great burst of sound came out, and from the church emerged the altar boys in their red and white cassocks, two of them swinging brass balls on long chains from which the scent of incense wafted. Behind them Father Filippo was carried in a kind of sedan chair, then came four men carrying a large brocade canopy over the priest, who now held up an ornate gold object. I couldn't decide what it was, but Paola crossed herself, so it had to be some kind of religious relic.

They took their places behind the altar boys. Then the trumpets blasted again, the band struck up, and the procession started to move forward. I noticed a strange thing. There were few men among the waiting crowd. Then I saw why—a group of men came marching up holding ancient battleaxes and crosses. They were dressed in white robes and wore pointed hoods that hid their faces. The effect was quite alarming. I realised that the only similar thing I had seen was the clothing of the Ku Klux Klan. I glanced at Paola.

"The Society of Saint George," she said. "A devotional society of the men of this town. It is an honour to be invited to join."

I noticed then that their white tunics had a star on the breast. A many-pointed star.

As the procession moved solemnly away to the slow beat of the drum, the townspeople came to follow. We took our places with the rest of the women. Our route took us at a snail's pace through the town. As we walked I had time to think. The many-pointed star was like the tiny replica that Gianni had given me. Was he saying that someone who was an important man in town had somehow been implicated in bloodshed? I glanced back at those hooded men. Which of them had something to hide?

Down through the village we processed until we came to the road that was lined with cypress trees, then on to a track through the fields and past several farmhouses before looping back again to the town. The weather that had started out brisk and bright was now clouding over. The wind had picked up, making the task of carrying the canopy challenging. The priest was finding it hard to keep his vestments in place.

"Let us pray that it doesn't rain," Paola said. "After two weeks of nothing but sunshine, surely God doesn't want to rain on us today."

We came up through vineyards and back to the road, then back to the piazza again. The canopy was carried to the steps of the church. The priest said prayers and gave a blessing. The band struck up a tune that was obviously a hymn as everyone started singing. I found myself watching the rapt expressions as the people sang. These were simple folk who really and truly believed. I felt a twinge of envy that I had never experienced such a feeling of belonging.

The hymn came to an end. The people dispersed. I noticed that Father Filippo had been left sitting on his chair, and I seized the moment. I went over to him. "Father, I am an Englishwoman," I said. "I came here to find out about my father, who was a British airman, shot down in the war. He wrote a letter to Sofia Bartoli, but nobody in this town knows anything about him. I wondered if you knew anything more you could tell me."

He smiled up at me. "The war. Such a tragic time. So much suffering. So much useless loss of life."

"Do you remember Sofia Bartoli?"

286

He was still smiling. "Sofia? Such a sweet young girl. How sad she was when her man— what was he called, now? Let me think . . . Giovanni? No, it was Guido. That's right—when Guido did not return and she realised he was dead."

"But my father," I said. "The British airman. Did she never mention him to you? Did you know about him?"

He frowned, trying to concentrate. "You are not from around here?" he asked.

"No, Father. From England."

"England. A long way away. A heathen land where they do not have the true faith."

I realised then that his mind had gone. He remembered Sofia, but if she had told him about my father, then that memory had long been lost.

I tried to think what I might ask him that could jog his memory, but at that moment some of the men came up to him. "Come, Father. We will take you to your place at the table. I am sure you are hungry."

Father Filippo smiled. "Food is the one pleasure left to an old man," he said as they helped him to his feet. He glanced back at me. "It was such a long time ago," he said. "Old memories can only open old wounds. Sometimes I give thanks that my memories have faded."

CHAPTER TWENTY-SEVEN
HUGO

December 1944

Christmas was almost upon them. Sofia reported that Cosimo had shot a wild boar in the forest. "We have to keep it a secret," she said, "because we are not allowed to own weapons, and if the Germans found the boar, they would take it from us. They love their meat. But our men will cut it up in the forest and deliver a portion to each family in San Salvatore so we can each have some meat for the holiday. And guess what I will do? I will make a wild boar ragu. The tin you gave me contained tomatoes! I am so excited. And I'll make a chestnut cake. A real holiday feast."

After she had gone Hugo pictured her face, her joy. *She finds happiness in such small things,* he thought. He found himself comparing her to Brenda, who never seemed excited by anything these days. He knew she found life at Langley Hall boring. She found their county set boring. But it wasn't as if they were in the middle of the Sahara. There was a fast train to London from Godalming, and she certainly went up to town enough, shopping and even going to clubs. She drank a lot, any kind of cocktail, and he was pretty sure she had used cocaine. He saw her as a trapped animal in a beautiful cage.

He shut her image from his mind and thought instead about Sofia. He wanted to give her a Christmas present. He had not managed to catch another pigeon. In fact, he rarely saw birds now that the temperature had dropped and there was a frost at night. He found it hard to keep warm, even when wearing his own and Guido's clothing at once and lying on the sheepskin. He tried to move more during the day, and spent hours hopping around, poking about the rubble. The bombing had been thorough. Not much had survived, apart from the walls of the chapel. He found odd pages of books, now so damaged by rain that they were barely legible. He found an almost complete missal with a battered leather cover. He was going to leave it but then changed his mind. It didn't seem right to leave something so old and sacred to be destroyed by the weather. He picked it up and tucked it inside his bomber jacket. He wondered what other valuable and rare objects had been left behind by the monks when the Germans had turned them out. Sofia had said that the Germans had taken the paintings from the chapel. He hoped the monks had been able to take their chalices and other precious objects, because there certainly wasn't anything precious to be found lying amid the rubble. *Just more bodies, probably,* he thought.

He was making his way back when he saw it—the sun sparkled on something that looked like a coin. He bent with difficulty and picked it up. It was a holy medal—a woman stretching out her hands with tiny words written around her. *La Madonna*, he thought, and realised he had his Christmas present for Sofia. He returned to his sanctuary and sat polishing the medal on his shirt until it looked almost new. Then he thumbed through the pages of the missal. The end sheets were marbled. He tore one out carefully and drew a little Christmas scene for Sofia: the holy family, the shepherds and their sheep, the ox, and the ass. Then he added a hillside with San Salvatore in the background. He was quite pleased with the result. He folded the drawing and placed the medal inside it. Then he tucked it inside the leather cover of the missal.

"I regret that I shall not be able to come on Christmas Day," Sofia said the next time she visited him. "It will be impossible. We go to Midnight Mass on the holy eve, and then we celebrate with neighbours for much of the night. Then the whole village is out and about during the next day. Much celebrating, although God knows we have little to celebrate at the moment. I will have to wait until all fall asleep on Christmas night, full of wine and food and happiness. I am sorry to leave you alone at such a special time, and I will come as soon as I can. I will bring you some of the wild boar ragu, although I do not think the pasta will taste as good when it is no longer hot. But I have brought you enough now to keep the hunger away." She unfolded the cloth and he saw that she had brought him a big slice of polenta, some olive tapenade, a small piece of sheep's cheese, and a dried apple. "These will keep," she said. "And for now here is some soup."

He ate it, touched by her concerned face as he swallowed each mouthful. "Have you ever tried to paint or draw, Sofia?" he asked suddenly.

"Me? When I was a child. One of the nuns liked my drawing of a donkey and pinned it up on the wall. But that was the extent of my artistic career." She laughed.

He had an absurd desire to sweep her away to England, to install her in his studio at Langley and teach her to paint, but he stopped himself from voicing this ridiculous notion. Why offer someone something she can never have? Why give false hope? *To get through this time of darkness,* came the answer.

"When the war is over I shall return to San Salvatore," he said, "and I will bring my easel and my paints and I shall let you paint whatever you want. Then I shall hang it on my wall at home."

She giggled. "It will be another donkey. That is all I know how to draw."

"But it could be a blue donkey. A polka-dot donkey. A flying donkey. Lots and lots of flying donkeys."

"You are absurd, Ugo." She laughed and slapped his hand playfully. Then a spasm of guilt crossed her face. "Sorry. I should not have done that."

"Don't apologise. I like it when you laugh. It makes me feel that I am still alive—that there is still hope."

"Me too," she said. "When I think that I will see you soon, I, too, feel that I am still alive."

Instinctively he took her hand. "You are the only reason I am alive, Sofia," he said. "You are the only reason I want to stay alive."

"No, don't say that. Your wife. Your son. Your family. They are your reasons."

He shook his head. "No. If I do not return they will cry a little, say what a brave fellow I was to give my life for my country, and then go about their lives as if nothing had happened. I don't think there is anyone at home who would truly weep for me."

"I would," she said. "If you died, I would truly weep for you."

And he noticed she had not pulled her hand away. In fact, she was clasping his hand as fervently as he clasped hers.

• • •

He awoke to the sound of bells. It was quite dark, and he had no idea of the hour, but the bells continued to echo across the frosty countryside. *The Germans,* he thought. *The Germans have returned to the village.* But then he thought, *No. The bells are ringing for Midnight Mass. It's Christmas Day.* And he lay back, smiling to himself, recalling memories from the distant past: Hugo at five or six awaking in the cold, grey dawn to find the stocking at the foot of his bed bulging with presents. And Nanny poking her head around the door. "So did Father Christmas come, then?"

"Yes." He could hardly say the word, he was so excited. "Look at all the things he brought me."

"Well, aren't you the lucky boy? And I rather think there might be something else downstairs. We'd better get you washed and dressed."

And there was: a fat, cream-coloured pony. *Happy times,* he thought. *When Mother was still alive and Father had not yet gone off to war and I had been promised a brother or sister.* Only something had gone wrong and mother and child had died in childbirth. Suddenly it was just Father and Nanny. And the next year he was sent away to school and Father went off to war, and he had never really felt safe again.

He lay listening until the last chimes of the bells died away in the still night air.

"Happy Christmas," he said out loud, and then fell asleep.

When he awoke again he was aware of distant noises—the sound of drums and then trumpets. It immediately brought to mind an invading army, Roman or medieval. But Sofia had told him that everyone would be out and about with much celebrating. Maybe the village band and a procession was part of the "much celebrating."

He washed himself at the rain barrel and wished he had a comb in his pocket to sort out his hair. He wet it and ran his fingers through it to smooth out the curl. The day was exceptionally clear and bright. And still—so still that his breath seemed like the only sound in the world. The drums and trumpets had ceased, and he pictured everyone in the village sitting around long communal tables, passing great bowls of food, talking and laughing as if they had not a care in the world.

They will be feasting until late in the night, he thought. *Sofia might not come at all.* He had to accept that and hope she wouldn't take the risk when people were going home from their celebrations.

Darkness fell. He settled himself in his bed and lay back, longing for a cigarette, a glass of Scotch, a pork pie, a sausage roll, a chocolate bar—all of the little things he had taken for granted all his life.

He thought he heard angels singing and opened

his eyes in disbelief. "And there were shepherds abiding in the fields, keeping watch over their flocks by night," he muttered, the words of the gospel coming back to him. He looked up to see an angel coming toward him, singing in a high, clear, sweet voice. She held up a lantern that illuminated her face.

"*Mille cherubini in coro ti sorridono dal ciel*," she sang. A thousand cherubim serenade you from the sky. Then she dropped to the floor beside him.

"Oh, you are awake. I am so glad. See, I bring you good things for Christmas. Come out and enjoy your feast."

He dragged himself from his bed and perched on the bench beside her. She was unwrapping dishes from the thick cloth.

"Wild boar ragu and pasta," she said. "And ewes' milk with honey and pepper. And chestnut cake. And a little flask of grappa. Eat, eat."

He gave a chuckle at her insistence. *The typical Italian mother,* he thought, *even though she is so young.* He needed no urging. The food was still warm. He ate, using the last of his polenta to wipe the plates clean. The grappa was raw and stung his throat as it went down, but it spread a warmth through his body.

"You like it?" she asked shyly.

"Magnificent. A true banquet," he said, and she gave a delighted laugh.

"We had such a good time today in the village. First a beautiful Midnight Mass. Everyone singing, and Father Filippo gave us words of such comfort. Then we joined with other families to celebrate. There was enough to eat and everyone was happy. Just like old times." Then her face became solemn again. "Cosimo gave me a gift—a bottle of limoncello he had been saving in his cellar. I didn't want to accept it, but we were in company and I did not want him to lose face in front of other people. So I made him open it right away and drink a toast to our missing loved ones, those who had not returned home yet."

Her face became wistful. Then she smiled again. "And I have brought a small gift for you, because at Christmas one should give gifts."

She handed him a tiny angel carved from wood. "It was part of our Christmas scene," she said.

"You should have left it where it belongs, Sofia," he said as she put it into his hand.

"But there are other angels, and I wanted an angel to be looking after you. The crib is very old. Many generations, and each one added to it, until now." She curled his fingers around it. "Keep it and know that all the time I pray that your guardian angel looks after you."

Hugo felt tears welling up and blinked them away.

"I have a gift for you, too," he said.

"A gift? For me?"

"Of course. It's Christmas. One has to give gifts. You said so."

"Is it another pigeon? Another tin?"

"Nothing as useful, I'm afraid. Here." He handed her the missal.

"It's an old book." She looked at it in wonder.

"I found it among the rubble," he said. "It seems to be almost intact. Open it."

She did and found the folded paper.

"Carefully," he instructed.

She unfolded it and gave a little gasp of excitement. "It is a Miraculous Medal, just like the one I put into Guido's pocket when he went off to war. How did you know?"

"I found it among the rubble," he said. "I cleaned it up a bit. I remembered you said you had no medal for *la Madonna*. And I drew a picture for you." He realised as he said it that he sounded like a hopeful little boy.

Sofia spread out the folded sheet and held it up to the lantern light. "It's the nativity," she exclaimed. "The Virgin and Saint Joseph and the infant Jesus. And shepherds and sheep. Oh, and it's my home. Look at the church tower. It's amazing. You are a true artist, Ugo. I will treasure this forever."

He felt absurdly happy. She moved over to sit beside him and gently stroked his hand. "You are a good, kind man. I hope your wife learns to treasure you."

They both looked up as they heard the low-pitched vibration of approaching aircraft.

"The Allies. They come to bomb the German winter line again." She looked excited.

The noise grew in intensity until it rattled loose stones. Then there was a sudden whining noise followed by a deep, booming thud.

"They are dropping bombs," she said. "There must be a convoy on the road." She started in fear as a second thud came, making the whole hillside shake.

"Too close," she exclaimed. "Hold me, Ugo. I am frightened."

She nestled up against him and he wrapped his arms around her, feeling the softness of her hair against his cheek.

"Don't worry. You are safe with me," he said.

I could stay like this forever, he thought. No sooner had this thought formed itself in his head when there was a screeching whine closer still. The dull thud of the explosion made the ground tremble. Sofia screamed and clutched at Hugo, burying her face in his jacket collar as they felt the blast. Stones rained down from the damaged walls, bouncing and thudding around them. Hugo flung himself on top of her to shield her. Then the floor was tilting. The lamp fell with a crash and they were in complete darkness. He could hear and feel rubble sliding past them. It felt as if the whole chapel was imploding. They were sliding, being swept along with cascading stones. Sofia cried out. Hugo grabbed at the side of the altar and hung on for dear life while the world crumbled around him.

CHAPTER TWENTY-EIGHT

JOANNA

June 1973

As the procession disbanded in the piazza, we stood watching while people hurried off in all directions. I looked at Paola, wondering if we, too, would be going home.

"They go to bring the feast," she said. "We have been invited to join the Donatelli family this year. Maria Donatelli kindly invited us because it is a long way for me to walk down to my house and then back to the piazza with the food. We will wait for them at their table."

I followed her across the piazza to a table with a white cloth. *"Famiglia Donatelli"* was printed on a card. I now saw that every family had reserved a table. I looked around to see where Cosimo and Renzo would be sitting. Men were passing carrying trays of carved lamb. I watched them place the trays at tables in front of the town hall. There was no sign of Cosimo or Renzo yet. I realised that they must have been among those dressed in the robes and hoods. People were arriving at our table now, bringing huge mounds of pasta, risottos, platters of salad, breads, a big ham. I was introduced and found myself sitting amid a loud crowd of many generations. The youngest was Angelina's daughter and the oldest a shrunken little man with no teeth whose food was cut up for him. Everyone laughed and shouted, and this was repeated at all the other tables. The noise level in the piazza was overpowering. I looked around, wondering if any occasion in England would produce such obvious joy and celebration of family. I felt uncomfortable among them, although they were kind enough to include me, constantly pressing food on me and keeping my wine glass full.

Suddenly I felt that I had to get away. I excused myself on the pretext of finding a lavatory. As I stepped into the shade at the edge of the piazza, I saw someone coming up behind me. I stepped aside to let him pass, but instead he stopped and faced me. It was Renzo. He took my wrist again, held up my hand, and compared it to his own, now wearing a ring.

"Yes, they are identical," he said. "Incredible." We stared at the rings, comparing them. He was still frowning, as if he couldn't believe what he saw.

"And there are letters inside mine," he went on. "I only noticed them yesterday. 'HRL.' Do you know what they mean?"

"Yes, I do. Hugo Roderick Langley. My father's initials," I said.

He shook his head. "So I have to agree that this ring came from your father. It's hard to believe that he was here and he knew my mother, but now we have proof that what you say must be true. I must apologise for my rude treatment earlier."

"There is no need to apologise. I'm just glad that somebody now believes me."

Renzo looked at me and I nodded. He gave a little laugh. "To think we had no idea. When my father finds out, he will be so surprised."

"Don't tell him," I said quickly.

He gave me a questioning look. "Why? Why should he not know?"

"Because . . ." I hesitated. "Because we don't know what really happened, and until we do, I'd like to keep this to ourselves."

I was still unsure what to do and whether I could trust Renzo. I had learned the hard way that not all men are trustworthy. Then I realised I had no way of finding out any more about my father and Sofia if I did not share some of what I knew.

"I'd like to show you something," I said. I held up my wrist. "This medal on a ribbon was among my father's things. I am sure that your mother gave it to him. He was not religious and would never have chosen to wear something like this."

Renzo took my wrist again, holding it up to look at it. I was horribly aware of his touch, but he seemed not to notice that he was so close to me. "Interesting," he said. "I'm not sure which saint this is."

"Paola said it was Saint Rita," I said.

He shrugged. "I'm not exactly a student of saints. The older generation believes there is a saint for every problem. Frankly I haven't found them to be very effective in solving mine."

"You have had problems?" I asked.

Renzo shrugged. "I have had my share. Only small setbacks compared to the sufferings of the world, I suppose. Mainly problems of love." He stopped, frowning again. "I should not bore you with this, Signorina Langley."

"No, please. Go on. And do call me Joanna."

"Very well, Joanna." He shrugged. "There was a girl here when I was eighteen. I was sent to Florence to school, you know, and when I came home I told my father I wished to be a chef. He thought it was a stupid idea. I was going to inherit all this land, the prosperous vineyards. He wanted me to study agriculture, so I had to agree, and did a course on viniculture at the university. Then I came home and fell in love. I thought Cosimo would be happy, but he didn't like her. She wanted to be a fashion designer, and miraculously she got a place at the fashion institute in Milan. Off she went and of course she never came back. I hear she's quite famous now."

He broke off and looked at me. "I don't know why I'm telling you my life story."

303

"Maybe because you sense that I've been through similar experiences."

"You have?"

"Yes. The man I thought I was going to marry dumped me for someone who could advance his career."

"I was always told that English men were cold and proper," he said. Then he corrected himself. "But not all English people, I have to admit. I met an English girl once when I was working over there. She was very nice—funny and warm and not at all stuffy as the English are supposed to be. I thought I might stay in London and marry her. But then Cosimo had his stroke and I had to leave her and come rushing home. I feel that any time I fall in love, it is doomed."

"There is still plenty of time," I said.

"For you, maybe. I have already turned thirty. In our culture this is a hopeless case. An old bachelor, like my father."

We had been walking in the shade up the narrow street, and I saw that the little park was up ahead of us. "There is something else I'd like you to see," I said. "Can we sit in the park and I will show you? Maybe you can help me figure it out."

We left the houses behind. Renzo followed me along the sandy path to the bench in the shade of the sycamore tree where the old couple had been sitting. He sat beside me and I opened my purse.

I took out the cigarette packet on which my father had sketched the woman.

He gasped as I handed it to him. "Yes, this is her. My mother. Exactly as she was. That smile. Did your father draw this?"

"He must have."

"He has captured her so well."

There was no sound apart from the cooing of a pigeon in the tree above us and the chirping of sparrows as they pecked in the dust. It felt as if we were alone at the edge of the universe.

"I don't understand," he said. "Your father gave my mother his ring, which must have been a prized possession. He took the trouble to draw a picture of her. So it is clear that he had feelings for her. And she gave him a medal. That must have meant that she had feelings for him, too. So what happened? What went wrong? Did he leave her and go back to England, so she chose the security of a German instead?"

"There is something else I want you to see— the letter I told you about." I pulled out the letter my father had written.

Renzo examined the envelope. "Yes, the address was correct," he said. "That was the house where I was born. And it was posted . . . after she went. Not at this address." He sighed.

"Now read what my father wrote."

He opened the letter. He started it, then looked up. "He wrote good Italian."

"He studied art in Florence before the war," I said.

"He was an artist?"

"Not when I knew him. He taught art at a school, but I didn't know he had painted until after his death when I found some really lovely paintings."

He went back to reading the letter. I heard the small intake of breath as he came to the part at the end. "Our beautiful boy?" he asked, looking at me.

"I wondered if that meant you, whether you had to be hidden at a time of danger."

He shook his head. "I told you before. I was never hidden. I lived with my mother and my great-grandmother until my mother left us. Then I continued to live with Nonna until she died soon after the war ended. That was when Cosimo took me in. He took over my mother's land and he managed to buy the land of those men who were killed in the war. So he became prosperous enough to give me a good education."

"Is it possible that your mother could have had another child? A child with my father?"

"How could this be?" He shook his head. "We would have known."

"How old were you? Three? Four? Maybe a child of that age doesn't notice if an adult gets fatter."

"But Nonna would have noticed. Every woman

in the town would have seen. Nothing gets past the women of San Salvatore, I can assure you. They know everything. And if she had given birth, where would she have done this?"

"It comes back to the question of how my father was here and yet nobody knew about it. Would it have been possible to have hidden him away in your house?"

Renzo frowned at this, considering. "I suppose it might have been possible. We had a big attic, and you had to climb a ladder to reach it. My mother went up there from time to time to bring down things that might be useful to us. There was also a cellar. I didn't like to go down there because there were rats and it was dark. But the wine and olive oil were kept down there."

I looked at him hopefully. "So someone could have been hidden in your cellar?"

"Except how could your father have been brought in? The only door to the house opens to the street."

"At the back what is there?"

"Windows and the town wall below. Besides, Nonna would have had to be in on it, and I remember her as a strict, correct, and demanding sort of person. I don't think she would have permitted a foreigner to be hidden in what was her family home. She would have gone straight to the priest and confessed to him."

"Wouldn't your mother have done the same?"

I asked. "She must have been religious, or she wouldn't have given my father this medal."

"I suppose so. And the priest must never reveal the sanctity of the confession."

"I talked to Father Filippo," I said, "in case your mother had told him something important. He remembered her fondly but was hazy about details."

"Yes, I heard that his mind is failing. Such a pity. What a fine old man."

"She would have taken an awful risk to hide an enemy pilot in her house, risking her son and her grandmother's lives," I said.

"Not only that, but there was the German, remember. The German she ran off with? But perhaps he came to the house after your father had gone. How was your father rescued? Perhaps the Allies came and found him and drove him away, leaving my mother."

"Yes, I suppose that is possible."

We looked at each other, our brains each trying to make sense of things.

"I am sorry I cannot help you," Renzo said at last. "Truly I have almost no memory of that time. I know I was sick for a while and my mother took care of me. I remember the German in our house—the one she ran off with. I remember we ate rabbit and chestnuts and anything else she could find for us. She'd go off with her basket and look through the woods for something to eat because the Germans had taken all we had. And I have to believe now that she and your father did meet and clearly he felt that they had fallen in love. But the beautiful boy . . . I have no idea what he meant by that. And I am afraid now we will never know." He looked up at me, as if processing this. "If there was a child and he was hidden, then surely he must have died. No good can come from this search. You should go home. Leave this place. I have a feeling it is not safe for you to be here."

A cold wind sprang up, snatching at the letter in my hands. Out over the hills the clouds were building. Suddenly I felt uneasy sitting here with him, two people together on a bench with nobody else around. I wanted to ask him what he meant by "not safe." Did he know something, or was he saying that the police might want to pin the murder on me?

I stood up. "I should be getting back. Paola will worry about me."

"Yes." He stood up, too. "And I should be helping Cosimo. He will not be pleased that I am talking with you. He thinks you mean trouble here."

"I don't want to cause any trouble," I said. "I only wanted to know the truth. But it seems now that I never will."

We started to walk together. "Do you think the police will let me go soon?" I asked.

He shrugged. "Who knows? I think it must be quite obvious to anybody but an idiot that you had no reason to kill Gianni and that you were certainly not strong enough to have put him into the well. But unfortunately some of our policemen are idiots. But don't worry. We will do what we can for you, I promise. Such treatment should not happen to a stranger."

Our footsteps echoed back from the walls on either side of the narrow street. In the distance we could hear laughter, and someone had started playing an accordion. Voices were raised in song.

"They seem to be enjoying themselves," I said.

He nodded. "In a place like this people expect little and are delighted by small things. Not like in London, where one must spend money to have a good time and nobody ever laughs. In the restaurant where I worked it was as silent as the grave. People whispered. Nobody laughed."

I thought about this. "That's true," I said. "If someone talked or laughed loudly everyone would look at them."

"And yet you live there."

"I have to finish taking my bar exams," I said.

"Bar? You wish to work making drinks?"

I laughed then. "No, that's what we call the exam to become a lawyer. Called to the bar. Silly, isn't it?"

"So many silly expressions in English," he said. "I was constantly puzzled about what people meant. So you take the exam to become a lawyer?"

I nodded. "And when I have passed . . . if I pass, then I can practice law wherever I want. But I haven't yet found a place where I feel at home."

"Not where you grew up?"

I shook my head. "I never felt that I really fitted in," I said. "My father came from a noble family. He was Sir Hugo Langley. We owned a beautiful big house called Langley Hall and a lot of land before I was born, but my father had to sell everything because of the taxes owed on the estate. So we lived in the lodge and he was the art teacher at the school that took over our house."

"That must have been hard for him," Renzo said, "to be reminded every day of what he had lost."

"Yes, I'm sure it was. My mother was from a less noble background and was quite happy to look after us. But she died when I was eleven, and after that life was quite bleak. I attended the school, but the rest of the girls were rich. And they were not interested in their studies. They either teased or despised me. So no, I don't think I'd want to go back there."

"So we both grew up without a mother. It is never easy. There is always something missing," he said. "Sometimes I used to wake up from a dream that my mother had kissed my cheek as she used to when I was sleeping."

"Your mother clearly loved you," I said. "Do you really believe that she would just abandon you if she didn't have to?"

He stopped, staring out ahead of us to the laughter and song in the piazza. "It is what I have been told. What everyone believes," he said. "Now I'm just not sure."

CHAPTER TWENTY-NINE

JOANNA

June 1973

We had reached the alleyway where Renzo's old house stood. Renzo sensed me looking at it. "Do you think we should take a look at my house and see if there was possibly anywhere that someone could have been hidden?"

"But won't the occupants all be at the feast in the piazza?"

He gave me a conspiratorial grin. "Exactly. What better time to look around?"

"But we can't go in without permission. And won't the door be locked?"

"I doubt it," he said. "Nobody in San Salvatore locks their doors. Any stranger would have to enter the town along this street and would be noticed. And nobody here would rob a neighbour. It is against our code. Come on. Let us give it a try. If we are caught I will say that I am showing the young lady from England where I used to live. No harm in that, is there?"

We hurried down the alleyway and Renzo tried the handle on the front door. It was made of carved wood and looked very old. The door swung open easily.

"Hello? Is anyone here?" Renzo called. His voice echoed up a stairwell. There was no answer. He gave me an affirming nod. "Let's go."

First he walked me around the ground floor. A formal living room at the front looked on to the alleyway. It was full of heavy, dark furniture and felt oppressive to me. At the back was a dining room that had a wonderful view over the vineyards that sloped down to a small valley and the olive groves that climbed the hill beyond. I went over to the window and looked out. Yes, he had been right. The window opened to the sheer drop of the town wall—not a place where one could climb in. Next to this was a very old-fashioned kitchen with a big cast-iron stove and copper pots hanging in a row. And on the other side of the kitchen was a room that now contained easy chairs and a TV set. So San Salvatore had entered the modern age!

"This used to be my mother's bedroom," he said. "At least during the time I remember. We slept down here because it was warmer and we did not have enough fuel to heat the upstairs. My little bedroom was behind it." And he showed me a tiny box room that looked out on to the alley. He had moved me along quickly, presumably because he was beginning to feel uneasy about snooping in someone's home, but I had glanced out of the window of the room that used to be his bedroom. This window also opened onto the wall, but the top of the wall was built out a little here so that one could step down on to it. Not much use, however, as it was still a sheer drop.

We went up and peeked into three bedrooms. Renzo pointed to a square on the ceiling he said led to the attic. Might it have been possible that someone could remain hidden up there? But Sofia would have had to come up with good excuses as to why she kept needing to go up and down. And if she brought my father food, wouldn't the old grandmother have noticed that?

We came down and Renzo opened a small door that led to a flight of dark stairs descending into blackness. I hesitated. "I don't think I want to go down there," I said. "It looks awful. Is there a light?"

"I'm not sure. I don't think I ever went down."

A cold draft of dampness and mould wafted up toward us. Renzo looked at me and nodded. "I have to agree it seems most unpleasant. And the same would apply here as to the attic—my nonna would have seen my mother taking down food. I think we had better get back before we are caught."

He had just finished these words when there was a sound like a truck running into the side of the house, followed by a rumble. Everything started to shake. I heard things falling and

315

crashing. For a moment it felt as if the walls were coming down on us. I grabbed on to Renzo. "What's happening?"

"Only an earthquake," he said.

The shaking ceased and I realised that he had his arms around me.

"Only an earthquake?" I demanded. "Only?"

He laughed, releasing me. "They are rather common in this part of Italy," he said. "There. It's over. We are fine. Let's go back to the others."

We arrived back in the piazza to find chaos. Jugs of wine had spilled on to white tablecloths. Babies were crying. Old women were praying and moaning. Others were rapidly clearing up the mess.

"It is over," the man with white hair who had entertained me the other night said to the crowd. "Forgotten. Let us enjoy ourselves again."

"The mayor," Renzo said to me. "The most important man in this town. He is well respected here. He led us through the wartime and was sensible enough to appear to get along with the Germans. I think it saved us from more grief."

I looked at the old man with interest. One who got along with the Germans? Might he have betrayed his own people to save his skin? I took this one stage further. Might he have betrayed Sofia, knowing that she was hiding a British airman?

I had no more time for these thoughts as Paola

came toward me. "Where have you been? I was so worried. And then the earthquake . . ."

"I'm sorry," I said. "Renzo took me to show me the house where he lived with his mother during the war."

Paola turned to stare at Renzo. "I see," she said. "Oh well. No harm done."

At that moment Renzo's name was called—or rather bellowed—across the piazza. Cosimo was gesturing to him. "Where have you been, boy?" he shouted. "Wandering off and leaving your old father to fend for himself?"

"Father, you are among a hundred people. Any one of them could have helped you," Renzo said.

"And during the earthquake? If I'd had to move swiftly to escape? What then?"

"I think the open piazza is probably the safest place in town," Renzo said.

"Oh, so now you choose to be flippant and disrespectful to your father, do you?" Cosimo came toward him, glaring at him. "Is it this German girl's influence? I knew she was trouble the moment she came into our town."

"She's not German, Father. She is English. And I was not trying to be disrespectful. I was merely stating the truth. And anyway, the earthquake has passed and you are quite unharmed, so all is well. We can get back to our celebration, okay?"

He took the older man by the arm and glanced back at me with the hint of a grin. As they walked away I heard Cosimo say, "The sooner she is away from this place, the better."

I went to rejoin Paola's group. The women were still talking about the earthquake, recalling quakes of times past, villages that had been destroyed, people who had been buried alive. They spoke fast and in their strong dialect, so most of it went over my head, but I nodded agreement as if I understood. I wondered how long the feast usually went on, but the matter was settled for me by Angelina's baby, who started crying.

"Mamma, I think I should take her home," Angelina said. "It's getting cold out here and I think it might rain."

"All right." Paola got to her feet. "We will come with you. I will make sure you are home safely and then I think I should pay a visit to Francesca. She did not come, I think. Of course I can understand why she stays away at this time of grief. But I will bring her some of our vegetables and maybe some biscotti to cheer her up, poor soul."

"Who is Francesca?" I asked.

"Gianni's widow. I think the poor thing has suffered much during her marriage. She may be glad to be rid of him, but then how will she live now? Who will tend to the sheep and make the cheese, eh? It is too much for one woman, and I don't think she can afford to pay a man to do the work, even if she can find one around here who is not working for Cosimo."

We took our leave of the people at our table. I had never been hugged and kissed by strangers before. It was a weird sensation, but not unpleasant, to feel that I was part of a big, warm group.

We walked together down the path and left Angelina at the farmhouse nursing her baby.

"I will now go to Francesca," Paola said. "You should take a little sleep. We have had a long day."

"Oh no," I said. "I am not tired. Would you like me to come with you?"

A big smile crossed her face. "Oh yes. I should like that very much. I always like company, and seeing a young, fresh face like yours will cheer up Francesca in her hour of grief."

In truth my volunteering to come with her was not entirely selfless. I wanted to have a chance to speak with Gianni's widow. Maybe he had told her some of the things he'd wanted to share with me. Paola put together a big basket of food: fruit and vegetables from the garden, baked goods, and some of the leftover ragu.

"She won't feel like cooking, the poor soul," she said.

We set off along the track away from the village, then we turned off up the hill to our right. It was a steep climb. I had offered to carry the basket and now regretted it. I realised how unfit I still was. If I stayed here for long I'd make sure I took plenty of good walks, I decided. Then it struck me that I didn't want to leave, regardless of the unpleasantness with the police. In spite of getting nowhere in my search for the truth, I liked being here. I liked being with Paola and feeling that I was part of a family.

Gianni's house was at the edge of the woodland that crowned the hills. It was a humble sort of place, built of old stone, with a slate roof, and looking as if it might fall down at any moment. Chickens wandered around outside the house. A dog was chained in the yard. It rose up, growling as we approached.

"Francesca," Paola yelled in her big voice. "It is I, Paola Rossini, come to pay you a visit."

The front door opened and a thin woman in black came out. She looked as if she had been crying constantly for some time. But she managed a weak sort of smile. "Paola. It is good of you to come."

"I was concerned when I didn't see you at the feast day."

"How could I come and be joyful when one of the people eating and drinking there had killed my husband?" she demanded.

"You don't know that, Francesca. It could well have been an outsider."

"What sort of outsider? Which outsider would

know about your well? They say he was jammed in there with his head down and left to drown. What kind of monster does that?"

"Maybe Gianni had made enemies," Paola said. "He was not always wise in the company that he kept."

"Gianni was always looking for a deal, that is true," she agreed. "But he stayed away from criminals, from Mafia and gangs. There were rumours about him that just weren't true. He liked to talk big, you know. Liked people to think that he lived with danger and intrigue. But it just wasn't true. He was quite a timid man. But it does no good talking about it, does it? I don't suppose they will ever get to the bottom of the murder. And where does it leave me? With no man to look after the sheep, to lift the heavy pots that make the cheese. I'll have to sell up, if anyone will buy. Make do with my chickens and our few olive trees." As she finished this tirade she seemed to notice me for the first time, standing back in the shadow of a cherry tree. "And who is this?" she asked.

"This is the young English lady who is staying with me," Paola said. "She was kind enough to carry the basket for me up the hill."

I felt those dark eyes analysing me critically. "The one who . . . ?" she began.

"That's right," Paola said. "The one who found your husband's body with me."

"It must have been a shock for her," Francesca said.

"A shock for both of us," Paola said. "I thought my heart would never start beating again. The poor man. What an end."

"As you say, what an end. A most brutal and vicious man must have done this. And for what? Because Gianni wasn't always wise in what he said?" She stopped, her hands toying with the apron she wore over her dress. "You'd better come in and have a glass of wine with me."

"Of course," Paola said. She motioned me to follow and we stepped into the darkness of the house. It was cramped and spartan inside but spotlessly clean. We sat at a wooden bench in the corner. Francesca took an earthenware jug from a shelf and poured us glasses of red wine. Then she put a plate of olives and some coarse bread out on the table. "Your health, Signorina," she said, still examining me as if I was a creature from Mars.

Perhaps I am the first foreigner she has met, I thought, but then I reminded myself that she had seen plenty of Germans during the war. That might have made her suspicious of all foreigners.

The two women talked. They spoke so rapidly and in their Tuscan dialect that much of what they said was lost on me. I found my attention wandering. I stared past them out of the window. There was a good view of San Salvatore from here. I picked out Sofia's former house with the peeling yellow paint. Then I stared a little more intently. The windows at the back certainly opened onto the parapet. But from here it looked as if a stairway went down the outside of the wall just to the right of her house. So there was a way to bring up someone she wished to hide. I couldn't wait to tell Renzo.

Finally, and to my relief, Paola got up. "I should be getting back to my daughter and the grandchild," she said.

"Will you be attending the dancing in the piazza tonight?" Francesca asked, looking at me as well as Paola.

Paola chuckled. "I think my dancing days are over. But if the young lady wishes to go, I have no objection."

"Oh, I don't think it would be right for me to attend alone and to dance with strangers," I said. "The police inspector already thinks I have a bad character because I had a glass of wine with the men of the town without a chaperone."

"Why was an inspector from the police talking to you?" Francesca asked. "Why did he concern himself about your character?"

I realised instantly that I had opened up an embarrassing topic. I could hardly say that he was trying to pin her husband's murder on me because he thought Gianni had tried to force himself on me and I had killed him in self-defence. I tried to come up with a reasonable thing to say. "He was being unpleasant to everyone," I said. "He tried to make me confess to your husband's murder because I was the one who found the body."

"How ridiculous," she said. "These police are idiots. Why should you have any reason to kill a man you had never met?"

"He was among those men at the table, I suppose," I said. "I did exchange a few words with him. I said I was interested in seeing the countryside, and he offered to show me his sheep and how he makes cheese."

"I see." She was still frowning. "And why did you come to San Salvatore, Signorina?"

"My father was a British airman whose plane was shot down near here. I wondered if anybody knew anything about him."

"In the war?"

"Yes. I don't know any details. That's why I came to find out."

She waved a hand, dismissing this. "We were only children during the war. We learned to survive and hide away."

"Yes. It seems nobody ever knew anything about a British pilot who survived a plane crash."

"And was taken away by the Germans?"

"Why do you say that?" I felt my pulse quicken. "Do you know that to be true?"

"I think Gianni mentioned it once. They came for him, I'm pretty sure of that."

324

"Was he alone?"

"I have no idea. I was up at my uncle's farm at the time. But what you said just jogged my memory about something Gianni said. He was only a boy himself at the time, but he ran errands and he saw a lot of things that other people didn't. He always did like spying on other people, and look where it got him."

She put a hand up to her mouth and sobbed. Paola came around to comfort her. "Don't worry, Francesca. You have friends here. We will make sure you are all right," she said. "We'll take our leave now. But you are welcome at my house any time."

"You are a good woman, Paola. May the saints watch over you."

We left her standing at the doorway and watching us as we walked back down the hill.

CHAPTER THIRTY

HUGO

December 1944

For a long moment they lay huddled in complete darkness until the movement around them ceased.

"Are you all right?" he whispered to her.

"I think so. Just very afraid. You saved us. What was happening? It felt as if the whole building was falling down to hell."

"The bomb must have disturbed the foundations."

Their voices seemed to echo in the darkness.

"Is it safe now, do you think?" she whispered. "Have they gone?"

"Yes, they have gone." He stroked her hair and she snuggled against him.

"How will I get home if I cannot find my lantern?" she said.

"We'll find it. Don't worry." He eased them upright, reached for his lighter, clicked it, and held out the small flame, looking around. The lantern had fallen on its side and rolled a few feet away from them. He retrieved it and relit the candle.

"Why did they drop a bomb on us?" she asked

as he set the candle upright and held his lighter flame against it. "How could they do such a thing?"

"The pilot might have seen the light of your lantern and thought this was still an enemy position, I suppose," Hugo said.

"My little lantern? A pilot thought that was a danger?" She smiled.

"You'd be surprised how small a light can be seen from up in a plane," he said. Then he added, "Sometimes an airman just wants to turn around and go home, so he drops the last bomb where he thinks it can do no harm, in the woods or fields."

"Did you ever do that?"

"I am a pilot. My job is to fly the plane, not drop the bombs," he said. "And I flew only light bombers with very few bombs. We tried to make them count."

He positioned the lit candle back inside the lantern, then he held it up to examine the damage. The small light threw out long shadows on to newly fallen masonry. The walls were still standing, although there were now gaping holes in them. The rubble on the floor had shifted, and the whole floor now lay at an angle.

Sofia stood up. "I hope it's still solid enough to walk on." She took a few steps, then she stopped. "*Gesù Maria*!" she exclaimed.

"What is it?" He hauled himself to his feet.

"Look here."

He made his way over to where she was pointing. On the floor, against the side wall of the chapel, a gaping hole had now opened up and a flight of steps went down into darkness.

"There must be a crypt of some sort," Hugo said. "Did you ever visit it?"

"No. I only came here once for a feast day," she said. "We did not have much to do with the monks. They were shut away from real life up here."

"Until the Germans turned them out and they found out exactly what real life is all about," he added.

"Should we go down and explore?" she asked. "It may be dry and snug down there for you."

Hugo was loath to go down into that rectangle of blackness. Cold, thick air crept up from it, and he smelled musty dampness. "I think we should wait until daylight," he said. "We don't know how stable it is down there. The whole ceiling might be about to come down."

"I will return in the morning if I can get away," she said. "I will tell them I need to check on my turnip fields. The harvest may be this week. And besides, it is the day after the feast. Everyone will sleep late."

"All right." He found he was smiling in anticipation at seeing her again so soon, although he didn't share her enthusiasm for exploring some old cellar. "You should go home now then so that you get some sleep. Be very careful as you make your way to the door. The floor may no longer be solid."

"I will take great care," she said. "And I will be impatient to return so that we can find what lies beneath us. Is it a treasure trove, do you think?"

"I doubt it. I expect your monks were simple men. I have certainly found no gold vessels or ruby rings as I have searched the rubble outside. And their bowls and plates were of crude pottery."

"All the same," Sofia said, "it is exciting, is it not?"

"Yes," he agreed, wanting her finally to have something to look forward to. "It is exciting."

Hugo found it hard to sleep for the rest of the night. He was conscious of lying in an unstable place that could collapse at any moment and wondered if he should move outside. But the bitterly cold wind swirling around the ruins did not make that seem an enticing prospect. He sat up, wishing desperately for a cigarette. Instead he found the flask and swigged at the grappa. It warmed him but did nothing to dull his anxious mood. He fought against sleep and was glad when the first streaks of morning appeared over the eastern wall.

Hugo waited until it was completely light, then

picked his way around the outer wall and made it safely to the front entrance. He saw then that the bomb had not landed directly on the damaged building. It had struck the hillside, cutting out a chunk of soil and rock so that the monastery now perched at the edge of a precipice. *At least no German lorries can drive up from the road anymore,* he thought. The flight of steps was unharmed.

He washed, had a long drink of water, and then returned to the chapel. He stood for a long time at the entrance to the crypt. Sofia was right—it was enticing, but at the same time alarming. A cold draft crept up from it, although Hugo couldn't imagine where a draft could be coming from deep within the earth.

He was still standing and staring when Sofia arrived out of breath and with glowing cheeks. "There is a stiff wind today," she said. "It was hard to walk up the hill. And see, I have pulled up one of my turnips. We will wash it and then you can eat it."

"Raw turnip?" He made a face.

"Oh, but yes. It will taste good. Crisp and refreshing." She put it on a fallen beam. "Have you been down there yet?"

"No, I waited for you. I wanted to make the discovery together."

"I brought another candle," she said. "It will be very dark down there." She gave him an excited grin. "Are you ready? I am so curious about what we shall find."

"Probably a basement where the monks stored their old prayer books and habits and unwanted furniture," Hugo said.

"But no. It is below a chapel. There may be the tomb of a saint. Or holy relics. I have seen the head of Saint Catherine in the cathedral in Siena."

"Only her head? What happened to the rest of her? Was she beheaded?"

"No, her head was taken off after she died and put into a gold and crystal case. It is still miraculously preserved for all to see. It grants miracles."

"Poor Saint Catherine," he said. "I'm glad I'm never going to be a saint. I wouldn't want my head cut off after death."

This made her laugh. She went to slap him, then thought better of it, the intimacy of the prior night forgotten. "Your lighter, please." She lit the candle. "I will go first and see if the steps are safe."

"Be careful," he called, but she was already descending into darkness.

"It is good," she said. "The steps are not too steep and they are fairly clear. You can hold on to the wall as you descend. Come slowly."

He followed her, taking one step at a time, feeling the solid coldness of the stone wall against his palm. He heard her gasp but was focusing so completely on not tumbling and making his splinted leg hold his weight that he didn't look up until he reached the bottom. He let out a sigh of relief and looked up. Then he saw what had made her gasp.

It was a perfect little chapel with a carved and vaulted ceiling. Lining the walls were what looked like tombs—of long-dead monks, presumably. At the base of the steps lay several thick slabs of masonry. Sofia was holding up the candle, trying to get its light to reach the far corners. At the far end was an altar on which stood a tall and very realistic crucifix. There were saints in niches, and on the walls hung several big paintings.

"This is why the Germans never looted this chapel," Sofia said, shining the candlelight on the thick blocks of stone around the steps. "See. This must have blocked the staircase from above, and now it has fallen. Perhaps this chapel has not been used for centuries. Or perhaps the monks had a secret entrance from their other buildings." She went ahead of him, gazing up at the walls. "Look at this!" Sofia held up the candle to one of the paintings. "Is it not lovely? It shows the three wise men coming to visit the baby Jesus." She moved on. "And over here is Saint Sebastian, poor man."

Hugo turned away from the latter. He could see

it was painted by a master, but the image of the corpse tied to a post and shot full of arrows was just too graphic.

"They must be very old," Sofia said.

"Yes. Renaissance," Hugo said. "I wonder if they are signed. The magi painting looks like the work of il Perugino."

"Would that not be amazing? Works of the masters right here, and we are the only ones who know about them."

"Yes," he agreed. "Amazing."

Instinctively she put her hand on his arm, looked up at him, and smiled. "I am so glad we are sharing this moment together."

He wanted desperately to take her in his arms and kiss her, but he merely returned her smile. They continued around the wall, Sofia examining each tomb and reading out the Latin for him to translate. "Albertus Maximus, prior, 1681 to 1696," he said of one of the inscriptions.

"You are such an educated man," she said. "You know Latin."

"We had seven years of it rammed down our throats at school," he said. "But your Mass is in Latin. And you speak Italian, which is very close."

She shrugged. "I don't listen to what the priest says," she said. "When Father Filippo gives me the absolution after confession, I have no idea if he's saying I am forgiven or I am going to hell."

"Have you told him about your visits to me?"

She hesitated. "Not really. Only that I found you and helped you once. Not that I come every day and feed you. Because it is not a sin, is it? Jesus said to feed the hungry and welcome the stranger, and I am doing both."

"Quite right." He started to move on.

"Look at this," he called to Sofia, pausing at a small door recessed into the wall. "You were right. There is another way into the crypt. Those stairs have probably been blocked for ages."

"Try it. See where it leads." She reached for the handle before he did. She jiggled it but it didn't move. "It's locked," she said in disappointment. "Who knows where it might lead?"

"Wherever it led is now only rubble," he said, and started to move away. Sofia stayed staring at the door, as if willing it to open, then she sighed and came to join Hugo. At the back of the chapel was an intricately carved stone screen and behind it a small side chapel with an altar, still laid with an altar cloth and a prie-dieu before it. Above the altar was another painting. Sofia held up the candle, and this time they both gasped. It was a small painting in a gilt frame. The subject was an expected one: baby Jesus in the arms of his mother. But it was quite unlike any Renaissance painting Hugo had seen before. Instead of the stylised child, often proportioned like an adult and with an expressionless, rather mature face, this was a true baby. He had a round face topped with a mass of golden curls. His little face was alight with joy as he reached out chubby hands toward two adorable cherubs, their tiny wings fluttering as they hovered just out of his reach, almost as if they were teasing him.

It was Sofia who spoke first. "Oh, what a beautiful boy," she said. "Isn't he the most beautiful boy you ever saw?"

"Yes." Hugo could hardly make the word come out, his throat was so constricted with emotion. "This is the most amazing rendition of Madonna and child I have ever seen. In some ways it is so modern, with the use of light and the realism. But you know, I'm wondering if it might even be Leonardo. The Virgin's face has that wonderful serenity to it of *The Virgin of the Rocks*."

"Leonardo da Vinci?" Sofia was whispering, too.

"It could be."

"Then we must take good care of it. We must make sure the Germans never find it."

"Yes, we must," he agreed. "Could you maybe take it to your house and hide it in the attic?"

She looked horrified. "It is not mine to take. And what if the Germans decide to search the village and it is found? Then it will be lost forever. No, better to try and hide it here. Who would want to come here now when it is just a ruin?"

"All the same," he said, thinking as he stared at the picture. "Perhaps we should block off the steps again and hide them."

"But you should stay down here. It is dry and warmer than up above, and you will have the beautiful boy's face watching over you while you sleep. We would have good warning if the Germans were coming, and you can think of a good place to hide the painting. Saint Sebastian over there they can have!"

He laughed at this. "Yes, I find him quite gruesome."

"So you will stay down here now, no?" she asked. "You will be warmer and blessed by all these holy saints and by the Child Jesus."

"I will try sleeping down here," he said. "The wind has been so cold lately."

"I will bring down your things for you."

"No need. I can come up and carry them down one by one. I can throw down the blanket."

"I do not want you to risk a fall. I can do it. You stay below and catch."

She put down the candle on one of the monk's tombs, then picked up her long skirt and ran lightly up the stairs.

CHAPTER THIRTY-ONE

JOANNA

June 1973

I studied the town on the hill as we walked. Yes, it did seem there was a way down the wall from close to Sofia's house. An agile person could have climbed out of a window, made their way along the top of the wall, and then come down into the vineyards without too much chance of being observed. I remembered Renzo saying that his mother had left with her basket to forage in the woodland. My gaze went through the vineyards and then up through the olive groves to the woods that crowned the hilltop. Beyond them a rocky outcropping topped with an ancient ruin rose above the trees. I stopped to stare at it. It was little more than a pile of rubble, and it was hard to tell what had once been a building and what was part of the rocks themselves.

I thought of Sofia and her basket. Would it have been possible to hide someone up there?

"That old ruin," I said. "Was it a castle once?"

"A monastery," Paola said. "I remember the monks there when I was a child. Such a beautiful chapel it had."

"When you were a child?" I blurted out the words. "It was still a monastery when you were a child?"

"Oh yes. Until it was bombed in the war."

"The Germans bombed a monastery?" I asked, horrified.

"No, not the Germans. The Allies. The Americans, I think."

"They bombed a monastery? That's terrible. Was it by mistake?"

"Oh no. The Germans had turned out the monks and used that site for their big guns. It commanded a good view of the road in the valley and also of aircraft flying overhead. So of course the Allies had to take it out. Such a shame to destroy a holy site like that, but they had no choice, did they? In those days it was kill or be killed."

I was still staring, trying to picture those remnants of standing walls as a once-beautiful monastery. It would have been simple enough to have hidden anyone up there, but surely they would not have been sheltered from the elements among those rocks. Still, it was somewhere I needed to check out for myself. But not that day!

Paola paused and sniffed the air. "We should hurry. Thunder is not far off," she said, and quickened her pace. We were still a good way from Paola's house when we heard the first distant rumble. The wind swirled around us, suddenly cold and fierce. The heavens opened and the rain came. We were drenched within a minute and arrived home looking like drowned rats.

"Oh, Mamma," Angelina cried as she met us in the hallway. "Look at you! I was worried when I heard the thunder."

"We are just a little wet, my darling, but nothing that dry clothes and a good glass of grappa won't heal." She put a comforting hand on my shoulder. "Go and put on dry clothes, Joanna, then we shall hang your dress inside the bathroom and it will soon be dry."

"All right," I said. It was a daunting prospect. It was raining so hard that the drops pinged loudly on the tile roof and bounced up where they hit the ground. I sprinted across the garden along a path that was now a series of puddles. I reached my little house, lifted the latch, and let myself in with a sigh of relief. As I closed the door behind me, I froze—surely I had locked my door when we left early that morning. Surely I couldn't have been careless enough . . . and yes, the key was still in my purse. Then I remembered Renzo saying that nobody in San Salvatore locked their front doors. There must have been an extra key hanging in Sofia's house—easy to find.

Maybe I'm worrying for nothing, I thought. Perhaps Angelina had needed something from this little house—there were spare linens in the big wardrobe. But also perhaps someone had used the knowledge that we were all at the festival to see if my room could be searched. It could have been the Carabinieri. Or not. I opened a drawer carefully. Yes, my clothes had been moved. I retrieved my spare shoes and found that the things Gianni had sent me were still hidden in the toe. So the searcher had not done a very good job, had he? Or he had found the things but saw no need to disturb them, letting me think that I was still safe. An alarming thought. I checked my other possessions, but nothing else was missing. And of course the incriminating letter, along with my passport and wallet, was safely with me in my handbag. So somebody might know what Gianni wanted to talk to me about. But they would also know that he never reached me and that I probably would not be able to interpret those three objects.

I collected some dry clothes, wrapped them in a towel, and ran back to the farmhouse.

Warm and dry and after a glass of grappa, I was feeling better. After the feast we were not hungry and had a simple meal of leftover soup and bread. I made sure my door was locked when I went to bed. I lay there listening to the storm moving off until the growls of thunder receded into the distance.

The next morning I awoke to the more familiar bright blue sky. The air smelled fresh and the colours were so brilliant after the rain that I had to shade my eyes to stare out across the countryside. Paola announced at breakfast that she had to work on her vegetables. She'd noticed that the insects had been having a feast. If the aubergines were ripe, she'd make an aubergine Parmesan for dinner.

"I suppose I had better see if the inspector from Lucca has made up his mind about whether I am free to go," I said.

"Oh." Paola's face fell. "So soon? You wish to go so soon? Just when I have found another daughter?"

"I'm really liking it here," I said. "But I need to know that the police don't consider me a suspect in the death of Gianni. And I should be returning home soon. I have to get back to my studies."

"But you will stay at least a week," she said.

That fact struck me with surprise. Had I been here less than a week? It felt as if I had lived here for a long time.

"Oh, of course. At least a week," I said.

"How can I teach you to cook Tuscan food if you run away so quickly?" She put an arm around my shoulders and gave me a squeeze. "And I need to fatten you up. You need meat on these bones or you will never find a husband."

"Perhaps she already has a man in mind, Mamma," Angelina said, looking up from where she was breastfeeding the baby.

"Is that right? There is a young man waiting?" Paola asked.

I shook my head. "No young man waiting."

"Of course. You need to pass those exams first. When you are a rich lawyer you'll have men lining up to marry you," Paola said.

"She doesn't want men to marry her for her money, Mamma," Angelina said. "She wants to marry for love. You can see that she is a romantic, not a practical person."

"Money doesn't hurt, either," Paola said. "But perhaps you come from a family with money so there is no problem."

I shook my head. "No family money, I'm afraid. My father was almost penniless when he died. I will have to make my own way in the world, or marry a rich man."

"She should make eyes at Cosimo," Angelina said, chuckling. "Fifty-five and not married and owns all this land!"

"Cosimo? She should set her cap at Renzo, the heir. Much more pleasing to the eye, eh, Joanna?"

I felt myself blushing. She chuckled. "I notice things. I see the way you look when he speaks to you. And you go off together at the *festa*?"

"We were just speaking about his mother and whether he had any memory of meeting my father."

"And had he any such memories?"

I shook my head. "No. But we are now sure that they did know each other. And now Gianni's widow says that my father was taken away. Maybe that was what happened. He was taken away by the enemy, and she gave up in despair and chose the protection of a German. Or . . . or she was betrayed and taken away, too. I suppose now we'll never know."

"You never asked your father about this? He never spoke of it?"

"He never did," I said. "My mother told me he was shot down and badly injured in the war and almost died, but I never thought to ask her for details. And I'm sure my father wouldn't have shared anything about Sofia with my mother." *Which is why he kept his memories shut away in a little box in the attic,* I thought.

We finished breakfast. Paola put on her sun hat and her apron and went out to work in her garden. I volunteered to help her, but she brushed me aside. "You are here on holiday. Enjoy yourself. Go."

I left her tying up beans and set off up the hill. It was going to be a hot day. Already I could feel the heat of the sun on the back of my neck. *I will try to see Renzo,* I thought, *and suggest that he comes to the monastery with me.* The thought gave me a jolt of pleasure. I shook my head. Would I never learn? Renzo was the son of a man described as dangerous—a man who might have

343

ordered the death of another who crossed him. He also happened to live in a village in Italy. Hardly suitable boyfriend material, even if he hadn't turned out to be my brother. Besides, he had hardly seemed to notice when I grabbed on to him during the earthquake.

I reached the town piazza. The remains of yesterday's merrymaking were still much in evidence. There were banners and flags looking very sorry for themselves after the rain and now trailing from rooftops or lying over tables that had not yet been put away. I went into the office of the Carabinieri and found that the inspector had not yet arrived and it was not known when he was expected. As I came out of the building again, I noticed that the yellow building at the edge of the piazza was the post office. It occurred to me that I should telephone Scarlet and let her know that I was still in danger of being arrested. Just in case . . .

I went in, paid, and was shown how to use the telephone. The post office employee was very excited about putting through a telephone call to somewhere as far away as England. He insisted on doing everything himself, and it took a long while before he finally handed the phone to me. I heard it ringing at the other end. I waited a long time and was about to hang up when a voice said, "Do you know what bloody time it is?" And of course I realised that Italy was an hour ahead of

England. It was ten o'clock here but only nine there—the middle of the night as far as Scarlet was concerned.

"It's me. Joanna. I'm sorry. I must have woken you," I said. "I forgot the time difference."

"Jo? Is something wrong?" she asked. "It's not like you to waste money on a phone call. Are you still in Italy?"

"Yes."

"Have you found your long-lost brother and your father's former love?"

"No, but I'm getting there," I said. "And as to whether something is wrong, I wanted to make sure you knew in case I'm hauled off to jail."

"Jail? Did you rob a bank?"

"No, I'm a suspect in a murder."

"Bloody hell," she said. "What's all that about?"

"A man's body was found in the well beside the little room where I'm sleeping," I said. "I think the police might want to pin it on me because it's more convenient than finding out the truth."

"Mafia, I suppose. Isn't that what always happens there?"

"It could be something like that. The man had shady dealings, so I'm told." I kept quiet about the letter. "I have to see the inspector again today, and he's going to decide whether I have permission to leave or not."

"You poor thing. Can't you just hop on the next

train and be safely in Switzerland before they realise you've gone?"

"Not as easy as that," I said. "I'm in a place that has two buses a week. And it's not on a proper road, so I'm stuck. But if you get a cryptic message from me asking you to feed the hamster or something, then go and find Nigel Barton and tell him I'm in trouble."

"That's funny," Scarlet said.

"That I'm about to be accused of murder?" I exclaimed.

"No, Nigel Barton. I think he's quite keen on you. He showed up last week saying he had news for you about those paintings you gave him— something about cleaning them up successfully. I told him where you were and that I didn't know how long you'd be there." She paused. "I think the paintings were an excuse."

"Oh golly," I said. "That's the last thing I need—a keen solicitor."

"You could do worse. His dad and granddad own the business."

"Why is everyone so eager to marry me off to someone who will inherit something someday?" I snapped.

"Whoa, what brought that on?" she asked. "Only joking, mate. Anyway, apart from being accused of murder, are you having fun?"

"Strangely enough, yes," I said. "I'm having a good time. I'm learning to cook Italian food.

And there was a big festival yesterday. I like it here."

"A few days in Tuscany and she's turning into an Italian housewife," Scarlet teased. "But listen, take care of yourself, okay? If someone's been killed then a murderer is still at large. It's probably a local vendetta and nothing to do with you, but someone may think you know more than you do."

"Yes, I'll be careful," I said, thinking how close she was to the truth. I wanted to tell her that, but I glanced out of the little cubicle to see the postmaster loitering nearby as well as an old woman, her arms folded impatiently. I had to keep silent for now.

"Call me again when you have more news," she said. "And not so early in the morning next time. We were striking a set until two."

"I'm sorry. And I will call you again, although the only phone in the village seems to be this very public call box."

"I'd better send Nigel Barton out to rescue you." Scarlet chuckled. "I can just see him riding up on his white horse."

"Ha ha. Very funny. See you soon."

"Yeah. See you soon."

I stood staring at the telephone after I hung up. She had been my one tenuous connection with home, and now I was on my own again in a world I knew nothing about. I had heard of the bribery, corruption, and intimidation in Italy. Places where the Mafia ruled. What if the inspector was in the pay of the real killer and had been told to pin the crime on me? That seemed all too possible. Paola was my ally, but how much influence did she have in town? And the only other person I could turn to for help was the adopted son of a man who could well have ordered the killing himself.

I came out of the post office to see one of the Carabinieri officers beckoning me. "The inspector has arrived," he called. "He asks for you."

I took a deep breath and followed him. The inspector was seated at the desk again.

"Signorina Langley," he greeted me in Italian. "Did you have a pleasant weekend?" He smiled, revealing a couple of gold teeth.

"Yes, thank you," I replied. "I attended the festival in town. It was very beautiful." I stammered the words as slowly as I dared with an awful English accent. I wanted him to think that if he needed to ask more questions he would have to find Renzo again.

"Am I at liberty to go home now?" I added.

He spread his hands. "I am not yet satisfied that you did not have a part in this killing. Why did you come to San Salvatore? I ask myself. It is not a beautiful tourist town. Were you maybe sent here to lure poor Signor Martinelli to his death? Paid money to do so?"

I took my time to understand this. "I have said before, I know nobody in this town. I came to find out the story of my father in the war. But nobody here knows of my father. That is all. Now I wish to leave again and go home to my country."

"I have more people to question today. It seems this man had many dealings with outsiders—not all of them above the law. But do not worry. I shall get to the bottom of this. Maybe there are other fingerprints on that well. Maybe not. But if you are innocent, as you say, then you will be on your way home in a few days."

He was about to dismiss me when there came the sound of raised voices in the hallway outside. The young Carabinieri agent poked his head around the door, looking extremely embarrassed. "Inspector, there is a gentleman and he says—"

"He says he must speak with the inspector immediately," said a deep, rumbling voice, and Cosimo himself came into the room. In spite of his stick he moved remarkably quickly.

"Signor di Georgio, isn't it?" The inspector had gone quite pale.

"Of course," Cosimo said. "I am well known to your superiors in Lucca. I come about this unfortunate young woman. My son tells me he has spoken with her and he is sure that she has no connection to this crime. We do not want her to have a bad opinion of Tuscany, do we? We do not wish her to go home and say that the law in Tuscany is full of idiots, that they do not know how to solve a crime like Mr. Sherlock Holmes does. So I am here to say you must let her go when she wishes to leave. Maybe we will get to the truth about Gianni Martinelli one day. Maybe not. The sort of men who carry out such crimes are not always easy to track down, as you know."

There was a long pause. The inspector looked uncomfortable. He did not want to surrender his authority, but he also did not want to go against Cosimo.

"Give me a few more days, I beg of you," he said. "The young lady will be quite safe here. She can enjoy the Italian sunshine."

"My son has to go into Florence tomorrow," Cosimo said. "He is willing to drive this young lady to the train."

"I will take the matter into consideration," the inspector said. "That is the best I can promise."

Cosimo put a hand on my back and steered me out of the room. "Do not worry, my dear young woman," he said. "I can promise you that you will be able to leave with my son in the morning. Enjoy your last day in San Salvatore."

I found that last sentence quite ominous, although I'm sure I was reading more into it than was meant. I came out into blinding sunlight and wondered where to go next. Then I came to a decision. I needed to talk to Gianni's widow. She was the one person who had actually heard of my father. Maybe she knew more. Maybe she even knew why Gianni came to see me that night and met his end.

CHAPTER THIRTY-TWO

JOANNA

June 1973

The dog rose barking as I approached Francesca's house. He looked so menacing that I was reluctant to come any closer. I wasn't sure how long that chain was. I hoped she would hear the noise and come to see what was happening. Finally, a curtain was drawn back and a face peeked out, and then the front door was opened.

"It is the English signorina," she said. "You have come for Paola's basket, no doubt. She will need it. And her bowl, too. The ragu was excellent. Please thank her for her kindness."

Her accent was so strong that I had trouble understanding her.

"Come in, please." She motioned me toward the door. The dog didn't take his eyes off me for a second as I entered the house.

"Will you take some coffee with me?" she asked.

I wasn't a big fan of the thick black espresso that was drunk here. It seemed that milk was only mixed with the coffee at breakfast. Any time after that it was a sign of weakness to water down the coffee. "Thank you." At least it would give me an excuse to stay and talk.

She ushered me to the bench at the table. I sat and watched as she poured the liquid into a tiny cup. "Signora," I began hesitantly. "I wanted to talk to you about my father and the war. I think you know more than you said yesterday in front of Signora Rossini."

She looked uneasy. "I only know what my husband told me—that he had seen the Germans driving off with a prisoner. He thought that prisoner was an Allied airman. He wore a leather jacket like those who fly aeroplanes."

"Did your husband say anything about Sofia Bartoli?" I asked.

Now she really did look surprised. "Sofia Bartoli? The one who went with the German officer? What has she to do with this?"

"I think she helped to hide my father," I said cautiously.

She shook her head. "I know nothing about that."

On the path up the hill I had weighed whether I would put her in danger if I showed her the contents of the envelope. I decided to take the risk.

"Your husband pushed a letter through the bars of my window on the night he died," I said. "I have to think it was meant for me."

I handed her the note. She read it, then half

laughed as she shook her head. "The stupid man. I told him he should have left well alone."

"You know what he was referring to, do you?"

"I know very little," she said. "I know he used to run messages for the local partisans. He was proud of that. Only a boy and already doing his part to win the war. He said to me once when he was drunk—which he often was, God rest his soul—that if the inhabitants of San Salvatore knew the truth, things would be very different.

" 'What truth?' I asked him.

" 'About the war,' he said. He said one day he'd find a way to let the truth out, and when he did, it would change everything."

She fiddled with the objects on the table, moving the sugar bowl and a spoon around as she talked and not looking at me. She was clearly uncomfortable with talking about this, but I had to press on.

"Do you know what he meant?"

"Not exactly. When he was drunk his conversation wandered. And when he was sober the next day and I asked him what he had been talking about the night before, he struck me across the face and told me to mind my own business about matters that didn't concern me." She paused and looked up. "He struck me frequently. He was a violent man as well as a stupid one."

"I'm very sorry. It must be a relief for you in a way that he is gone."

"A relief?" She glared at me. "A relief? To be left alone in poverty? How can I carry on the farming alone? At least he was useful in some ways. He made good cheese."

The absurdity of this almost made me grin. I stifled the smile. "So Gianni had run messages in the war and had seen something that was important, something that other people didn't know about."

"That is what I believe," she said.

I opened my purse and removed the three objects. I put them on the table. "Did he ever show you these? Do you know what they mean?"

She stared at them. "Well, that is the star of the Society of Saint George. It is the order that the respected men of the town belong to."

"And it was a secret sign of the partisans during the war?" I asked.

"Maybe. I was only a young girl, I didn't know about such things. But this"—she picked up the banknote—"this is German money, surely. And the cloth? A dirty old piece of cloth? What is that supposed to mean?"

"I think it is stiff with blood," I said, and watched her drop it hastily. "Maybe Gianni was trying to tell me that someone gave information that resulted in death and was paid for with German money."

"Oh." She looked up at me, digesting this. "So that's what he was hinting—that someone was not the hero he claimed to be and one day Gianni was going to make sure he paid well for his silence."

"Cosimo?" I asked. "Do you think he meant Cosimo?"

"It's possible." She glanced around nervously in case anyone was listening at the window. "We all heard about his bravery during the war. And he certainly profited afterward. But if my husband was foolish enough to have blackmailed him, then he paid for it with his life." She sighed. "I told him to leave it alone. He never listened to me."

I was coming to terms with this. I had heard how Cosimo had survived the massacre of partisans. What if he had not survived it but orchestrated it and been well paid? Gianni might have thought this was a good time to tell me about it so that someone outside the village knew. And when I was far away, then he'd blackmail Cosimo. As Francesca had said, foolish man.

"Would you like to keep these things?" I asked.

"No. You take them." She pushed them back toward me. "Destroy them if you are wise. They can only bring more grief. The past has gone. My husband is gone. And I would like you to go now, too. Go home to your land and forget about this place."

There wasn't anything more to say. I got up, thanked her for the coffee, and went out. The dog rose, his fur still bristling, but he didn't growl as I passed him. I started down the hill but then I turned and headed up toward the woods. I didn't know what I hoped to find. If my father had erected a little shelter there it would have been found or disintegrated long ago. And local people would have talked about it. Unless . . . I stopped at the edge of the woodland. Unless they all knew what had happened to my father. Unless they were all in on a secret and had agreed to stay silent. In which case I'd go home never knowing.

I entered the leafy coolness of the glade. It was quite pleasant among the trees, broad oaks and chestnuts still flowering. Birdsong rang out around me. A pigeon cooed in a melancholy fashion on a branch above my head. I followed the barest hint of a path through the trees, still trying to get my thoughts in order. Cosimo had become the richest man in the town after the war. Gianni might have been foolish enough to have seized upon the opportunity of my arrival and threatened to blackmail him, which was why Cosimo was so anxious for me to leave before I asked any more questions. And Renzo—Renzo was Cosimo's son and heir. Surely he must know what had happened in the war and also what had happened to Gianni. I saw how he obeyed his father's every wish, leaving his studies in London to rush home to his side, helping him around.

The best thing for me to do would be to take

Cosimo's offer and let Renzo drive me to the station as quickly as possible. Whatever had happened to my father, nobody was going to share that information with me. Suddenly I sensed a watchfulness in the woods, as if all the living creatures were alert. I was afraid. What if I was being followed all the time? What if someone had overheard my conversation with Francesca Martinelli and had followed me into the woods? How convenient that my body wouldn't be found for days . . .

I pushed blindly through undergrowth. Twigs scratched my cheek and brambles caught on my skirt, but I kept going until I came out to the olive groves, breathing heavily and glad to see Paola's farmhouse on the hillside opposite. I think I must have run all the way home.

CHAPTER THIRTY-THREE
HUGO

December 1944

Hugo spent the night in the crypt. He wasn't at all happy about being in the presence of dead monks, a crucifix, and sundry saints, but it was good to be out of the wind. He made his bed on the other side of the carved screen knowing that he could see the Child Jesus through the holes in the carved stone. He lay down and had the best sleep he'd had since leaving his base near Rome.

He was glad of his protected spot when the next violent storm blew in sometime in the middle of the night. The wind howled down the staircase, and he heard the crash and thump as more pieces of masonry were dislodged from the walls above. Sofia did not come that night. He fed himself with the turnip (it was surprisingly good) and the remains of the Christmas feast.

With daylight he made his way up the stairs and examined the lie of the land. The intense rain had washed away more of the hillside, and the steps now clung to what was an impressive drop. He needed to warn Sofia not to attempt the climb in a strong wind. She was so light and delicate, she might be blown over. He waited for her all morning but she didn't come. He kept a watch on the road for any signs of Allied troops moving in from the south, but the higher mountains to the north were now well and truly covered in snow and he realised that Sofia might have been right—the Allies might not risk the advance until the weather became more spring-like.

He retreated to the shelter of the crypt. Darkness was falling when he heard the sound of footsteps crossing the floor above. He stood up to greet Sofia. She came rushing down the steps and put a finger to her lips.

"Your knife or your gun," she whispered. "Have them ready. I think I was followed."

He went to find them, checking that the gun was loaded.

"It had better be the knife," she whispered. "The gunshot might be heard from far away."

He examined the knife in his hand. He had never stabbed anyone in his life and couldn't picture doing it now. He tried to imagine grabbing a German soldier from behind, holding his head, and calmly slitting his throat. Could he do that?

Sofia must have realised what he was thinking because she said, "Give it to me. I have killed pigs on the farm. I have no fear of killing a German."

She snatched it from him, then she went back

up the stairs. Hugo felt like a coward and made his way up behind her as fast as he could. The sun had just set and the sky was streaked blood red. With the knife in her hand and the walls glowing pink, she made the most dramatic image.

She turned back to him. "Stay hidden. I may be able to bluff my way out of this. We shall see who it is."

She positioned herself near the doorway. He heard feet coming across the forecourt, then Sofia stepped out. "Gianni!" he heard her say in a surprised voice. "What are you doing up here?"

"None of your business, Signora Bartoli. What are you doing here?"

Hugo peeked out and saw a skinny boy of about eleven or twelve. His voice was still unbroken, and he looked defiant and afraid at the same time.

"If you must know, I came to see whether the latest bomb uncovered more of the monk's kitchen. I have been up here several times and found tins of food and preserved fruits. I thought maybe some new items might now be found."

"I'll help you look," he said. "My mother would welcome a jar of preserved fruit."

"You are very kind, but I'm sure your mother wouldn't want you risking your life by coming up here. See how the new bomb has blown away more of the hillside. You are so light you could get swept away."

"I'm tough," he said. "I can handle it."

"So what are you doing here?" she asked. "Did you come up for a dare?"

"No," he said. "I thought I might find the boys up here."

"The boys?"

"Yes, you know, the local partisans. I overheard someone say they were planning something big. You know, an attack on the road maybe, and I think they might be meeting up here. I want to join them."

"You? Join the partisans? You're only a boy. They wouldn't want you."

"But I could be useful. Run errands for them. Spy out places for them."

"Gianni." Sofia put a hand on his shoulder. "From everything I hear, these are ruthless men taking big risks. They might well kill you rather than worry that you would give them away."

"They are our men, our neighbours, on our side."

"I wouldn't quite say that. Some groups of partisans are communists. They want the Germans gone, but they also want our government overthrown and a communist rule by the people."

"But the ones I'm talking about are men from around here. We know them."

"I think you should stay well away. No good comes from eavesdropping," Sofia said. "But now that you are here you can help me look for more items we can use . . ." Her voice became fainter as she walked away with the boy. Hugo waited impatiently, and just as the last glimmers of daylight were fading he heard their footsteps again and Sofia saying, "Go home now before it is quite dark. I'm sorry we didn't find any food for your mother. Tell her I will bring her some of my turnips when they are harvested."

"Are you not coming with me?" he asked, his voice sounding young and uneasy now.

"Of course. You go down the steps carefully and I will join you at the bottom. I left my basket in the old chapel where I was saying a prayer when you arrived. It is still a house of God, you know, even though its walls have been damaged. Go carefully now."

Sofia came rushing back into the chapel and up to Hugo. "I have to go with him. There is food in the basket. And you may be in great danger. The partisans . . ."

"I heard," he said. "They may plan to meet here."

"I will keep my ears open," she said, "and try to come and warn you. But you also must be on the lookout and ready to hide if necessary. If you could get that door open, maybe you would have an escape route."

"I've tried," he said. "It won't move."

"Then maybe you should no longer stay down

here. You would be trapped. At least you were hidden in your little spot under the altar."

"Yes," he agreed. "You'd better go or that child will come back looking for you."

"Take care, Ugo." She reached up and kissed his cheek. Then she ran out.

"Sorry, Gianni," he heard her calling. "I could not find my basket in the darkness. It is nothing but rubble in there now. And unstable. I shall have to come back for it in the morning."

Darkness had fallen. Hugo got out his lighter and made his way down the stairs to light his candle. He felt horribly vulnerable, trapped. If he stayed down here he would not be able to run if he was found. He lit his candle and carried his belongings upstairs and back to his former hiding place. It was cold and damp and uninviting, but he set up his bed and then dragged over more splintered pieces of wood to conceal himself. In the daylight he'd have to do a better job, and maybe close up the crypt again. The thought of the partisans finding the painting and maybe even taking it to sell or barter made him want to go down and take it off the wall immediately. But his candle was burning low—who knew how much fluid remained in his lighter? He couldn't chance finding himself down there in complete darkness, possibly becoming trapped. He retrieved the basket and ate the soup that

Sofia had brought for him. Another bleak thought struck him. If the partisans were really going to use this as a meeting place, then Sofia could not risk coming here again. He would have to come to a decision and take action soon. He could now put some weight on his injured leg. Maybe it was time to go and trust his luck.

He settled himself in the narrow space and spent a miserable night alert for the smallest sound. At some time during the long hours of darkness, he thought he heard gunshots, or it could have been thunder. The night dragged on for an eternity, and he was relieved to see the first streaks of cold daylight. They wouldn't come during daylight, he was sure. This site was too open and exposed. That gave him time to think and plan. He went down the steps and stood in front of the painting of the Child Jesus. Even in the semi-darkness it seemed to glow with an inner light. It still took his breath away. *I must find a safe hiding place for it,* he thought. He moved around the small crypt. There was space behind some of the tombs, but any thorough search would uncover the painting quickly. There was also a gap behind the altar. *A possibility,* he thought.

He was still down there when he heard footsteps up above. He swore under his breath, realising he had left his revolver and knife tucked with his belongings. Looking around, he could come up with nowhere to hide other than behind the carved stonework screen—hardly a secure hiding place. "Caught like a rat in a trap," he muttered.

He heard the feet come to the top of the steps and saw a shadow blocking the daylight. A voice called softly, "Ugo? Are you down there?"

"Sofia?" He let out a huge sigh of relief and hurried to meet her. "I didn't expect you again so soon, and in daylight. You mustn't take such risks, please."

"Bad news," she said, gasping as if she had run all the way. "Terrible news, Ugo. Gianni was right that our local partisans were planning a raid. But someone must have tipped off the Germans. They were waiting for them, and all were slaughtered except for Cosimo."

"How come he managed to get away?" Hugo, who had taken a dislike to Cosimo without ever meeting him, was instantly suspicious.

"It was a miracle. The first bullet just grazed his shoulder. He flung himself to the ground, and the body of one of his comrades fell on top of him. He said he lay there while the soldiers went around driving their bayonets into the bodies to make sure they were really dead. He didn't dare move for hours. When daylight came he crawled out and made his way home. I've never seen a man look more exhausted and distraught."

"So someone tipped off the Germans. That means you have a spy in your midst."

"Maybe not in San Salvatore. These men come

from other villages, too. Some are not even originally from around here—they are soldiers who fled from their regiments rather than be taken prisoners of war by the Germans. One of them could have been planted as a spy."

"All too easily," he agreed. "But at least this is good news for me, for us, isn't it? They will not be using this as a meeting place."

She shook her head. She was crying now. "But it is worse than you think. German trucks came into the village first thing this morning. They questioned everybody about the partisans, and they said they were going over the bodies and if they identified one of them as coming from this village then we would all be shot."

"And Cosimo? Did they find him?"

"No. He escaped out into the fields when someone saw the trucks coming. He will have to stay hidden, I think."

"This is terrible," Hugo said.

She nodded. "It is more than terrible. The major in charge also asked us about an English airman. They said your plane had just been discovered and there were only two bodies in it and nobody in the pilot's seat. They asked if anybody had seen or heard any rumour of an Englishman hiding out. Nobody had seen anything. Nobody said anything. Then this German said if it was found that any of us had helped an enemy, the whole village would suffer. You should have seen his face. He was actually looking forward to massacring all of us, I'm sure."

She stared at him, her eyes bleak and hopeless.

"Then I must get away now," Hugo said. "And you must come with me, Sofia." He took her hand.

She turned away. "I can't leave my son, or my husband's grandmother."

"Bring Renzo with you. You want to save your son, don't you? The neighbours will take care of the old lady, and it won't be for long. We'll go south. We'll find a way."

"But how can you walk? Your leg still is not strong enough."

This was all too true.

"Where is the nearest transportation? Are there no buses, trains?"

"There is a train line down in the Serchio Valley, about ten miles from here. The train goes to Lucca. I do not know if that is still in territory controlled by the Germans. And I do not even know if trains are still running. And to travel you must show documents. They would find you."

"Then we must try to steal a German car or truck."

"And how is that less dangerous than staying where I am and praying that nobody has seen me?" Her voice was shrill now.

"And if they decide to shoot the whole village?" His voice had risen, too, echoing back from the walls. "I want to save you, Sofia. I want to protect you. I'll give myself up to them. I'll say I was hiding out in the countryside and nobody aided me."

"No." She grasped at his arm. "No, I can't let you do that. I won't let you do it."

"But I would be a prisoner of war. And I'm an officer. Officially they have to treat me properly and take me to an officer's prison camp."

She shook her head violently so that her shawl fell to her shoulders. "They would kill you right away. I know it. They are retreating and scared. They will not want to take prisoners along. I don't want to lose you, Ugo."

"I don't want to lose you, either." He wrapped his arms around her. She buried her head in his jacket as she had done when the bomb had fallen. They stood there together in silence. He stroked her hair gently as if she was a child.

"There must be a way," he said angrily. She looked up at him. "Is there no one around here who has a car or truck?" he asked.

She shrugged. "All taken from us. Besides, there is no petrol. Some farmers still have a horse or donkey. I know of a farmer who has a cart to take his produce to the market in Ponte a Moriano. I have heard that he has taken black market items before now. But he charges much money and I have none, and nothing to sell."

Hugo frowned, thinking desperately. Then he

pulled his signet ring off his little finger. "Take this. It's gold." He put it into her hand and closed her fingers around it. "I don't know if it will be enough, but tell him we just want to borrow the cart. We will leave it where it can be found and he can collect it."

She nodded solemnly. "I don't exactly know where he lives, but someone in the village will. It is too bad that Cosimo has to hide out, because he would know. He knows of black market dealings, I am sure."

"We don't want Cosimo to know anything," Hugo said sharply. "We don't want anyone to know. We can't risk them going to the Germans."

"Perhaps you are right," she agreed. "Very well, I will try. I will do my best. But it will not be easy. I do not think the Germans will leave us alone now. And if they identify one of those men as coming from our village then it will all be over. We will be slaughtered like animals."

"Surely they wouldn't go through with that?" he said. "Not women and children?"

"Oh yes. They have done this in other towns. All the population slaughtered because these people have aided the enemy. I am sure they would do it."

"Then for God's sake go and find this man today. I will make myself ready to leave. And I will keep watch. I can see the road from here. If

German vehicles are coming I'll go down into the forest to wait for you."

She nodded, clearly trying to come to terms with the burden of so much worry at once.

Hugo grabbed her arm. "And, Sofia, if it is not safe don't come again. Save yourself. Save Renzo. That's all that matters. I love you. I know I shouldn't because you are a married woman and I am a married man, but I do. I'd do anything in the world to protect you."

"I love you, too, Ugo," she said in a small voice.

He took her face in his hands and kissed her tenderly on the lips. He felt desire stirring in him but broke away hastily. "Go now, while there is still time."

Tears were running down her cheeks. "God protect you, Ugo," she said.

"And you," he called after her as she ran out into the night.

CHAPTER THIRTY-FOUR

HUGO

December 1944

After she had gone he remained rooted in place, trying to think clearly. He was a British officer, combat trained. He should be able to come up with a good plan. He had six bullets in the chambers of his revolver. At least he could kill the first six Germans if he took them by surprise. But then they would take reprisals against the village. Sofia had to find the man with the cart and make him lend it to her. The ring was a good one. Heavy twenty-two carat gold. Worth a lot. A simple farmer would be tempted, surely.

Then his eyes strayed to the painting of the Child Jesus. He had to protect that, too. No German was going to loot it! He lifted it down from the wall with difficulty, surprised at how heavy it was. He wondered if the frame was actually made of gold and not gold leaf. Held close in front of him, the child seemed almost to be exchanging a secret joke with him. He had an overwhelming desire to take the canvas from its frame, roll it up, and stuff it into his jacket or parachute pouch. But his artist's training would not let him do such a thing. The old paint would crack and the painting would be ruined. And it was certainly too large and heavy to carry with him. It had to be hidden until the Germans had finally retreated northward.

He went back to the little door in the wall. It was made of solid oak, with carved panels and a keyhole big enough for an ancient key. He fetched his knife and tried prying the lock, then cutting out a section of the door, but the attempts were futile. The wood was too thick and the door was snugly built into the stone. He was loath to carry the painting upstairs, where it would be exposed to the wind and weather. In the end he tucked it behind the altar. At least nobody would find it unless they searched well. Then he went back upstairs to keep a lookout.

It was a blustery day with clouds racing in from the west and the promise of more rain. Hugo scanned the countryside in all directions, but nothing moved on the road, and the surrounding fields were empty and bare. *A desolate landscape,* he thought. It echoed his mood. He looked over the recent landslide down to the track. *Could I make it down to the road if Sofia has to bring the cart that way?* he wondered. A little voice in his head whispered that he should just run for it now and not put Sofia at any more risk.

He returned to the rubble beside the chapel to see if he could salvage anything of use—

something that could be used as a weapon, maybe. But the walls had already collapsed in the first bombardment. Nothing much had shifted when the latest bomb fell. In truth there was nothing left to destroy. Bending with difficulty, he idly turned over smaller pieces of masonry, not knowing what he hoped to find. Then he found himself looking at a large iron ring poking from beneath the stones. Intrigued, he lifted more masonry away and pulled out a key ring with several large keys attached. He held it in his hand, staring for a long moment while his heart beat faster. Surely he couldn't be lucky enough to have found the key to the door?

He made his way back inside, moving as fast as he could, not even noticing the pain in his wounded leg. He was brought back to sanity when he almost tripped going down the steps into the crypt. He had to steady himself against the wall, and so took the last steps at a more careful pace. One by one he tried the keys in the lock, and at last the biggest one fitted. He turned it and heard the lock click. He pushed but the door didn't budge. It must have jammed when the building shifted during its collapse. He threw his shoulder against it and felt it move, but still it wouldn't open. Gritting his teeth with frustration, he tried again. At last it opened, scraping against the stone floor with a loud screech that echoed alarmingly through the crypt. Hastily he reached for his lighter and poked his head around the door. Then he snapped the lighter shut and sighed. There had once been a passage, but it was blocked with rubble only a couple of feet beyond the door. Barely enough room for a slim person like him to squeeze around it. A door into nowhere.

Hugo swallowed back his disappointment, but then an idea came to him. A door into nowhere. He squeezed around the half-open door and checked the rubble beyond. The passage was well and truly blocked. He examined the back of the door, then nodded. It could work—the best solution for now. He extricated himself again and went back upstairs, although his leg was already giving him signals that he had done enough and needed to rest. There was certainly plenty of lumber to choose from. Shattered pews and kneelers, smashed altar tables, and carved pieces that must have been parts of the high altar once. He chose four relatively straight and sturdy lengths and then worked to prize out the nails from the shattered wood. It was long and tedious work. Then he carried his materials downstairs with a good, round piece of marble that had probably been part of a saint's statue. He squeezed around the door, noting dryly how good it was that he had eaten so little for a month now and was horribly thin. Then he set to work building a crude frame into which the painting could fit on the back of the door. He had never been much of a carpenter—he had never needed to be, with plenty of servants to do the manual work—and there was much swearing as he tried to hammer rusty nails through varnished wood and into a solid door. But in the end he achieved what he had envisioned. He lifted up the painting and pushed it into the enclosing wood frame. "*Va bene*," he said out loud in Italian. He now hammered short pieces diagonally across the corners to hold the painting in place. Even if anyone managed to force the door open, they would only see a blocked passage. The painting would be safe until Sofia could return and the Germans had retreated.

Hugo felt very satisfied with himself as he came wearily up the steps. If only he could protect the rest of the artworks in the little crypt. He imagined Germans hauling off the other big paintings with delight, taking down the crucifix, even knocking down the saints and the marble figures on the tombs. Then another idea came to him. The former door to the chapel that had fallen when the last bomb hit—it might just fit over the opening that led down to the crypt. He picked his way across unstable rubble to where it lay, and then attempted to drag it along the floor. It was large and incredibly heavy. His leg sent out waves of pain every time he bent and then pulled at the door. His forehead was soon coated in beads of sweat, and he felt nauseous. He had to admit defeat and realised he needed to wait for Sofia. But he had no idea when she could come or how quickly he'd have to leave once she got there.

He went to lie down, the revolver and knife at the ready by his right hand. The rest of the day passed and Sofia didn't come. He agonised over what that might mean. She had not found the farmer with the cart, or the Germans were still in the area and were watching her. It could be something as simple as her son being afraid and not wanting to leave her side. This reassured him a little. He would just have to be patient and pray that the Germans had not identified any of the bodies of those dead partisans as coming from San Salvatore.

Night fell. Hugo was now desperately hungry. He stuffed the remaining parachute into its pouch. Silk might be a good thing to barter, given Sofia's enthusiasm for it. In the morning he would scatter the items he had acquired over the ruins so that all traces of his occupation there were removed. He dozed, then jerked awake again at the smallest of sounds. But he must have finally fallen asleep because Sofia was suddenly beside him. He felt her soft hair touch his cheek. He opened his eyes, not knowing if this was reality or just one of his dreams about her.

"Ugo, *mio caro*," she whispered, her face only inches from his.

Instinctively he took her into his arms and felt her body warm against his. Then he was kissing her hungrily, the pent-up desire mingled with his fear, and she was responding, her slender body pressing against him. His hand fumbled with her skirts, felt the flesh of her upper thigh, tugged at her underpants. And he realised she was unbuttoning his trousers. Then he rolled on to her, the pain in his leg forgotten, the Germans forgotten, the war forgotten.

Afterward they lay together in silence, their breathing in harmony.

"Ugo, I must move," she said at last. "The rocks dig into my back."

"The next time we do that it will be in a big, beautiful bed with a feather mattress," he whispered in her ear as he helped her to sit up. "Much more comfortable."

"You can believe there will be a next time?" she asked.

"I can. We will get away, Sofia. You and I. And if your Guido is truly dead . . ."

She put her fingers to his lips. "Don't go on. Who can think about the future?"

"What about the cart? Did you find the farmer?"

"Not yet. I could not leave the village. It is so bad, Ugo. The Germans are not going to leave us.

One of them has come to stay at my house. He has taken the best bedroom upstairs."

"In your house? Oh, that's terrible, Sofia. For God's sake, take Renzo, go find the cart, and we'll leave immediately."

"I wanted to go yesterday, but this German asked me where I was going. I told him my turnips were almost ready for harvest. I was going to check on my field, and if they were ready I had to arrange for a cart to take them to market."

"That was clever."

She shook her head. "He said he would send one of his men with me to help me dig up the turnips." She paused and sighed. "I told him that was not necessary, I was strong, I was used to hard work. But he said he wanted to help in return for giving him accommodation."

"So he sounds like a decent sort of man, then."

She turned away. "Who knows? It may be that they have been instructed not to let any of us out of their sight. And I don't like the way he looked at me. He watched me going upstairs. I could feel his eyes on me."

"You took an awful risk coming here now," he said. "What if he checks on you at night?"

"I locked my bedroom door," she said. "I have brought Renzo to sleep with me. I just pray that he doesn't wake before I get back."

Hugo felt impotent rage building inside him.

"Then you should return immediately."

"I am afraid I could only bring you a little polenta and a few cold beans," she said. "The German ate two helpings of the stew I had made. I told him we had almost no food and he said not to worry, he would bring me more. He said his men were good to those who cooperated. I told him I had no choice. I had to protect my son and the old woman. Then he smiled and said, 'You have no reason to fear me.' I wish I could believe him."

"Will he be in your house all day, do you think?"

"He knows I must go to my field. If he sends a man with me I will tell that man to keep digging while I go and arrange for the cart to market. And even if he insists on accompanying me to the old farmer, he will not speak our language, and he will certainly not speak my Tuscan dialect. I can arrange for the cart in front of him."

Hugo put his arm around her. "You are very brave, Sofia. I feel so helpless and useless stuck here. I should be protecting you. Instead you are risking everything for me."

"And for me, too, now. I realise I must get my son to safety. And myself." She stood up, adjusting her skirts and wrapping her shawl around her. "Let us hope I can take the cart tomorrow. Then I can load it with turnips and you can hide among them and we will be free."

"You make it sound so easy."

"We must trust in God. That is all we can do," she said.

Hugo pulled himself to his feet beside her. "Before you go, I need you to help me with one thing. That old door—we can cover the opening to the crypt and disguise it."

"And the painting?"

"I have hidden it, Sofia. A perfect hiding place. Behind the secret door."

"The door in the wall?"

"Yes, I have the key. I will take it with us and give it to you when it is safe for you to return."

"You are so clever, Ugo. Our beautiful boy will be safe and dry down there."

"Yes," he agreed. He went over to the great door. She bent beside him, and together they manhandled it across the rubble until it was in place over the opening. It fitted perfectly. They looked up at each other and exchanged a grin of conspirators.

"You go," he said. "I will cover it with rocks and wood, and nobody will ever know it was there."

"Yes," she said. She came to him and kissed him, full and hard on the lips. "Until tomorrow, *amore mio*."

CHAPTER THIRTY-FIVE

JOANNA

June 1973

"Oh, there you are," Paola said, looking up from the beans she had been retying. "I was beginning to get worried about you. I thought you had gone up to the town, but then Renzo came seeking you and said that you were not up there."

"Renzo came?" I blurted out the words.

"Yes. Looking for you." She misinterpreted my alarm. "I think you might have made a conquest there, *mia cara*." She gave me a knowing little smile.

"Did he say what he wanted?"

"He didn't. Maybe just to enjoy your company, to get to know you better."

"Oh no. It's not like that," I said. "He must have wanted to arrange a time to meet me and take me to the station tomorrow."

"Tomorrow? So you will really leave so soon?"

"I think it would be wise," I said. "If I stay longer then I fear that the inspector may still try to say that I killed Gianni. He may also try to say that you helped me. It is better for everyone that I go when I can. And Cosimo told me that his son

382

has to drive into Florence tomorrow and will give me a ride to the train station."

"So soon." She came around the table and embraced me. "I will miss you, little one. You have become a second daughter. And Angelina has enjoyed your company, too. She says I am old and boring and it is good to speak to someone her age."

"I know. I have enjoyed every minute with you, especially your cooking. And I am sorry that I will now never learn to become an Italian cook."

"We will have a good meal tonight if it is to be your last," she said. "A mushroom risotto, perhaps, before the aubergine Parmesan and panna cotta, definitely. You can help me to prepare them, if you like. We will start with crostini. Perhaps Signor Renzo will want to help us, too?"

"Renzo?" I asked.

"Yes, I invited him to join us for dinner, and I know that he loves to cook."

I could tell from her face what she was thinking: she was playing matchmaker with Renzo and me. On any other occasion I might have welcomed her help, but now I knew what I did, I didn't want any more to do with him. The chats we had, his taking me to his old house—they were probably designed to find out what I knew and what I didn't know. He was just following instructions from Cosimo. I took this one stage further—had he also witnessed Gianni pushing the envelope into my room and now wanted to retrieve its contents or find out what it said?

I couldn't stop him from coming, but I would have to tread very carefully this evening. I put my purse back in my room, locked the door again, and came to help Paola in the garden. Later I had a rest, locking myself in, but I slept undisturbed and awoke feeling refreshed. Heading over to the farmhouse to see if the preparations had begun for dinner, I was startled to find Renzo standing close to my door.

"Oh," I gasped, and took an involuntary step back.

"Sorry if I startled you, Joanna," he said. "Paola wanted me to pick more asparagus and see if any more tomatoes were ripe. I came early to help prepare the meal. She is making a real feast for you."

"I know. She told me. She is so kind."

"She has become fond of you," he said. "She is sorry you have to leave so soon."

"I am, too, but it's better that way, isn't it?" I said. "I would rather be far away from that inspector. He still seems to think I might be somehow involved with Gianni's murder, which is ridiculous. I only exchanged maybe a dozen words with the man at a table full of other men."

"Quite ridiculous," he said. "But I, too, am sorry you are going to leave. I would like to have found out the truth about your father and my mother. And the beautiful boy. I can't stop thinking about it. If your father was in this area long enough for my mother to have a child, how could they possibly have kept both those things secret? And would he have hidden a child where nobody else could find him, only to write to her about him months later?"

"Perhaps the child was given to a family in the hills to look after?" I suggested. "She was going to reclaim him later, but she never did."

"Then why does nobody know about this? Surely the family would have told someone? They would have said, 'A British airman left a baby with us. Now we have to find his mother.' There would have been talk. Old memories would have been jogged."

"Yes," I said. "And yet nobody in San Salvatore seems to know anything about a British airman. And everyone believes that your mother ran off with a German."

"It's strange," he said, straightening up from where he had just picked a big ripe tomato, "but old memories are beginning to come back to me. I remember I was sick for a while. I'm not sure what it was. Measles? Something like that. Anyway, I couldn't leave the house and my mother went out every day looking for things for us to eat. Mushrooms, chestnuts—once there was a pigeon, I remember that. I wanted to go with her, but she said that I had to stay indoors because of my chest. I watched her going up the hill with her basket. She was worried about me and hated to leave me. But we had to eat, didn't we?"

"She was worried about you?" I stared at him. "Renzo, everything you say tells me that your mother loved you dearly. She would not have abandoned you, I'm sure. She would not have run off and just left you behind. I'm sure she must have been forced to leave against her will."

"But everyone said . . . ," he began hesitantly. "I've always been told . . ."

"You know what I think?" I said. "I think someone betrayed your mother and my father, maybe for money, or maybe out of jealousy, or maybe to save their own skin. And the Germans took her away." I realised as I said it that I might just be causing him more grief. What if the person who betrayed her was Cosimo? Then I remembered that Gianni had seen the British airman being driven off, and he was an opportunist and a sneak. Perhaps he had tipped off the Germans that a British airman had been hiding out. "Did you see her go, or had she just gone by the time you woke up in the morning?"

He frowned, trying to recollect. "No, I was there, I'm pretty sure. Yes, she came over and kissed me and told me to be a good boy and that she'd be back soon. She was crying. There were teardrops on her cheeks. And then she wanted to say more and kiss me again but the soldier shouted at her and . . ." He broke off, a look of wonder on his face. "It wasn't the soldier who was staying at our house—the nice one. It was another soldier. A big man. I remember that he seemed to fill the whole doorway. And he yelled in a fierce voice."

"You see?" I smiled at him triumphantly. "Your mother and my father were innocent. They loved each other, and they were betrayed."

"Yes," he said softly. "I have to believe you."

"Are we ever going to get those tomatoes for tonight's meal?" came Paola's big voice across the rows of vegetables.

Renzo grinned to me. "The slave driver calls. Come and help prepare the meal."

I followed him along the narrow path, now more confused than ever. Had Cosimo betrayed Renzo's mother and then felt guilty enough that he had adopted him? Perhaps Renzo knew no more than I did.

Renzo fell back to wait for me. "I've been thinking," he said. "My mother always went up the hill with her basket. It is possible that your father was hidden somewhere in the woods or even in the old monastery. We should go and look tomorrow before you leave us."

"I was wondering about the old monastery myself," I said. "But it just looks like piles of ruined stone. Could someone really have sought shelter up there?"

"I went up a couple of times when I was a boy," Renzo said. "It's all fenced off and nobody is supposed to go there because the hillside is in danger of collapsing. But of course when we were boys we had to do it on a dare. There truly wasn't much to see. The walls of the old chapel still stood, but there was no roof. And the floor was piled high with rubble. The rooms of the monastery were completely flattened. If your father hid out up there, then he would have had a miserable time."

"He'd been to a British boarding school," I said. "He was probably used to a miserable time."

This made Renzo throw back his head and laugh. "You English and your boarding schools," he said. "Was your school also like that?"

"I didn't board at the school I told you about, but it was certainly not a good experience for me. I couldn't wait to leave."

"So you, too, have had your share of miserable times?"

"Yes, you could say that."

He put a hand on my shoulder. "Perhaps it is time to put the past behind you and to look forward to the future. You will be a rich and famous lawyer. You will travel and marry an equally rich man and have the perfect two children and live happily in one of those big, draughty English houses."

I looked up at him, horribly conscious of his hand, warm and comforting on my shoulder. "I'm not sure that's what I want at all," I said.

"So what do you want?"

"I'm not sure. I'll know when I find it."

Renzo released me and stood aside for me to enter the house first.

"*Allora.* Now we get to work," Paola said. "With so many courses to prepare I need much assistance. First we make the toppings for the crostini."

"What is a crostini?" I asked.

"Like bruschetta, but instead of being baked, the slices of bread are grilled," Renzo said. "More chewy and less brittle." He turned to Paola. "And what toppings have you in mind?"

"The fresh asparagus, naturally . . ."

"Wrapped in prosciutto crudo, naturally?" he said. "And fennel? I see you have fennel growing in your garden. Should I dig up a bulb and slice it thinly with some pecorino?"

"That would be a wonderful idea," she said. "And I have a good tapenade here."

"And will you allow me to make the risotto?" he asked. "It was one of my specialties when I was sous-chef at the restaurant in Soho."

"With pleasure," Paola said. "But you must show the young lady how you prepare it. She

389

wants to learn how to cook our Italian food, you know."

He looked at me with interest. "You want to learn to cook? Lawyers don't need such skills. They can employ a cook, surely."

"Not this lawyer," I said. "At the moment I am still a poor articled clerk, earning almost no money until I pass my exam. And even if I get a good job, I think that coming home to cook a good meal would be very relaxing."

"You are right," he said. "When I am cooking I think of nothing else. It is as if all the troubles of the world are shut out and it is just me and the food."

Paola frowned and Renzo translated for her.

"You should speak Italian to the young lady," she said. "How else is she going to improve? And already she understands quite well."

"All right. In future, only Italian, Joanna, *capisci*?" he said, giving me a challenging look.

I was given the herbs to chop up for the sauce to go on the aubergine—oregano, Italian parsley—and then lots of garlic to crush. I was concentrating hard when Renzo came up behind me. "No, that is not how you hold the knife," he said. His fingers came over mine. "Straight. Up and down. Swift motion like this. See?"

"Renzo, you will distract the young lady from her task if you flirt with her like that," Paola said.

"What does this word mean?" I asked. When Renzo translated I felt myself blushing.

"Flirting? Who was flirting?" he demanded. "I only wish to correct the way she cuts parsley. If she wants to cook well she must develop good skills."

"You say what you like," Paola said, chuckling.

"I say what I observe. See, her cheeks have become quite pink."

"But she did not push me away, so she must have liked it," he replied. "Now let me see you cut, Jo."

I realised he was using the abbreviation of my name that only a few people had used in my life. Scarlet was one and Adrian was another. But coming from Renzo it sounded right. I started cutting, making smooth and even chopping motions. He watched, nodding. "You learn quickly."

"It's a shame she is not going to stay longer. You and I could teach her much," Paola said. "Instead she goes back to London and to her diet of roast beef and sausages."

"Yes, it is a shame," Renzo said.

I had to agree with them. I went back to chopping my herbs.

CHAPTER THIRTY-SIX

JOANNA

June 1973

By eight o'clock the meal was ready.

"I think outside, don't you?" Paola said. "Since it is such a beautiful evening."

So a table was laid with a white cloth out in the garden under the cherry tree. This time there were no simple ceramic beakers, but silverware and crystal. I took my place looking out away from the farmhouse. The sun was setting over the western hills, and bats flitted through the pink twilight. The air was scented with honeysuckle and jasmine. It was almost like being in a dream.

Angelina came to join us, bringing olive oil and a plate of olives. It turned out that Renzo had brought wine from his father's vineyards. We started with a crisp white as Paola brought out the tray of crostini. I had to try one of each topping as I had done my first night in San Salvatore in the piazza. The asparagus wrapped in slivers of uncured ham and drizzled with truffle oil; the thin slices of fennel, which was another new flavour for me; the sharp sheep's cheese served with fig jam. All of these tasted like little miracles and frankly would have been enough for a grand evening meal on their own.

But then we had Renzo's risotto—creamy rice with mushrooms cooked in a rich broth. When Renzo saw my nod of appreciation he said, "In London I used to make this with seafood. You should try it. The fish broth and the mussels and shrimp are just perfect. It is too bad I can't make a trip to the coast and bring back the right ingredients to cook for you."

"I can't imagine it would be much better than this," I said. "I grew up being forced to eat rice pudding at school, and I've shied away from rice ever since."

He laughed. "The English unfortunately don't know what interesting things can be done with simple ingredients. Give them cabbage or Brussels sprouts and they boil them to death."

"Maybe you can come back to England one day, open your own restaurant, and educate everyone," I said.

I watched the joy drain from his face. "Maybe," he said. "But I don't see that day happening. My father's health does not improve, and frankly he needs me here. Family comes first, does it not?"

I thought about this—a strange notion to me. I certainly had not put my father first in any of my decisions. Maybe I had failed him. I didn't like to think about it, but I pictured his body lying cold in the grass. And now it was too late to say I was sorry.

"But we can fix these gloomy thoughts," Renzo said, "with another good wine. This is the pride of our vineyard. In England the only Italian wine you know is the rough Chianti that comes in a straw bottle. But this is from our premium grapes, perfectly aged in oak barrels. You will taste the difference."

The white wine was already having its effect, and I hesitated as I took a sip of the red. *I don't have far to walk home,* I told myself. The first taste was smooth and rich, like drinking red velvet. "Oh," I said, and Renzo smiled.

"Now you will go home and be a wine snob and say to your friends, 'This is not like that cheap Chianti that they produce, the wine in the straw bottle,' " he said.

"I doubt that I could afford to buy this in England," I said. "Wine is very expensive."

"You are right, you couldn't buy this in England," he said. "We only produce a few cases of this wine, and it goes straight to our preferred customers in Rome and Milan. Film stars, racing car drivers, and millionaires."

"Then I am indeed honoured." My gaze met his and I felt a shiver go down my spine. I tried to make light of it. "But don't top up my glass or I may not find my way home."

"Don't worry, Renzo will escort you," Paola said.

That did bring me back to reality. Renzo walking me back to the little house, past the well into which Gianni had been stuffed head first—and the high probability that Renzo knew something about this. Had he been sent to get me drunk? To gain entrance to my room and find the envelope that Gianni had pushed through my window?

"What's the matter?" Renzo asked me, as if reading my thoughts.

"Just that I am sad I will be leaving all this beauty tomorrow."

"And I am sad that you are going," he said. "Perhaps you can return in less worrying times."

"I doubt that," I said. "The inspector might invent new charges against me if I come back."

He laughed, but I sensed that I wasn't too far from the truth.

I got up to help Paola clear away the dishes, but she waved for me to stay seated. "Why else do I have a daughter?" she said. "You are the guest. Sit. Talk with Renzo."

As they disappeared into the house, I grinned. "I'm afraid Paola is trying to do some match-making."

"She has a good heart," he replied. "And her judgment is not bad, either."

I chuckled nervously because I was highly conscious of his presence across the table from me, his crisp white shirt unbuttoned at the throat, his unruly black curls, and his eyes that sparkled as if they were on fire. It must have been the wine, but I wanted him to take me in his arms and kiss me.

That ridiculous thought was banished by Paola coming back with the big dish of aubergine Parmesan. I didn't think I had any room for another mouthful, but once I took my first bite I had to finish my plate. So rich, so creamy. And the aubergine tasted like a really good meat.

We finished the meal with the little dishes of panna cotta—smooth and white and slipping easily down the throat, and to accompany it a glass of limoncello, the local liqueur. A soft, velvety darkness had fallen over the land. The night air was full of the sound of crickets and frogs. Renzo stood up. "I should probably be getting home," he said. "My father will wonder where I am." He looked at me. "May I escort you to your room first?"

"Oh no," I said, laughing. "I must help Paola and Angelina with the washing up. We must have made a lot of dishes dirty."

"Of course you do not need to do this," Paola said. "Let the young man escort you if he volunteers. I know if a handsome man offered to escort me to my room I would not say no. Unfortunately such offers do not come anymore." And she laughed.

I had no choice. Renzo offered me his arm. I

took it, giving him a nervous smile. "Honestly, Renzo, I can find my way to my room unaided," I said. "And I'm sure Cosimo will be pacing the floor waiting for you to come home."

"Let him pace," Renzo said. "Did it not occur to you that I might want to spend some time alone with you?"

I looked up at him then. He was giving me a little half-smile. "I don't know what it is about you," he said. "I find myself strangely drawn to you. Maybe you remind me of the girl I once knew in London, the one I might have married if things had been different." He turned to face me. "Do I not detect that you are also a little attracted to me?"

"Maybe a little," I said, trying not to ignore the warning alarm going off in my head. *Cosimo's son, remember.*

"Then perhaps it is in our shared history," Renzo said. "Maybe it is the story of my mother and your father finally being completed. It is fate. Destiny. There is nothing we can do about it."

"Do you think so?" I asked.

"How do I know?" he said, smiling at me. "I just know that at this moment I want to kiss you. Is that all right with you?"

He didn't wait for an answer. He took me in his arms and his lips moved toward mine. I could feel my heart racing, the small frisson of danger mingling with my desire for him. I don't know where it might have led, but suddenly the ground beneath our feet was moving. It only lasted for a few seconds, but Renzo held me tight until the rocking stopped.

"Was that another earthquake?" I asked.

"Just an aftershock," he said. "Don't worry."

"Isn't there a song that goes something like, 'I felt the earth move under my feet'?" I laughed, a little shakily.

"Now you know it really happens," he said.

"Joanna? Renzo? Is all well with you? It was only a small earthquake," Paola called from the open door.

"All is well," Renzo responded, releasing me. "I think I'd better go," he said, "before the earth moves under our feet again." He touched my cheek. "I will see you in the morning. Sleep well."

And then he went. I let myself into the little room, locked my door, undressed, and lay on my bed staring at the ceiling. Was it possible, just possible, that Renzo really did have feelings for me?

CHAPTER THIRTY-SEVEN

HUGO

December 1944

As soon as Sofia had departed, Hugo got to work lugging pieces of masonry, as big and heavy as he could carry, to pile on top of the old door. He was still working when the sun came up. He admired his achievement—the area now matched the rest of the rubble on the floor. No one would ever suspect that an entrance to the crypt lay beneath. The beautiful boy was safe.

Then he attacked the next phase: hiding any trace of his occupation of the chapel. He had already been wearing all the extra clothes to keep out the cold, so set about dismantling his shelter, hurling the pieces of wood around the chapel. He took the blanket, sheepskin, bowl, and spoon and scattered them around the rubble, then tossed a few rocks on to them for good measure. When he was done he looked around in satisfaction. Nobody would ever know that he had been here.

All he had to do now was wait. He didn't think it was likely that Sofia would be able to bring the cart to him that very day. He also didn't think she'd risk being out at night. It would be too suspicious, and how could she see to drive the wagon in the dark without lanterns? But tomorrow, at first light—that would be logical if she was going to market with a load of turnips. He ate the last crumbs of bread, drank some water, and fantasised about reaching a town to the south, an Allied camp, hot food, a real bed, safety for him and for Sofia and her son. When darkness fell he went and recovered the sheepskin to sit on and dozed sitting up. The night seemed eternal. When the glow of dawn came in the east, he got up, then wondered if he should make his way down the steps to wait for Sofia in the forest. He decided against this in case she came by the other side of the rock, up the track to the precipice, and he somehow had to clamber down to meet her. He wasn't sure he was up to that feat and decided to go around and scout out the best way down, just in case.

As he came out of the chapel and stood blinking in the bright daylight, he saw a movement among the trees. His heart leapt and he waved. The next thing he knew, two German soldiers emerged, their guns pointed at him. One of them came nimbly up the steps.

"You are the Englishman?" he asked.

Hugo thought of lying. His Italian was now quite fluent, and he had even picked up Sofia's Tuscan dialect. But they would want to see his papers. They would search him and find his logbook and identity tags.

"Yes," he said. "English pilot. Officer."

"Give me your weapon, then put up your hands."

He had no alternative but to obey. He handed over the revolver. The German did not ask for his knife. "You come with us now. *Schnell.* Run."

"I have a broken leg," he said, lifting his trouser to reveal his splint. "Leg *kaputt.* Can't walk fast."

There was a rapid conversation between the two men. Even with his scant knowledge of German, picked up on a couple of skiing holidays, Hugo sensed that one of them wanted to shoot him on the spot. The other disagreed, and Hugo thought he understood that their colonel would want to question him first.

The German standing in front of him motioned for him to move with his weapon. Hugo went down the steps as slowly as he dared, hanging on to the railing and lowering himself from step to step. He had the knife in his pocket. There was a slight chance he might be able to use it. At the foot of the steps, the two men conversed again in low voices, and he could tell they didn't agree about something. But the one who had remained at the foot of the steps prevailed.

"Keep your hands on your head. March," the senior soldier barked at him.

They forced him ahead of them through the trees, one of them digging at his back with the barrel of his weapon. Hugo's leg began to hurt him, and he stumbled a couple of times.

"Do not play tricks or we will shoot you now," one of them said.

On the other side of the trees an open military vehicle was waiting. The soldiers ordered him into the back seat. "Keep hands on your head. Do not try to escape, or Heinrich will be happy to shoot you," the one who spoke English said. He climbed into the driver's seat, and the other soldier slid into the back beside Hugo, his weapon thrust into Hugo's side. They drove off, bouncing over the ruts between the olive trees.

For the first time since the shock of being caught, Hugo's brain began to work. He scanned the fields for any sign of a cart. Had they captured Sofia and made her tell them where he was hiding? Had her son inadvertently given her away? His heart was thumping so loudly in his chest that he found it hard to breathe. If only she was safe, nothing mattered. They did not turn downward toward the road in the valley. Instead they went up through the vineyards and joined the road he had seen on the hilltop when he first arrived—the narrow dirt road lined with cypress trees that led up to the village. Hugo prayed he was not being taken up to the village to be paraded until someone confessed to helping him, or to be forced to watch the whole village slaughtered before he met his own end.

He heaved a small sigh of relief when they turned away from the village, heading north along the ridge. He scanned the countryside to both sides. No sign of a cart and horse. No sign of anybody moving in the fields. If he encountered a sympathetic officer, a soldier of the old school, he had a chance of being treated as a fellow officer and prisoner of war—just the slightest chance of remaining alive. He tried to think of Langley Hall, his father, his wife and child. Instead all he saw was Sofia's face—so lovely, so gentle—and his heart ached at the thought he'd never see her again.

After a few miles they joined a wider road, this one paved and no longer tree-lined. The wind sweeping down from the north was brutal. Hugo could see a town silhouetted on the hilltop ahead. Several German military vehicles were drawn up beside the road. Hugo's car stopped and there was a brief exchange. As they spoke Hugo noticed the men glancing up nervously. He could not turn round, but he could hear the reason for their concern—the deep thrum of approaching aircraft.

Soon the low drone became a roar. The German soldiers who had been standing around rushed for their vehicles or fled into the fields to hide among the vineyards. The first wave passed overhead, their shadows making black crosses on the fields. Big American bombers. There was a whistling sound and a bomb came down, striking near the head of the convoy of German vehicles. A petrol tank exploded, and Hugo felt the blast sucking air from his lungs. A second bomb landed just in front of them. The driver of his vehicle swore and abruptly put the car into reverse, throwing Hugo and the soldier guarding him off balance. It was only a fraction of a second, but Hugo decided to take his chance to escape.

As he attempted to clamber out of the vehicle, there was a deafening roar of aircraft noise overhead. One of the fighters at the rear of the formation had broken off and was coming in low over the road. A machine gun spat out bullets. His driver flew upward as he was hit, then slumped forward. The vehicle careened wildly across the road. A second bullet struck the man beside Hugo. The vehicle crashed into a burning lorry and rolled over. Hugo was thrown out. He was still conscious and trying to crawl away when the petrol tank exploded and he knew no more.

CHAPTER THIRTY-EIGHT

JOANNA

June 1973

As soon as I awoke the next morning the first thing that came into my head was that I was leaving San Salvatore today. Renzo would drive me to the station, and I'd never see him again. And it occurred to me that I might have misunderstood Cosimo's desire to get rid of me in a hurry. Maybe it was not a fear that I knew something dangerous—maybe it was that he sensed Renzo was becoming attracted to me. It was quite a coincidence that everyone Renzo fell in love with was somehow whisked away from him. *Was that Cosimo's doing?* I asked myself. Had he arranged for the local girl to attend a fashion design school she couldn't possibly afford? And bringing him back from England when he had a stroke was understandable, but keeping him here, needing his assistance every moment, was that really necessary? Cosimo was clearly one of those people who see themselves as the centre of the universe and see others only when they can be useful.

This thought led to another one: Renzo had

mentioned that Cosimo had been in love but the girl had rejected him. Might that girl have been Sofia, and to get his revenge he tipped off the Germans about her and my father? That would definitely explain why Cosimo had smeared her reputation and why he wanted me to go so quickly.

I was still trying to make sense of these thoughts when I went over to the farmhouse to take a bath and then joined Paola and Angelina for breakfast. The meal was a solemn one. Paola looked as if she might burst into tears at any moment. "And I haven't taught you anything about mushrooms yet," she said. "The little wood mushrooms, so delicious. And ravioli . . . we haven't learned to make ravioli." She reached across and took my hand. "Promise me you will come back, *cara* Joanna. We will have such a good time, no?"

"I hope so," I said. "I hope it will be possible when this sad time with Gianni is over."

"Too bad you are not a lawyer here in Italy," she said. "You would know how to speak to this police inspector so that he listens and sees the truth."

"Unfortunately we don't know the truth," I said.

"Whatever it is, it can have nothing to do with you," she said firmly.

That's where you're wrong, I thought but didn't say. We finished the meal. "I must go and pack,"

I said. I went back to my room and folded my clothes neatly in my suitcase. Soon I'd be back in grey and rainy London, buying a pre-cooked steak and kidney pie from Sainsbury's for my dinner and wondering what my future would hold.

I hadn't quite finished when I heard a tap on my door.

"Come in," I called, and was startled when Renzo entered, not Paola.

"Are you ready?" he asked. "We have to hurry if we wish to see the monastery before we drive to Florence. My father insists I see a man about our grapes before this fellow leaves for his afternoon snooze."

"I just need to pack these last few items," I said. "Shall I leave them until we get back?"

"Or finish them now. Whatever you want," he said, and sat on the bed. It would have been disturbing enough at any time to have Renzo sitting on my bed watching me as I crammed undies into a suitcase. Now, knowing what I knew, fearing what I feared, it was almost unbearable. I picked up the spare shoes, the ones with the items from Gianni in the toes, and stuffed them with undies and stockings. Renzo said nothing as I put them into my suitcase. I finished, looked around the room, and closed the suitcase.

"There," I said. "All done and ready to go."

"*Bene*," he said. "Good. Now let us go on our adventure."

We cut across the vineyard between the rows of vines and picked up a track that went up the hill between olive groves. In the distance we heard a shout and saw a cart going up the hillside on another track, the man exhorting his horse to move faster. Renzo stared at it, frowning.

"A cart," he said. "Something about a cart."

"What about it?"

"A flash of memory returning. Something about a cart. A man came to our door and said he had brought the cart and he wanted payment first. But my mother had already gone and he went away again."

"Do you think she was planning to escape with this cart?" I asked, looking up at him hopefully. "Maybe she and my father were going to escape together, or maybe she had arranged the cart to transport my father to safety."

He shrugged. "Who knows? There is nobody alive to tell us now. That is what is so frustrating, to realise that we shall never know."

I nodded agreement. We walked on in silence. "Did you sleep well last night?" he asked.

"Very well." I gave him a little smile.

He smiled, too. "I'm sorry the earthquake interrupted us. And now there is no more time." He paused. "I was wondering, if I managed to come to London someday, could I see you again?"

"If Cosimo would let you out of his sight for that long," I said without thinking.

He frowned. "I am not a prisoner of my father, you know. It is just that with his limited mobility I have to do things he would otherwise have done. But I go to Florence on occasion. And Rome. So why not London? I am sure his wines are not well enough represented in Harrods."

"Why not?" I laughed. "And yes, I would like it if you came to visit me."

"You must leave me your address."

"I don't know where I'll be," I said. "I've been sleeping on a friend's couch since"—I was about to say, "Since I came out of hospital and my boyfriend went off to marry someone else"—"since I had to give up my last flat," I finished. "But I've just inherited a little money from my father. I'm hoping it will be enough for a down payment on a small flat somewhere."

"In London?"

"Yes."

"But you hate the city," he said. "I can tell that you hate the city."

"I have to work, and it would be lonely living out in the country."

"I see." He looked at me and I thought for a moment he was going to say something, but then he looked away and stomped on up the hill. "This is quite a long way," he said. "I can't believe my mother came up here with her basket to the woods every day. They were strong people in her generation."

He was right. The steep climb was making me perspire, and I was finding it harder to chat easily. I was glad when the path entered the woodland at the crest of the hill. Here it was cool and quiet, soft underfoot, and smelled sweet. The band of trees was not very broad, however, and we came out on the other side to see the rocky pinnacle rising above us. All around it was a fence with signs saying "Danger. Keep Out. Unstable Rocks" every few feet.

I glanced at Renzo. "Is this all right?"

"We'll have to see, won't we?" he said. "Come on, here is where we can get through the fence." He led me to a section where one could squeeze through. Ahead there were steps cut into the turf. A riot of poppies bloomed along with other wild flowers. With the crag towering over us it was a brilliant spectacle, and the thought came to me that my father would have loved to have painted it.

The first steps were quite easy. Then a second flight went almost vertically up the rock face. These steps had crumbled in places, and the rock beside the stairs had fallen away so that they hung out over a sheer drop. I swallowed hard but wasn't going to let Renzo see that I was afraid.

"You go first and I'll be right behind you to catch you," he said.

That set off an alarm bell in my head. Had this been the plan all along? Take the English girl up to a place where no one comes and throw her off a cliff?

"No, you go first," I said. "I want to see which steps are stable and which aren't."

"Oh, you want me to plunge to my death, do you?" He turned back to me, laughing.

"Rather you than me," I replied.

"That's hardly true love, is it?" he asked. "What about Romeo and Juliet?"

"They were too young to know any better," I replied.

"All right. I'll go first. Stay over to the right side of the steps," he said, and started upward.

A stiff breeze swept in from distant mountains. Far below on the left side I could see the remains of an old track leading down to a road in the valley. Tiny lorries and cars the size of Dinky Toys made their way along the road. After Renzo had gone three or four steps, I followed him, holding on tightly to the rusted iron railing on the right. We both came safely to the top and stood on a former forecourt to admire the view. On all sides of us were range after range of forested hills. Hill towns like San Salvatore perched precariously on the tops of some of them. Old fortresses rose out of woodland.

It felt as if one could see to the end of the world.

"Beautiful, is it not?" he asked, putting an arm around my shoulder.

It should have been the most magical moment, standing close to him and sharing this view, but I couldn't quite shake off the tension.

"We shouldn't stay long," I said. "We might be seen and get into trouble."

"And they would fine us a few hundred lira for trespassing. So what?" He laughed. "Relax, Joanna, enjoy this while you can."

Again the choice of words made me glance up at him, but he was gazing out with a look of pure delight on his face.

"You wouldn't have been happy if you had stayed in London," I said. "You love it here."

"Yes," he said. "I do. But I also want to further my career. If I had come home as an accomplished chef, I would have opened my own restaurant. I could have turned our little town into a tourist destination."

"You could still do that," I said. "You cook very well. Your food is delicious."

"But I do not have that certificate that says I am trained in a culinary academy, do I? One needs that piece of paper."

I thought of my bar exam. One needs that piece of paper. Of course.

"Let's explore," I said.

"Tread carefully," Renzo warned. "These paving stones are uneven and some are loose. Here, take my hand." His hand felt warm and firm in mine. I began to let the tension slip away. We made our way toward the buildings. Small trees and shrubs had sprouted up between the cracked stones, and on the pile of rubble to our left there were now bigger trees growing. A creeper with bright blue flowers covered much of the rubble. We stopped, staring around.

"Nowhere anybody could hide out here," Renzo said. "It would have had to be the chapel."

On the right what used to be four walls rose up. Curved marble steps led to a gaping hole where front doors had once been. We stepped inside. It was cool and in dark shade where we stood, but the sunlight was striking the opposite wall, where the remains of a mural were still visible. A woman with a crown on her head still smiling sweetly. Clouds. Angels. I looked down, ready to go forward, but the floor was covered in rubble. Great beams lay across roof tiles and stones.

"I don't think my father would have found much shelter in here, do you?" I said.

"At least he would have been out of the wind," Renzo said. "He could have built himself a little shelter with all these stones."

"Then where is it?" I asked.

He looked around and shrugged. "There have been earthquakes since he was here. Anything

413

would have fallen down. Come on. Let's take a look."

Again he took my hand and we clambered over mounds of rubble. But there was nothing. No discarded tins or cigarette packets to indicate an Englishman might once have been here.

I sighed. "I don't think there is any point in staying any longer. If he hid up here he was found by the Germans. He escaped and made his way back to England. But there is also no proof that your mother ever came up here, either."

"We might have got it completely wrong," Renzo said. "Perhaps he hid in the woods—built himself a little shelter of branches. Or she might even have risked hiding him in our cellar."

I shook my head. "Then the people of San Salvatore would have seen the Germans taking him away. And you would probably have all been executed for hiding an Englishman."

"True. Very well, we have come. We have seen. And now it is time to drive to Florence, I am afraid. The very least I can do is treat you to a lunch in a good restaurant before you catch your train home."

"Thank you." I hesitated, still reluctant to move. Did I sense my father's presence here? Maybe if I had been closer to him . . .

As I went to move forward I was jolted off my feet. My first thought was that one of the great beams had shifted beneath the rubble. But as

414

I went down on all fours I could feel the whole floor shaking.

"Another earthquake!" Renzo shouted. "Can you make it to the door? We don't want stones flying off the walls and coming down on us."

But it was impossible to stand. The floor danced as if it was alive. Around me I heard stones thudding down from the tops of the walls. I crouched, covering my head and waiting for it to stop. Then there came a deep rumble and a thud. And miraculously the shaking stopped. I looked up and saw Renzo staggering to his feet.

"Wow, that was a big one," he said. "Are you all right?"

"I think so. It was impossible to move, wasn't it?"

He nodded. "I hope the town is not damaged." Then he added, "I hope the staircase hasn't fallen and we find ourselves trapped up here."

"Cheerful thought," I said, and he laughed.

I stood up and tried to move toward him. Stones rolled away as I stepped on them. Then I stopped, staring. "Renzo. Over here. Look."

He came to where I was pointing. In the floor beside the right-hand wall there was now a gaping hole. And what's more, steps led down from it.

"It must have been the former crypt," Renzo said.

"You don't suppose my father hid down there, do you?"

"Then why was it all covered up again?"

"An earthquake after he left?"

"Possibly. Do you want to go down and see? The floor up here might be very unstable. It could cave in if there is another aftershock."

"Let's just go a little way and see what's there," I said. "You smoke, don't you? Do you have matches?"

"Yes, in my pocket. I'm game if you are."

He picked his way over to the opening and started down the steps. They were now covered with rubble where the floor above had fallen in. Renzo kicked some of it down, clearing a path for me. I followed step by step. When we were in almost total darkness Renzo lit a match. I heard him say what was probably a swear word in Italian.

I could see what he meant. It was a perfect little chapel with a carved altar at one end, statues of saints in niches, and several large paintings on the walls.

"Look at these," Renzo said, holding up the match to the nearest painting. "They are magnificent. So lucky that the German soldiers didn't find them. They looted any art they could get their hands on."

The match went out. I waited halfway down the steps until he had struck another, then came to join him. It smelled damp. A chilly draft curled around our feet, making it feel strange and spooky. I moved closer to Renzo. "Any sign of my father?"

He had advanced around the room. "There is a door over here. Perhaps it leads somewhere where your father could have hidden."

He wrestled with the bolt and opened it. It would only open a foot or so.

"The passage behind it must be blocked," he said.

"Let me see if I can squeeze through. I'm slimmer than you," I said.

"Be careful."

I squeezed around the door. "You were right," I said. "The passage behind is blocked, but there is something stopping the door from opening. Wait a minute. Light another match for me."

Renzo did so. I bent to pick up the object that was lying at my feet. "It seems to be a painting," I said. I struggled to lift it as it was jammed so completely between the door and the massive pile of rubble. "I can't budge it," I called back. "Let me see if I can move some of this rock."

As I tried to clear rocks away, more cascaded down to join them. I was in danger of starting a small avalanche and trapping myself behind that door. "It won't . . . ," I began, giving the painting a savage jerk. Then I almost fell over when it came free in my hands. "I've got it," I yelled triumphantly.

"Pass it through to me," Renzo said.

As I went to do this I had a sudden sense of fear. Was this all part of a plan? He'd take the painting and shut me in, and no one would ever find me. *Ridiculous,* I told myself. I had to start trusting again sometime. I had to believe, to take a leap of faith. I handed him the painting. As I squeezed myself out around the door, I heard him gasp.

"We've found it, Joanna. It's their beautiful boy."

CHAPTER THIRTY-NINE

JOANNA

June 1973

We carried the painting over to where the sunlight came down the steps.

"Oh." There was nothing more I could say. The radiant child, laughing as he held his chubby little hands out to the fluttering cherubs—I had never seen anything more exquisite.

"So they were down here," I said. "And I bet they hid that painting away so that nobody could steal it before the war was over and they could come back to rescue it."

"Yes," Renzo said. "That must have been true. Behind the door of a passage that went nowhere. And only someone as thin as you could squeeze around. Quite safe where nobody would ever find it."

"As you say, quite safe," said a voice from above. Cosimo stood at the top of the steps, his large shape blotting out the sunlight.

"Father, how did you get up here?" Renzo asked.

"With difficulty, but I made it. I drove up in

the Land Rover and hauled myself up the steps. I wanted to make sure you were safe after the earthquake." He was speaking calmly, evenly, but I could hardly breathe. "Hand the painting up to me, boy."

"It's magnificent, Father. There are other paintings down here, but this one—this is the most beautiful I have ever seen." Renzo started up the steps with the painting. "Look. Isn't it magnificent?" He held it up to Cosimo.

"It is indeed. We must decide what should be done with it. Now come up quickly."

I looked up and saw that he was now holding a gun. "The young lady will have unfortunately had an accident. She was warned about coming up here. So dangerous."

"What are you talking about, Father? Put that thing away," Renzo exclaimed. I could hear the shock in his voice. "Why are you behaving like this?"

"She has been asking too many questions," Cosimo said. "She wants the truth about what happened in the war. Why does she ask these questions?"

"I told you. I wanted to find out about my father," I called up to him.

"No, I don't believe you. There was no English airman. Sofia ran off with a German."

"No, she was taken away because you betrayed her!" I shouted up the stairs. Renzo was still standing halfway up the flight, between me and Cosimo.

"That is not true. I loved her. She spurned me, but I took in her son because of my love for her."

"I think you wanted her land," I said. "You felt guilty so you took in Renzo."

"You talk rubbish," Cosimo said. "Get up here now, boy."

"No, Father. Put that gun away. Joanna knows nothing that can harm you."

"Ask him who killed Gianni Martinelli!" I shouted before I realised that it would have been wiser to stay silent. My voice echoed around the crypt. "Gianni was the only one who knew the truth about what happened."

"What truth?" Renzo demanded.

I glanced at Renzo, trying to decide whether to remain silent, whether I could trust him to protect me from his father.

"Gianni liked to run messages and spy on people," I went on, speaking fast and in English. "He saw the massacre. He saw that Cosimo betrayed the partisans to the Germans."

"No, that can't be true. It can't," Renzo said.

"Get up here instantly, boy!" Cosimo bellowed. He was waving the gun.

"I'm not going to let you shoot anyone, Father. Have you gone mad?"

"And I'm not going to lose everything I've

worked for all these years." I heard the click as the gun was cocked.

"No," Renzo said. "I've suspected things about you, but I've stayed quiet out of loyalty. But not this. You are not going to harm her." He dropped the painting and bounded up the rest of the flight of steps. I picked up the painting as it came bouncing down toward me. The beautiful boy smiled at me. I clasped it to me as I made my way up the steps. Over my head I could hear grunts and an animal-like growl. Renzo and Cosimo were locked in combat. Renzo was taller, but Cosimo was a big bull of a man and still very strong despite his stroke. Renzo had his hand on Cosimo's wrist, trying to make him drop the gun. It went off, the sound of the bullet ricocheting from the walls. Pigeons fluttered upward, alarmed. Renzo and Cosimo were staggering on the uneven floor, slithering over rocks and beams. Cosimo tried to slam Renzo against the wall. There was a grunt and a howl of pain, but Renzo didn't let go.

I had reached the top of the steps and started to creep around the outside of the wall toward the front door. I was close enough to see freedom ahead of me when I heard a shout.

"Hello up there? Anyone there? Joanna?"

Cosimo hesitated for a second. I fled out through the door to see Nigel Barton standing at the bottom of the steps. His face lit up and he waved when he saw me.

"Hello, Joanna. They told me you'd gone up here, so I thought I'd come and surprise you with the good news. But is everything all right? I thought I heard what sounded like a gunshot. But of course it might have been—"

"Nigel," I interrupted as I came down the steps as quickly as I dared. "Run back to the village and get help. There's a man with a gun. Go."

Nigel's mouth opened in surprise. "Are you sure? There really is a man with a gun? Then come down to me right now and I'll get you away from this awful place."

"Nigel, run!" I shouted. "Don't wait for me."

At that moment Cosimo staggered out of the door. The gun was still in his hand. I looked around for Renzo but didn't see him. My heart was thudding so hard that I couldn't catch my breath. Cosimo took aim and shot at Nigel but missed. The bullet pinged off the rocks. Nigel gave a little shriek of terror and fled down the last of the steps and into the woods. Cosimo now aimed the gun at me. "This time I shall not miss," he said.

There was a sound from deep within the earth. Pebbles bounced down the steps. The rock on which Cosimo was standing started to tilt. Cosimo turned to move out of the way, but his bad leg buckled under him. "Renzo, help me!" he called.

Almost as if in slow motion the chunk of

hillside gave way. Cosimo grasped wildly at air. He screamed as he fell down the cliff face, his body bouncing among pieces of rock and pebbles. Renzo appeared in the doorway. Blood was running down one side of his face. He staggered toward me. "He knocked me out," he said. "His own son. Are you all right?"

I nodded, still not able to find words. "He fell," I said at last. "The rock collapsed and he went . . ."

Renzo made his way cautiously to the edge of the parapet. Cosimo's body lay far below, half-covered with rock and turf. Renzo crossed himself. "He was an evil man, I know that now," he said. "But he was always good to me. The best of fathers. May he rest in peace."

"You fought for me," I said. "You wouldn't let him kill me. You were very brave."

"I couldn't believe he'd do it," I said. "I knew his dealings were not always straight. But I had no idea . . . but that's not true. When I learned about Gianni's murder, somehow I sensed he was responsible. But the partisans in the war . . . he really was evil, wasn't he?"

I put my hand gently on his arm. "But he was your father and you loved him. I'm sorry you had to go through this. Come on. Let's get you back to the town and have this cut stitched up."

"Don't forget our beautiful boy," Renzo said.

"As if I could." I realised I was still clutching

the painting to me. Renzo helped me down the steps, and we made our way toward the valley, where we were met by several men running toward us.

"There was a mad Englishman," one of them said. "We did not understand what he was shouting about, but he said something about Joanna and a gun so we came and . . ." He stopped when he saw Renzo with blood streaming down his face. "Where is this madman with a gun?"

"It was Cosimo," Renzo said. "He tried to kill Signorina Joanna. We fought. He hit me with the gun and knocked me out."

"Where is he? He must be stopped," one of the men said.

"He's dead. He fell from the heights. The hillside collapsed and he went plunging down."

The men crossed themselves. I noticed that none of them said, "May he rest in peace."

Then their gaze turned to what Renzo was carrying.

"We found this in the crypt under the monastery." Renzo held it up for them and they gasped.

"Magnificent. A work of the old masters," one of them muttered.

"I remember that there were fine paintings in the monastery before the war," the oldest man said. "We thought the Nazis had taken them all."

"There are more in the crypt," Renzo said, "but none so fine as this."

"Will it make San Salvatore rich, do you think?" one of them asked.

"How can you talk like that?" another man snapped. "This belongs to our heritage. It belongs in a museum in Florence."

"Florence? Why not Lucca? Is Lucca not as good as Florence?"

And they were off in lively dispute. Renzo grinned at me. We started up the hill to the village. The doctor cleaned Renzo's cut and put three stitches in it. "You were lucky you did not lose your eye," he said. "Or bleed to death from the vein in the temple."

"Yes, I was lucky," Renzo said. There was a note of bitterness in his voice.

At that moment there were raised voices outside the door, and the doctor's wife came in looking worried. "There is a mad foreigner outside," she said. "He claims he is the signorina's lawyer and—"

She didn't have a chance to finish because Nigel burst in. "Oh, there you are, Joanna. Thank God you're safe. What on earth was going on up there? What madman was shooting? Have they caught him yet? Mafia, I suppose. The whole place is teeming with gangsters, so one hears. Let's get your things. I have a car. I'll drive you back to Florence and we can go home."

"It's good of you, Nigel," I said, "but as you can see I am quite unhurt. And as for the man with the gun, he is dead."

"Thank God," he said. "Can we go now? We can take the night train back home."

I glanced at Renzo, who was looking rather pale, with the row of stitches making a black line above his eye. "I don't think I'd be allowed to leave right away," I said. "I'm sure there will be an inquest at which I'll have to testify."

"Not if you are out of the country before the police come," Nigel said.

"But I want to testify," I said. "I think it's important that this business is sorted out. It has to do with my father, you know."

"Oh, I see." His face fell. "Well, I suppose I had better stay, too, to defend you in court, if necessary."

I looked at his earnest face and had to laugh. "Nigel, are you qualified to practice international law? I'm sure I won't need anyone to defend me because I was a victim, not a suspect. And Signor Bartoli here can translate for me."

Nigel looked at Renzo, then back to me.

"So you don't want me to stay, just in case?"

"It is very kind and I appreciate the offer," I said, "but I'd like to get everything sorted out before I come home, and I'm sure you'd rather go back to England."

"Well, if you really don't want . . . Oh, all right." He looked crestfallen.

"It was extremely kind of you to come over here so quickly after I telephoned Scarlet," I said. "I suppose she was worried that I was in trouble with the law."

He looked puzzled now. "I don't know what telephone call you are speaking about. I went to Scarlet's flat last week to find you, and since I learned where you were in Italy I arranged to take a few days off and bring you a piece of good news myself."

"Good news?"

He smiled now. "Yes. Your paintings."

"My father's paintings? They are worth money after all?"

He shook his head. "No, not your father's paintings unfortunately. I'm talking about the family portraits. We had them cleaned and then one of them warranted further inspection by experts—the portrait of your ancestor namesake, Joanna Langley. It turned out it was painted by Thomas Gainsborough. A hitherto unknown portrait by him."

"Gainsborough? Are you sure?"

He nodded excitedly. "Once the painting was cleaned, the signature was quite visible in the lower corner. And there is a reference in his diary that a J. L. came to sit for him and had good bone structure."

"Golly," I said.

"Golly indeed. It is a major find. It could bring a serious amount of money at auction. Several hundred thousand pounds at least."

"Several hundred . . ." I couldn't even stammer out the words.

He nodded. "At least."

I was about to say "Golly" again but swallowed it back.

"So do I have your permission to put it up for auction at Christie's?" Nigel said. "I think we should get the wheels in motion right away while the discovery is still newsworthy."

For a moment I was tempted to keep it, to have my lookalike gazing down at me from my wall. But then my sensible nature prevailed. "Oh yes. Absolutely."

"Jolly good. Well, that's that, I suppose. I'll see you back in England, then," Nigel said awkwardly. "And if you need anything, here is my card. Don't hesitate to call me."

"Thank you," I said. "Thank you for everything you have done."

He blushed like a schoolboy.

After he had gone and Renzo and I came out of the doctor's office, Renzo gave me a questioning look. "That Englishman, he is your boyfriend?"

"Oh gosh, no. He's my father's solicitor. He was handling the estate. And one of the paintings is valuable. Isn't that amazing?"

"He likes you, I think," Renzo said. "Do you like him?"

"I'm sure he's a very nice person," I said, "but not my type."

"Good," Renzo said. He picked up the painting from where it lay on a side table. "I suppose this should be delivered to the mayor. He will decide what should be done with it."

I stared at it with longing. I knew I would have to give it up, but I didn't want it to be so soon. "Could we not keep it, at least until things have sorted themselves out?"

Renzo was also gazing at it. "I think we can. We will take good care of it, won't we? I am not sure now if we should call the Ministry of Art and Antiquities. After all, it was the property of the monks."

"Do you think any of the monks are still alive?"

"I know that several were killed trying to resist the occupiers," he said, "and the others will be old men now. But they were Franciscans. This part of Italy is crawling with Franciscans. It will be up to them whether they wish to donate the painting to the state and have it shown in a gallery like the Uffizi."

I nodded, my head trying to come to terms with famous paintings both here and in England. It was almost too much to take in, given the shock I was still feeling.

"Do you still plan to drive to Florence?" I asked.

"Oh, Florence. I had forgotten all about it," he said. "No, I will telephone the wine dealer, and he will have to wait."

I realised that the wines and the olives and all of Cosimo's businesses now belonged to Renzo. I wondered if he also realised it.

"Will you come to my house?" he asked. "We both need a glass of wine, I think."

"Yes, please."

We walked through the village. Renzo brushed aside questions that had already filtered through the village grapevine. He told people he was upset and needed to be alone and poor Joanna was shocked and could not talk. We left the village street behind and went up a straight gravel driveway lined with cypress trees. Inside wrought-iron gates, not unlike those of Langley Hall, was an imposing Venetian-style villa. A fountain played in the courtyard surrounded by orange and lemon trees. Pigeons fluttered at the lip of the fountain. We entered into a marble foyer. A female servant appeared, and Renzo gave her an order I couldn't quite understand. Then he led me through an ornate drawing room and out on to a terrace beyond. A grapevine on a trellis gave shade. Renzo offered me a wicker rocking chair. I sat. Below us the panorama of the landscape spread out as far as the eye could see.

Renzo sat beside me. For a while neither of us spoke.

"You saved my life today," I said. "Thank you. And in spite of everything, I'm sorry about your father."

He nodded, choking back emotion. "Whatever kind of man he was, he was also my father and he was good to me. Of course I will miss him, but I had no idea, no idea. I knew his deals were not always quite straight. I knew he was a bully and made sure he got what he wanted. But that he was a traitor and a murderer? No. Never." He brushed away a tear that was trickling down his cheek. Then he took a deep breath. "And I did suspect that he had some part in the death of Gianni. I don't know if he carried out the murder himself or if he had one of his men do it for him. But the next morning when I saw him at breakfast he looked pleased with himself. As if a load had been taken off his mind."

I reached across and put my hand over his. "You don't know how relieved I am that you weren't part of this. All this time I was afraid that maybe you'd had a hand in the murder, or at least knew about it."

"Is that what you thought of me?"

"Only until I realised the truth," I said. "When you tackled your father and tried to wrestle the gun from his hand, I knew I'd got it wrong."

We looked up as there were footsteps on the terrace behind us. The servant came out bearing a tray with a wine bottle, glasses, and the

432

obligatory dish of olives on it. She placed it on the little table in front of us and retreated without saying a word.

"She doesn't know yet," Renzo said. "I hadn't the heart to tell her. She worshipped my father." He paused. "He was always good to his workers. They will be devastated to know this." He poured me a glass of wine. "I think we need to steady our nerves, don't you?" he said.

Frankly I didn't feel like drinking or eating anything. My stomach was still tying itself into knots. After a while I turned to Renzo. "When it comes to an inquest, what are you going to tell them?"

"You mean should the truth about my father be made public?"

"That's exactly what I mean. Are you going to tell them he was responsible for the deaths of many men, for the death of Gianni, and almost for my death, too?"

Renzo sighed. "I suppose I must."

"Gianni's death is being linked to his underworld dealings, isn't it? And nobody knows that the partisans were betrayed in that German massacre."

Renzo looked wary. "Are you saying I should say nothing?"

"It's up to you. You say your father was liked by his workers, respected in town. Perhaps that is the memory you'd like to live on."

"I'll have to think about it," he said. "Of course we could say that he followed us and the hillside gave way. But your Englishman ran screaming about a man and a gun."

"My Englishman could have been in a panic and misunderstood."

Renzo sighed. "I think the truth should come out, however painful it will be for me. Too many people have suffered because of my father."

"You're a good man, Renzo. I'm glad to have met you," I said.

A worried frown crossed his face. "You're not leaving now, are you?"

I smiled at him. "As I said to Nigel, I might be called upon to give evidence at an inquest, and who knows how long that will take? Long enough to learn how to make Paola's ragu, at any rate."

Renzo smiled back. Then a thought struck him. "At least we now know that Cosimo did not betray my mother. He loved her. So perhaps she was not betrayed by one of our own. Perhaps it was as simple as the German who was billeted in our house watching her going up the hill and following her one day."

"Yes," I said. "That is probably what happened. So the Germans came for both of them. My father managed to escape, but who knows what happened to your mother? Do you think we would have any way of finding out after all this time? Old records?"

"I suspect they shot her," he said. "I've known in my heart all this time that she was dead." He gave a long sigh. "If only that cart had come a little earlier. If only they could have got away . . ."

"Then they would have married and I would never have happened," I said. "And I wouldn't be sitting here with you."

"So some good did come of it," he said.

CHAPTER FORTY

HUGO

Early 1945

Hugo opened his eyes to a soft touch on his cheek. A young woman with dark hair and a sweet face was standing over him.

"Sofia?" he whispered.

"My name is Anna," she said in English. "You are awake at last. That is good news."

"Where am I?" He took in the white ceiling and the white curtains around his bed.

"You are in a hospital near Rome."

"How did I get here?"

"You're a lucky man. You were found when the Americans advanced toward Florence. God knows how long you'd been there. They almost gave you up for dead, but then they felt a heartbeat and rushed you back to a field hospital. They transferred you here after a few days when you'd been stabilised. You've been in a coma for a couple of weeks. Head injury, collapsed lung, and a real mess of a leg. Yes, I'd say you're lucky to be alive."

He tried to move and found that he couldn't. "I need someone to write letters for me."

She put a hand on his shoulder. "All in good time."

"Have the Allies taken the area north of Lucca now, do you know?"

"I really don't know exactly how far they've reached. All I know is we are advancing steadily and the Germans are retreating as fast as they can. But I believe they haven't quite been driven out of that area in the mountains yet. There's still a lot of snow."

"I need to find out about the village of San Salvatore," he said. "I need to know if they are safe."

"I'll ask for you." She gave him a smile. "Now rest and I'll see if you are allowed a drink."

"Whisky and soda," he said.

She laughed. "You'll be lucky."

Later she returned. "The village you asked about is still in territory that is being fought over. It's close to the Germans' fortified line."

"So I couldn't get a message there yet?"

"I'm afraid not. But everyone is optimistic that we are nearing the end, in Italy at least. And with any luck you could be going home if you continue to make progress. How about that, eh?"

He tried to smile.

The next day an American army surgeon came to see him. "I've patched you up to the best of my ability," he said, "but that leg of yours is a nasty mess. I gather it is an old wound that has

437

healed badly. You'll need to have it cleaned out of pieces of bone and reset. I imagine they'll want to do that at an English hospital and not try to do anything here. So it will be a question of waiting until there is a ship that can take you."

Every day he felt a little stronger. He was allowed to sit up, to walk with crutches. He wrote a letter home to his father, wife, and son. Daily he asked for news on the fighting at the front and whether the area north of Lucca was now in Allied hands, but the answers were always uncertain. He longed to write to Sofia but didn't dare risk it. If there was still a German presence in her area and she received a letter from an English pilot, it could be a death sentence.

And so he waited impatiently for something to happen. In the middle of February he was taken to Civitavecchia harbour and on to an English ship bound for Portsmouth. The journey was a long and tedious one, dodging enemy ships and then battling gales in the Bay of Biscay. He was taken straight to hospital in Portsmouth where his leg was operated on. Again he wrote to his father and wife. And at the beginning of March he received an answer, but not from his family.

Dear Mr. Hugo,
I have taken the liberty of writing to you as there is not a family member at Langley at the moment to answer your letter.

May I say that I am so glad and relieved that you are safely back in England and not in some foreign hospital. I wanted you to be stronger and on the road to recovery before I shared the news with you. Your father died two months ago. His chest became progressively worse, and during the brutal cold in early January he caught pneumonia. I think the worry about having you reported missing contributed to his death. I am sorry he never lived to know that you were safe and coming home. So you are now officially Sir Hugo Langley, although I don't suppose that brings you any comfort.

There is talk that the army regiment may be pulling out of Langley Hall at last. Thank God for that, although I fear they have made an awful mess of the place. It really does seem as though the war will soon be over. It hardly seems possible, does it, after so many years of hardship and worry?

I am going to see if you are allowed visitors, and if so may I take the liberty of coming to visit you? They are not restricting travel so much these days. I'll bring you some good food. I expect you need building up after all that time hiding out with nothing to eat. Cook has done

wonders with our limited rations plus
what the estate brings in, although I'd
truly be glad to see the end of rabbit pies.

Well, I won't tire you anymore, but
hope to visit you soon.

Yours truly,

Elsie Williams, housekeeper

Hugo folded the letter, his head a jumble of
thoughts. He smiled fondly at memories of Mrs.
Williams. When he'd been growing up she'd
been Elsie, a new housemaid, a cheeky young
girl who was kind to him after his mother died.
Then, years later, the old housekeeper had retired
and Elsie had taken her place. Always kind and
cheerful, that was how he remembered her. Such
a contrast from Soames, the butler—stiff, rigid,
and humourless.

Then his thoughts turned to his father, and he
wondered whether he felt any grief. His death
was not unexpected after all, and his father
had always been a remote sort of man, shying
away from affection or any sort of closeness.
Duty, honour, doing the right thing—they were
what mattered to his father. And now he was
gone. Hugo tried to picture himself as lord of
the manor. Sir Hugo Langley. It seemed highly
improbable. *How Sofia would laugh,* he thought.
If only . . .

Elsie Williams came to see him a few days

later. She still looked plump and cheerful, fresh-faced and young-looking for her age, as if the war had not affected her at all. She brought a hamper packed with good things: calf's foot jelly, a game pie, homemade elderberry wine, and a jar of strawberry jam from last summer's crop. She laughed when she held up this treasure. "We all saved our sugar rations for a month to make that," she said. "My, did we have a bumper harvest last year. I helped Cook to hull all those strawberries. I've been helping her quite a lot recently since we've no kitchen maid. I never realised how much I enjoy cooking."

"It's very good of you, Elsie," he said. "Although I must apologise. I should be calling you Mrs. Williams."

"Only if you want me to call you Sir Hugo," she replied. Then her face became sombre. "I'm sorry to be the bearer of bad news about your father. In truth he had been going downhill for the past few years. And having his house occupied by a lot of louts really grieved him, too."

"A lot of louts?"

"That army regiment. You should see what a mess they've made of the place. I think it almost broke your father's heart. You know how proud he was of the house and the grounds."

Hugo realised there was one subject they hadn't broached. "And my wife and son? You haven't even mentioned them."

"That's because they've been gone from the house for a while," she said.

"Gone? Where?"

"I couldn't tell you, sir. I know she has left you a letter, but I didn't think it was my place to open it. She told your father she was going away, but he never told me where. Maybe she was nervous being close to the south coast when those doodlebugs and V-2s started coming over. She never looked happy and it was hard to please her."

"And my son? Is he away at school?"

"No, sir. He was attending the village school until recently. Your father was most put out. He wanted Teddy to go to the same school that you were sent to, but Mrs. Langley wouldn't hear of it. She said she'd been doing without a husband, she wasn't going to do without a son as well."

"I can understand that," he said. "Oh well, when I finally get home I expect it will all be sorted out. And when the war ends, we can choose a school for Teddy then."

"You really think it's going to end soon?"

"I'm sure of it," he said. "The Germans are retreating all over Europe. We've got them licked, Elsie. It's only a matter of time."

"Praise the Lord for that," she said, "and for bringing you safely home. I was so worried about you, Mr. Hugo. When we got the telegram that you were missing, well, we feared the worst. And what good news when you finally wrote that you were alive."

"Only just," he said. "I was extremely lucky. That the American troops found my body in the midst of a German convoy and, what's more, discovered that I was still alive—well, that was nothing short of a miracle."

"You must have had an angel watching over you," she said. And Hugo's hand went instinctively to where his breast pocket would be.

He was allowed home in April. The banks were covered in primroses. There were daffodils and crocuses blooming in cottage gardens, and the fruit trees were a mass of pink and white blossoms. As the taxi drove up the drive to Langley Hall he saw what Elsie had meant about the place being destroyed by louts. Heavy army vehicles were parked all over the south lawn, their tyres leaving deep gouges in what had once been immaculate grass. The north lawn had been ploughed up and was now growing vegetables. The house looked in need of a coat of paint, and some of the windows were boarded up with plywood. He got out of the taxi and went up the steps to the front door. Immediately a sentry stepped out to intercept him.

"Oy, where do you think you're going?" he demanded.

"Where am I going?" Hugo regarded him with

distaste. "I am Sir Hugo Langley and this is my house."

"Not this part of it, mate," the man said. "Right now this is the property of His Majesty's government and the East Sussex regiment. Your bit is the wing over there."

Hugo swallowed back his anger. "I thought you were supposed to be moving out."

"We are. They were going to send us over to France, but it seems they don't need us. Doing very nicely without us. So I reckon we'll be going home soon."

As Hugo went to walk away the man called, "So where have you been? Having a good time on the Riviera?"

"Flying bombing raids. In Malta since 1941, then in Italy, then in hospital for three months while they rebuilt my leg."

The man stood to attention and saluted. "Sorry, sir. I didn't see the uniform. I didn't realise."

Hugo went around to the side of the house and in through what had once been a servant's entrance. It felt wrong to be sneaking into his own home like this. He wandered around, recognising objects of furniture but experiencing a jolt of unreality that nothing was in its proper place and none of the rooms were familiar to him. On the table in what was now serving as a drawing room, he found the letter addressed to him.

Dear Hugo,

As I write this I don't know whether you are alive or dead. They say you are missing. I have to think that means dead. I have stayed on here dutifully, but now I have to think about my own happiness and that of our son. I have met someone. He's an American major. A wonderful person, likes to laugh and dance and makes me feel alive again. I am going to America with him as soon as they can find a place for me on a ship. I have instructed your solicitor to start divorce proceedings. I'll happily admit to being the guilty party so there is no stain on you or your lofty family.

It never really worked, did it? I saw the fun, creative side of you when we were students together in Florence, but when we came back to England you tried to be your father—stuffy and boring and correct—and I never felt that I belonged at Langley. Not the sort of life I would have chosen. And poor little Teddy, so lonely and always teased by the village boys. I want a better life for him, too.

Please forgive me. I wish you all the best,

Brenda

Hugo stared at the letter for a long while. At first he felt indignation that his wife should betray him with an American. But then elation took over. If Sofia's husband did not return he was free to marry her. As soon as the war ended and he was allowed to travel, he would go back to Italy and bring her home. He sat down immediately at the writing desk and wrote her a letter.

CHAPTER FORTY-ONE

HUGO

Spring 1945

Weeks passed and there was still no letter from Sofia. Hugo told himself that the postal system in Italy was just not up and running yet. Maybe her letter had got lost in the mail. He'd wait until the official end of the war and then write again. Or better still, he'd go over and surprise her.

But then he had a visit from the family solicitor, Mr. Barton.

"I'm sorry to meet in such distressing circumstances," he said. "I understand you will not contest the divorce your wife requests?"

"I will not," Hugo said.

"Then that matter can be taken care of simply. But your father's death has created the serious matter of death duties. I am afraid they are quite considerable based on the size and value of the estate."

"What do you mean when you say 'quite considerable'?" Hugo asked.

"Almost a million pounds."

"A million pounds?" he demanded. "Where am I going to get that sort of money?"

"If you can't raise it I'm afraid the estate will have to be sold."

"But that is monstrous," he snapped. "Unfair."

"It's the way the law works I'm afraid."

"Could some of the land be sold off for building?"

"Possibly. Although I doubt it would bring in enough."

"I'm going to make it work somehow," Hugo said. "I'm not selling off a home that has been in our family for nearly four hundred years. I'll see if I can get a loan to have houses built on the far field of the estate. People will need new homes after the war."

But gradually he had to face reality. No bank was willing or able to lend him money to build houses, and no one wanted to buy part of the land so far from a train station. The regiment withdrew from Langley Hall, leaving damage throughout the house and estate. Hugo walked with Elsie Williams, the housekeeper, through the newly abandoned rooms. All around him was decay and destruction. Men had taken potshots at statues and ripped the wallpaper. They had even used dressing rooms as urinals—the floors were stained and rotting. The roof had leaked and allowed damp into upstairs ceilings. The main boiler had ceased to function. Good furniture had been piled willy-nilly into small bedrooms where the woodworm had found it.

"It's hopeless, isn't it?" he asked Elsie.

For once she couldn't give him a cheerful answer. She looked as if she was fighting back tears herself. Instinctively he put a hand on her shoulder. She smiled up at him.

Later, the letter to Sofia was returned unopened—"Not known at this address. Return to sender" stamped on the envelope. He told himself that she had probably got news that her husband was alive and had gone to be with him. A happy ending for her. He tried to believe it. He wanted to go back to San Salvatore to find out for himself. It didn't take him long to find out how impossible that would be. The war had officially ended in Europe with the German surrender on May 7, but Europe was in turmoil and no civilian travel was allowed. Hugo had been invalided out of service and thus was now a civilian. He appealed to old RAF friends to see if they could find out any more, but none of them was stationed anywhere near San Salvatore. Finally, he wrote to the mayor, and this time he received a short answer:

> Signora Bartoli is no longer in this village. She was seen driving away with a German officer and since then nothing has been heard of her.

It was the final straw. He returned to his solicitor.

"Very well," he said. "Put the house up for sale."

Later that summer, Hugo stood outside Langley Hall looking up at it as the last items of furniture were carried out. The servants had already left. He felt horribly alone, almost as if he had died. In truth he wished he had died that spring. Why had he been discovered among the German dead if only for all this heartache? It made no sense.

Elsie Williams came out of the servant's door carrying a suitcase. He watched her coming toward him, her face not cheerful at this moment but stoic and resolute, her chin held high. He thought how sad it was that she'd be going off to work somewhere else and he wouldn't see her again. During the summer he had come to rely on her sensible countrywoman's judgment, her sunny disposition.

"I'm so sorry this had to happen, Sir Hugo," she said as she caught up with him. "It's just not fair after all you've been through."

"You're right, Elsie," he replied. "It's not fair. But then nothing has been fair for a long time, has it? All those chaps I flew with who went down in flames. All those poor sods sitting at dinner in their houses who were blasted to pieces by doodlebugs. And the poor, damned wretches in the concentration camps. None of them deserved to die."

She nodded. "You're right." There was a long pause, then she said, "I hear you're planning to stay on."

He sighed. "The school has offered me accommodation at the lodge if I become the art master. Since I have no other options at the moment, it seemed like the easiest thing to do. At least until I find my feet again." He looked down at the pitifully small suitcase she was carrying. "What about you, Elsie? Where will you go? There isn't really a Mr. Williams, is there?"

She laughed. "Oh no, sir. It's just the convention, isn't it? You know that. Housekeepers and cooks are always called 'Mrs.' out of respect. And as for where I'll go, I'm not sure. I expect I'll find another situation, although one hears that many of the big houses are going to be closed up or pulled down. I expect I'll find something."

"You have no family, do you? I seem to remember that you were an orphan when you came to us."

"That's right, sir. I have no family. I don't even know who my family was."

Hugo looked at her and felt immense pity. Here she was, cast out into the world with no place to go and she was not complaining, just facing it stoically. He opened his mouth and was surprised to hear himself say, "You know, Elsie, you could always stay on here."

She looked surprised, then shook her head.

"Stay on here? Oh no, sir. They made it quite clear they will be hiring their own staff for the school."

"I meant with me," he said.

"With you? At the lodge?" She gave a nervous little laugh. "I don't think there would be room, for one thing, and you don't need a servant."

He felt himself turning red. "I'm putting this badly. What I meant was that you and I have always got along well. You're a kind and decent person. And recently I've come to value having you around. You've been a great comfort to me. And you have nowhere to go and I have nobody. If we got married it might solve things for both of us."

"Married, sir?" She opened her eyes wide in astonishment, then shook her head. "That would never work, would it? I'm a good deal older than you. You can't be more than, what, thirty-four?"

"Thirty-five," he said.

"And I'm already forty-two, sir."

"Not an unsurmountable gap, surely."

"I don't think you should make a hasty decision on something as important as this, not when you've had so much thrown at you and you're on the rebound after Mrs. Langley left you. And I wouldn't want you to make such an offer because you felt sorry for me, either."

"I don't feel sorry for you, Elsie," he said. "Actually I envy you. You seem to be able to make the best of the bleakest of situations. I think you're just what I need right now. Of course you might not find me much of a catch . . ."

She blushed then. "I've always thought you were very handsome, Mr. Hugo. In fact, when I was younger I used to keep a picture of you in my room." She paused, shifting awkwardly from foot to foot. "But then there's the matter of class. You're a baronet, an aristocrat. I'm a servant. Think of the talk."

Hugo put a hand on her shoulder. "I have a feeling the war will have changed things. No more class distinction. And anyway, who cares if there is talk? Let them talk. I think we might be happy enough, don't you?"

"I've always been very fond of you, Mr. Hugo," she said. "And the chance to have my own home, not living under someone else's roof—well, it's very appealing, I must say. But I don't want you to do something you'll regret later."

He smiled at her then, putting his finger under her chin. "No regrets, Elsie, I promise you. And for God's sake put down that damned suitcase so I can give you a kiss."

CHAPTER FORTY-TWO

JOANNA

June 1973

A week later I was reluctantly preparing to go home to attend the auction of my painting when the man from the post office came up to Renzo and me. "I have received a telephone call from the home where Father Filippo resides," he said. "It seems he is failing fast and would like to talk to Signor Bartoli and the young lady from England."

Mystified, we drove in Renzo's Alfa Romeo to a nearby town. The home was a pleasant, modern building a little away from the town centre. We were escorted to Father Filippo's room by a young, fresh-faced nun. "He is very weak," she said, "and in distress. His mind may be wandering, but I hope you can put him at peace before he goes."

Indeed, the old man looked almost transparent as he lay under white sheets. His eyes were closed. Renzo said softly, "Father, it is I, Renzo Bartoli. I have come as you wished and brought the young lady from England with me."

The old priest's eyes fluttered open. "It is

good," he said. "I want you to hear my confession before I die—you and the young lady, since it concerns her. I am responsible for the deaths of your mother and the Englishman. I betrayed them, and it has been on my conscience all these years."

"How could you have done that, Father?" Renzo asked gently.

"I had to weigh what was best," he said, his breath coming raggedly. "The German commandant came to me. He said he suspected that someone in the town was hiding an English airman. He was going to execute us all, every man, woman, and child, unless someone confessed. Sofia had told me in confession about the Englishman. I know the seal of the confessional is sacred, but this was many lives, many innocent lives against her one. I told him what I knew, but I begged him to spare Sofia and take me instead. He wouldn't agree. So with the heaviest of hearts I gave him your mother, Renzo, so that others could live. I have never known since whether I did the right thing or not."

"You did what you thought was best, Father," Renzo said. "There was no right answer."

"This is true. But all the same . . . That sweet young woman. How I have wept for her all these years and prayed that she is now an angel in heaven."

"I'm sure she is." Renzo's voice cracked.

"And the young English lady. The Germans took her father, too. I'm sorry."

"But he escaped, Father," I said. "He came home and married again and I am his daughter."

"So that is good." He gave a faint smile. "So something good happened." His eyes fluttered closed.

Renzo leaned down and kissed his forehead. "Go in peace, Father. There is nothing that needs to be forgiven."

A sweet smile came across the priest's face. It took a while for us to realise he was no longer breathing.

That evening Renzo and I were sitting on the terrace. This time we were drinking a glass of limoncello after a meal that he had cooked for me—mussels and clams in a cream sauce, Florentine beef steak, and a rich almond cake with gelato for dessert. I was feeling content—more content than I had felt in years.

The distant hills were bathed in pink twilight. Somewhere far off, a bell was tolling. Otherwise there was silence.

"So this is all yours now," I said, motioning toward the vineyards and olive groves. "You'll be a rich man."

He looked around. "Yes, I suppose I will. But now I know the truth, I think I must give back the land that my father took after the war—the land of those brave men who were killed in the massacre. It's only right, don't you think?"

"Yes," I agreed. "I definitely think it's right."

"I'll still have the vineyards and the olive press," he said. "I won't exactly be poor." He looked directly at me. "Neither will you, so it seems."

"No, you're right. I still haven't digested that fact."

"You could buy back your family home. You could become mistress of Langley Hall."

For a moment an image flashed into my mind. I saw myself saying to Miss Honeywell, "I'm sorry but I'll need you out by the end of term. I'm coming back to live here." Then I laughed. "It's funny but all my life that was what I dreamed of doing. I was driven to succeed so that I could buy my father's house back for him. And now he's dead and I can't see myself as lady of the manor. I don't quite know what I want to do yet."

"Joanna," he said slowly. "You didn't need to stay here. You could have gone home with the English lawyer. But you sent him away, saying you would be needed for inquests. I wondered if that meant that you didn't want to go."

"You're right," I said. "I don't want to go. I like it here. I like being with Paola and learning to cook and feeling that someone cares about me."

"And me?" he asked. "Does part of your reason

for staying mean that you do not want to leave me?"

"Yes," I said carefully. "I think it does."

He leaned toward me, put a hand under my chin, and pulled my face toward his. Then he kissed me hard and with longing. When we broke apart he laughed uneasily. "It is lucky we are on a terrace where we can be observed, or I don't know where that would have led."

"I'm a respectable young English lady," I replied. "I expect to be courted properly."

"Of course, my lady." He laughed, his eyes flirting with me.

I looked at him, suddenly struck by a thought. "You could go back to London to finish your studies and then open your restaurant."

"We could turn your Langley Hall into a hotel and restaurant," he said.

"We?"

"Am I moving too fast? Maybe just as business partners, you know."

"Why England? It's rains too much. You could open your restaurant here as you once dreamed. You could turn this house into your dream restaurant. Imagine the diners sitting here on your terrace and feasting their eyes on the view before they feasted them on the food."

"I would need to return to England first to finish my apprenticeship," he said. "And you should pass your exam. And then, who knows?"

He reached across and took my hand. We sat there side by side on the terrace not saying a word while the sun sank behind the western hills and one by one lights twinkled on in the world spread out below us.

AUTHOR'S NOTE

The village of San Salvatore cannot be found on any map. It exists only in my imagination, although it is based on Tuscan hill towns I have visited. The German Gothic Line, north of Lucca, was real.

ACKNOWLEDGEMENTS

Pier-Raimondo and Cajsa Baldini were wonderful hosts in Tuscany and were kind enough to read my manuscript and offer suggestions. Penny and Roger Fountain were perfect hosts in Lincolnshire and found WWII museums where I could check out a Blenheim bomber, as well as experts on the Blenheim to answer my questions. They even attended an air show to take pictures of a Blenheim actually flying for me.

ABOUT THE AUTHOR

Rhys Bowen is the *New York Times* bestselling author of the Royal Spyness, Molly Murphy, and Constable Evans mystery series, as well as the #1 Kindle bestseller *In Farleigh Field*. She has won the Agatha Award for Best Novel and has been nominated for the Edgar Award for Best Novel, among numerous other awards, nominations, and starred reviews. Bowen was born in Bath, England, studied at London University, married into a family with historic royal connections, and now divides her time between Northern California and Arizona.

Books are produced in the United States using U.S.-based materials

Books are printed using a revolutionary new process called THINKtech™ that lowers energy usage by 70% and increases overall quality

Books are durable and flexible because of Smyth-sewing

Paper is sourced using environmentally responsible foresting methods and the paper is acid-free

Center Point Large Print
600 Brooks Road / PO Box 1
Thorndike, ME 04986-0001 USA

(207) 568-3717

US & Canada:
1 800 929-9108
www.centerpointlargeprint.com